Born and raised on the Wirral Peninsula in England, **Charlotte Hawkes** is mum to two intrepid boys who love her to play building block games with them, and who object loudly to the amount of time she spends on the computer. When she isn't writing—or building with blocks—she is company director for a small Anglo/French construction firm. Charlotte loves to hear from readers, and you can contact her at her website: charlotte-hawkes.com.

Also by Charlotte Hawkes

Christmas with Her Bodyguard
A Surgeon for the Single Mum
The Army Doc's Baby Secret
Unwrapping the Neurosurgeon's Heart
Surprise Baby for the Billionaire
Falling for the Single Dad Surgeon

Reunited on the Front Line miniseries

Second Chance with His Army Doc
Reawakened by Her Army Major

Available now

Discover more at millsandboon.co.uk.

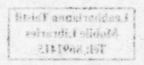

SECOND CHANCE WITH HIS ARMY DOC

CHARLOTTE HAWKES

REAWAKENED BY HER ARMY MAJOR

CHARLOTTE HAWKES

MILLS & BOON

First Published in Great Britain 2020
by Mills & Boon, an imprint of HarperCollins*Publishers*
1 London Bridge Street, London, SE1 9GF

Second Chance with His Army Doc © 2020 by Charlotte Hawkes

Reawakened by Her Army Major © 2020 by Charlotte Hawkes

ISBN: 978-0-263-27983-2

MIX
Paper from
responsible sources
FSC
www.fsc.org
FSC™ C007454

Printed and bound in Spain
by CPI, Barcelona

SECOND CHANCE WITH HIS ARMY DOC

CHARLOTTE HAWKES

MILLS & BOON

To Helen,
I've never walked, talked, and laughed so much.
Thank you. xx

CHAPTER ONE

IT COULDN'T BE HER. It wasn't possible.

Kane Wheeler stopped dead in the corridor of the large, city hospital that was Castleton University Teaching Hospital, and practically glowered through the glass doors to the ward. Something surged inside him. Sharp. Edgy. Altogether too dangerous.

Yet it wasn't exactly *impossible* either.

Mathilda Brigham. *Mattie.* His first and—aside from his career in the army—his *only* love.

He'd known she was a doctor, of course. The last time they'd been together—or at least the last time that Mattie had been *his*—she'd been about to go off to university to begin her dream of becoming a doctor. But that had been fourteen years ago. A lifetime.

He'd seen her twice since then, neither an occasion he cared to dwell on, though she hadn't seen him. How long had she been working here in Castleton? In a hospital that was hours away from the life she was supposed to living with her perfect earl—the man to whom she'd been married for the past four years.

That rough, unsteady thing moved through him at the thought of Mattie with…*him*, George Blakeney, but Kane fought it off. He'd learned long ago that emotions like anger—and guilt, and love, for that matter—served little purpose.

Besides, didn't Mattie deserve happiness? And if her earl made her happy, then it was better than he himself could have managed.

George Blakeney, son of a duke and from one of the wealthiest families in the area. The perfect match for the independently successful daughter of a brigadier, so far removed from a kid from a bad family in the back streets who had so very nearly ended up in juvie for a momentary lapse in judgement.

There was no bitterness in that. It was merely a fact. The kid he'd been would never have been right for a girl like Mattie, however much she'd tried to claim otherwise. And as much as he'd made a success of his life since then, it still didn't make him Earl Blakeney—a man who might as well have been handcrafted for a woman like Mathilda Brigham.

Which surely only made it all the more inconceivable that she was here, a good hundred or so miles from the vast Blakeney Estates. Not even close to Heathdale, where they'd both grown up. Mattie brought up by her loving family in the posher Lower Heathdale, and him barely dragged up, along with his two brothers, by his waster father in the lower-class town, Heathdale.

Then again… Kane gazed into the ward… Castleton was a big city with a large military population and a large RAF base down the road, from which he was due to fly out on arguably his biggest mission to date in a few days. Even though Mattie had left the army when she'd married, it would stand to reason that a teaching hospital like Castleton would value her experience and expertise and secure her for a few months. But he wouldn't have thought she'd readily have left Blakeney. Or any children.

She might have kids with him!

Kane swayed slightly, as if drunk, although he hadn't touched a drop in months. And when he did, he never over-indulged. He was always in control, anything less was unacceptable. One misjudged moment now and his career trajectory—the only thing that had mattered to him for the past fourteen years—could nosedive faster than jumping out of a plane with no parachute. But right now he felt light-headed. Dizzy. Out of control.

He leaned his hand on the doorjamb as he stared in. Not wanting to stay but unable to tear himself away. Mattie was engaged in an animated conversation with a patient. Even from a distance he could see that she was employing her own unique blend of humour, professionalism and charm to reassure and settle the patient and his wife. Indeed, the couple was looking less stressed and more bewitched as the conversation went on.

Something pulled at his mouth in spite of everything. It was so characteristically *Mattie*. He'd always known she'd be an amazing doctor, just as he'd kept up with her career as an amazing army officer—until she'd given up the latter for her marriage, that was. Being a doctor and a countess was one thing, apparently, but being a captain and a countess wasn't as widely appreciated.

Kane allowed his eyes to roam over her, as much as he knew he probably shouldn't. He didn't know whether he was looking for proof that she'd changed or evidence that she was still the same, but either way there were clues to both.

She still carried herself with a bearing he'd always admired, though her long, blonde hair, which had once tumbled down her back and over her shoulders, was now a touch darker and scooped up into a tight bun, as he suspected she had become accustomed to doing during her decade of service.

He let his eyes drop lower to the top she wore. Feminine

and pretty, yet practical and professional, it didn't cling
to the curves he knew lay beneath, but it was fitted, and
it flattered her body perfectly. And then there were the
tailored trousers that moulded themselves to the swell of
her hips and reminded him of how it had felt when those
long legs of hers had been wrapped around him, drawing
him inside her.

Dammit.

Kane slammed his fist against the wall in disgust and
swivelled on his heel to march up the mercifully deserted
corridor. He had absolutely no right to think about her
that way any more.

In fact, he was better not to think of her *at all*. The way
he'd been avoiding doing so for the last fourteen years. No,
that was a lie. But he thought he'd exorcised her, at least for
the last four years. Certainly ever since he'd stood in the
plush hotel that had hosted her wedding rehearsal dinner
and watched her on that stage with her groom-to-be, both
staring at each other with unmistakeable love in their eyes.

For one moment he had actually thought she'd spotted
him. But then she'd turned back to her husband-to-be,
reaching out to hold his arm as though he was the only
man in room. The world. A simple, instinctive gesture
that had left Kane feeling as though his very heart had
been ripped out.

He'd felt mad and sad all at once, but had also felt a
strangely bitter-sweet kind of emotion that at least Mattie
was happy, even if it couldn't be with him. Which was why
he'd left without speaking to her and without even finding Hayden—Mattie's older brother and at one time his
best friend—to ask why his old friend had invited him to
Mattie's wedding rehearsal in the first place.

Whatever the reason, seeing Mattie's obvious devoted-
ness to her fiancé had made anything else irrelevant, and

Kane had slipped out of the room before she'd even turned back to the crowd.

He'd concentrated on his life and on his army career. And whilst he was careful about his personal life, he wasn't exactly a monk. He knew of at least a couple of engaging, equally career-minded female friends who had made it clear they were interested in dating him, if he ever wanted to call them up.

'Kane?'

Kane stopped, paused, then swivelled around to stare back down the corridor to where Mattie was standing immobile, as though rooted to the spot, and ignored something that kickstarted deep in his chest.

'It *is* you,' she muttered, and even from a distance he could see the stunned expression playing over her striking features.

Suddenly his hands itched to smooth it away and he had to clench them into fists and punch them down, deep into his pockets in a very non-military way.

Thank God he wasn't in uniform.

'Hello, Matz.' The name that only *he* had ever used for her. He couldn't help himself. 'It's been a while.'

'Fourteen years.' The words were clipped, sharper.

As though it still mattered.

Kane hated it that his heart twisted in some perverse hope. Of course she didn't care, she was just surprised, even shocked, and he was just reading into it what he wanted to see. He had no idea how he managed it when so many emotions were charging through him right at this second, but he folded his arms across his chest and affected a lighter air.

'And you're still chagrined?'

'Of course not,' she answered quickly—too quickly— and her voice sounded thick.

He had to remind himself that didn't mean anything either.

And if he saw her eyebrow quirk slightly at his choice of vocabulary—using words his younger, uneducated self never would have known—then so be it. He wasn't that uncultured kid any more. He'd changed; in ways he doubted she could even imagine.

'I never thought… That is, I didn't expect…' She stopped, lifted her head and straightened her spine as if she'd given herself some kind of pep talk. 'What are you doing here, Kane?'

'Just visiting…someone.' He didn't think she'd detected the momentary hesitation when he'd stalled. Wanting, for a split second, to tell her more.

Suddenly needing to unburden to someone—he refused to admit it was only because it was *her*—that he was here visiting a former army buddy. The only other survivor of a mission gone wrong a few years back, and who was only in this hospital now because he'd let the guilt of it eat into him.

Kane slammed the shutters in his mind in an instant. He had no intention of following his old buddy down that dark path. And baring his soul to Mattie wasn't going to help anyone.

'Which ward?'

She bit her lip, her brow furrowing in a hint of irritation. It was a mannerism so painfully familiar that it caused a sharp band to tighten around his chest. Still, he was fairly certain her question had slipped out before she could check herself and it felt as though there was some comfort to be drawn from that.

Still, saying anything to her about his visit was bound to have her demanding to know how he—army-hating as he had been as a kid—had even come to sign up. And then he'd have to tell her where he'd disappeared to all those years ago. And why.

He'd have to explain himself, the colossal error of judgement he'd made, and how Mattie's own father had been the one to drop everything and rescue him. And how they'd agreed that the feisty eighteen-year-old Mattie—always scrappy despite being a couple of years younger than him—should never, *ever* know.

Oddly, a part of him actually welcomed the prospect to explain it to her after all this time. But another part—a greater part—balked at the idea. Why rake up a past that could only make her think worse of him than she'd probably thought all this time?

It wouldn't have changed anything back then, and it would change even less now. She was married, he reminded himself.

She belonged to someone else.

And he fully intended to respect that. But no one else had ever come close to knocking Mattie off that pedestal in his head. Since they'd been kids, whenever he had been around her, he'd felt his world contracting until it had been just the two of them. Which was why, if he stayed in her company too long, it would surely get harder and harder to remember the outside world.

'Good to see you, Mattie,' he said grimly, this time avoiding using his pet name for her, which had somehow felt too...*intimate*. 'I'll let you get back to work.'

And then, with the same force of will that had got him out of multiple difficult situations over the years, including one firefight in hostile territory from which not a single one of his section had been expected to escape, he turned and walked away.

'Kane. Wait.'

She hurried up the corridor before she could stop herself. Her mind was screaming for her to stop but her traitorous body wouldn't listen, intent instead on rushing headlong into her past. If the ground had opened up and sent her twisting and spinning, hurtling downwards to the centre of the earth, she couldn't have felt more shocked.

She caught up with him as he reached the double doors at the far end of the corridor. Placing her hand on his arm, she pretended she didn't feel the terrific jolt of electricity as she made him turn back to her. He stared at her fingers on his forearm but he didn't shake them off, and she couldn't seem to make herself let go.

As if she was frightened that, if she did, he would slip away from her again.

She had imagined this moment a hundred—a thousand—times over the years. She'd played it over and over in her head. She'd rehearsed what she would say until the words were honed to a shine even more impressive than that on a pair of bulled army parade boots. But at this moment her faithless mind had gone blank.

She was a doctor, an army major. She'd fought in dangerous combat zones and saved countless lives. She'd had hundreds of men and women under her command. However, right now she felt like the eighteen-year-old whose heart had just been shattered into a million tiny fragments.

And Mattie still didn't know why. She just knew that it wasn't because he'd been a couple of years older than her and so had grown tired of her, the way people—usually jealous girls in her year, though never her own family—had always warned her he would do.

She had no idea how long they stood, immobile, staring in silence at each other. Fourteen years had done nothing to diminish the effect Kane Wheeler had on her. If anything, his hold seemed to be greater than ever right at this moment. She couldn't move, couldn't talk, she couldn't even breathe.

Seeing him had been like wallop to the solar plexus. All her worst, long-buried fears had screamed up to the surface, bursting through her like an explosion of lust.

'Go back to work, Matz,' he growled eventually.

The low growl—the voice she hadn't heard in fourteen years and the only one to have ever called her by that name—spiralled through her like the hottest, deepest coil of smoke. If she hadn't been gripping his arm, she was certain that her legs would have buckled beneath her.

Mattie gritted her teeth, hating herself for her weakness, and hating Kane even more for doing it to her.

And yet…there was another chunk of her that didn't hate him at all, that had never hated him.

Kane Wheeler.

Her first love. Worse, in some respects, her *only* real love. *And wasn't that the kicker?*

Fourteen years, her fair share of boyfriends and George—her ex-fiancé, and the kindest, sweetest man she'd ever known—but, in the end, none of them had come close to prising open the death grip hold that Kane still had on her heart.

Kane. The man who hadn't even wanted her back, hadn't loved her, and who had so easily, so devastatingly, betrayed her.

All the more shameful, then, that her heart was currently hurling itself—with suicidal recklessness—into the wall of her chest, practically winding her.

'Practically a decade and a half, and that's all you have to say to me?'

'What would you like me to say?'

Scores of questions cracked through her like thunderclaps, each one echoing more loudly than the last. Mattie bit every one of them back.

'Why are you here, Kane?'

'I already answered that,' he told her calmly, and she might actually have believed him if it weren't for that hectic glitter in his all-too-familiar eyes.

Pools of deep, rich brown that actually seemed to turn black sometimes, when his emotions ran high.

Like now.

Her heart slammed forcefully against her chest wall yet again, and she pretended not to notice. Yet, despite all her internal commands to move away, her legs wilfully ignored them, and her arm refused to drop away.

'What about you, Mattie? What brings you here, so far away from where you should be?'

Where she should be?

'Do you mean on operational duty?' Mattie frowned.

She could have told him about Operation Strikethrough. About the fact that she'd been chosen out of any number of majors in the Royal Army Medical Corps to run end-to-end simulations in support of light and armoured infantry, trying new tactics for the first time since the end of the Cold War. She almost did tell him, out of sheer pride. Just as she almost told him that, at the end of the three-month exercise she would be due for promotion to Lieutenant-Colonel.

But something had stopped her.

In all likelihood, that *something* had been her memory that a row between their teenage selves about the army—and the fact that her joining up would have torn them apart—had been the last time they had ever spoken. Kane had been so anti any authority back then, including her military-orientated family. She was the daughter of a brigadier and he was the son of a man who'd fought in back-room pub brawls just for enough beer money to drink himself into a stupor every night.

In typical teenager-in-love fashion, she'd been naïve to think that their vastly different backgrounds didn't matter back then. But surely he wasn't still so entrenched in his views all this time later?

Yet whilst she wasn't afraid to tell Kane, she found that

she simply didn't want to cloud this moment with an old, long-buried disagreement. She didn't care to examine that choice in too much depth, which begged the question, *What did she want?* In the end, Mattie settled for a half-truth.

'No, I don't mean on operational duty.' His lip curled slightly in disgust. 'I mean that I thought… I *heard*…you gave up your army career.'

Her heart stopped thumping and simply…*stopped.*

He couldn't know about George. Surely?

'You…heard?' she managed, her tongue sticking uncomfortably to the roof of her mouth. 'How? From whom?'

His gaze was all too sharp. Too piercing. She couldn't breathe. Her chest was pulling so tight she was afraid it might suddenly snap.

Abruptly, he shook his head.

'Rumour.' He shrugged. 'Someone back in Lower Heathdale maybe? I really wasn't that interested.'

She wasn't sure she entirely believed him, but at least her heart was slowly thudding back into life.

'What did they say?' She barely recognised her own voice.

'You were getting married and you were leaving the army for your husband. Some earl or something.'

She made a strangled sound in her throat. They were venturing into territory she wasn't ready for.

Not yet.

'Were they lying?' he demanded.

As if her answer mattered to him.

And how she *wanted* it to matter to him. But she couldn't afford for it to matter that way because she wasn't ready to explain herself. She didn't want to make some throw-away remark as though calling it off four years ago, on the eve of her wedding to gentle, loving George, hadn't been the hardest decision she'd ever had to make.

She waited for the familiar punch of guilt that she'd always felt when she thought of her ex-fiancé but, for once, it didn't come. Instead, her body was blazing. Singing. A veritable orchestra playing with all the fanfare of the *Last Night of the Proms*. All because of the man standing right in front of her now. Which could only say something deeply worrying about herself as a woman.

'Were they lying, Mattie?' Kane ground out.

'No. They weren't lying.'

That *had* been her intention. It just hadn't happened. But she didn't say that.

'Why would you give up the career you'd dreamt of all your life for a wedding?' he demanded. 'Just because your husband is an earl?'

Without warning, he plucked her hand from his arm as if he couldn't bear her to be touching him a moment longer. Then his palm stilled as it held her fingers and he lifted her hand to examine it. Deep furrows pulled between his eyes for a fraction of a second before he quickly smoothed them out. His eyes raked over her face, leaving it feel as though a fire was raging under every inch of her skin.

'No ring?' Was it her imagination or was his voice deliberately neutral? 'Why not?'

A thousand little detonations went off inside Mattie at the unexpected contact, yet she couldn't pretend it was an intrusion. Still, it was easier to tell herself that her body was reacting out of shock, rather than anything else. Certainly not some kind of chemistry. Just as she told herself that she wasn't leaving her hand in his because she *liked* it, but rather that snatching it back would only have proved to him that he was getting under her skin.

She wasn't even sure that *she* believed her excuses.

'Not married,' she managed, at last.

The silence was so long that, for a moment, she wondered if she'd suddenly lost her hearing.

'No perfect husband?' His voice snagged over her.

Rough, like sandpaper, making her skin prickle and her voice choke up.

'No husband.'

And just like that something…*shifted* between them. She felt it with every raised, fine hair on her skin, and in every cell of her body. And she felt it in the way the air thickened around them. As if creating some bubble around her and Kane. An airwall between them and the rest of the world.

He took a step nearer to her. So close she could feel the heat seeping from his body into hers. Melting her. He dipped his head, centimetres from hers, then stopped, his warm, vaguely minty breath dancing over her skin.

He was going to kiss her and, heaven help her, she wanted him to.

'What went wrong?' he asked softly, making her blink.

What was wrong with her? He was after answers and all she could think about was kissing him. She was such an idiot.

'That's none of your business.' She sucked in a sharp breath.

What was she going to tell Kane? That she'd spent ten years thinking she'd got over him, thinking that she'd found the perfect man in George Blakeney, only for her to look up and imagine—at her damned *wedding rehearsal dinner*—that she'd seen Kane standing in that room.

As shameful as that was.

She could still remember that awful night with heart-breaking clarity. Even now, if she closed her eyes, she could remember exactly how she'd felt standing on that stage next to her future husband, a gentle sort of happiness fizzing inside her as they'd addressed their guests and looked forward to their wedding the following weekend. She recalled smiling out into the sea of loving, happy, laughing faces, all the well-wishers who had travelled so far to be with them, and how that bubble had popped in an instant the moment she'd thought she'd seen Kane standing at the back—as bleak and imposing as ever.

Worse still was the dangerous thrill that had rushed her entire body at the thought that he had finally, *finally* come back to her.

She remembered swaying. Clutching at George's arm just to stop herself from toppling off the stage. She'd turned to look at George and then back into the crowd, and in that instant Kane had disappeared. Gone up in a puff of smoke, which was apt since he'd never really been there in the first place. She'd been imagining him, conjuring him up because really, deep down, however happy she'd been with George, there had always been that cloud, hovering just in her periphery. However much she'd loved her fiancé, there had always been that little piece missing.

She'd spent fourteen years pretending otherwise, but the simple fact was that Kane Wheeler had stolen the very core of her heart years ago, and she'd never really had it to give to anyone else.

But that didn't mean she had to stand here like the gauche, helplessly-in-love teenager she'd once been. She was a successful doctor. An army major. It was time to act like it.

'You were right, Kane,' Mattie bit out. 'I should get back to work.'

'Mattie…' His voice corkscrewed around her, twisting her, bending her to his will the way he always had done.

She couldn't let him.

It was…*interesting* to see you again.' She forced herself to take a step back and break all contact. It made things a little better, though not enough for her liking.

'I'll buy you a coffee,' he announced abruptly, his tone suggesting that his brain hadn't entirely engaged with his mouth when he'd blurted out the offer, such as it was.

It was ignominious how tempted she was to agree. Had it ever been so hard to shake her head instead of nod?

'Sorry, but right now I have work to do. A long shift so I won't even be finished until the early hours.'

What did she say that for?

'Tomorrow night, then.'

She wanted to say *yes*. Oh, how she wanted to.

'Tomorrow night, I'm meeting friends. And, Hayden, it's a celebration.' *Stop waffling*, she ordered herself. Sucking in a breath, she made her brain focus. 'Thanks for the offer, though. Perhaps we'll run into each other again in another fourteen years.'

And then, before the less rational part of her brain could talk her round, she turned and left.

Walking away from Kane for the first time ever.

CHAPTER TWO

'PATIENT IS ASHLEY, a female in her thirties. Traumatic c-spine injury. Knocked off her bike at approximately eleven o'clock this morning; driver witness reported she was travelling downhill at approximately twenty miles per hour and was thrown over the handlebars, landing head first. No loss of conscious noted at the time, and when we arrived she had a GCS of fifteen out of fifteen. She's able to move her extremities and is tender to palpation over the second vertebra. She also has a fractured left clavicle.'

'Okay, thank you.' Mattie nodded.

'We also brought in her cycling helmet, which had broken into three pieces on impact.'

'Great.' Again Mattie thanked him, handing the helmet to one of her team. It could come in useful in assessing exactly how her patient had landed.

Finally, she approached the woman.

'Okay, Ashley, sweetheart. I'm Mattie, your doctor. I'm just going to check you over.' Her head, which had been crowded with thoughts of Kane only moments before, instantly cleared as she focused on her patient.

She ran through her thorough checks efficiently as her team moved around slickly, all knowing their jobs with nominal direction from her. At length she concluded her obs and stepped away to brief the ward sister in a low voice.

'Can you page Ortho, please? She's got a C2 fracture and she's unstable, so we need some portable c-spines, then get her in for CT and MRI. No evidence of intra-abdominal injury but there's a mid-shaft fracture of the left clavicle.'

The positive was that the patient's obs were stable and she seemed neurologically intact, but Mattie knew that if her patient moved, she could sever her own spine. Not to mention lose her ability even to breathe. But this was her job. It was what she loved to do, even in these circumstances.

For the next few hours Mattie concentrated on the busy A and E department. After her cyclist came a broken leg, then a cardiac arrest, a duodenal fistula, and if each one kept her brain whirling, and mercifully well away from Kane, well, so much the better.

Now, finally, she had her last patient of the shift, and one of Mattie's more unusual cases. Another female, but this one was an elderly woman with a knife embedded in her back.

Her husband hovered, stricken, at his wife's bedside. He started talking to Mattie the moment she approached them.

'I didn't mean it… I just… She was just…' He faded out as the young paramedic placed his hand on the older man's arm to calm him.

'It's all right, Vern. Let me explain to the doc, okay?'

The older man bobbed his head unhappily.

'This is Dot, eighty-two, she has a stab wound to her back with the knife still in situ. Dot and Vern were preparing veg together for their family, who are visiting tonight, when Dot tried carrying a pan of water from the sink to the hob.'

'It was heavy,' Vern added, agitated. 'Really heavy. I *told* her to leave it and wait for me.'

'I *will* explain…' the paramedic began.

Mattie moved swiftly to interject with a gentle smile.

Right now she wasn't interested in apportioning blame as much as treating her patient, but clearly the old man wanted her to understand the circumstances, and it was going to be quicker to listen than to argue.

Plus, a part of her thought it was lovely that he was caring and concerned. Once upon a time, in what felt like a lifetime ago, she'd thought that she and Kane would grow old together. Still caring for each other, like this couple did.

She'd forgotten that. So why was it there, in the forefront of her brain, right now? She thrust it away.

'It's all right, sir. Do you want to briefly tell me what happened?'

The man nodded gratefully, his shoulders sagging slightly.

'I was chopping carrots. That's my job, you see. Peeling and chopping the veg whilst Dot deals with the meat.'

'Of course.' She smiled again.

'So Dot tried to carry the pan, but she isn't as steady on her feet as she once was, you see? And she slopped a bit over the edge and onto the floor.'

'I see.' Mattie nodded encouragingly.

'So she slipped. In the water, see?' He gestured to the floor as though that might somehow better illustrate what had happened. 'And I went to catch her. See?'

'With the chopping knife still in your hand?' she asked, more for the sake of clarity than anything else.

'I never thought.' He looked distraught. 'I just wanted to catch her before she hit the floor.'

'Of course you did,' she soothed. 'Can you tell me about the knife, Vern? Was it a long knife? A serrated knife?'

'About this big…' He gestured again with his hands.

'Dot has a two-centimetre laceration on her right side, just above the iliac crest, and you can see the knife still in situ. We didn't want to turn her over because this was the position she was in when we arrived, but I'm sure there are no wounds to the front. Dot isn't on any medication, and there's no volume issues.'

'Thanks,' Mattie acknowledged. 'Vern, sir, would you like someone to bring you a tea or a coffee whilst we just check on your wife?'

A and E might be bustling, but it was going to be far easier to examine Dot if her husband wasn't hovering. Which wasn't to say that she didn't feel for him, he was clearly worried, but she could do with ten minutes without him there.

'All right Dot,' Mattie told her patient when Vern had finally been led across the room and her team could get on with their job. 'We're going to roll you over now, just to check there are no injuries elsewhere, and get you across to the bed. We'll be as careful as we can be, but I need you to try to stay still, all right? Good. That's good.'

Mattie glanced at her team.

'Okay, ready, steady...'

And perhaps it was the twisted way a medical mind seemed to work, looking at life in a skewed way from the rest of the world, but when she looked at the older couple—with the bizarreness of their situation juxtaposed with the sheer banality of the fact the accident had occurred when they'd simply been making a meal together in domestic harmony—all Mattie could remember was the time when she'd thought she and Kane would grow old together like this couple. And how much it had hurt when he'd walked away from her without a second thought.

Seven years of practically back-to-back tours in multiple war zones, seeing atrocities that the average person couldn't even have imagined—the human body ripped apart in ways she hadn't even known it was possible to survive—and that experience still ranked as one of the worst days of her life.

Which was why, tonight she was going to meet her

friends to celebrate her upcoming promotion, and Kane Wheeler wasn't going to take up another moment inside her brain.

And if she could even pretend that was the case, she was making progress.

'My little sister, Major Mathilda Brigham, soon-to-be Lieutenant-Colonel Mathilda Brigham.' Hayden Brigham raised his glass proudly, his rich voice just about heard over the deep pulse of the music's bass line. 'To Mattie.'

'To Mattie,' the handful of close friends chorused loudly, before each taking a drink.

Tucked away as they were in a booth in the quieter part of the club, Mattie was still trying to convince herself that Kane didn't deserve another moment's thought. But it wasn't that easy. He lingered around the peripheries of her mind and if she was being entirely honest, despite her pep talk to herself earlier, she hadn't exactly been chasing him off.

And it doesn't matter how much you shake your head like that, a little voice whispered in her ear, *it isn't going to shake him off.*

It wasn't as if she'd never moved on with her life these past fourteen years—because she *had.* She'd dated, even got engaged. It was just that ultimately no other man had made her want to want to bend in her dream career as army doctor, the way that Kane had when they'd been kids.

Even George. She'd been prepared to give up the army because it had been expected of her, because she'd known that if it had been the other way around George would have given up anything for her, and possibly because she'd wanted to prove to herself that she had well and truly moved on from Kane.

In short, all the wrong reasons. Which meant her marriage to George would probably have unravelled at some point anyway, even if she hadn't seen Kane—or had imagined that she'd seen him—at her wedding rehearsal.

It also meant that she'd vowed to herself that she would never give up either part of her career for any man again. *And yet…* The encounter yesterday, and the way she'd reacted so viscerally, had only proved to her that she had never quite exorcised Kane Wheeler. Some might say she'd never had closure, others might say that she had always been looking at her youth through a rose-tinted rear-view mirror.

Either way, maybe yesterday had been her chance to knock both on the head. Maybe going for a coffee with Kane would have allowed her to see that she'd built that typical youthful first love into something far greater than it had ever really been. Maybe she'd have seen Kane in a different light—one that wasn't tinged with the adoring glow of a teenager.

And maybe she was lying to herself all over again.

'Mattie?' Hayden's concerned voice penetrated her musing. 'Everything okay?'

She blinked. Forced a smile.

'Everything's great.'

'You just wish Mum was still alive to see this? She'd have been so proud of you, Mattie.'

She swallowed hard. Her head had been so full of Kane that she hadn't even stopped to think about her mum. Her sudden death eight years ago had been so devastating to them all, but perhaps to their father most of all. He'd held it together, of course, with his proud stiff upper lip, but Mattie wouldn't have been surprised if that was where it had all started to unravel for him.

As much as he had been a brigadier, her mum had been the real rock of the family. Had trying to suppress his own grief to appear strong for her and Hayden been too much? Was that when his Alzheimer's had started?

God, but it was such a hateful disease.

She chased the moment away hastily. Nothing was going to cloud tonight. She had so many other things to be grateful for, not least a great career, a wonderful upbringing, and a loving family. How many times had she heard them say how proud they were of her? How lucky she'd been. This promotion wasn't just hers—it belonged to all of her family for their unwavering love and support all her life.

And who cared about Kane-ruddy-Wheeler?

'Just that this promotion hasn't been announced yet, Hayd.' She leaned against her brother to be heard as she waved her hand in a mixture of pride and embarrassment. 'I have to get through the next three months running medical simulations thousands of miles away in the middle of the Canadian prairies first.'

'You say it like they're going to be just any medical simulations.' Her brother shook his head, half grinning and half grimacing. 'But you're going on Operation Strikethrough, Mattie. You've no idea what I would give to go on a brand-new experimental brigade exercise like that. Especially after being deskbound for the past few months.'

'You've got Operation Ironplate,' she said placatingly, not surprised when he pulled a face.

'Three months putting in infrastructure into a new African nation is hardly the same as test-driving a new brigade tactic for the entire British Army.'

'Well, if you didn't go cutting the cords on your parachute to save some poor kid who has passed out on his first jump, you probably wouldn't have ended up breaking your leg.'

Then she laughed, the sheer absurdity and the sheer *Hayden*-ness of her brother's actions making her chest swell.

'I know, I'm a true hero.' He pulled a face at her before

his own grin returned. 'But you're going to have infantry and light armoured, you'll be trying out completely new tactics for the entire British Army, after thirty years of fighting using post–Cold War strategies.'

'I know. Incredible isn't it?' Mattie breathed, unable to help herself.

'And *you're* the doc chosen to run end-to-end simulations for them.' He squeezed her shoulders. 'Stressing the old medical chain until it breaks and then finding a way to rebuild it. Every major and colonel I know has been after that plum job.'

'Yeah, well, I got lucky.' Mattie wrinkled her nose as Hayden threw his arm around her shoulders.

'Nope, you've done enough tours of duty, flown out into enough war zones, and saved enough lives on the operating table, you're definitely the best man for the role.'

Mattie cast her brother a grateful look. She needed this. Her brother…and this camaraderie. To remind her that she had a good life. She didn't need Kane bursting back into it and turning it upside down. She had better things to focus on.

Like her promotion.

And her brother's respect meant a lot. As an army engineer, Hayden had been on just as many tours and been even closer to the sharp end than she had. But promotion in the Royal Army Medical Corps was different from promotion within the Royal Engineers, and she knew her brother was on track to becoming a full two-star general one day the way he was going.

'So, congratulations, Mattie.' One of her other friends reached behind Hayden and clapped her on the back. 'Can't think of any better doctor or officer to lead the medical unit.'

'Yeah, thoroughly well deserved,' another two echoed across the table.

'Thanks guys.' Mattie nodded, emotion bubbling inside her at their warmth.

Then, as the group split down to try to talk over the music, Mattie leaned to her other side to Bridget, the only one of her friends who wasn't from the military world. Bridget was a nurse, working for an NGO.

'You okay, Bea?'

'Sorry?' Bridget strained to hear.

Mattie leaned closer.

'I asked if Hayd has been looking after you?'

'Yes.' Bridget nodded, her voice so low that Mattie had almost had to lip-read rather than hear her friend over the music. 'But you didn't really have to task your brother to babysit me.'

If Mattie hadn't known better, she might have actually thought Bridget was blushing. But that was impossible—the young nurse didn't do any kind of relationship.

'I *did* have to.' Mattie pulled an apologetic face. 'We were supposed to be working together at Jukrem camp—until I got called away for this new mission. I was really hoping to be able to show you the ropes out there.'

'It doesn't matter. I need to learn to be bolder, anyway.' Bridget smiled, but Mattie could tell it was forced. 'Stronger.'

It was odd. When it came to working in war zones, or inhospitable environments, with malaria, or TB, or any one of a slew of diseases most of her colleagues wouldn't have a clue how to deal with, Bea was a wonder. Strong, confident, funny. But when it came to confidence in a social setting, like a bar or a nightclub, she seemed to press herself into the surroundings as though she wished she were some kind of chameleon.

'You're stronger than you realise, Bea,' she told her friend softly. 'You know what they say, fake it until you make it.'

'Yeah, well, I don't know how to fake it.'

'Sure you do.' Mattie laughed. 'Pretend you're that bush-veld lizard you told me about. The one that pretends it's a boogies-oogie beetle, or something like that, to frighten away prey.'

'*Oogpister beetle*,' Bea corrected automatically, but it raised a chuckle from her just as Mattie had intended. 'I don't know what I'm more impressed with—your analogy, or the fact you even remembered my story.'

'Both,' she confirmed promptly, eliciting another chuckle. 'But either way my brother will be there for any advice and support. Don't be afraid to use him.'

'Well, thanks.' Bridget flushed then shook her head. 'Anyway, enough about me. Can I get you a drink to say congratulations?'

'Actually, it's traditional for me to buy you guys the drinks since it's my promotion.' Mattie laughed, standing up and leaning over the table to address the group. 'Same again?'

She was lucky to have such good friends, Mattie thought five minutes later, standing at the busy bar and watching as the flirty bartender got her drinks. She smiled back without fully engaging. The guy was cute, and definitely giving her more than just passing banter, but she wasn't interested in some one-night stand. Her mind more focused on the new role she would be taking up in less than seventy-two hours.

The role that would lead to the biggest promotion of her career to Lieutenant-Colonel in the Royal Army Medical Corps. The culmination of everything she'd been working towards for years. The only thing that mattered in her life.

'Hello, Matz.'

Mattie didn't turn.

But she exhaled. As though she'd been holding her breath ever since their encounter the previous day. And it was useless to pretend her ears—and something wildly traitorous inside her chest—hadn't been straining for this moment ever since then.

'Has it been another fourteen years already?' she asked, but this time there was no bite to her words.

Perhaps there should have been.

She'd turned her head over her shoulder, raising her voice slightly to be heard. It was the closest she could come to bringing herself to face him without turning around.

'I couldn't wait that long,' he murmured.

Enough to send a fresh trail of goose-bumps zigzagging over her skin. None of it helped by the heat from his chest that seemed to seep into her back, spreading a warmth which she couldn't even pretend was unwelcome.

Something suspiciously like *desire* beginning to flood its way through her very veins.

'Hayden is here,' she managed, by way of distraction. 'If you want to say hi.'

'I didn't come here to talk to your brother.'

She swayed. *Dangerously.* Almost leaning back into him. This had always been Kane's power over her, and it revealed rather too much that she wasn't immune to it even now.

She would call him a loathsome man, except that *loathing* wasn't the sentiment that filled her at all. Not even close. Especially when he reached around her body to lean his hand on the bar top in front of her. And still, somehow, managed not to quite make contact.

Her body practically hummed with electricity.

'How did you know I'd be here?'

'You told me you were going to be out celebrating,' he replied, and what did it say about her that she could actually hear the shrug in his voice, even though she couldn't see him? 'This town doesn't exactly have that many places you could go.'

That much was true but, still, it made her feel good that he'd taken the effort to track her down. Her head was spinning. Did she stand her ground, or did she give into this *thing* that roared and howled inside her?

Did she give into wanting Kane?

Determined not to turn around until she knew what she was doing, Mattie forced herself to concentrate on the bartender, who was thankfully almost finished making her drinks. Although now, it seemed, she was also going to have to contend with a female bartender who, having caught one glimpse of Kane, was already sashaying over, ignoring the clamour of customers who had been waiting far, far longer.

'What can I get you?' The pretty girl simpered and sizzled, pouting in a way that Mattie knew—with perhaps a hint of envy but no real jealousy—would have made her look like a constipated duck had she herself ever had the nerve to try.

Who knew it was even possible to sound so seductive whilst still being heard over the thumping music?

'Two margaritas.' His smile was audible in his voice. And altogether too close to her ear.

A thrill rippled through her, unsolicited.

She hated it that she could conjure up that sensually crooked mouth as surely as if she'd been staring right at it. Was it any wonder that the poor bartender could barely contain her swoon? And the girl hadn't even heard the last part of Kane's words, when he'd dropped his lips to brush her ear, his low voice setting off those faithless goosebumps all over again.

'What do you say, Matz? For old times' sake?'

'I'm not drinking with you,' she muttered. Rather weakly to her own mind.

'Oh, don't worry.' Amusement laced his words. 'They use proper agave tequila and a quality agave syrup here, none of that overly sweet triple-sec stuff that you and I used to drink as kids.'

'You can't appeal to my sense of nostalgia,' she lied. 'Besides, it isn't the ingredients I object to. It's the company.'

'Liar.' He laughed. Altogether too low, and too male.

It cascaded through her. Right down to between her legs. Once she'd been the only person who could ever make Kane laugh. Who else had made him laugh in the last fourteen years?

'Is that why you can't turn around, Matz?'

And then he placed his hand lightly on her shoulder, making her pulse flutter at her neck, and it was a fight—an actual tussle between mind and body—not to let her head tilt to one side and rest her cheek against that hand.

How could he read her so easily? Know just which buttons to push? She was a successful, independent woman, who had flown into perilous combat zones and performed life-saving operations under fire. She hadn't felt these precariously jelly legs and erratically pounding chest since she'd been a teen. Yet here she was, fighting to control her own body's perfidious responses.

Fighting, but not succeeding.

In all these years she had never been able to decide between the part of her that had never wanted to see Kane again and the part of her that had fantasised about this moment. It was pathetic, really. *She* was pathetic.

So why did she feel so alive?

The male bartender finally made it over with the collection of drinks for her group, the female one following closely behind with the two Kane had ordered, and they set them all down on the bar. Mattie's brain spluttered back into life and she reached for her money, but before she could open her purse Kane reached his other arm over her shoulder and handed a note to the guy.

'No change,' he murmured discreetly as the guy tipped his head in tacit gratitude and the woman hovered for a moment before apparently accepting defeat.

Finally, *finally*, Mattie turned to face him, and it was so much worse than the previous day.

Yesterday she'd still been in shock at seeing him again. Today everything about him seemed so much…*more*.

He'd always been dark, dangerous, edgy, but now he seemed positively lethal. She had probably noticed yesterday, though it hadn't quite registered. He was unlikely to be any taller than he'd been almost a decade and a half ago, yet it seemed as though he was. He was certainly bulkier. He'd always been lean yet muscly but now he seemed to be more of a powerhouse of a man.

It suited him. As her body was only too eager to point out. She licked her lips, trying to eradicate an odd, parched sensation, and when his eyes flickered down to watch the movement, something turned round and round inside her.

'You shouldn't have paid,' she managed. 'You…'

She tailed off uncomfortably.

'I can't afford them?' he finished lightly, reading her mind far too easily. He cocked one eyebrow. 'That was a lifetime ago. I'm not that poor kid from the worst part of the estates any more.'

'No, of course not,' she conceded quickly, angry with herself for not stopping to think.

That had always been the problem with Kane. People had judged him without actually knowing. They had made assumptions. Usually, they had dismissed him. No one had ever really wanted to see a spark of decency in any kid from the Wheeler clan. The son of Mick Wheeler, a man who was feared only a little more than he was hated across affluent Lower Heathdale and struggling Heathdale

town alike. And the younger brother of Richie and Rob-
bie Wheeler, who were feared and hated across the whole
damned county.

Even she had dismissed Kane, until she'd been acciden-
tally paired up with him for a school project and had seen
a different Kane Wheeler that no one else seemed to have
bothered to look for. For two years they'd been inseparable.
Even Hayden, initially disapproving and protective of his
sister, had seen a different side to Kane.

Or at least they'd thought they had. Right up until the
night her father had offered him money to leave town and
never come back. And Kane had taken it.

Without even a goodbye.

Something somersaulted inside her and she told herself not to react. Not to be bitter. But then she realised it
wasn't bitterness, it was pain, running along scar lines that
were so deep she had forgotten they were there. And then
something else unfurled inside her.

Hurt.

And shame.

She'd thought that Kane had loved her. Wholly, loyally,
unconditionally. Turned out she'd been wrong.

'Kane…'

'Stop overthinking things, Matz.'

She stopped, the words evaporating on her lips.

Was she?

'Where's your group?'

'My group?'

'I presume you're not drinking all of these yourself?'
He leaned over to scoop up into his large hands the collection of drinks she'd ordered. 'You get the margaritas,
and I'll carry this lot over.'

'Carry them over?' she said weakly.

It was like the cogs in her brain had been frozen in position and she was desperately trying to work them loose.

Her thoughts were all over the place, skittering like a puppy on ice.

She was lurching wildly from old feelings of resentment to old feelings of…well, not *love*, of course. That would be insane. But…*lust*. Yes, that was what it was. Old-fashioned, unadulterated *lust*. Possibly with a generous dusting of nostalgia.

As ludicrous as she knew it was, it was far easier to hold onto that notion of *lust* than the truth of anything else. The truth of anything deeper. But once that proverbial seed had been sown in her head, she realised her mistake too late.

Because now her mind was running riot with a hundred other ridiculous notions.

Like how much harm could come of indulging that lust. Just for one more night…

She tried to put on the brakes, but her thoughts were like a runaway train of carriages, with no way of halting them.

Indulging in this lust for each other would be foolhardy. Ludicrous.

Mattie knew it down to her very bones, yet all she could think was how in a matter of days her three-month posting at the Castleton University Teaching Hospital would be over and she would be beginning her three-month stint in a field hospital thousands of miles away.

So what harm could one night do?

'This is insane,' she muttered, though more to herself than to Kane.

And if he read her lips as the words were snatched away by the loud, sinuous bass of the music, he didn't respond.

She had to stop this before it started. Reaching up her hands to push him away—at least, that's what she was telling herself—Mattie watched in horror as her palms flattened against his chest. Her fingers spread out like they were blooming over him, feeling their way.

And how they revelled in what they felt.

One more moment...

Snatching her hands back abruptly, Mattie glowered at him, but for once he merely stared back at her wordlessly.

'Get the rest of the drinks, Matz,' he growled at last, and she couldn't stop a kick of triumph at the realisation that he sounded as off-kilter as she felt.

But before she could answer he turned around, with her drinks still in his large hands, and began to move through the crowd. All she could do was grab the remaining glasses from the bar and plunge in after him.

Like she always had done.

CHAPTER THREE

'ARE YOU SURE you know what you're doing?'

Mattie sucked in a breath and reminded herself that her brother was only looking out for her. Like any good brother would.

'I'm not doing anything, Hayd,' she replied, shocked at how hollow the words actually sounded. 'I haven't seen Kane for over a decade. We're just having a drink.'

She couldn't blame Hayden for his sceptical glance.

'You don't have to tell me everything, Mattie, we're not kids any more. But you don't need to lie to me either.'

She flushed, hating herself for not being able to stay cool and collected.

'I'm not lying.' Why did she sound like they were teenagers again? 'Fine, so I bumped into Kane yesterday in the hospital. But apart from that, I haven't seen him since I was eighteen.'

'Mattie...' For a moment she thought he was going to tell her something, but then stopped himself. Instead, he shrugged. 'If that's how you want to play it. It's your life, Mattie.'

Why did she get the impression that she was missing something?

'I thought you were going to tell me how stupid it would be.'

It sounded even lamer aloud than it had in her head.

'Do you need me to tell you that?' her brother asked her evenly.

'No.' *Yes.*

'More to the point, do you *want* me to tell you that?'

'No.'

And there it was. The truth—at last. She didn't want to hear Hayden tell her how stupid it would be to open herself up to Kane Wheeler again because she already knew that for herself. The simple truth was that *knowing* it didn't make her want it any less.

She needed to do this. She needed closure.

'You're right.' She forced a bright smile to her lips. 'It's my life. Just as you live your life. Speaking of which, you and Bridget seem to be getting on even better than I'd expected. She's funny, isn't she, when you get past that initial shyness?'

If she hadn't known better, she might have thought her brother actually blushed slightly. For a fraction of a moment. But that was impossible, he didn't do relationships. Or at least he'd had a few carefully chosen female companions but he didn't do *attachments*, however much they'd pushed him. Hayden was all about his career. Arguably even more than she was.

Except right now when, despite the fact that this night was about her friends taking a rare opportunity to get together and celebrate her career—this incredible promotion—the thoughts she was fighting in her brain were all centred on one man.

Kane.

The way it had been all those years ago.

Surely she ought to feel some shame that the focus and drive that had served her well these past years had faded so easily. But then Kane had always burned brighter than anything else in her world.

Hadn't that always been part of the problem?

Abruptly, she felt him there. At her side. So damned close. And she told herself that his proximity didn't have to mean a thing, but it didn't work. Because she couldn't seem to think straight.

'So how do you want this to go, Matz?'

Something darted through her. Twisting and turning as it moved. Starting fires everywhere it paused.

'I don't want this to go any particular way,' she tried, though her tongue felt too thick and too heavy in her mouth.

'Liar,' he whispered. 'You don't *want* to want it to. But that isn't the same thing.'

She hated that he was right. That he knew her so well.

And at the same time it was the thing she loved the most.

'Not here, then,' he offered instead.

It was all she could to offer a curt nod.

'Come on,' he muttered, lifting his hand to the small of her back to guide her discreetly away from the group.

She didn't even try to resist him. She just marvelled at the way her skin seared under the heat of his palm. Blasting through her. Her body soaring in a memory she'd pretended had long since died.

'Kane…' she began, finally turning when she knew they were deep enough into the crowd that her group—her brother—couldn't see them. Lost on the crowded dance floor and hidden in plain sight amongst a sea of moving bodies.

But his mouth crashed down on hers, snuffing out whatever words she'd been about to say next—not that she had any idea what they might have been. Devastating and divine. And in that instant Mattie knew she'd been toppled.

Perhaps a part of her had hoped that her memories of Kane were unrealistic, the proverbial rose-tinted glasses.

Had she almost imagined that the reality wouldn't live up to the perfect image she'd built in her mind, thereby finally releasing her from the prison of her past?

If she had, it was a fatal mistake on her part. Because Kane's kisses weren't merely hot and wild. They were scorching. Torrid. Feral. As addictive as they had always been, and she felt him everywhere.

Every square millimetre of her body was alight whilst she was practically dancing in the blaze, as though her body was coming back to life when she hadn't even realised it had been dormant all these years. A conflagration. And every wicked sweep of Kane's tongue was like a hefty slosh of gasoline on the flames.

His hands cupped her jaw as he angled his head for a better fit and Mattie found herself pressing up against him, desperate to get closer. The drag of his mouth over hers. The warm waft of his breath on her skin. It was all so wonderfully, painfully familiar.

Like coming in from the cold and finding herself somewhere warm. Somewhere *right*.

Her fingers ached as if they, too, needed to discover if that solid chest felt even better than she remembered. And a pulse blasted right through her, straight down to her core, at the memory of how it would feel when Kane touched her right *there*.

Because this madness wasn't going to stop here. Just with one kiss. This was the man she'd once loved with every fibre of her being. Every inch of her naïve teenage heart. He would be her death the way he'd always been— even if she no longer harboured ridiculous notions that he would be with her forever.

Which was why she wrapped her arms around his neck and clung on, as though he was a liferaft in this sea of heaving bodies. No one was paying remotely like any attention to them and yet, to Mattie, the entire world felt as though it had zeroed in on her. On Kane.

She had no idea how long they stayed like that. His mouth tasting hers. His tongue teasing hers. She only knew she never wanted to it to stop. But it finally did, when he wrenched his lips from hers as though it was as much a torture for him to do so as it was for her.

Somehow that simple fact helped her.

'We're getting out of here,' he growled, taking her hand in his larger one and leading her off the dance floor and to the doors, leaving her with no option than to obey.

Not that she wanted to do any such thing. She'd taken that leap now and let him kiss her. She wasn't about to look back.

'Where are we going?' she managed, a little breathlessly so it was a wonder he heard her over the music.

Either way, he barely turned.

'A hotel. There's one around the corner.'

A thrill went through her. She told herself it was just echoes of the past. The unexpectedness of the moment being just like that first time they'd ever slept together as teenagers. The bed and breakfast they'd gone to a couple of towns over. Far enough that no one would ever recognise them but not so far that they felt as though they were doing something so very wrong.

And far more special than the back seat of a car like she knew most of the girls in her class had managed. Far more magical.

But tonight wasn't about being special, Mattie reminded herself firmly as she hurried down the stairs with Kane. And these butterflies dancing dizzily in her belly weren't magical. Tonight was about finally laying those old ghosts to rest. Finally cutting those invisible ties. After that, she would be free. Able, at last, to move on with the rest of life.

And if there was a part of her that remained sceptical that she could be so clinical, well, she wasn't about to let it have a voice.

Kane used his body to pin Mattie to the wall of the hotel room the instant they tumbled inside. Her hands slid down to his backside to pull him to her, the hardest part of him against the softest part of her, and they both groaned. He plundered her mouth, again and again, revelling in every greedy little sound as her lips slid, plump and perfect beneath his touch, and her tongue scraped over his, making wordless demands of her own.

He scarcely remembered taking her hand and leading her out of that nightclub, or the way he'd had to fight with every inch of his self-control to keep his hands—and his mouth—off that lush body of hers long enough to get to them the closest hotel. One of only a couple in town, and hardly the kind of five-star resort spa to which she was probably accustomed.

But it was clean, and close. Most importantly, it had a bed.

She tugged at his shirt, hauling it roughly over his head as his fingers worked the zip at the back of her dress, then he stepped back long enough to slide it from her shoulders and let it fall, like a shimmering waterfall, to pool at her feet. Then, as she stood there in a lacy whisper of a bra and matching thong, and a pair of the sexiest heels he thought he'd ever seen, her eyes black with desire, she reached out and cupped him through his trousers.

It was all Kane could do to keept himself in check. He had no intention of embarrassing himself at the door of the hotel room.

It was years since he'd felt this out of control. Fourteen years, to be exact. The realisation should have impacted on him, but it barely registered. He had Mattie back in his arms—something he would never have believed even possible twenty-four hours ago—and right now absolutely nothing else mattered.

He pressed against her again, needing to feel her breasts against his chest, her legs wrapping around his waist. And Mattie—*his* Mattie—was only too obliging. He didn't dare speak, not convinced that his brain could even form a coherent sentence right at this moment, but it didn't matter. Words weren't necessary.

She tasted of magic. Black magic. Her light perfume—incredibly, the same one he'd bought her as a teenager—was utterly intoxicating. And it was doing…*things* to him.

Sliding his hands down her body, Kane fought to take his time reacquainting himself with her sensual curves. Touching, tasting, teasing. When she dropped her hand between them, cupping him and making him feel like he was going to go off at any moment, he caught her wrist in his fingers and lifted it to pin both her hands above her head.

'Kinky,' she teased, so that he could feel the curve of her mouth against his lips.

'Not especially,' he murmured. 'But if that's what you're after, I'm sure I could tie you to the bed whilst I lick you until you scream my name.'

Which wasn't necessarily a bad idea, Kane thought as Mattie sucked in a soft breath at the mere idea. Especially as he felt like some randy teenager again and wasn't entirely convinced he'd last too long once he slid inside her.

Matz. Mattie. *His* Mathilda.

This wasn't some random attraction. An unexpected opportunity presenting itself. This felt like coming home. The sensation moved within him as though it had been cramped up in some tiny hole for far too long, and was only now awakening from its long, self-imposed hibernation. It was stretching out, it was reaching into every corner of his being, and it was settling there as though this—here, with Mattie—was the way it was always meant to have been.

He unhooked her bra, slipping it from her, and then he bent his head to draw one perfect nipple into his mouth. Mattie gasped, arching her back, and he drew whorls over her soft skin with his tongue, up and around, taking his time, while she laced her fingers through his hair and made the sweetest sounds. And then, when he was satisfied on one side, he turned his attentions to the other.

'Kane,' she muttered at length. The undisguised *need* in her voice playing havoc with his self-control.

Slowly he lifted his head from her breast and began to make his way lower, trailing kisses down her stomach, over the creamy swell of her abdomen and lower still, until he could smell the sweet scent that was essentially *her*. And it drove him half-crazy.

Without even bothering to remove that whisper of lace, he reached down and traced her swollen, molten core. Her legs quivered instantly, and Kane loved it that she couldn't even begin to disguise her reactions to him, even as he was barely capable of reining himself in. Still, he made himself take his time, letting his calloused palms graze up the back of those smooth, shapely calves.

'Old bullet wound,' she muttered, when his fingers slowed over a long, thick, welt of a scar.

His heart stilled, caught in the crosshairs of a memory so vivid that it almost knocked him backwards. For a moment he could hear the firefight. Smell that distinct odour. Taste the sand in his mouth and his nose.

And then he squeezed his eyes closed and it was gone. He was back in the hotel room with Mattie, and that was all that mattered. He concentrated on her leg, stroking the scar almost reverently.

'Is that so?' he asked. 'Another round and you could have been killed. Makes you a hero.'

'No, I'm definitely not a hero,' she bit out harshly, despite her ragged breathing. 'We were retrieving a couple of casualties from a previously deserted village. I just got clipped getting on a heli. It was the guys who covered us in the firefight who were the real heroes.'

Kane didn't answer. At least, not with words. Instead he lifted her leg and kissed the scar. One day he would tell her the truth. That he'd been one of the guys in that village, in that firefight. Their two buddies dying in front of them and no one wanting to risk coming in so close to the enemy and during the back end of a sandstorm.

And then the heli had appeared seemingly out of nowhere, and Mattie had jumped out of the back like some kind of angel.

She'd saved more than just the casualties' lives that day.

One day, he would tell her. *Just not today.*

Pushing the memory from his mind, he continued his exploration of her body. Tracing his hands up her velvety, lean thighs, following closely with his lips, leaving a trail of feather-light kisses. Then, finally, when he could hardly make himself wait any longer, he rested her leg on his shoulder, hooked her pretty underwear to one side, and buried his head in her honeyed heat.

Finally.

And his glorious Mattie cried out, her hips moving and bucking until he had to take them in his hands and hold her steady, licking deeper into her, sucking that sensitive bud and gently grazing the soft skin with his teeth. Not hard. Just enough. Driving her—both of them—wild. She was coming apart under his mouth and he couldn't get enough of her.

'Kane... I can't...not like this...' she gasped, even as her hands gripped his shoulders as though a part of her thought to push him away but the rest of her couldn't bring herself to do any such thing.

He wanted to tell her to relax, but that would have meant lifting his head from her sweetness, and he didn't think he could stand to do that. Instead, he licked deeper, sucked harder, until her fingers were biting painfully into his muscles, until she was trembling in his hands, and until she was crying out for him.

And still he didn't stop. He didn't wait for her to come back down, he simply kept going, driving her through one orgasm and straight on to the next. This time, as she began to fall, moving hotter and wilder, he plunged first one finger inside her, and then another, propelling her on until she screamed his name and her legs buckled beneath her.

His.

And he realised he was never again going to allow her to be anyone else's.

By the time Mattie came back to herself the second time, she was already sprawled over the hotel bed and Kane was moving over her, finally naked. She reached for him instinctively.

'That was…' She shook her head, tailing off.

For over a decade she'd told herself that she was remembering Kane through the sentimental, syrupy glow of a nostalgic first love. That being with him couldn't have really been *that* spectacular. That earth-shattering.

But after this, *tonight*, there was no way she was ever going to be able to tell herself that lie again. Because nothing, *nothing* had never matched this incredible gift that Kane had just given her.

Worse, she knew now that nothing ever would.

'Mattie? Everything okay?' He paused, bracing himself above her as if he was about to stop.

She had the terrifying premonition that if he did stop, she would die.

'Everything is perfect,' she whispered, looping her hands around his neck and pulling him down to her.

And when he gathered her in his arms, rolling them both over so that she was astride Kane, with him nudging at her heat, she had the feeling that it really *was* perfect.

'I can't promise you I'll last,' he warned her grimly, making her feel more wanted than ever.

'All the more chance to do it again and again.' A soft laugh escaped her throat. 'All night if we have to.'

'I don't think one night is going to be long enough.'

It was enough to make her body soar even as a hundred new questions began to swarm in her head, but he didn't give her chance to dwell on them. Taking hold of her hips in his large hands, he shifted her until he was sliding inside her. The way she'd never thought Kane would ever do again. Hotter, tighter, and even better than everything she'd pretended not to remember all these years.

And then he began to move. In and out. A slow, lazy rhythm that seemed to pulse right through her, and for the third time that night her world began to spin. Mattie could feel herself losing her grip, and nothing had ever felt more *right*.

She flattened her hands on his chest, tipping herself forward and lodging him that bit deeper, making them both groan, loving how Kane began to move faster as though he couldn't help himself.

'Let go,' she whispered, letting her hair drop to brush over his chest the way she had so many times all those years before.

It was like flipping a switch. Without another word, Kane gripped her more tightly around her hips and began to plunge deeper as everything left in Mattie burst into bright, magnificent flames. A searing, perfect fever that seemed to consume her whole. She was splintering with every thrust, shattering into a million perfect fragments that she didn't think she would ever be able to piece back together.

And she didn't care.

All she could do was cling on for the ride, as Kane finally drove his way home.

CHAPTER FOUR

'THEY'RE COMING IN NOW, ma'am.'

'Thank you, Corporal.' Mattie acknowledged the young girl as her team looked out at the skies.

In a short while the low-flying Hercules C130 would fly by, dropping three seven-hundred-and-fifty-kilogram pallet-loads of supplies by parachute. From saline drips to MRI scanners, and from stretchers to generators.

It was up to her team to retrieve the pallets, load them onto the back of an army lorry and get them back to the location they had identified for a field hospital. Then set them up for a strata one medical facility comprising an eighteen-by-twenty-four tent for one resuscitation bay, one field surgical table and one ITU bed.

The ultimate test was that the first 'test' casualties would be arriving one hour from 'drop-off' and the field hospital would have to be up and running by then. A hectic but well-organised and practised set-up that would entail full attention from the moment the pallets were parachuted in. And Mattie welcomed it.

Anything to keep her mind from wandering back to the weekend. That perfect night when it had just been Kane and herself. Even now, two days later and thousands of miles away, her body still ached deliciously. Muscles she had forgotten about reminded her of the way they had made love, over and over. Relearning each other, their shape, their feel, their taste.

They had taken their time, relearning what the other liked. Even now, she could still hear those impossibly carnal groans as she'd tightened around him.

And then she thought about when she'd knelt down in front of him in the shower later that night, the hot water running over their bodies as she'd reacquainted herself with the taste of him, the way she'd done when they'd been teenagers.

Only this time she'd had a few tricks. It was odd because she hadn't really enjoyed it with any other man. It had always felt like such a powerless, surrendering position to be in. But Kane had always been different, and she'd thrilled in those impossibly feral noises he'd made as she'd used her tongue like a weapon against him.

The way he'd stared down at her with such a black, lust-filled, carnal expression when she'd taken him into her mouth, and the way he'd reacted—like he was shaking from the inside out—when she'd grazed her teeth down his length. It had made her feel like the most powerful woman in the world to know that she was doing that to Kane, having that effect on him. She'd deliberately ignored all his warnings for her to stop until he'd been helpless to do anything but brace his hands on the wet tiles and let her have her way.

And then he'd carried her back to the bed and punished her with his all-too-clever hands and his all too wicked mouth. Taking her in every way possible, making her splinter apart so many times she'd thought she'd never be able to piece herself back together.

Or ever want to.

If there had been any way that she could have stayed with him in that hotel room forever—ignored her orders to fly out here—Mattie knew she would have done so. Willingly.

And she hated herself for it.

That night was supposed to have been about closure. Nothing more. It certainly hadn't been about picking up where they'd left off fourteen years ago. It wasn't as though he'd even *tried* to explain what had happened back then. And yet, whatever she'd tried telling herself in that night-club about taking just one weekend to indulge in whatever that...*thing* was between her and Kane, she now feared that one weekend wasn't enough.

Three months, Mattie told herself desperately. Three months to get her head in order a few thousand miles away from home on this prairies exercise where she couldn't give in to this outrageous urge to call Kane.

And it would be all too easy to do.

His mobile number might be tucked safely in the jewellery box in her accommodation back in the UK—she hadn't wanted the temptation of bringing it out with her, focus was key for this exercise—but she had memorised it on sight. Her thirsty brain soaking it up in an instant. As though a traitorous part of her had needed more. Had needed *him*. And this time that perfidious part wasn't simply going to leave it alone or let her stuff it back in that deep, dark hole inside herself, like she'd done with it over a decade ago.

She was out here for a reason. To do a job. And she'd be damned if she didn't do the best job that she possibly could.

Fighting to tune her brain back to the present, Mattie grasped at the first conversation she could hear going on around her.

'So, we're going to be dealing with IED cases?' One of the newer members of the team was posing the question in general.

It was the distraction Mattie needed.

'IEDs, yes.' She stepped forward. 'But also routine small arms fire, indirect fire, sprained ankles, musculo-skeletal injuries. It's a bit of confidence and morale for the front-line troops that medical support isn't far away.'

'Yes, ma'am.' The young lance corporal nodded, and Mattie had to quash the urge to tell him to use her first name.

With the medical corps, consultants and surgeons working so closely alongside combat medical technicians, unlike the rest of the army they tended to have a more re-laxed approach to rank in the field. But all that would be changing for her now that she was months away from pro-motion to Lieutenant-Colonel. Her new role would mean that she would be moving out of the field and more into training roles.

It was going to feel strange, but she was oddly excited. Or she had been until she'd started wondering how it would fit in with Kane. One thing they hadn't done at the week-end had been discuss anything personal. As though nei-ther of them had wanted the real world to encroach on their perfect bubble for fear that old prejudices would mar the moment.

'We might even get some routine infectious diseases, which is why it's always a fine balance knowing what equipment we might need and what we can reasonably carry, as well as how long we can reasonably sustain our-selves.'

'Squeezing the most capability out of the least equip-ment?'

'Exactly,' Mattie agreed. 'For Operation Strikethrough, it's about testing the support network, but right now this part is for us to test our own teams, especially in the space available. This part of the exercise gives us the chance to iron out any potential problems so that when we're doing the main battlegroup roles next month we know what works at our end so that we can really test them in their new tactical approach.'

'Yes, ma'am,' the young man agreed.

'Major Brigham.'

Mattie turned as a runner raced up from behind her. 'Message from the radio-operator, you're needed back at the main field hospital at Brigade.'

'Now?' She frowned. 'We're about ready for the pallet drop.'

'Sorry, ma'am, they said it was urgent. They're sending a helicopter for you now.'

'I've got this, Mattie.' Alex, the major she had appointed to run this part of the exercise, stepped closer to her. 'You go. Shall I drive you to the landing site?'

'Dammit, I really wanted to be here for this part.'

'Yeah, that's because you've run so many of them.' He grinned. 'But now you're getting this promotion you're going to have to learn to take a step back. This hospital's going to be my baby now.'

Mattie wrinkled her nose.

'Fine, I'm going. You'll take care of it, right?'

'I learned from the best.' He laughed, then turned and headed off to brief the team.

Mattie turned to her driver and smiled.

'Okay, let's go.'

'Give me the sit-rep, Kath,' Mattie directed her second-in-command, Major Katherine McDonal, as she arrived back at the main field hospital.

'New orders from Brigade. The exercise has been going much smoother than expected. Early training has bedded in and Infantry and Light Armoured are advancing quickly. If they keep it up there's going to have to be a hiatus.'

'But Brigade want to keep up the tempo,' Mattie guessed. 'They're bringing forward the casualty scenarios?'

'Right.' Kath nodded. 'However, Amputees for Armies aren't going to be able to get out until next week, as previously planned, so they need us to come up with a few more scenarios to throw at the guys for now.'

Mattie's mind began to race. There were several medical situations she could create, but it depended what Brigade's overall picture looked like.

'Do they have anything particular in mind?'

'Possibly bringing in the Engineers for some kind of bridge collapse.' Kath shrugged. 'They're sending you a liaison from Mechanised Infantry.'

Mattie groaned.

'Oh, God, not Percy Copperhead? He's an oxygen thief. The only reason he got to Major is because his father was a divisional commander. I know it doesn't happen that often, but the guy's the epitome of the worst elements of nepotism.'

'He is,' Kath agreed. 'But I think he knows exactly what you think of him because he isn't coming in person, he's sending his company sergeant major instead.'

'I guess that's him trying to make a point and insult me.' Mattie pulled a wry face. 'But I'm guessing his CSM is the one who really runs that unit anyway. The place would fall apart if Percy was really in charge.'

'Funny you should say that…' Kath laughed '…but I had the same thought. So I asked around, and from what I can glean the guy is as solid as they come. A real straight shooter who knows his stuff. Should suit you a lot better.'

'Great. Okay, when is this guy—do we have a name?—heading in?'

'No name, but the guy's already in transit so he should be here by seventeen hundred hours.'

'That's in fifteen minutes. Brigade must really be panicking,' Mattie mused, consulting her watch. 'Okay, you crack on with what you were doing before, I'm going to see if I can't grab my first coffee of the day then have a look in Triage and the ICUs.'

'Okay, I'll know where to find you,' agreed Kath. 'Try to grab some scran as well—I'm willing to bet you haven't eaten yet.'

Mattie's stomach rumbled on cue.

'I'll see what I can do.' Mattie laughed as she left the room. 'I just hope the CSM that idiot Percy's sending me is going to live up to his apparent reputation.'

Heading down the corridor, she was about to peel off to the doors leading outside and to the mess area when a commotion at the end of the hallway caught her attention. By the looks of it, it was a gunshot wound to the chest, and as this wasn't in any of her scenarios for her own hospital, she knew it was a genuine casualty.

'What happened?' she asked, forgetting her other plans and racing towards the incident.

'Gunshot wound to the upper right quadrant of the chest from three hundred to four hundred metres. Penetrating front to back.'

Meaning that the round would have lost a significant amount of velocity before it had hit the casualty, Mattie calculated quickly.

'Combat medics describe open sucking chest wound. Used the casualty's field dressing to occlude it, as well as some other materials to hand.'

'BP?' she asked.

Good, so at least that suggested no significant loss of blood and therefore no vital organs had been hit.

'Stable. Slightly elevated pulse and breathing.'

'From the mask I'd say oxygen saturations are down?'

'Slightly.'

So probably a small hole. If it was much bigger the air would have wanted to move out of the chest wound instead of the airway and breathing would be a more serious problem. Still, she suspected the exit wound would be enlarged and jagged, experience having taught her that it was likely the bullet would have destabilised as it had penetrated the chest tissues, and therefore turned sideways slightly.

'Let's have a look and get him to CT,' Mattie instructed, taking up position on one side of the gurney and running her fingers over the tissues of the chest.

It felt like bubble wrap under the skin and seemed to confirm the pneumothorax diagnosis.

So much for her coffee and food, but this was what she loved doing. What she lived for—saving lives.

'All right, so the left side looks normal, as expected.' She eyed the monitor a short while later. 'Right side we have collapsed lung, clouding suggesting haemo-pneumothorax, and soft-tissue distortion suggesting surgical emphysema. However, there appears to be no bone damage, with the round apparently entering and exiting between the ribs, so that's good. Let's get him into surgery, shall we?'

Some wound exploration, cleaning and insertion of a tube to drain the blood and air, and reinflate the lung. Hopefully the kid should be okay. It wasn't a great thing to happen to him, but she'd seen a lot worse.

'Ma'am, the liaison from Strike Brigade arrived whilst you were in surgery.' One of the junior NCOs from Command post was waiting for her when she got out.

'Thank you, Corporal,' she acknowledged. 'Please tell him I'll be right over.'

She didn't wait for the confirmation before popping into ICU to check on her patient one more time. She would have preferred to hold on just a little longer to be sure, but it probably wasn't the best idea.

Percy would probably think she'd deliberately kept his company sergeant major waiting, but that was too bad. She wasn't here to pander to Major Copperhead's ego. Hopefully, the liaison would know that. Still, it would be better to leave her patient with her team and go and find out what new scenarios Strike Brigade wanted to put into play.

Hurrying down the labyrinth of corridors that led to the command post on the other side of the hospital, Mattie practically burst through the doors.

'Sorry to keep you waiting. Surgical emergency.'

She froze in shock.

It couldn't be. It wasn't possible.

'Ma'am, this is WO2 Wheeler, Strike Brigade liaison for the new medical scenarios. Sir, this is Major Brigham, CO of this field hospital. She'll be running the medical exercises.'

Mattie didn't speak. She didn't even move.

She couldn't.

All she could do was stand and watch as Kane rose and, after barely the briefest hint of a pause, saluted. She had no idea how she managed it but she braced in acknowledgement, still reeling.

She needed to collect herself. Get herself straight. Mattie forced herself to focus on her colleague, her tone as light as she could manage.

'Thank you, Sergeant. We'll be in my office but unless it's urgent I don't want to be disturbed.' She turned stiffly to Kane, careful to afford him the courtesy her soldiers would expect from her to do with any warrant officer and company sergeant major. 'Mr Wheeler, come through.'

Then, without waiting to see him follow, she forced her wooden legs to turn and step through the doors, concentrating on placing one foot in front of the other as she made her way down the corridor and into her office. She made her way around the desk as though it was the only thing protecting her from the enemy.

As Kane followed her in, he closed the door carefully

behind them without waiting for her to instruct him to do so. His one indication that whilst he might have followed protocol out there in front of her men, he wasn't about to in here, away from prying eyes.

And she wasn't about to pull him up over it.

'What the hell, Kane?' Mattie choked out instead, her throat constricted and painful. 'You're a WO2? In fact, you're Percy's CSM? You never once mentioned it...that night.'

Everything inside her screamed and railed but she stoutly quashed it. They couldn't afford for anyone else to hear even a raised voice, certainly not the actual subject matter.

'And you're not just Dr Brigham. You're *Major* Brigham. In fact, as I understand it, you're *Acting Colonel* Brigham, Commanding Officer for this Three Medical Regiment. You never thought to mention that.'

Vaguely she recognised that he was making some point, but she didn't know what it was. And she was too caught up in the heat flooding her body to press him. The inconvenient truth was that whilst they'd...she refused to say *made love* again and again that night, neither of them had done a whole lot of talking.

'Did you know?' she pressed instead.

'Of course I didn't know.' Kane's voice cracked through the air like a whip. Low and powerful.

'You must have,' she insisted desperately, because they were in an impossible situation and it couldn't merely be coincidence. Or fate. That felt somehow...inadequate. 'You knew I always intended to join the army as a doctor, whereas I had no idea you'd even contemplated joining the military.'

'If you're looking to lay the blame somewhere, Mattie,' he growled, 'I suggest you stop now. There is nothing to be gained by it. But, for the record, I told you I'd heard you left the army a few years ago. I even told you that… the day we met at the hospital.'

Oh, Lord, how she didn't want this to be happening. A perverse part of her wanted him to tell her it was all a bad dream, take her in his arms, and make love to her the way he had, over and over, the previous weekend.

But she didn't want that, she reminded herself quickly. And even if a weak part of her *did* want that, he couldn't do it. Not here.

Not ever.

She was a major in the army, and he was a warrant officer. He might be one of the highest-ranking, most respected non-commissioned officers in the British Army, but he was still non-commissioned. And she was commissioned.

A relationship between them simply couldn't happen. Not if they both wanted to keep their careers in the army.

It *shouldn't* have happened that night, then.

A fresh wave of grief swelled and crested above her, then crashed. As destructive and terrifying as the one that had engulfed her fourteen years ago. It was all she could do to fight not to be dragged under.

'You told me you'd heard a rumour,' she muttered thickly.

'And you never corrected me.' He gritted his teeth. 'You never told me you were still in.'

'I assumed you'd realised.'

And, if she was honest, she hadn't discussed it because she hadn't wanted to resurrect an old row. It was also the reason why she'd hadn't told him the celebration in the nightclub had been about her promotion. She'd just been holding her breath, expecting someone to say anything at any moment. But they hadn't, they'd already done the congratulatory part by the time Kane had arrived, and they had just been enjoying the evening.

It had felt as though she'd managed to get away with it. Like meeting Kane that day had been *fate* and that they were meant to have that one night together.

Now she just felt guilty…and maybe a little ashamed. But why should she? It wasn't as though she could ever have anticipated that, of all people, anti-establishment Kane—the boy who had wondered time and again why she had wanted to follow in her father's footsteps—could have ended up joining the army himself.

Fourteen years ago the idea would have been preposterous to him.

In fact, it *had* been preposterous to him.

'How could I have possibly known that it mattered?' she hissed. 'You'd always known I wanted to be an army doctor—ever since we were kids it was all I ever wanted to do.'

'I know that.'

'I even remember suggesting, several times, that you could join the army yourself.' She heard the lift to her voice, as if she wasn't quite in control, but she couldn't seem to stop it. 'You always told me that it wasn't for you, that you would never want to be a soldier. I pleaded with you, Kane.'

And how she'd pleaded.

She'd been desperate for him to join up when they'd been teens. She'd wanted them to have a life together, and even though Kane had never wanted to go to university, she'd begged him time and again to speak to her father, to ask him to guide him on the way to becoming a non-graduate commissioned officer.

He'd been a bright kid at school, even if he'd been the wild kid. The rebel. He could have got good A-levels if his dad hadn't pulled him out to earn a wage, just so that the old guy had more drinking and gambling money.

But Kane had been a hard worker. Focused and trustworthy. He could even have taken night courses for those missed A-levels. Her father would have helped him.

'You told me you would never, *ever* join the military. And nothing I said ever changed your mind.'

'So I was wrong,' he clipped out curtly. 'Turns out joining the Infantry was the greatest thing I could have done.'

But she didn't miss the strange, bleak look that flashed across his eyes for a split second before it was gone.

She frowned, trying to work out what she'd seen. But she couldn't. It was like only having a few pages from a book and trying to work out what the whole thing had been about.

'How? How did it happen, Kane?'

'It isn't important.' He shot the question down with all the deadly force of a surface-to-air missile.

Shutting her out, unequivocally, and it hurt. Far more than she should let it. The ground was shifting beneath her and she struggled to try to get the conversation back onto something more solid.

'Nevertheless…' she offered weakly.

'*Nevertheless* what, Mattie?' he demanded. '*Nevertheless* I should have known that, even though you'd left your career for your new husband, you signed up again when the marriage went wrong? How could I have known?'

She blinked, the conversation moving too fast and skipping too many facts for her to follow. Her chest was aching with the effort of containing her hammering heart. It didn't help that his eyes had locked with hers, virtually rooting her to the spot.

Her mind raced back to that moment at the hospital when she'd first spoken to him again after so many years. He *had* mentioned he'd heard about her engagement when he'd told her he'd heard a rumour she was leaving the army. He *had* demanded that she confirm the rumour, but before she'd said anything more, he'd spotted her ringless finger, hadn't he? And she'd been so frantic to change the topic of conversation—before he'd realised that she hadn't married sweet George because a weak part of her had never stopped loving *him*, Kane—that she'd merely confirmed she wasn't married and moved on.

Did he really think she'd got married and then…what? Divorced?

The blood hurtled through her veins, but the thoughts in her head were still jumbled. Confused.

'You never told me, Kane, but who did you hear the rumour from?' she asked slowly, barely recognising her own voice.

He stopped, his eyes catching hers, refusing to let them slide away. Pinning her where she stood. The silence in the room so tense it almost suffocated her. And all she could do was wait.

'You,' he said eventually. 'I heard from you when you announced that you were leaving to concentrate on being a civilian doctor.'

Mattie didn't answer, she merely shook her head adamantly. But the hammering was making its way into her brain, pressing on her temples. There was only one time she could think of that she'd made any such kind of public statement.

'What do you mean, *I announced it*?' she asked carefully.

His face shuttered down. Effectively locking her out.

'Forget I said anything.'

She knew this side of Kane. This so-called stubborn streak that people had always taken to mean that, once he'd taken a stand, there was no talking him around. But Mattie also knew that it was less about blind stubbornness and more about trying to protect himself.

And with an upbringing like his, he'd needed to protect himself from a lot.

Nonetheless, her legs were still threatening to skitter away from underneath her. Very un-major-like. Certainly uncharacteristic. She didn't know how, but Mattie drew herself up to her full five-foot-seven height. It might have worked had Kane not been a full eight inches taller. She still had to tilt her head up towards him, which did nothing to lessen the aura of power that swirled around him.

'You were there,' she whispered at last. 'At my wedding rehearsal. Weren't you?'

How did her voice sound so...*normal* when her tongue felt too thick, too heavy for her own mouth?

'I thought I saw you,' she pressed on when Kane didn't answer. 'But then...you were gone.'

He still didn't answer, and the silence pulled between then, taut and close. She tried again.

'I thought I'd imagined you.'

Still he didn't react, and Mattie hated it that she couldn't read him. That she had no idea what he was thinking.

How could she bring herself to tell him the rest, if she didn't know what was going on in that closed-off head of his? How could she admit that she'd called off the wedding to George because she'd finally accepted the fact that no one else would ever claim her heart whilst it had still been trying to cling to the memory of Kane?

She needed something from him. Anything.

'Why didn't you say something, Kane? Anything?' She could hear her voice rising and she fought to pull it back under control. 'What were you even doing there?'

'What does it even matter now?' he demanded, his voice too gritty, too raw for her to bear. 'You married him, and it fell apart. You moved on. It happens.'

'It *doesn't* happen,' she choked out. 'At least, not like that.'

'I'm not entirely sure I understand what you're saying.'

He lifted his shoulders, as if it didn't matter one way or the other.

But it *did* matter. At least, to her. He stared at her and she shook her head, searching for the right words.

'My marriage didn't fall apart,' she choked out at last. 'My engagement did.'

Another icy fog of silence swirled around the room. Mattie tried not to shiver, but it was hopeless.

'Say again?' Kane rasped eventually.

She didn't think she could until she heard the words dropping awkwardly from her lips. 'I never left the army because I never married. I called it off after that night... after the wedding rehearsal.'

'Why?'

She'd known the question was coming but she couldn't bring herself to answer it. How could she tell him the truth? What would be the point?

Because when it had come down to it, the only reason her marriage to dear, sweet, kind George—who had to have been the most perfect man alive—had fallen apart was simply because he hadn't been Kane.

As shameful as that was.

And now that they were in the situation they were in... what difference did it make anyway?

CHAPTER FIVE

MATTIE WASN'T JUST not married *to her precious earl...she'd* never *married him*.

The revelation rolled round and round in Kane's head until he couldn't think of anything else. He wasn't even sure that he was still breathing.

And she *had* seen him that night after all. He hadn't just imagined her staring right at him. But all this while that he'd told himself she'd turned to her fiancé without even appearing to take a second look in his direction—effectively dismissing him from her thoughts, her life—the reality was that she'd thought she'd simply imagined him.

What the hell was he supposed to take from that?

The fact that Mattie had accepted the idea that her subconscious had conjured up an image of her first boyfriend on the night of her wedding rehearsal dinner. And the fact that she had ended up not going through with her wedding. Those two thoughts raced through Kane's head, so utterly neck and neck that he couldn't tell which thought was chasing the other. Or even if they were connected at all.

Questions jostled for room in his head, elbowing each other out of the way as they tried to get to his tongue. To spill out into the silence. But Kane didn't want to let them. He needed time to absorb this new revelation. He needed to think.

Mattie, it seemed, had other ideas.

'How did you know I was getting married?' she demanded, and he tried not to read too much into the breathless tone. 'How did you even get inside? It was a private party.'

He had no intention of replying so it was something of a shock when he heard the words leave his own mouth, as gravelly as his voice sounded.

'Hayd contacted me.'

She stared at him for a long moment.

'My brother invited you?'

Had it been an invitation as such?

He'd never really thought about it, preferring to shut the whole incident from his mind.

'He told me you were getting married,' Kane offered evenly. 'And he told me that he was going to the rehearsal dinner at the hotel.'

'I didn't even know you two were in contact. He never told me.' She sounded annoyed and distraught all at the same time. 'He never even mentioned you to me.'

Kane didn't answer. He didn't know how to. How was he supposed to tell Mattie that Hayden's call had come out of the blue? That he hadn't spoken to her brother, or indeed had any contact with Hayden since the night Kane had walked away from the Brigham family—from Mattie—for good?

'We weren't in contact.'

'You must have been.' She shook her head, clearly trying to make sense out of it.

He wished she could. He'd been trying to, and failing, for the past four years.

'I had no contact with Hayden either before or after. Just that one call. One time. Maybe he thought I'd talk to you, I don't know. I just know that when I saw you there, looking so happy, I left. And I never heard from your brother again.'

And had then spent four years pretending he wasn't kicking himself for not doing more. Pretending that he hadn't tormented himself with what-ifs. A thing he worked hard never to do in any other area of his life.

A part of him had harboured the idea that maybe Mattie's father had played some part in getting his son to contact Kane and alert him to the wedding. After all, he was the only one of the Brigham family who had known where Kane had gone. And why. Without Mattie's father's help, he would never be where he was now.

The high-ranking officer hadn't pulled strings, of course, he had always had far too much integrity for that. He'd merely opened doors for Kane that would otherwise have remained firmly locked. It had then been up to Kane himself to walk through them and prove he was worth talking to.

But he couldn't explain any of that to Mattie. Not just because he didn't want to drop a bombshell that although she'd clearly had no idea where he'd been these past fourteen years, her father *had* known. But also because he was still ashamed of the actions that had led to him leaving without warning in the first place.

Anyway, she wasn't asking about what had happened fourteen years ago, but was asking how he'd come to be at her wedding rehearsal four years ago. And he wasn't sure he could give her the answer she wanted. Even to him—and even though he couldn't make sense of *why*— it sounded as though Hayden hadn't wanted his sister to marry her Earl Blakeney.

'I don't have the answers you want, Mattie,' Kane managed, wondering how he didn't burst into flames at the sheer effort of shutting it down. Especially since he desperately wanted to have that conversation, too.

'But we're not here to rake over our past personal life. We're here for Operation Strikethrough. So that you can

set up the medical scenarios that will test our infantry pla-
toons to their limits.'

He could see the emotions buffeting Mattie. The same
emotions that were tearing through him. But he couldn't
let them in. He *wouldn't*. It would serve no purpose now,
too much time had passed.

'So we're just going to…what? Pretend the other night
didn't happen?' Sharpness pierced her tone, striking him.

He had no idea how he pretended it didn't score a direct hit.

'I don't see what choice we have, Mattie.' It took everything in him to keep his tone neutral. Distant. 'I'm a
warrant officer, you're a major. I've led seminars on what
would happen if any of my NCOs were caught having a
relationship with a commissioned officer, even a colour
sergeant with a lieutenant. You know what would happen
if they discovered anything between you and me.'

'You don't have to remind me.' She straightened her
shoulders. 'I'm well aware. One or both of us would lose
our careers. I *have* briefed my own share of subbies on the
consequences of fraternisation with privates or NCOs.'

'Even if anyone found out about what happened between
us at the weekend—which they won't, of course, but even
if they did—there could be no fallout.'

They hadn't known the situation then. They'd had no
idea the other was also in the military. But they did now.

'It just can't happen, Mattie.' He didn't know whether
he was trying to convince her or himself.

'It wasn't going to,' she snorted.

But he could tell she was lying, though it gave him little comfort.

'Then surely that's all the more reason to lock it away
and pretend it didn't happen, don't you think?' No reason
for her to know that he had to bite every unpalatable word
out. 'What's the point in dissecting it further?'

She glared at him and never before had he so fervently wished he could read what was going on behind those deep pools of hazel.

'No point at all,' she clipped out at length. 'You're right. We just need to get through the next couple of days and then…'

'Then?' he prompted, when she appeared to falter.

She squared her shoulders and her black gaze jolted through him, leaving him feeling even more wretched than ever.

'Then I don't imagine we'll cross paths again,' she managed. 'You're infantry, I'm medical. After all, we haven't until now.'

Something slithered and twisted through him but he refused to acknowledge it. He dipped his head instead, his voice even.

'I don't imagine we will.' And even though it scraped against everything else he wanted to say, he pushed past it.

Neither of them spoke, each lost in their own thoughts.

'So, that day back at the hospital…' Mattie broke the silence suddenly. 'You said you were visiting someone. I assumed it was a patient in the main hospital, but I'm guessing now it was someone in the military wing.'

He hesitated, weighing up what to tell her. What harm could it do?

'One of my former men,' Kane confirmed after a moment. 'He was also a buddy. My OC was hardly going to make the trip, even though it was about ten minutes from barracks, so I thought I would.'

'Major Percy Copperhead?' She pulled a face, though he doubted she'd intended to. 'He's an idiot.'

At least he wasn't alone in his distaste for the man.

'He is,' Kane concurred. 'In fourteen years I've known a few idiots—there are plenty of good officers, don't get me wrong, but a couple of bad ones. Copperhead takes the prize, though.'

'At least it isn't just me, then.' Mattie forced an awkward laugh. 'So you've been in the army for fourteen years?'

From the moment he'd walked away from their relationship without even a goodbye.

Kane didn't need to hear the words aloud to recognise the unspoken question in her tone.

She was piecing it together yet he couldn't answer her. He *wouldn't.* Because that would mean diving into a part of his past he was still desperate to keep locked away. He was still so ashamed that he wanted to pretend that it had never happened. Even with Mattie.

Especially with Mattie.

So, instead, he picked out a document from his folder and turned to the third page.

And he certainly wasn't about to let her know that it damned near killed him to do so.

'I assume you read our original brief?'

For a fraction of a moment he thought she blinked, but then it was gone and she was making her way around her desk to locate the files.

'Outlining the medical scenarios the division wants to test? Yes, originally there were two parts to it, the first one being individual scenarios testing the combat medical guys.'

'Right. The second exercise is more a front-line exercise, role one support with mass casualties. Setting up a medical search team to follow the infantry in, we had a FIBUA location in mind.'

They both knew that training for fire fights in built up, urban areas, was essential, so he could understand Mattie's frown.

'Had?'

'Depending on how the main operation is progressing,

there's a chance we have to bring forward that scenario, which would mean choosing a new location. From our POV that scenario will be a chance to look at command and control aspects.'

'So plenty of casualties, a tactical environment, with your guys under pressure,' Mattie confirmed. 'From our perspective it will be more about seeing the medical treatment the medics can provide and we've got about one hundred and forty medics taking part.'

'For a lot of these guys it will be the first chance they'll have had to see real-life amputees made up to look like the accidents have just happened. We've got another infantry unit coming in to keep them under constant fire to really ramp up that pressure. It's going to be about making sure they can keep calm and seeing how fast they can select a good building in which to set up medical treatment facilities.

'And stressing the new tactical set-up?' Mattie surmised.

Kane bowed his head.

'Right.'

'Okay, so all of that seems as expected as we'd planned for them next week, using exercise casualties from this hospital. Amputees for Armies are being flown in next week, and we have HFMSs, high-fidelity mannequin simulators.'

'I'm familiar with them,' he confirmed. 'Full-size dummies, computer controlled, which you'll make up to look like injured soldiers—even those caught by IEDs or mines and losing limbs.'

'They can recreate physiological issues such as blood pressure, heart rate, breathing, as well as normal and abnormal heart sounds, lung sounds and pupil findings,' Mattie continued, clearly beginning to find her feet now they'd moved away from the personal and into the medical side of the operation.

It was ridiculous that he couldn't seem to do the same. Couldn't stop his eyes from wandering to her lips and remembering how soft and plump they felt. Or following the sweet curve of her neck and recall how she'd quivered in his arms when he'd kissed that sensitive hollow by her collarbone.

Not to mention the primal, caveman part of himself that was barely containing itself from stripping her and throwing her on her desk, hearing her scream his name again as he buried his head in the sweet heat between her legs.

The way he'd promised himself he would do the moment this exercise was over, when he'd thought all he had to do was return to the hospital and find her there, waiting for him.

When he'd planned to tell her everything.

'The mannequins can vary blood pressure, heart rate and breathing, and many of them can simulate going into cardiac arrest,' she continued, oblivious to his wild, uncontrollable thoughts. 'Depending on how far you want to test your different level of medics at section level, platoon level or company level, HFMSs can even respond to medication and oxygen administration, receiving electrical cardioversion and procedures such as diagnostic peritoneal lavage and central lines.'

'Okay.' Moving forward, Kane tried to get a grip of his wayward thoughts and settled in front of the large map on the pinboard on the side wall of the room.

He did it more to move away from her than because he needed to. Because if she got any closer he knew he would smell that familiar, vanilla scent of her hair, as tightly scraped back in that bun as it was. And his fingers were already itching with the desire to pull it free and tunnel his fingers into its luxurious silkiness.

'So,' he managed, 'to summarise, we can't get the Amputees for Armies flown in any earlier than scheduled, but we should be able to use the HFMSs and your guys made up to look like casualties. I suggest we go through each potential scenario one at a time, decide on what can best be gained by it, and then feed it into a new time and grid reference.'

'Fine.' Mattie whipped through the pages, annotated with her own notes, before standing up and moving to join him at the board. 'Starting with the incident on page four, where you've highlighted a bridge collapse.'

He sidestepped again. Like a besotted teenager next to their crush. It might have even been comical, if it wasn't so damned tragic.

'Yeah.' He coughed brusquely. 'We're looking at setting up a tank fall so the Engineers can have a play with their toys.'

'How about if we use it to introduce a crush scenario? We can have a two-stage approach, with stage one concentrating on your medics and soldiers in the field, right up to extraction using one of our MERT helicopters. Stage two will be for us back at the field hospital.'

The Medical Emergency Response Team were always an essential part of any operation, as was the field hospital.

'Okay.' Kane nodded, taking his own notes. 'I'm aware that there are arguments and recommendations for leaving crush victims in situ if they have been trapped for more than fifteen minutes, but on the other hand there's an argument concerning crush syndrome for releasing them as soon as possible.'

'Yes, so let me explain,' she began, her evident passion for her work making him smile despite everything.

He cocked an eyebrow at her.

'In layman's terms, Mattie,' he cautioned.

At least she had the grace to flush. But that only made

him wonder if the stain was spreading down her deliciously creamy chest. To the gentle swells that he ached to touch again.

To taste them again.

'Right. Of course. When the human body is crushed, in this instance between a vehicle and a bridge deck, it is subjected to pressure. Muscular compression damages the muscle cells and leads to a process called rhabdomyolysis.' She eyed him briefly before hastily skating over the explanation he knew she'd been about to give him.

If he didn't know better, he'd say she was talking for the sake of it. That, in reality, she was finding this conversation as distracting as he was. And he could have sworn her breathing was a little shallower than it had been. A little more rapid.

'Okay, the point is that rhabdomyolysis causes organ dysfunction such as acute renal failure, so the likelihood of developing acute crush syndrome is directly related to the length of time the body is under compression.'

'So you're looking for the guys to release the victim or victims as soon as possible,' Kane surmised, his brain clouding over as she shifted, subconsciously, closer to him.

'Irrespective of how long they've been trapped.' She nodded a little jerkily. 'But they will need to apply tourniquets.'

'Right.' It was impossible to concentrate when he felt her in every part of himself, like this.

'Your guys will need to administer pain relief. I know they'll each have the lollipop lozenges with fentanyl, but in this instance you're going to need the section medic to administer a strong intramuscular morphine shot.'

Everything was falling away. Her office. The hospital, even the fact that they were on a military training ground. There was only Mattie.

'Testing that long flight scenario requiring inflight operation on the MERT, I would put with a forward unit, so arguably this location here.' He pointed to the map, indicating the grid reference.

His hadn't intended it—at least, not on any conscious level—but his hand brushed hers as he moved.

He might as well have self-combusted.

'Agreed.' She swallowed. Hard. 'I'll send a couple of Directing Staff there on your instruction. And the veterans who have already suffered life-changing injuries will act as serious casualties for the simulations.'

There was a roar in his head. A rushing noise, drowning out everything else. He fought to maintain some semblance of restraint, but she was leaning into him now. Her warmth, her scent were irresistible.

'Yeah, once they fly in, your medical staff who aren't on the exercise can decide how best to make them up.'

His voice cracked, but she didn't notice. She was too intent on staring at him, her voice growing softer, murmuring the words as if on autopilot.

'Multiple casualties, some big pyrotechnics to make the scenarios as realistic as possible.'

Kane snaked out his hand and slid it around the back of her neck, tugging her to him. She didn't even pretend to resist, her hands circling his upper arms, her papers floating to the floor with a soft swishing noise.

The kiss was hotter, and wilder, than even he had remembered. Carnal, feral, savage. He ravaged her mouth with his own, dragging his tongue across her lips, dipping into her mouth then out again. And she met him stroke for stroke. Like she was caught up in the same madness that was sweeping him away. He kissed her, over and over, plundering and demanding. Imagining that somehow, some way these kisses branded her and made her *his*.

And then he was scooping her up, his hands holding her backside as she wrapped her legs around him. He carried her to the desk, his mouth never leaving hers. The heat from her body, so hot and inviting, even through their clothing, was making the blood roar in his ears. Making him want to taste her again, just like the other night. He reached down between them and ran his fingers up the seam of her trousers, right where she was molten for him, and the soft, greedy sound she emitted made him ache almost painfully.

He wasn't prepared for her to tear her mouth from his.

'Wait.' Her breathing was ragged, wrecked. And Kane found that he liked that rather too much.

But, still, he wasn't sure he could wait at all. He moved his hand and ran it over her core again, and her eyelids fluttered down as she bit her lip.

God, but she was beautiful.

And then she drew back, sliding her hands over his arms, as if testing out the muscles, and then she moved them to his chest, letting her palms glide down his pectorals, his abs, until she was suddenly cupping his sex, sliding down the zip of his trousers without preamble and slipping her hand inside.

'I rather think, Kane,' she told him, in the sexiest, most commanding voice he thought he'd ever heard, 'that you took charge last time. Now it's my turn.'

Before he could speak, her hot fingers closed around him, applying just the right amount of pressure, and then moving up, down *so damn slowly*. He bit back a deep groan. It had to be the most perfect torture he'd ever known in his life. She was taking charge, as though she couldn't wait another moment to touch him, to taste him, to do whatever it was that she wanted to do to him. And he feared he might let her. Right here and now.

What was it about this one woman that had him—had always had him—so crazy and unbridled?

He pulled her body to his and she fitted against him like

she always did. Like she always *had*. Kane forgot what the rules were, what he could do, and what he couldn't. He forgot that this couldn't happen. He simply knew that wanted her with every fibre of his being, and what was even more incredible was that she wanted him, too.

A loud knock on the door jarred them both back to reality.

As Mattie sprang backwards, he kept his back to the door, aware that his body was a giveaway sign of what had just been happening.

'I'm sorry to disturb you, Major Brigham,' the voice began, 'but ICU called to say your gunshot patient has developed complications, and you might want to see him.'

It was like a switch being pushed in her, Kane noted as she acknowledged the corporal before turning back to him.

'I really do have to go and attend this.' A statement, not a question. 'I'm sure Mr Wheeler has a couple of notes he wants to finish up here for now, but if you wait outside, Corporal, perhaps you can escort him to the mess hall for something to eat or drink whilst he waits?'

'Yes, ma'am.'

'Mr Wheeler?'

'Yes, that would be fine, thank you, Major,' Kane answered. Polite without the deference of the young lad at the door. Nothing anyone would be unhappy about.

Except him.

Because now, more than ever, it was apparent to Kane that there was no future for him and Mattie. As long as they were both in green, they couldn't be together.

It would have been different if they were both commissioned officers, the way she'd pestered him to do back when they'd been little more than kids. Back then he would only have pulled her down. Now, despite fourteen years of working his way to one of the highest non-commissioned officer ranks in the British Army, the problem still remained.

He was proud of who he was, and how far he'd come. But it still wasn't good enough for Mattie, an acting colonel.

The irony wasn't lost on him.

CHAPTER SIX

MATTIE HAD NO IDEA how long she'd been avoiding returning to Kane. Or, more precisely, she knew *exactly* how long.

Not because she didn't want to go back into that room, but more because she wanted nothing *more* than to return. Her whole body felt tight, and coiled, and needy.

But giving in to temptation with Kane the other night, before they'd known about…*this*, was one thing. Now, here, it was different. She took her career seriously, and more than that she loved it, which was why she'd always taken its rules seriously. Including fraternisation.

She had never, in her entire career, had a workplace relationship—not even with a fellow commissioned officer, however brilliant any of them might have been. She'd never even been tempted. But, then, none of them had been Kane, had they?

And hadn't earlier on proved beyond all doubt that, where he was concerned, she lacked any kind of resistance whatsoever?

Which was why she'd been hiding out back here. She'd dealt with her gunshot patient's complications a good hour ago. Thankfully it hadn't been as troublesome as everyone had feared, and the young patient was now back in ICU, recovering.

And now all she could think about was how a few minutes longer in her office and she could have been naked on that desk with Kane driving into her, without a second thought for her career. A career she'd spent nearly fourteen years—ever since an officer cadet at medical school—painstakingly building up.

It was unprofessional, *reckless*, and she ought to be ashamed. Instead—and this was the worst thing about it—all she wanted to do right now was rush straight back to her office and pick up where they'd left off.

Not only had she never had a relationship with a fellow officer before, but she had also never avoided a colleague or a mission before now.

Right now, she found herself in a consultation room with a young squaddie who had come in a few days earlier complaining of a rash on his body. What had concerned her the most had been that the rash had precisely matched the shape of his body armour.

In consultation with the specialist dermatologist on her team, the two of them had agreed on a prescribed cream, but the follow-up had been set up to ensure that the rash wasn't getting worse or changing properties.

To be fair, any one of her team could have dealt with the young lad but she'd chosen to do it herself—her mind only too aware that Kane was still on the other side of the hospital, waiting for her. Which was all the proof she needed that she was putting off the inevitable.

'Okay, Fusilier, can you strip off your top half, please?'

The lad stood, peeling off his jacket and T-shirt without a trace of bashfulness. Particularly when he moved his fingers to the button of his trousers.

'You want me to take these off, too, ma'am?' he enquired casually. 'Only the rash went down there...if you remember?'

Mattie felt her lips quirk.

Oh, the confidence of youth.

'Okay, then. I'd better see.'

Peering closer, Mattie inspected the site. Interestingly, the skin was beginning to peel and the skin beneath was clear and healthy.

'And you have no other symptoms?' she checked for the third time in the last ten minutes.

'None. I feel great. And the itching has stopped.'

'All right, then, just keep applying the cream to the affected area only. Come back and see us in another two days.'

The lad began to put his clothes back on.

'So what is it?'

'We still have no idea,' she told him honestly, making her notes as she headed for the door. 'But we've taken a swab and if there's anything to tell you when the results come back, we'll call you straight in.'

'Thanks, Doc.' He grinned as she opened the consultation-room door for him, letting him out before she followed.

'No problem.' She headed for the desk, and her next patient.

'Are you still here?' Kath's voice had her swinging around, trying not to look guilty.

'Just doing a few routine consults.'

'And the liaison from Battle Group?'

So much for trying not to look guilty.

'In the mess hall, last thing I knew,' she admitted, aware that her long-term colleague was casting her a shocked look.

'Geez, Mattie, that isn't like you.'

She knew that. But it didn't really help.

'Listen, everything is under control here, and you still have that liaison to deal with, don't you? Or is there another reason you don't want to go back there?'

Mattie swung around sharply.

'Another reason?'

'Word is he's a bit of a hottie.' Kath grinned. 'One of the nurses was in the command post before you arrived the first time and took a bit of a shine to him, and the sergeant who was driving him from the Helicopter Landing Site said she wouldn't have kicked him out of bed.'

'Not exactly appropriate.' Mattie frowned, even though she felt like the biggest hypocrite around. She might have known Kath would call her out on it.

'Neither is ducking around here, trying to avoid talking to the guy. So unless you want to tell me what that's all about, I suggest you go back over there.'

With that, she pulled the list of new patients out of Mattie's hands, spun her round and guided her back down the corridor.

'Come on, I'll walk with you. I should have got off shift a couple of hours ago, as it is.'

'Fine, I'm going,' Mattie grumbled. 'How do you get all this gossip anyway?'

And more to the point, were there any whispers about her right now?

Kath laughed, unoffended.

'Because I'm a civilian doctor playing at being a reservist. You're the army doctor with rules and regulations stamped right through you like a stick of rock.'

'Right,' Mattie agreed grimly.

Except that what had happened in her office just over an hour ago had been so far removed from rules and regulations that she would have been risking her job. Or Kane his.

'Unless you're telling me you're considering breaking the rules where this guy is concerned. I also heard that he's only around his mid-thirties, which means his career has been soaring for him to get to WO2 already.'

Mattie mumbled something incoherent. She'd already

worked that out for herself, but it didn't help matters. If anything, it made them worse because it only made him more successful, and therefore that much more attractive to her.

Her main concern was that if she returned to a private room to finish ironing out the new scenarios with Kane she would find herself in yet another compromising situation with him before she could say *Case simulation zero one*. Again.

Worse, some insubordinate side of her *wanted* it to happen again.

They were at the mess doors before Mattie could find another excuse. And then, like a parent waiting to watch their kid go into school on the first day, Kath gave her a gentle push and waited at the doors until she stepped inside.

She saw Kane immediately.

'You're still in here?' She would never know how she made her objecting feet cross the room towards him and fold themselves over the bench so she sat on the opposite side of the table from him in an otherwise empty mess hall.

In a couple of hours it would be heaving again. Just not now.

'Where else was I to go?' he enquired smoothly, before lowering his voice so it was just loud enough for her to hear. 'Besides, after…before, I thought it might be advisable to continue the discussion in a more public setting.'

No one could overhear them where they were, but they could be seen. Privacy to talk, without the temptation to touch. It made complete sense, so why did she feel so suddenly deflated? Mattie forced a bright smile.

'Yes. Right. Good idea.'

He eyed her darkly but said nothing. There was no need to feel this urge to fill the silence.

'We have less than twenty-four hours to get through. Then you'll be back at Battle Group.'

And this time she wouldn't harbour any foolish notions that they could pick up where they'd left off that night in the hotel. She had to put it out of her mind. Just like she had fourteen years ago.

Because back then it worked out so well, a little voice needled in her head, but Mattie resolutely ignored it, although it made her stomach hurt.

'Why didn't you tell me that you'd joined up?' she asked. 'More than that, that the army has been your career for the past decade and a half?'

'I didn't think it mattered.'

'You're a CSM, Kane.' She shook her head. 'To make that rank in such a short time means you must have been flying from practically the moment you went on your recruits course. People are in for eighteen, or twenty years and they don't even make it half as far.'

'I got some lucky breaks.'

'It's more than that,' she snorted. 'You've dedicated your life to it. And you always dismissed the military. You hated my father being a brigadier, and you slated my dream of being a doctor in the army.'

'I was an arrogant kid who thought he knew it all.' Kane barked a humourless laugh. 'An idiot.'

'So what changed?'

He sucked in a breath, his wide chest expanding even further.

'*I* did, Mattie.'

'You?'

'People can, you know.'

Of course she knew that. But it hardly clarified anything for her. Everything was still as murky and confusing as ever.

'I always thought my father paid you to leave.'

He pulled his lips into a thin line, but it took a while for him to answer.

'I always wondered what he'd told you,' he remarked evenly.

It didn't answer her question.

'He didn't tell me that. I just thought maybe he had, and that's why you hadn't said goodbye.' Still, he didn't answer. She tried again. 'What I mean is, *did* he pay you to leave?'

The distant clatter of the cooks across the mess hall stopped the silence from being too oppressive. Still Kane didn't answer, and Mattie wondered if she was about to go insane with the need to know.

'Did he pay you, Kane?' she pressed at last.

Kane eyed her for a moment longer.

'What *did* he tell you?'

'Nothing.' She blew out heavily in exasperation, thrusting aside the stab of grief that sliced through her. 'Although maybe that's because he started suffering from Alzheimer's six years ago. Or at least that's what we think, in hindsight. He's been getting progressively worse these last three years, though.'

'Oh, hell. I'm so sorry, Matz.' A genuinely sad expression clouded Kane's face. 'I hope you never blamed him for me leaving.'

If she hadn't have known how Kane and her father had rubbed each other up the wrong way, she might have actually thought it was more than just sympathy on Kane's part. That he was saddened on a more personal level.

She waggled her head from side to side, trying to shake off the melancholy.

'I didn't. I blamed you,' she told him simply. 'For leaving. And for taking the money, if there was any.'

'I'm glad.'

And she didn't doubt that Kane was sincere. She offered a wry smile.

'However much my father and I might have clashed when I was going through my rebellious teens, I always knew he had my back. He always loved me.'

'If it hadn't been for you, and Hayden, and your parents, I would never have known what a true, loving family could look like,' Kane said quietly, a moment of unguarded wistfulness.

Mattie thought her chest would crack open with the effort to contain itself. She stamped it down quickly.

'So, did he pay you, Kane?'

Another beat, and then…

'No.'

She wasn't expecting the numbness that crept over her so abruptly. Her throat suddenly tight. The answer she'd wanted to hear but hadn't really believed she would.

'He didn't?' she whispered.

'He did not,' Kane confirmed. 'What's more, if he had tried, I wouldn't have accepted it. No amount of money could have made me walk away from you.'

It was as if some giant concrete block had been sitting on her chest and she hadn't even realised it. But now it had lifted. Gone. Something was swelling inside her chest and she didn't care to evaluate that too closely, but either way she could breathe again.

'You *did* walk away from me, though,' she managed instead. 'So, if not for money…then *why*?'

'For your own good, Mattie.' His face shuttered instantly. Effectively locking her out.

Strangely, instead of making her back off, it sent a sliver of anger through her.

'What kind of answer is that?'

'The only one you're going to get.'

Her heart started thumping slowly in her chest.

'Well, that isn't good enough, Kane.'

'That's too bad.'

'It's been fourteen years.' She blew out a breath. 'And you still can't tell me? What can possibly matter that much?'

'Because it's my story, Mattie. My past. I don't want it all raked up now and, what's more, I don't believe it will achieve anything to do so.'

'It's *our* past,' she corrected furiously, reining herself in sharply as she cast a glance at the kitchen area.

But no one was watching. As far as they were concerned it was two senior ranking soldiers discussing a brigade issue. They couldn't know what the topic really was.

'I think I deserve that much.'

He snagged her eyes with his. Searching them. Making her feel utterly naked.

'What would be the point, Mattie?' he demanded hoarsely. Quietly. 'Two days ago, maybe I would have. When I thought that maybe things could be different between us the next time.'

'You mean when you thought I'd left the army?' she asked dully. 'Before I even knew you'd ever joined up?'

'Yes. Back *then*,' he confirmed.

'So you'd thought that maybe we could have a future? You really had intended to search me out the moment you returned from this exercise?'

'Why else do you think I gave you my number?'

'And would you have told me then? Would you have said that you were one of the most senior NCOs in the British Army?'

'I would have.' He dipped his head slowly. Once. 'But we both know that it's impossible now.'

How was it possible for hope to flourish in one part of her chest, only for it to be extinguished in another?

'Unless one of us leaves,' she posited carefully.

He studied her, his expression guarded.

'And have you any plans to do that?'

She stared at him. He couldn't be serious.

'You were going to once before,' he reminded her, seeming to read her thoughts. 'When you were marrying your Earl Blakeney.'

'True, but it would have been a mistake, I realise that now.' She shook her head sadly. 'I never wanted to leave—it was just what was expected of me.'

And she'd been trying to convince herself that she'd moved on. From Kane. Not that she was about to admit that now.

'I would have ended up resenting him for it sooner or later. And the marriage would have failed.'

'So you're saying that seeing me—or thinking you imagined me—at your wedding rehearsal saved you from making a mistake that would have hurt both of you?'

She couldn't be sure whether he understood too little or too much. Either way, she wasn't sure she wanted to go down that route.

'Remember that promotion I mentioned I was getting?' she asked, changing tack swiftly. The one he must have imagined was in a civilian capacity. 'Well, it's to half-colonel, back at Brigade.'

There was a beat.

'Congratulations.'

His voice was to level. Too even. As though he was picking his words too carefully. Guarding himself from the inevitable.

The way that she should be.

Instead, a complicated knot of emotions was moving inside her. Surging back and forth, even as her heart was numb.

'What about you? You're Company Sergeant Major. What's next for you? I heard that you've been inundated with offers to join the private sector.'

'Where did you hear that?' he scoffed.

'Kane, the instant you walked into my field hospital looking like…that…' she waved her hand to encompass him '…all the single female soldiers took notice. The rumour mill went into overdrive.'

'I'm flattered.'

'Oh, come on, you know as well as I do that half the girls fancied you when we were back in Heathdale. Even your family name didn't put them off.'

'Only half?' he teased, but it was a careful teasing, like he was really just changing the subject.

They both knew it.

'The point is, you could change career if you wanted. Leave the army and go into the private sector. There's a lot more money in that.'

'Of all people, I'd expect you to know this isn't about money, Mattie,' he chastised her gently, and heat raced to her cheeks.

He was right, she *did* know that. It had always been about being part of something special. More than just a family. Something that was bigger than her. Something that mattered.

She bobbed her head but didn't answer.

'We don't have a future, Mattie.'

He left the statement hanging, giving her a chance to refute it the way she wanted to. *Oh, how she wanted to.* But she couldn't. He was right, they didn't have a future.

She could feel emotion welling up inside her, threatening to effervesce and spill out everywhere. But, as Kane had said himself, what good would it do to give in to it? To let it out?

With a superhuman effort she pulled herself together, fighting through the threatening tears—and she never cried—to focus on the paperwork on the table in front of her.

'Okay,' she began, swallowing back a lump of…something

in her throat. 'So, the purpose of the medical simulations we run on these occasions won't be to train my medical team. We've run all the scenarios multiple times and the teams all know exactly what they're doing. The aim is to stress the new tactical brigade. To test them, and to find any weaknesses.'

She wouldn't have objected if Kane had taken the conversation back to the personal. But he didn't. As she'd known he wouldn't.

'Yes.' He offered her a half-smile. His only acknowledgement that they were trying to move past everything. 'You can benefit, of course. But initially the scenarios will test the individual soldier out there on the front line. It will test the company. But most of all for Operation Strikethrough, these initial scenarios have been designed to test and stress the new strike battalion's medical chain and handovers.'

'So we'll start with relatively standard scenarios and cas-evacs.'

'Some cas-evacs on the bonnets of four-by-fours to an FOB,' Kane agreed, indicting the Forward Operating Base and making notes accordingly, as she tried not to let her gaze linger on that hand that had touched her, held her, the way that no one else had ever quite managed before or since.

'And if that runs smoothly and the chain holds out, we'll also look to delay medical support for…shall we say forty minutes initially,' confirmed Mattie, as though she didn't feel broken. Exposed. As if she would never quite be right again.

'Keeping the patient alive and stable enough for transport. Consider nutrition, hydration, et cetera whilst the recovery vehicle finds a way in.'

'Right, so, like I said, we may need to find a new grid reference if things keep advancing the way they have been.

It's going to be our job to fly out and assess the site together, as well as assess the guys during the scenario itself.'

'I know.' She tried to tell herself that it was no big deal. She was a professional with over a decade of experience. She'd never let herself get into a compromising situation before. But, then, Kane had never been involved before.

At least they would be able to work through the assessment and feedback separately, feeding the findings up through the chain of command and letting them iron any issues out at Brigade level.

'Can you handle this, Mattie?' he asked, and she tried not to notice that he hadn't called her *Matz* in the entire time he'd been at the field hospital.

She suspected that, if it had not felt completely insane, he probably would have addressed her as *ma'am* as a way to keep that line of separation all the clearer.

He'd have to address her more formally if anyone else were to overhear their conversation. It worried her that she didn't know if she'd prefer that or not. He seemed to be finding this—resisting each other—far easier than she was.

Except that he was the one who had reached for her back in her office.

The thought left a warm glow as it wound slowly through her.

'Can you handle working together this closely?' he added, as though he thought she needed clarification.

'Of course I can handle it,' she bristled, despite the fact that she'd only just been asking herself the same question. But, then, he'd always known just how to push her buttons. 'The question is, Kane, *can you*?'

CHAPTER SEVEN

MATTIE SKIMMED THE notes of her fourth patient so far, before heading into the consultation room. Theoretically, as CO she had plenty of things to do other than routine examinations, but she'd always liked to keep her hand in, carrying out the occasional check-up to see what was going on at ground level in her hospital.

Besides, although the hospital was so often in a flurry of activity, there were sometimes a few days of downtime, especially just before or after a big exercise. And right now, doing an occasional consultation kept her mind from wandering to Kane.

She felt better this morning, although she didn't know why since she'd spent most of the night tossing and turning, pretending that she wasn't thinking about Kane, or imagining him on his own cot bed a few army tents over. By zero four hundred hours she'd given up trying to sleep and had dressed and slipped into her office to catch up on some admin, ploughing through a decent amount of work. Nonetheless, a corner of her mind had been distracted, thoughts of Kane weaving around her head.

By now he would be with Kath, her second in command, observing the medical scenarios she had set up for her own teams to keep them sharp and focused. It was part of his job as liaison, and it provided them with a chance for him to see what her unit practised, which could then be dovetailed into the scenarios they would work up for the infantry medics.

Mattie had almost been tempted to head down there and see him—see what he made of it, she corrected hastily. If wouldn't have been that unusual for the CO to attend, especially with the place enjoying this brief lull. But, in the end, she'd chosen instead to come to the walk-in clinic and spend a half-hour or so seeing what kind of cases were walking in at the moment.

Like this private who was apparently suffering from back pain. Satisfied with the notes, she went into the consultation room, smiling at the young lad sitting side-on on the examination bed. He looked as though being in the field hospital was the last place he wanted to be, but was in too much discomfort to avoid making the visit any longer.

'Hello, Private, what brings you in today?'

'Yeah… Hey, ma'am… I guess… I guess I've got a bit of a sore back.' He pulled a face.

'Upper or lower?'

'Um…around here…' He reached round carefully to indicate.

'Is the pain new?' Mattie asked.

The lad shook his head.

'It's been hurting me for a while now, maybe eight months on and off, but it's getting pretty bad now, and the pain has started shooting down my leg.'

'Right.' Mattie nodded. 'Done anything particularly strenuous recently?'

Again the young private shook his head.

'I'm always in the gym, working out, you know? Some weights, and lots of PT. Nothing unusual.'

'Jumping out of planes?'

'Yeah. Sure.'

'Okay, let's give you a physical. Check your reflexes,

muscle strength and stuff. Which leg is experiencing the shooting pain?'

'Left.' He tapped his thigh.

'Okay, let's start with your right leg. Lift it up, bending your knee so that's against your chest, and try to resist as I push down. Good. Okay, try the left leg. Good.'

For the next few minutes Mattie went through a series of tests, chatting to him as she went and eliciting more information. Ultimately, everything seemed to confirm her original suspicion that he had a herniated disc.

'Okay,' Her test complete, she sat back on the chair opposite to chat to him. 'So, I suspect you have a bit of bulging in one of the discs between your vertebrae. It can press on the nerve and cause some of the pain you've described for me.'

'That goes away by itself, right?' the lad asked hopefully.

Mattie smiled. They were all the same, soldiers.

'It should do,' she told him. 'But only if you take care of it. That means getting you on the timetable with the physical therapist for some rehab, and accepting you'll have some limitations on what you can do whilst it heals.'

'So I'm out of training?' He pulled a face. 'It isn't that bad really, ma'am.'

'If you want to heal fast, then you'll listen,' Mattie told him firmly, knowing how these guys could feel pressure to get back to their units before they'd given their bodies chance to fully heal. 'I'll be passing it along the chain of command so that your CO knows you need time to heal, but ultimately the more you take care of it now, the faster you will actually be able to get back out there.

'Do I need an X-ray to confirm it?' He pulled another face.

Mattie smiled. 'No, don't worry. An X-ray won't detect a herniated disc. It might just rule out other causes, but at this stage I don't have any reason to suspect anything else.'

He blew out heavily.

'How long, then?'

'Piece of string,' she told him, not unkindly. 'Come on, let's get you out of here and into the physical therapy unit. With any luck they might even have a slot this morning.'

As she walked the private out and tasked one of the nurses with getting him an appointment with the physio, she turned back for her next patient's notes, only to find Kane standing there.

'Mr Wheeler.' She plastered a friendly smile on her lips, aware that there were plenty of ears around right at that moment.

'Major Brigham,' he acknowledged.

'I trust you had an informative morning with Major Donal. I know she ran through some of the scenarios we've been practising here, so that you see how we can dovetail with medical situations for your guys.'

'Yes, I have some thoughts on how we can integrate it. When you're available, I'd like to go back to the map and run you through where our different units are going to be, and when.'

'Of course.' Mattie nodded. After all, dealing with this mission for Battle group was the priority. 'Give me a moment.'

Reaching for the patient list, she made a couple of notes, nodded to the nurse, and gestured for Kane to join her.

'Shall we, Mr Wheeler?'

And her pulse wasn't really leaping in her throat at the idea of being alone again with Kane—away from all her sharp-eyed staff.

They might not have clocked anything yet but one wrong move, one misplaced word and they would instantly know something was amiss.

'I saw one of the scenarios you were looking at was apparently a splenic injury,' he remarked as they began their walk down the corridor past other colleagues.

'Yes, blunt splenic injuries were always notoriously challenging to manage when on deployment, not only because field posts may not have angiographic capabilities to confirm hemoperitoneum, in which case the casualty would need immediate evacuation for surgical treatment, but also because NOM of splenic injuries could put the casualty at risk of prolonged hypotension.'

'NOM?'

'Sorry, Non-operative management.'

'Right.'

'The other question concerns whether the need for immediate splenectomy can differ between those splenic injuries in a patient also suffering from severe brain injury and those patients with splenic injury with no severe brain injury.'

Reaching her office door, she opened it and invited Kane inside, before hesitating for a moment then propping it open slightly. When she turned, he was watching her, those deep cocoa pools drawing her in, leaving her breathless. She stopped, almost daring him to comment. But he said nothing, simply waiting for her to round her desk and take her seat before sitting down himself.

'I think we should start over. Yesterday was a bit of a...' She searched for the word, her normally sharp brain obviously still a little dented.

'Shock,' he supplied wryly.

'Shock,' she echoed.

'I think that's a wise idea,' he began seriously, before his lips twitched upwards. 'Hello, Major Brigham, I'm WO2 Wheeler.'

'Not that far back,' she objected, but he'd made her laugh and she felt a little of her awkwardness dissipate. 'Though I still can't believe you're an army guy.'

'No, I understand that.' He shrugged, and she appreciated that he still wasn't going to be drawn on his reasons.

It made her feel oddly shut out. He'd never shut her out once during their entire relationship all those years ago. Well, apart from the very end, of course, so that probably wasn't the best comparison to make.

Hurt lanced through her, cold and steel-like, and she tried to grab hold of it as though she thought she might somehow wrap it around her chest and protect herself. She told herself that as much as she longed to know his reasons, it was going to be better to leave well alone.

Far better to hold onto the knowledge that they had a job to do, and that people's lives in the future could hinge on how well she and Kane could pull things together now. And, despite everything else, she prided herself on being a good OC. Clearly Kane was a good WO2.

So, for now, that would he enough.

'Fine.' She made herself pick up her brief. 'Then let's run through the original exercise plans. Our main phase is running medical simulations with the battle group to test the support chain. This pre-phase now is about running our own medical scenarios to keep us sharp in a medical sense.'

'Right, so your main phase is obviously just a medical phase in our battle group's schedule. Brigade are now looking to break that element down further so that we have two distinct medical support chain phases.'

'Run me through it.' Clicking her pen, Mattie began making notes.

'Initially we'd be running the scenarios in the briefing.'

'Which means individual or small group scenarios.' Mattie nodded, not needing to check her notes but doing so anyway. To keep her fingers busy, if nothing else. 'To check how the support chain holds up with the new tactics.'

'Right. Then, depending how that goes, we'll tweak the

tactics or support logistics and keep running those scenarios until we know they're smooth.'

It was almost odd, seeing Kane flip so suddenly. A side of him that had always been there but which she'd never pictured in this military setting before—probably because he'd been so anti-establishment. Yet seeing him now, it was easy to see why he was already a WO2.

'Agreed,' she clipped out, pulling her head back to where it should be.

'But Brigade also want to see if we can look at how a mass casualty incident could be approached.'

'For this exercise?' She cocked her head at him, her mind already beginning to build up a possible event.

'Not necessarily. But possibly. You know how Brigade works.'

'Hurry up and wait.' She nodded. 'Yes. I know. So they want us to start drawing something up in case, but otherwise it can shelved for a future battle group exercise?'

'Pretty much.'

And Mattie couldn't say what happened, or how, but like a switch flicking on they were suddenly in a different place. Talking and tabling suggestions as though they were any OC and WO2. Not Mattie and Kane.

Their intimate history was no longer an issue. If anything, Mattie was shocked to find it made the process even easier, because they knew each other so well they could pre-empt what the other was thinking or read the other's body language.

And when that part of the discussion drew to a natural pause, it was startling to realise they'd been talking for almost ninety minutes. Yet when she stood up to stretch her legs, intending to move around the room, she found herself naturally drifting towards Kane.

'For the record,' she heard herself say quietly, 'I think

now that we're over the initial…shock of meeting out here, we will be able to work well together.'

He regarded her for a moment, his expression turning sober. Though she wished she could read exactly what was behind that slightly guarded expression.

'I really think we can, Mattie. The army is in your blood, it's who you are and you're very good at it, anyone can see that. And I know you don't understand how I came to be here, but I can tell you that the army saved me. I'm not here because my CO needed someone to fill a gap, I'm here because I'm good at what I do.'

'Obviously.' She eyed him with surprise. 'Did you think I didn't realise that? You wouldn't have made it to CSM if you weren't, and certainly not in under a decade and a half. You have to be exceptional at what you do.'

'Not bad for a Wheeler kid, eh?' He laughed self-deprecatingly.

Mattie didn't laugh with him.

'You were never like them, Kane,' she said after a moment. 'You always had the capability to make something of yourself. I just think… I just think that too many people around Heathdale were small–minded, saying that you'd never amount to anything, and you believed them. But I never thought that.'

He watched her again, those rich, brown pools swirling like a vortex. They would drag her under if she let them.

'No,' he said quietly. 'You never did, did you? You always believed in me.'

She bobbed her head in the fraught silence, not trusting herself to answer past the painful lump in her throat.

'I never wanted to let you down, Matz.' His harsh voice sliced unexpectedly through the air.

'Why did you leave?'

He looked simultaneously angry and sad.

'I had to.'

'Without a word of explanation? Without saying goodbye?'

'You think leaving was me letting you down.' He exhaled heavily, his fist thumping heavily on his lap. 'But that isn't what I meant. I let you down before that. Leaving was the solution, not the problem.'

'There you go, talking in riddles again,' she said quietly. 'But you never actually tell me anything.'

'I can't tell you,' he growled, his eyes glittering with fury.

But not at her, she realised. At himself. At his past.

'Can't?' She dropped her voice again, not wanting to attract any attention from out in the corridor. 'Or won't?'

He studied her, as if the words were taking their time to permeate his brain. As if he was really evaluating them. And then, for the second time in two days, he swept the proverbial rug out from beneath her.

'I did something…' He lifted his hand. 'Before we started dating. Before we even met. I was fifteen, but I committed a crime.'

'*You* did?' Mattie sat up straighter in her seat.

She knew what his father was like. What his brothers were like. But not Kane. Still, he'd been fifteen, it surely couldn't have been that serious.

'It's something I'm ashamed of, even to this day. But that night—the very night I told you I loved you—what I'd done years before caught up with me. That's why I left.'

'You ran away?' She was confused.

'No,' he answered instantly. Vehemently. 'I did not run away.'

'But you left?'

'I faced up to it, Mattie. I took responsibility. In doing so I was offered a way out that I hadn't been expecting.'

The army, she realised abruptly. Plenty of lads joined the military because it was that or juvie. Or crime. Some ended up bringing their problems with them, but many of them went on to become incredible soldiers. She'd just never considered Kane would be one of them.

He must really have been some soldier to get past that start to where he was now. Yet she could well believe it.

But that meant that he had even more to lose than she did if either of them crossed that line again. All the more reason for them snuff out this chemistry that they shared and concentrate on the task at hand, hammering out the smoothest, most successful operation phase that they could.

'Then you deserve everything you've earned,' she said sincerely. 'I'm full of admiration. And I'm even impressed with your CO. I thought Percy Copperhead was a snob who would have been hung up on things like that. I thought he'd sent you here to try to undermine me.'

She probably shouldn't have admitted it. She wouldn't have admitted it to anyone else. But, then, she wouldn't have been in this position with anyone other than Kane. Besides, he'd finally shared a confidence with her, and it felt like they'd turned a corner. Being open with him could surely only help them to get things back on track.

'Oh, no, the guy's a first-class oxygen thief.' Kane laughed abruptly. 'If it was down to him, I'd be thrown out of the army even now. As would half the lads in the company, even though a raft of them were true heroes in multiple tours over the last ten years. But Copperhead only took over as CO a couple of months ago, it was my old CO who championed his guys.'

Why didn't that surprise her?

'So sending you here…?'

'Gets me out of his face. He likes yes-men around him, and I'm not one of those.'

'No,' Mattie snorted. 'You're not. So, if we really want to hack the guy off then we just need to make this the most enviable phase of the exercise.'

'Couldn't hurt,' Kane agreed.

'No more…*this*…' She waved her hands between them, hoping Kane understood all the words she couldn't bring herself to say aloud.

Chemistry. Passion. Lust.

She refused to acknowledge any other L-word because that, obviously, wasn't applicable here.

'It's still going to be there, Matz,' Kane answered in a low, only half-regretful tone that spiralled heat straight through her to pool right between her legs. 'We just have to move past it.'

'Ignore it,' she suggested.

'Use it to our advantage.' He shrugged. 'We understand each other in a way no one else will understand. Anticipate each other.'

'Even now, over a decade later?'

She already knew the answer, yet some perverse part of her wanted to hear him say it.

'If you have to ask the question then think back to last weekend in that hotel room,' he growled deliciously, 'and then decide how well I know you.'

It was thrilling. Exhilarating. And entirely the opposite of what they were trying to achieve.

'This isn't exactly *moving past it*.' She arched her eyebrows at him, even as she bit her tongue to stop herself from flicking it out to moisten her dry lips.

He countered her with a look that was so sensual she wanted to walk round the desk and straddle him, there and then.

'Then start trying,' he told her.

'Fine.' She didn't need to tell him that it seemed the more they tried, the harder it became. 'Tomorrow morning we're running a medical scenario on a MERT if you want to come. I'm sure you've observed before but might help give you an idea of what goes on when your guys hand

over the injured soldier to us. We'll be running two casualties from the same scenario with very similar injuries.'

'What is the benefit of that?' he asked curiously.

'The casualty who is slightly more severely wounded
will receive textbook treatment on the ground before our
MERT team arrives, whilst the casualty who's slightly
less severely wounded will have mistakes made by the
combat medics.'

'Okay.' Kane nodded. 'So that way, when we run the
simulations in my setting for my men, your teams will already be prepared for any less than optimal treatment on
the ground?'

'That way we can be sure the test is on your men rather
than my medics. Which is the goal of this new phase.'

'Call it a pre-phase.' Mattie offered a smile. 'The original first phase, which is the one we'd already planned, is
geared around testing the medical support chain for the
battle group rather than the medical knowledge of either
your guys or my medical staff.'

'Which it is still intended to be, it's just a matter of
whether we need to find new grid locations. And the pre-
planned second phase, which should also be changed, is
going to be a full mass casualty event, same grid locations
as those already planned with the Engineers.'

CHAPTER EIGHT

HE HADN'T INTENDED to join her, yet Kane found himself falling in step as they ran over the rough terrain together.

He'd been following her for four miles so far, ever since his alarm had gone off half an hour earlier and he'd decided to see if a run would clear his head. At first he'd thought it better to stay back, off Mattie's radar. But following that delectable body, clad in tight running gear that moulded itself to every delicious curve, had definitely not been helping to keep his libido in check.

At least running alongside her meant he couldn't stay just the right distance behind her, ogling her like some kind of hyped-up teenage boy. It'd been altogether too tempting to pull her into the nearby treeline and take her up against one of those silver birches. All he could think of was the way her long legs had appeared even longer, reminding him of the way she'd wrapped them around his hips that night at the hotel. Locking them over his back and using them to pull him deeper and deeper inside her.

God, he was losing it again.

Concentrating on his running, Kane willed his body back into submission. No easy feat when her ragged breathing was now causing a slightly different memory. The damned woman was enough to drive him insane.

And he wasn't even sure she knew it.

Mattie swung her head round, saw him running beside her and slowly—reluctantly, he thought—pulled her earphones out of her ears.

'I thought you'd be in the gym.'

'I've always preferred running.' He shrugged, then frowned. 'Why?'

'I don't know...the muscles.'

She flushed as she said it, the tell she'd been trying to hide. The giveaway that she'd paid him more attention than she wanted to admit to—thinking of him the way he'd been thinking of her. Kane barely supressed a grin.

'That's just genuine physical work,' he told her. 'No hours of weights in the gym.'

At least out here they were safe. Safe to talk in privacy, but also safe that it wasn't intimate. Nothing could happen.

'If the offer is still on the table for the MERT ride-along, I'd like to see that.'

'What changed your mind?'

He couldn't tell whether she was hacked off or happy about it and, for some reason, that got under his skin.

'I figured it could only help me to know what to focus on for my guys if I saw for myself how their packaging of the casualties affects your team.'

It was a valid reason, and one he certainly *should* have in the forefront of his mind. If was just a shame that the main reason started with *Spending more time* and ended on *with Mattie*.

Even the thought of her was helping to elevate his temperature, and as much as he'd like to blame it on the run, he couldn't. With an irritated grumble, Kane hauled off his running tee and tucked it into the rear waistband of his shorts.

'Do you really need to take that off?'

'Sorry?' He turned to look at her, assuming that this was her idea of a joke, getting him back for earlier.

Instead, he realised that her expression was deadly serious, and slightly anguished.

She wanted him, too.

'I do,' he replied with nonchalance.

If she wanted his chest covered, she could always order him to do it. He'd spent years thinking he'd lost her and missing her in a way he'd never dreamed possible. Now it was Mattie's turn to wonder at things that might have been.

The fact that she didn't told him everything he needed to know. Instead, they ran in quiet companionship together. Their step and their breathing reaching an easy harmony.

'It's so quiet,' he observed after a while.

'Peaceful,' agreed Mattie. 'And beautiful. Like those flowers over there. Whatever they are.'

He followed the direction of her gaze.

'Lupins.'

'Sorry?'

'The flowers. They're lupins.'

He couldn't help smiling as her head swivelled around, knowing what she was about to say even before she said it.

'I read it.'

'You read it?'

'In a book about this place,' he continued, with deliberate nonchalance. 'I like to do that when I go somewhere new. It's good to learn new things.'

An echo of something she'd once said to him as kids, he wondered if she remembered it.

'Yes,' she managed quietly, telling him that she did remember. 'I know.'

'Some things don't change, Matz.'

She looked at him and paused before answering.

'And some things do. It isn't always easy to see which it is. Or if it's for the best.'

'Sometimes it's better to just let your gut tell you.'

'So, what does your gut tell you, Kane?'

He shrugged, not answering for a moment. Another time he might have offered a dismissive quip. This time he didn't want to.

'I don't know,' he admitted at last. 'That's why I'm out here, running. Trying to clear my head.'

She eyed him again, but this time her gaze was softer. He thought it might be his undoing.

'I thought you were going to just say, *My gut's telling me I'm hungry.* Or some other clever remark.'

'I considered it,' he answered wryly. 'I opted against clever remarks, for the truth.'

She bobbed her head but didn't answer. They were all alone out here, no one was round. No one could even see them. For a moment he wanted to just grab her, kiss her and tell her everything was going to be okay.

But it wasn't. Because nothing had changed.

Except for the fact that he could no longer pretend he was over her.

'We get such odd periods through a day in this place.' Her soft voice broke through his thoughts. He realised she was trying to keep the topic light. Or, at least, not intimate. He welcomed it. 'Sometimes there's so much downtime you think you're going crazy, and other times it's so completely full on that you think you must already have *gone* crazy.

'That's life in the army.' He forced a laugh. 'I remember your father always used to say it, too. I'm so sorry about the Alzheimer's.'

And about the fact that she didn't know that it had been her father who had helped him to get into the army in the first instance. Yet she couldn't know. He'd already told her as much as he dared, and if there was a little shame involved on his part, well, that was his issue to deal with.

It was bad enough that he'd had to drag her father into his family's problems back then. He hated that pretty much thirty-five years on this earth still hadn't been long enough for him to work out a way to finally get away from the destructive impact his shameful family had on anyone around them.

Including himself.

Although the worst of it was that his actions that night had been of his own making. If he'd just called the police...

Even now he could hear it all. The shouts. The shots. The way the tyres had screeched in the night.

It was only when he felt a hand grabbing at his arm that he realised he'd been accelerating harder and harder, and now he could feel his breath ragged and painful in his chest.

It was almost welcome.

'Slow down,' Mattie grumbled. 'It's a training run, not a race.'

Abruptly, he slowed then stopped, fighting to regain his breathing as she bent over, her hands braced against her knees, her words choppy.

'What was all that about?'

'Sorry,' he managed curtly, steeling himself.

He didn't want all his doubts and regrets to be plastered all over his face when she eventually looked up again.

'I'm going back,' he barked. 'Get a shower before I go on that MERT shout later.'

'Kane...'

But he didn't wait. He couldn't afford to. They were a good few miles out from the hospital accommodation and, out here alone with Mattie, he feared he might be prepared to tell her anything.

Everything.

But he couldn't. Because right now she already knew that he had betrayed her. She didn't need to know he'd dragged her father—and ultimately Hayden—into the lie, too. So, instead, Kane concentrated on the run. The pounding impact of his body racing over the harsh terrain.

Cracking out a crushing pace was just what he needed to get his head back in order.

'Everyone has their job, don't they?' Kane yelled as the helicopter landed near the simulated blast site.

Mattie duly glanced at each member of the Medical Emergency Response Team.

She'd made a conscious decision to put the morning's odd run behind them. She wanted to pretend it was for the good of the exercise—and there was certainly an element of that to it—but deep down there was also the fear that if she pressed Kane on whatever this morning had been about, he would only back off from her all the more.

And it was pointless trying to tell herself that she didn't care. Clearly, she did.

Even though she shouldn't.

So, instead, she focused on his question, and the task in hand.

'Yeah, everyone knows their role. One of the paramedics will be charged with tourniquets, field dressings, log-roll. The nurse will be monitoring, so we know pulse rates, saturations, rhythms. Could be radial, femoral or carotid depending on degree of sickness.

'The doctor will be doing the ABCs, and the second paramedic will be putting in cannulas for fluids or bloods. So, yeah, everyone has their designated jobs.'

This time it might be a simulation scenario, but it was all too familiar to her. Over the last decade she had done this for real on multiple tours of duty, just as the four medics she was assessing today had done. However, she'd never worked with any of them before, which made today's simulation all the more important.

And the fact that Kane was on board, so very close to

her, only complicated things that little bit more. Not that she couldn't handle the pressure, of course. More that it was incredibly draining having her body on full alert almost every minute of the day. Attuned to his presence whether she wanted to be or not.

Surely this mini-exercise would be something she could get stuck into, and it would help her to clear Kane from her thoughts, even a little while.

'Okay, Sergeant Cole,' she shouted above the roar of the rotor blades, 'I'm designating you as the liaison for this shout. I'll be accompanying you on the ground but I'm there to observe only, so just continue as though you were alone.'

The sergeant confirmed her understanding, then they both covered their mouths as the helicopter descended, raising huge swathes of dusty air in its wake.

She'd be looking to see how well the sergeant liaised with the medics on the ground. The simulation was a bomb blast near the FIBUA, so Mattie was also keen to see how the medics on the ground had carried out their own medical procedures.

'I don't need to remind you that the point of the MERT crew is to essentially move the field hospital to the patient. As the doctor and medical staff on board you have the knowledge to treat, anaesthetise, even operate on the patient in-flight.'

She glanced around the group, hoping all of them could hear her—or at least read her lips—over the noise of the engines.

'But for the MERT crew to do a good job, the soldiers on site must have done their basics properly, which means applying combat application tourniquets in good time and tying them off tightly, getting the field dressings on, administering morphine, and ensuring they are ready with really accurate MIST handovers. That means we they need to have really identified the Mechansim of Injury, the Injury pattern, the Signs or observations, and the Treatment given. And that's what today is all about. Not us saving this guy, but us seeing if the lads out there, in the thick of the fighting, have done the best job they can do for their buddies, under the most intense circumstances.'

As the helicopter landed, Mattie followed the sergeant off so that she could continue assessing. Kane was only feet away.

'Okay, what have we got?'

'Patient one is a double amputee, mechanism of injury IED. Due to the loss of limbs there was no radial pulse, so we put a sternal IO into his chest to push fluids through.'

Which would have meant manually forcing the fluids through the injured soldier's sternum, an incredible painful procedure. Mattie continued to assess.

'Patient two was hit by an IED whilst travelling in a vehicle. The vehicle overturned and impaled him on some rebar. Although the rebar has been left in place, it was too long and had to be cut down. A field dressing was used to staunch the bleeding.

'Patient three has a gunshot wound to his chest. Entry wound but no exit wound. The wound has been cleaned and packed. He had no radial pulse and minimal external bleeding. Needle compression resulted in return of radial as well as easier breathing.'

Satisfied, the sergeant directed the lads to ferry the three casualties to the waiting helicopter, where the MERT team would be ready.

CHAPTER NINE

THE LULL OF the four-by-four had been almost soothing as they'd begun their recce the following day. A corporal was acting as their designated driver, and she and Kane had been in the back, sitting opposite each other on the hard metal seats that lined each side, ostensibly poring over the map and the potential sites. Going through the scenarios one more time to determine what kind of cas-evac would be ideal for each. Helicopter? Vehicle? Ambulance?

But a couple of hours in and the tension that had begun winding between them ever since they'd set off had become fraught, and thick.

It had started with the first sway of the vehicle as Mattie's leg had rocked against Kane's. She'd moved it away, trying to create some space, but as they'd moved from the level tracks around the hospital onto the more uneven ground of the landscape the rocking motion had grown more pronounced.

With every passing minute, and each brush of her leg against his, each moment of delicious friction, Mattie had felt her resolve slipping. She'd tried to focus on different things in the space. The jerry cans, the sticker, the stretcher behind Kane's head. Yet nothing had worked and, instead, all the professional attitude they'd been focused on had crumbled with each roll of the cab. Especially when Kane had snagged her gaze with his and slowly, slowly moved his thigh—hard and defined—to pin hers in place. As though his resolve was as fragile as hers.

As though he'd *wanted* as badly as she did.

There was no way that the corporal driving the vehicle would possibly have detected anything, and yet Mattie had felt instantly exposed. Edgy. Like they'd been teenagers caught necking in the back of a taxi. Except that it wasn't a taxi, they weren't teenagers, and they sure as hell hadn't been necking.

But she'd wanted to.

She *still* wanted to.

And now, several tense hours later, the four-by-four having left the main track for off-road terrain, and the wallowing becoming more and more pronounced, the contact was becoming almost unbearable.

'Bit rough, isn't it?' Kane murmured, pitched low enough for their driver not to hear in the front.

She blinked slowly, the tone sounding innocent enough but the glint in his eyes suggesting anything but. Despite everything they'd said the other day in her office, a wicked thrill poured through her in an instant.

She didn't mean to, but Mattie felt her eyes drop to his mouth. She'd avoided looking at him for the last few days but now that she was, she realised that the urge to kiss him, to taste him was right there. Like lifting a teacloth cover off a poorly concealed cake she'd been hankering over for too long.

And then she dropped her gaze again. Down the front of his jacket, which did little to disguise the well-built chest beneath, and the lower abs that she'd traced with her fingers, and then her tongue, that night back in the hotel.

And suddenly she was staring straight at the part of him that she should be looking at the least. The part that got her the hottest.

The vehicle lurched without warning, and Mattie shot her hand up to brace herself on the inside of the roof as they bounced along, helpless to stop her legs from banging against Kane's.

He lowered his hand, out of sight, to rest it on her thigh, steadying her. But the contact was scorching, branding her from the inside out. It was insane how badly she wanted to slide down her seat and make Kane's hand move higher. More centrally.

She wouldn't. Of course she wouldn't. But the need that pounded through her was incredible. Almost overwhelming.

'Sorry, ma'am...sir,' the young corporal designated as their driver apologised for the third time. 'The ground is a lot boggier than we thought.'

'Yeah, the map will show a lot of things, but it won't pick up weather-affected terrain,' Kane muttered as Mattie was flung towards him again. 'The place was probably bone dry a month ago.'

She braced her hand tighter against the roof, trying to give herself support. If she got thrown around any more, she was in danger of landing face first in Kane's lap, which was hardly going to help their efforts to ignore whatever this *thing* was between them. And they'd been doing so well over the past couple of days.

Yeah, keep lying to yourself if it makes you feel better, needled a wry voice inside her head.

Because, for her, every touch was reigniting the sparks she'd told herself she'd snuffed out.

Suddenly the vehicle wallowed heavily, and despite her best efforts Mattie pitched forward, slamming into the solid wall that was Kane's chest. Only his hands reaching out to grab her and steady her against him stopped her from sliding painfully to the floor.

'Thanks,' she muttered, wanting to move but unable to.

It was too intoxicating to stay here, pressed against him. She could feel his heart beating, strong and slightly too fast, echoing the pulse that drummed at her neck. Making her wonder if he could feel everything that she felt.

If he was as close to the edge as she was, so that a moment like this could undo all the good work they'd managed by avoiding each other the past couple of days.

'You okay, ma'am?'

The corporal's voice sliced through Mattie's thoughts, jolting her back into action. Hastily, she reached out and tried to lever herself up.

Only when she braced her hand this time, it was against a hard, muscled thigh—something decidedly *Kane*-like.

Shocked, she snatched her hand back as though burned, fire racing to her cheeks. It was one thing knowing he was as affected as she was, but it was something else feeling the indisputable proof of it so hot, and full of promise, against the palm of her hand.

Knowing she couldn't do a single thing about it.

'I'm sorry... I...'

'It's fine,' he cut her off tersely, jerking his head towards their driver in silent caution, but it was the look of intensity in his expression that reached into her chest and tugged. 'I suggest we stop and get out. Maybe have a look for ourselves rather than suffering this.'

Mattie fought to wrest her tongue from the roof of her parched mouth.

'I agree. At least it will afford us an opportunity to look for higher ground. It wouldn't take more than a few inches to get us out of this marsh.'

And give Kane and her a chance to get out of earshot of the young corporal, who would have to stay with the vehicle. Although what she was supposed to say after... *that* was unclear.

'Shall I stop, ma'am?'

'Yes, Corporal. Stop here.'

He obeyed, apparently only too eager to end the torture for himself, and Mattie took the chance to jump down from the back, giving Kane a moment longer to sort himself out.

Grabbing a day sack, she started to head off across the ground, knowing he would catch up with her when he was ready.

'The buildings should be over there...' She indicated a few moments later as he stepped alongside her. 'Just over that small rise.'

Her cheeks still felt like they were on fire, but there was no need to prolong the moment. In truth, the best thing they could do would be to get this mission done and over with. It was increasingly clear to her that the longer she and Kane spent together, the stronger their attraction was growing.

And the more she didn't want it to stop.

Forcing herself back into the moment, she turned to speak to Kane just as he was peering into the distance.

'It doesn't look promising.'

'Ground conditions are less than ideal,' she noted.

'For you medics perhaps,' he noted evenly. 'This is why the infantry come to places like this. To train over all kinds of terrain.'

'Yeah, yeah, you're all as hard as nails, I know.' And before she could stop herself, she was teasing him again.

Crossing that line. Again.

Biting her tongue, she concentrated on walking over the uneven terrain, reaching the top of the rise. Another step and she'd see over the low brow.

'Oh.'

Damn.

'That's disappointing.' Kane blew out heavily as they both stopped. 'You could lose whole tanks in those depressions. The helicopters will never be able to land.'

He was right. The ground had folds in it that would

never have been picked up on the map. Worse than that, though, was the fact that piles of stones lay where the collection of buildings was supposed to have been.

'They're more than just ruins.' Mattie exhaled. 'They've practically crumbled to the ground. There's no shelter there for any medical triage area. I don't mind rewriting scenarios on the fly, but there really ought to be something they can use as makeshift shelter.'

'Yeah, this location is a dud. Shall we try the next? The next one we identified is only a couple of clicks that way on the other side of that wood.' He gestured to a treeline further into the distance. 'We could walk it, or get back to the main track and see how far it takes us around by vehicle.'

There looked to be a path leading into the wood, or they could skirt around it as it wasn't too extensive. But time was running out and the vehicle was probably the best option.

Mattie worried at her lips with her teeth. She wanted to take a moment. It was just a bit too intense in that four-by-four right now, with Kane too damn close for comfort and the corporal seeing her every blush and flush, like there was something going on.

Especially when she and Kane had been doing so well at ensuring there was absolutely *nothing* going on at all.

'You want to just walk on a bit further?' he asked quietly.

She nodded, grateful that she didn't have to say anything for him to understand. They walked in silence to the ruins, and he stopped on a rock whilst she pretended to take a tour around them. Catching her breath.

'We'll find thd next location and confirm it as the new scenario site, then we'll be back at camp by nightfall,' Kane assured her as they finally headed back to the four-by-four.

'Right,' she agreed.

She hoped so. They'd packed for staying out for the

night, and normally she would have looked forward to the opportunity to be away from everything—even her beloved hospital—for a night.

But sleeping so close to Kane, with some random corporal acting like some kind of eighteenth-century chaperone— not that the poor kid knew it—wasn't going to be something she relished.

Climbing back into the rear of the vehicle, she shoved one of the bergens to one side and rammed her legs into the space, telling herself that it was for the best. At least this way no contact with Kane would mean no temptation. And that could only be a good thing.

The vehicle rumbled off, their young driver briefed on the new co-ordinates, but they hadn't been going for more than ten minutes when Mattie felt the vehicle pull to a halt. Carefully she leaned over the back of the seat.

'Everything all right, Corporal?'

'There are two tracks on the ground, ma'am, but only one on the map.'

Kane was out and taking a look before she could respond.

'My instinct would be to take the higher one.' He shrugged as he returned. 'But there's no clear indication which is best.'

Given the boggy nature of the ground, that would have been her instinct, too.

'Agreed.' She nodded. 'But if we need to get out and continue on foot, I have no issues with that.'

'Understood,' Kane confirmed, hauling himself into the front seat this time, and taking the lead as any other WO2 might have done.

Sometimes, Mattie decided, there were definite disadvantages to being the CO. Not least the fact that it wasn't always easy to just get in there and get your hands dirty.

And then, without warning, the four-by-four lurched

sickeningly, throwing Mattie from her seat and almost slamming her head against the metal frames on the side of the vehicle. When they jerked to a halt, the off roader was at a worrying angle.

'Are you all right, ma'am?' The corporal's agitated voice finally broke into the silence. 'Sir?'

Mattie had no idea how she forced her protesting muscles back into action and push herself back up and onto her own seat. It didn't mean she could talk, though.

'Fine,' Kane confirmed after half a beat. 'What about you?'

'Um…yeah…' the young lad began before catching himself. 'Yes, I think so, sir.'

Kane reached for the back door, swinging it open.

'Okay, let's assess the damage, shall we?'

Gathering herself together, Mattie followed him, leaping down on legs that she told herself weren't shaking—and if they were, it was only because of the violence of the accident and nothing whatsoever to do with Kane.

And when she turned back to look, she almost convinced herself that it was true. A rear wheel of the four-by-four had apparently opened up a narrow fissure, not even deep enough for a person to fall into but certainly deep enough to trap a wheel. So whilst there was no imminent danger of it opening up and pulling the vehicle in, there was clearly no way they were going to be able to drive out of the situation.

'It wasn't on the map, either ma'am,' the corporal told her anxiously.

'No, I imagine not. These prairies are extensive and not every square inch of it will have been mapped. We'll get to safety and call it in.'

'I suggest we try and push it out, ma'am,' Kane concluded after an initial assessment, before locking his gaze with hers. 'If that doesn't work, we can radio for backup.'

With anyone else she probably would have doubted their ability to succeed but, then, anyone else wasn't Kane. Brown eyes held hers as something lurched in Mattie's chest. She ruthlessly quashed it.

'You look the strongest, Mr Wheeler, perhaps you should take the rear.' Her voice was miraculously even and controlled. She'd never been more grateful for all her years of training. 'Corporal, you open the driver door and take that side, and I'll take this side.'

'Yes, ma'am.' The corporal scurried back around to the driver's door, opening it wide and holding the main body of the vehicle across from Mattie, as she did the same.

'Mr Wheeler, if you'd like to count us in when you're ready.'

'All right. One, two, three…'

The three of them pushed. The four-by-four rocked promisingly but didn't move.

'Perhaps you'd like to release the handbrake, Corporal,' Kane remarked dryly.

'Yes, sir. Sorry, sir.' The young lad went a fiery red and leaned into the cab. 'All done, sir.'

'Again, on three,' Kane said.

On his count, Mattie threw her full force into pushing the heavy vehicle but there was no doubt in her mind that it was Kane's input that ultimately, miraculously had the four-by-four moving. Not far, but enough to get the fourth wheel onto solid ground, although Mattie couldn't imagine them being able to push it much further given the rough terrain.

'Corporal, do you want to jump in and start the engine.' It was less of a request from Kane and more of a command. 'Move to the outbuilding over there, as we know that's safe ground. I suggest we follow on foot, Major.'

'I concur.' Mattie dipped her head, wishing she didn't

feel such a thrill at the idea of even a few moments alone with Kane.

Especially after that...*moment* when she'd been flung into his arms.

The young lad obeyed and within moments he was driving the four-by-four carefully over the terrain, leaving Mattie and Kane to follow on foot.

'You can call it in from the shelter,' she muttered quietly, in some kind of half-hearted attempt to keep things professional.

As though it could keep her head in the right place. Kane didn't seem to have read the unspoken memo.

'You okay, Mattie?'

'Fine,' she replied quickly. Too quickly. Too tightly.

'You got thrown around quite badly back there.'

'I said I'm fine.' She could see his head swivel towards her in her peripheral vision, but she ignored it.

She *was* fine...if she didn't count the way Kane seemed to constantly get under her skin.

'Have it your own way.' He sounded more amused than irritated.

'There's a bit of a grinding noise, ma'am,' the corporal suddenly called, as he stopped the vehicle. 'I just want to have a check.'

And then things happened so fast that Mattie barely had time to notice.

The lad jumped out of the four-by-four, slipping slightly as he landed. Spinning his body around, he reached out to grab the bonnet and the vehicle—its handbrake evidently not having been applied—began to roll back slightly.

As the corporal struggled to get traction on the wet grass and pull himself out of the way of the wheel, he twisted again, this time awkwardly, and then there was a loud cracking sound and a scream.

'He's broken his leg,' Mattie ground out, straightening up and beginning to run down the hill, Kane's boots pounding the ground next to her.

'Don't go in there until I've secured the vehicle,' he commanded.

As Mattie headed for the casualty, Kane yanked open the vehicle door and snatched on the handbrake. The bone sticking through the lad's leg and trousers were obvious the moment she arrived.

'Bring my medical grab bag,' she ordered, barely glancing up at Kane as she concentrated on the corporal. 'Okay, Daryl, isn't it?'

The lad made what sounded like a confirmation, though it wasn't clear over his cries of pain.

'Okay, Daryl, you have a compound fracture so what I'm going to do is stem the bleeding, immobilise the area, and see if we can't reduce your pain. But first I just want to check you for any other injuries. Does it hurt anywhere else?'

Quickly she began to check over his body. She suspected it was just the fracture of the lower leg, but she didn't want to miss any internal bleeding caused by some impact she hadn't quite seen.

'All right, Daryl, mate, it's going to be okay, Doc's treating you now.' Kane returned with her bag then knelt next to the corporal, taking his hand and beginning to talk, his low voice calm and soothing. Then he turned to her. 'What do you want me to do?'

'Can you get some scissors and cut his trousers? I want to pack this field dressing around the bone to staunch the bleeding and protect the injury, then elevate the limb.'

Dutifully Kane searched through her bag, quickly producing a pair of scissors and some field dressing kits. As he cut the trousers, she pulled off the soldier's boot and sock and checked for a pulse in the foot, relieved when she found it. At least the neurovascular state of his leg was good. She had known some soldiers who had ended up needing the foot amputated because a leg fracture had resulted in circulatory deterioration.

Pulling the field dressing apart, she lowered it around the protruding bone, working quickly and efficiently as she pressed it to the wound to staunch the bleeding.

'Right, apply pressure here,' she told him. 'Then I can pack the wound.'

'His breathing is becoming rapid,' Kane noted quietly, so that the young lad couldn't hear, and Mattie nodded grimly.

'His colour and temperature aren't looking too good either. I'm concerned about hypovolaemia.'

Ideally, she would give the lad oxygen, but she didn't have any with her. But she could give an intravenous saline solution to replenish his fluids, and she still needed to splint the leg.

'There's a box splint in the cab,' she told Kane. 'But I'd prefer to put his leg into traction. Can you see if there are any long sticks or branches by those trees? I need one longer than the other, one to run on the outside from the chest down to the ankle, and the other to run on the inside from the groin.'

'Diameter?'

'Enough to take some strain, maybe around five centimetres or so?'

'On it,' Kane confirmed, heading quickly towards the trees.

She plunged back into her med pack, talking to Daryl all the while. If she wanted to manipulate the corporal's leg she was going to need to administer some pain relief, and there was a morphine injector in her kit. And prepping a few bandages to use as ties would save time.

Kane was back quicker than she had hoped, bringing with him a decent selection of thick sticks.

'Great,' she approved, selecting the best, straightest two. 'Now, I'm going to need you to grab his ankle and pull the leg down.'

As Kane obliged, Mattie quickly set up the traction, constantly checking for signs of neurovascular compromise each time she made an adjustment. And then they were done, and whilst Kane called it in, she focused on keeping the injured man warm, and talking, reassuring him all the while.

'Okay, the heli-med will be here in ten. But we're going to need to get him off this patch of ground. They won't be able to land here.'

Mattie glanced around quickly.

'I don't want to put him in that vehicle, not the way it will toss him around. We're going to have to tab him out.'

'Understood,' Kane confirmed. 'I'll get the stretcher from the cab.'

By the time they'd loaded the corporal on the stretcher and carried him out of the dip to more level ground, she could already hear the helicopter in the distance.

Instinctively, Mattie stood over her patient, protecting him as best she could from the downdraught of the rotors, waiting as her guys jumped off the back and hurried over to carry out her handover with a few additional instructions besides. Before long, they were loading the corporal into the heli.

'Will you be returning with us, ma'am?'

She could feel Kane's eyes on her. Boring into her back. She didn't dare turn. Still, as she shook her head, she was grateful for the ability to keep her tone light yet professional.

'No,' she confirmed. 'We still need to determine the location for the new medical phase of the exercise. The first two locations didn't turn out to be appropriate.'

'Should we send out another driver?'

Mattie forced a bright smile.

'No, I'm sure Mr Wheeler can drive us.'

'Of course, ma'am.' His voice rumbled through her as potent as ever, but she made herself ignore it.

She ignored the niggling voice asking whether there wasn't a tiny part of her that was welcoming this opportunity to be alone with Kane again. Even though the rational part of her brain just said that she was courting disaster.

'Jolly good.' She offered a firm nod. 'Then I anticipate returning to the hospital tomorrow.'

'Jolly good?' Kane rumbled as the team jumped back onto the heli and it started to take off. 'I don't think I've ever heard you use those words before.'

'Leave it alone, Kane.'

'Jolly good,' he continued, without a hint of contrition.

She wanted to chastise him, but Mattie found she couldn't. She felt light suddenly. Free. The young corporal had been a decent lad, but it had been such a confining situation with Kane that she'd felt under scrutiny the whole time.

Maybe now she didn't feel her every word could be analysed she wouldn't feel so edgy.

Yeah. Right.

'Listen, the accident, not that it was anyone's fault,' she added hastily, 'has put us a couple of hours behind. The sooner we find and reach this third location and assess it, the sooner we can get back to the hospital.'

'You and I both know that isn't happening tonight,' Kane replied in a low voice.

And there was no reason for that to send such a thrill rippling through her.

No reason at all.

Mattie watched wordlessly as the chopper disappeared towards the horizon, more to rein in her racing heartbeat than anything else. Finally, she turned back.

They were alone. Just the two of them.

There was no one else around for miles and miles. The ultimate test of their resolve to concentrate on their jobs and resist each other.

'Well, *Mr Wheeler*,' she said pointedly, since there was no logical reason for them not to resort to first names as the corporal was no longer with them. Still, she softened her words with a smile. 'Perhaps you're right, but shall we continue? I'd rather not stay out here in the middle of... *nothing* all night.'

'We shall, *ma'am*.' He dipped his head as he swung up into the driver's seat, acknowledging the point she was indirectly making.

She climbed up into the passenger seat and turned to look at him, only for him to grin. That familiar, wolfish smile which made her imagine those straight, white teeth against her bare skin.

Doing things to her.

'Kane...'

'Actually, *ma'am*...' his grin pulled wider, teasing her '...I rather thought you might walk ahead of the vehicle back to the track.'

'You want me to walk us out of here?'

'Just to check the ground is solid enough for a heavy four-by-four,' he confirmed.

Mattie narrowed her eyes at him. It was a sound point but she just couldn't help thinking he was relishing the moment.

'Unless you want to drive, of course.'

They both knew, as CO, she couldn't do that. It was an odd quirk of the British army that a commissioned officer wasn't permitted to drive themselves around in military vehicles.

Any accident—even the one they'd just had involving the young corporal—would result in being called in front of the driver's commanding officer for an investigation pending disciplinary action. For the corporal, the CO would be his own officer-in-command, a major. For an NCO as senior as Kane, his CO would be a lieutenant-colonel.

But she, as a commissioned officer, would be called in front of the brigade commander—a general—and that could be the difference between her getting a promotion or not.

If she'd no driver and no choice, that would be different, especially in an exercise area. But when she was standing right in front of an NCO…well, it was pointless to risk her career just to prove a point to Kane Wheeler.

Glowering at him, because he was enjoying himself rather too much, Mattie swung back down and made a point of shutting the vehicle door as she turned her back. Not a slam, but loud enough to rock the four-by-four. She could hear Kane's deep, rich laugh as she stomped across the uneven terrain and stepped out in front of the four-by-four. Then, watching each step but more conscious of his eyes on her backside, she began to walk back to the track, making sure the ground was firm enough to take the weight of the vehicle as she went.

And if she put a little extra pizzaz into the swing of her hips, thrusting her hands into her pockets to hug the otherwise unflattering material tighter to her backside, *so what?*

Besides, Kane probably hadn't even noticed. He'd barely looked at her twice in the past couple of days and she hated to admit that it was galling to realise that he'd been finding it so easy to ignore the attraction that still burned low in her, whether he was around or not.

So, really, why not sashay a little? After all, what was the worst that could happen?

CHAPTER TEN

CONCENTRATE ON THE damned ground.

Gripping the wheel tighter, Kane fought to drag his gaze from that peachy derrière and back to the task in hand. The last thing he wanted to do was repeat the mistake the corporal made, but Mattie was hardly making it easy for him to stay focused. Especially because the fading light had caused him to have to turn the lights on, illuminating her—and her delectable rear—like a Christmas tree.

Worse, he didn't *want* to stay focused. He just wanted Mattie. And the more time they spent together, the stronger that emotion was becoming. It had been like a slow burn from the moment they'd agreed to keep things *strictly professional*. In some ways, he'd welcomed the challenge—being this close to her but controlling the tumbling desires. Proving to himself that he could. Like some exquisite torture.

But now it was just plain torture and there was nothing *exquisite* about it. Being cooped up with her in the back of the four-by-four for the past day, her leg or hand brushing him every time that corporal had driven over a bump—and there were plenty of them out here, in this rough terrain—had been enough to kill him. He'd spent most of the day uncomfortably hard.

And now she was swinging that backside from side to

side, practically driving him insane. He couldn't get them back to the main track quickly enough.

'Get in,' he growled to her, leaning out of the driver's window as soon as the vehicle jerked from the rough off-road terrain to the slightly less rough track.

'Problem?' She turned slowly, sweetly, before saunter-ing around to the passenger door and pulling herself up gracefully.

He wasn't fooled. So she *had* known what she was doing. Was it wrong that it gave him a kick, low in his gut, to know that she'd done it deliberately? That she'd *wanted* to turn him on. The corners of his mouth tugged upwards.

'No problem for me. You?'

She'd been doing such a good job of acting profession-ally over the last couple of days that he'd really started to believe she wasn't finding it anywhere near as difficult to resist temptation as he was.

Her gaze caught his. Sparkling. Fun. The Mattie he'd never been able to refuse. Never *wanted* to.

'None at all.' She grinned, and a lick of heat swept over him.

He could just stop the vehicle right here. No one was around. The temptation was almost overwhelming. Kane scrabbled to keep a grip on reality.

'That said, I want to check the underside of this vehi-cle to make sure no real damage was done in the accident, but the light is already fading. And out here it fades fast.'

'Oh, do you think there was damage?' she asked seri-ously, the sexual tension between them mercifully, regret-tably broken.

'I don't know.' He navigated the uneven ground around the hill. 'But it wouldn't hurt to check. Preferably on flat-ter ground and whilst we still have some light.'

Mattie peered through the windscreen, the land begin-ning to flatten and fall away as they crested the hill.

'Wait, what's that?'

He stopped the vehicle and followed the direction of her gaze, squinting to see better.

'Looks like a collection of old farm buildings,' he hazarded, turning as Mattie looked up from consulting the map.

'There looks to be something of a track although it isn't marked on the map. But this place is so vast not everything can be. Want to check it out? It's a damn sight closer than the area we were originally heading for.'

He revved the engine gently and guided the vehicle until they were on the new track. If nothing else, it certainly looked like a better place to spend the night than out in the open. Not that his mind really wanted to go there at this moment. Anyway, he'd been getting concerned that they wouldn't make it there before sunset, which made this a potentially better stop-over.

In silence they made their way to the cluster of buildings, somewhat reassured by the directness of the only slightly overgrown track. Pulling up outside it and climbing out, they made their way around the outhouses, which were in varying states of ruin.

'You know, this might actually make a good location for the new pre-phase,' Mattie said consideringly after several minutes. 'One of the buildings around that side still has its roof pretty much intact so it would an ideal spot to set up the triage and stabilisation section.'

'It isn't in a bad position for defending against tactical fire,' agreed Kane, circling back around the buildings as he headed back to the vehicle. 'And we already know there's an ideal landing zone back down the hill, where they can tab their casualties out.'

'It isn't too far off the designated route for the infantry?' she checked.

Kane slid the map out of his pocket, laying it on the bonnet to check.

'Less than a klick, so it's no big deal to bring them over this way slightly. See?'

She jogged across the path and peered over his shoulder, so close that he could feel her breast against his arm. The hear seared his skin even through the jacket and he heard her catch her breath. Then his brain cracked and went blank.

'Yes,' she managed thickly, refusing to meet his eyes. 'I see.'

'I'd like to drive it to be certain, but not at this hour.'

'So we're out here for the night,' she remarked, and he found himself listening for any indication of whether she was happy about that or concerned.

But her tone was frustratingly even, giving nothing away, so instead he tried to gather the map up without snatching, only to end up making a meal of folding it back up.

He cleared his throat.

'If we get the four-by-four into that first ruin, the ground's flat enough for me to check underneath.'

'Fine. I'll grab a bergen from the back and start setting up camp.'

Peeling off his jacket and hooking it over the wing mirror, Kane began working on the vehicle. Slowly, methodically giving himself a chance to get his head back in focus as much as anything else. He could hear the bustling sounds as Mattie set things up on the other side of the crumbling wall and it was almost…homely. Was that good thing or a bad one? He worked steadily, his head torch allowing him to finally complete the task. And there was nothing left but to rejoin her.

His heart kicked stubbornly.

'Good timing.' She glanced up as he walked through the half-doorway.

She'd laid out her bedroll and sleeping bag and had lit a fire for warmth. A small pile of logs sat next to it so they could keep feeding it through the night, which he had to admit wasn't a bad idea as the temperatures could drop considerably out here at night.

She even had a couple of rat packs by a gas burner, and he heard himself teasing her before he could stop.

'Cooking me dinner? From the kid who needed me to teach her to boil water?'

'Don't get used to it,' she quipped. 'I've left you to sort out your own bedroll and sleeping bag.'

Stepping forward, he dropped his rucksack and jacket on the other side of the fire from hers.

'Fair enough.'

'You know you have oil on your T-shirt?'

'I didn't know that, no.' He glanced down before peeling it up and over his head.

At least he had a spare in his bag. But when he retrieved it, standing up tall to pull it on, he became aware of Mattie staring intently at him.

Checking him out.

The air around them became heavy. Charged. And Kane couldn't help it, he slowed his movements, taking his time, loving the way her eyes darkened and her nostrils flared slightly as she drank in the sight of him. Like he was as pool of fresh, clear water in the middle of a desert.

The blood rushed through him. No one had ever had him as on edge as this one woman.

'Matz.'

She snapped her head up, her cheeks reddening slightly, which only fired him up all the more. Did that stain creep below her shirt? Over her perfect breasts? If he walked over there and hauled her into his arms, how long would it be before he could find out?

Because he wanted to. He wanted his hands all over her, closely followed by his mouth. From the elegant curve of her neck to the creamy swell of her breasts. And from the smooth expanse of her abdomen to the honeyed sweetness between her legs.

Lord, how he wanted to taste her again.

Realisation punched him in the gut—and lower—and he swung sharply away before his traitorous body betrayed him.

Being here alone with Mattie and in the middle of nowhere was a bad idea. Because out here there was no one to keep them in check. It felt like the brakes were off and he was already slipping down the hill. Slowly at first, but it wouldn't be long until he was careening out of control.

The last time he'd allowed himself to be out of control had been around twenty years ago, when he'd been stupid enough to let his brothers use him. When he'd been stupid enough to cover for them after he'd realised what they had done.

When he'd joined the army—when it had been that or face some kind of prosecution—he'd grabbed the opportunity to reinvent himself, to build a new life for himself with both hands. He'd sworn there and then that he would never do anything to jeopardise that, and he never had. Not in fourteen years.

But every time he was with Mathilda Brigham, all that went out the window whilst his common sense convoy became a runaway train.

And a crash was inevitable.

Mattie glowered into the fire and felt edgy. Restless. Unruly. No one had ever made her feel as wanton as Kane did. As he always had done.

She'd been fighting this pull ever since he'd walked into her field hospital, but she knew she'd been gradually losing the battle. And now they were here, alone, in the middle of nowhere, with no one around. It wasn't as though anyone was going to sneak up on them in a tank or a chopper.

It was just Kane and her.

And the darkness that had settled over them like a blanket, an inky blue, snuggly fleece, flecked with stars that shimmered and winked in the unending sky, seemed to add to the sense of intimacy. Out here there was no pollution. No light. No noise. Only the moonlight, slicing through the broken tiles in the roof above them and bathing the room in an almost romantic light.

Almost magic. Just as the air around them was thick with everything they weren't saying. Everything they weren't doing. And even though Mattie knew that they shouldn't, she couldn't seem to bring herself to stop.

Or, worse, to care about stopping.

Her pulse beat, wild and fast, at her throat. His eyes flickered to it, clearly able to see how he affected her as he swallowed. It appeared that her body wasn't alone in fighting a thousand desires that tumbled through her.

She *had* to resist him. She was an acting *colonel*, for pity's sake.

'I can't believe we've both been in for over a decade,' Mattie muttered. 'We must have been in the same theatres of war, surely? Yet we've never run into each other before.'

'Why would we? Infantry are front line, medical aren't.' He lifted his shoulders. 'And I've been in camps with ten, twenty, thirty thousand soldiers. Would it really be that surprising? Besides, what if we *had* crossed paths? What would that change?'

She tipped her head to one side thoughtfully as there was something in his tone she couldn't quite pinpoint.

'Perhaps not. But surely we would have at least *heard* the other's name mentioned. Realised.'

'I already knew you were in,' he pointed out. 'That was never an unknown for me. You, Hayd and your father.'

She paused sadly for a moment.

'Not my father. Not recently, anyway.'

'His Alzheimer's is really that bad?'

She could feel the hot prickling behind her eyes. Hating herself for the weakness, but it had come out of nowhere, almost blindsiding her. A rational corner of her brain was trying to say something, possibly that it was the tension of the last few days of suppressing this insane chemistry between herself and Kane that had really got to her.

Warning her that engaging in personal conversation with him was the last thing she should be doing if she wanted to avoid crossing the line with him again, the way they had back in her office that first day.

But she wasn't listening. Whether because she couldn't, or more because she didn't *want* to, Mattie couldn't be sure.

'I hadn't seen him as often as I might have liked. I'd always been too busy, but I guess that's a poor excuse.' She waited for Kane to answer, but he didn't. 'Maybe a perverse part of me felt as though I was being like him by saying the same.'

'Does it help?'

'The opposite.' She pursed her lips in an effort to control the welling sadness, 'I feel like I've let him down. Been selfish.'

The prickling was getting painful now and she dropped her eyes to stare into the fire, as though the dancing flames could somehow dry all the tears away before they fell.

She heard a shuffle, and felt Kane moving beside her, his strong arms wrapping around her and pulling her into the safety of his chest. And, for a moment, she felt safe, and seventeen, all over again.

She had no idea how long they stayed there, she warm in his arms.

'So where have you been? I mean, which tours?'

He named a few places. Something in his tone told her that they were operational tours that he was happy to forget but which, sometimes in the dead of the night, his brain remembered in all too startling clarity, and he would wake up in a cold sweat.

A sensation she knew well enough.

And then he mentioned another tour, the worst tour she'd ever known, and she froze in his arms.

'I was there, too. What year?'

For a moment, Kane hesitated, then he told her. It was as though an icy cold hand was creeping down her spine, spreading chill everywhere it touched.

'That was hell on earth,' she muttered thickly. 'There was an ambush in an abandoned village. Our guys went in to get the women and children but...'

She couldn't go on. Kane merely grunted but didn't speak. She realised he couldn't. His heart was pounding in his chest, thundering under her ear.

She lifted her head and stared into the flames and, for a moment, all she could hear was the crackling of the fire and a ragged voice. It took her a few moments to realise it was her own.

'I saw some of the guys in there. I didn't even think you'd make it out at one point.'

The air was thick with tension. A thousand memories, many of them bleak.

'We nearly didn't. We were pretty much pinned down, taking heavy fire with some really serious casualties. No one could get in to us, and we couldn't get out. And then, suddenly, this sandstorm came in and we decided it was all or nothing. We managed to get past the enemy, even got some distance away, though not far enough for any ambulance to risk getting into us. But then some crazy pilot flew in a chopper with a MERT team, led by the biggest badass army trauma doctor I've ever seen, to recover our two wounded.'

She blinked at him slowly, could feel the shock beginning to cloud her face.

He couldn't be talking about her...could he?

'The med team had barely got our buddies on board when the enemy tracked us, but the doc wouldn't get on until the rest of her team were safely on board. We held them off long enough for the chopper to get off the ground, but I saw the doctor get clipped by a round in the back of her leg just as she leapt on board.'

'Is that so?' Mattie asked faintly, her gaze caught with his. She wasn't sure if either of them were even daring to breathe, but she couldn't stop her hand sliding down to her calf to the scar from that bullet wound. The scar he'd felt that first night together back in the hotel.

Did he know that he was talking about her? Did he realise?

And if so, had he recognised her back in that hellhole? Because she'd had absolutely no idea that, crouched down by her heli—trying to give enough covering fire so that she and her team could get the injured soldiers out—one of the other men still fighting had been Kane.

Her Kane.

Leaving those guys on the ground had been the worst feeling she'd ever had to deal with—knowing she was leaving them to their inevitable deaths. There was no way they were going to make it out alive, but the chopper had been tiny. Too small for anyone but her team and the two casualties.

Few things haunted her—one couldn't afford to let them in this job—but that day did. Even now, she could remember that sensation as the adrenalin had kicked in and she—

her whole team—had been determined to save the lives
of those two injured soldiers. To make sure their buddies
hadn't died for nothing.

She'd had no choice—not that the knowledge helped.
Nausea swelled within her.

'Like I said, a hell of a leader,' he said quietly. 'Risking their lives to save our buddies. It gave us the morale
boost we needed. We just threw ourselves into that firefight knowing that even if we went down, at least two of
us had made it out.'

'I heard the firefight went on for eleven hours,' she told
him softly.

'Yeah, about that. But because of you we were determined not to give up. And then suddenly it was all over
and we'd won.'

'I know. We couldn't believe it.'

'Neither could we.' He grinned, a bitter-sweet twist of
his mouth. 'But want to know what the cherry on the icing
on that admittedly bloodied cake was?'

'Tell me.'

'Both our buddies made it. Thanks to you.'

'Thanks to *you*.' She shook her head. 'We weren't the
guys who tabbed out of an ambush, in the middle of a
sandstorm, with two stretchers.'

'And what difference would it have made if you and the
pilot hadn't brought the chopper through with the MERT
team?' he countered. 'No one else was coming. We knew
that. As far as the guys and I were concerned, that god-
forsaken, abandoned village in the middle of nowhere was
going to be our final resting place.'

'We kept up with your team.' Mattie nodded. 'We
couldn't believe you'd got out.'

She could remember the shock as her team had heard
the news back in the field hospital—such as it had been on
that tour. An initial numbness. And then a feeling of abso-

lute euphoria. It had been like their own personal miracle and they'd ridden that high for the rest of the tour.

'But we did.'

'Yes, you did,' she agreed fiercely, pulling out of his arms until she was sitting back on her heels, facing him.

She wasn't sure whose gaze was trapped in whose. Frankly, she didn't much care.

'Life is so precious, Kane,' she whispered. 'I know it, and yet I forget it. But every now and then something rams it home to me and I realise that we have to make the most out of this short time we have.'

'And everything we said back in your office?' he bit out, his hoarse voice scratching over her.

Inside her.

She swallowed, her head dipping closer to his. Inviting him without a word.

'Mattie.' He breathed her name and it sent charges of electricity through her. 'I need you to be sure about this. I want to hear it.'

'You don't need to hear anything, Kane.' She barely recognised her own voice. 'Don't they say that actions speaker louder than words?'

CHAPTER ELEVEN

THE SLOW BURN that had smouldered in him ever since he'd walked into her office in her field hospital had turned into a full inferno, ripping through him as though nothing could ever douse it.

As though he never *wanted* anything to douse it.

He was dimly aware of a muffled voice, deep inside his brain, warning him that if they did this, there could be no going back. That they could no longer pretend they were beating this...*thing* that arced between them. They could no longer profess that their army careers were the most important thing that mattered to them.

Everything would change. It would have to.

If he were a stronger man, a better man, he surely would have resisted. For both of them. Got them through this weak moment now that they'd found themselves alone in the middle of the deserted prairies where there was no chance of anyone intruding on them.

But he wasn't a *better* man. He never had been. It had been his distinct lack of respect for the law that had brought him to the army in the first instance—even if he hadn't knowingly committed the crime, a good man would have gone straight to the police when he'd realised what his brothers were doing. It was probably why a part of him had always felt like an imposter all these years, even when his career had started to soar.

Especially when his career had started to soar.

So now, as the moonlight sliced through the broken roof of the old building lending the space an ethereal glow, bathing Mattie in a romantic light, he felt a fervour pouring through his whole body. Dark and powerful. Filling him up and making him ache.

Making him yearn when he'd never *yearned* in his life. Except for Mattie.

Kane stopped thinking, he didn't allow himself another moment to second-guess, he simply reached out and traced that exquisitely perfect jawline the way he'd been aching to do for days. For all his life.

And he revelled in the feel of her skin, so smooth and soft, beneath the rough pad of his thumb. He wanted her. He couldn't keep away from her. Even when he knew that they were bad for each other. Even though he understood that there could never be a future.

Because neither of them would be prepared to walk away from the only careers they had ever known. Not even for each other.

But right here, right now, he was staring into those mesmerising blue eyes of hers, which were darker than usual, and glittering at him. And even though logic told him that it was a bad idea, and that nothing had changed since the last time they'd been alone, he didn't care. It was nonsensical, and reckless, but he felt as though everything was going to be all right as long as the two of them were together.

Because, really, when it came down to it, being apart hadn't allowed either of them to move on emotionally, had it?

Sliding his hand to cradle the back of her head, he hauled Mattie towards him, revelling in the way that she moved so willingly, pressing her body against his so that heat seared through the layers of clothing that separated them.

A part of him ached to tear them off, but Kane refused to rush. He indulged himself as she tilted her head back for him, allowing him to angle her head just right. He indulged himself as his tongue scraped hers, another shot of desire racing between them. And he indulged himself when she made those soft yet greedy noises in the back of her throat.

He had never been able to get enough of those sounds. He wasn't sure he ever would.

With his free hand he traced the line of her elegant neck, over her shoulders and down her arm, and it didn't matter that she was clad in the heavy material of her uniform, he could still remember how soft her skin felt.

Kane took his time kissing her. Tasting her. Teasing her. He was a man trained in any number of weapons, but right now those weapons were his mouth, his tongue, his teeth, and he intended to lay waste to Mattie with every one of them.

But it was harder to keep his control than he liked when she began winding her arms around his neck and moving to straddle his lap, making his body tighten. Ache.

'Did you think you were going to get it all your own way, Kane?' she growled huskily, hardly helping matters. 'Perhaps you're forgetting who is in control here.'

'You might be in control of this little recce party, *ma'am*,' he teased, dragged her lower lip between his teeth. 'But I'm going to be the one running tonight's entertainment.'

And then, before she could answer, he dropped his head to nuzzle at her neck. Kissing her, teasing her with his teeth, loving it when she dropped her head back, one of her hands laced through his hair, the other gripping his shoulder.

She tasted so damned good. So damned right. And the moonlight streamed in through the old ruin as if it, too, agreed.

And then he was moving his lips over skin, grazing her neck a little with his teeth as he made his slow, meandering way down to that sensitive hollow by her collarbone. He fought to keep control, to take his time. As if those little needy sounds she was making weren't driving him insanely wild with need. As if he didn't actually *hurt* with the urge to simply slide straight inside her. But not yet.

Not yet.

Slowly, deliberately, as though he was unwrapping a precious gift, Kane reached for the zip of her jacket and slowly began to lower it. The sound was especially loud, and loaded, in the silent night air, and somehow that only seemed to make the air pull tighter with delicious expectation.

Then, finally, he shucked the jacket off Mattie's shoulders, easing it down her arms and perhaps indulging a little too much in the way it made her straighten up and push her breasts harder against his chest. His mouth teased at her neck as he felt for the hem of her T-shirt and lifted that too, unhurriedly, up and over her head as she lifted her arms in unspoken compliance. And then there was only her pretty, lacy bra, doing little to cover the acres of lush, smooth skin that had haunted his nights for…*ever*, and that hectic glittering in her spellbinding gaze.

God, she was perfect.

He never seemed to get enough of her.

Kane hooked his finger around the lace of her bra, pulling it down and dipping his head, letting his tongue trace tiny whorls around one proud, taut nipple. Round and round, in more and more intricate patterns, as Mattie—

his Mattie—made appreciative noises and arched her back all the more. He ran his hand down her spine, able to feel the fire building up inside her—the same one building inside him—and with every sweep of his tongue he kept on stoking it. Higher, and higher, and higher.

Only when she tunnelled her fingers through his hair, almost as if a part of her was afraid he might stop before she was ready, did he draw one perfect nipple into his mouth and suck. Hard.

Mattie cried out, a low and throaty sound that rumbled right through him, straight to his sex. So tight it was almost painful. *Almost.*

'Don't stop, Kane.'

It was little more than a whisper. A plea into the night. But he had no intention of stopping. He couldn't have anyway, even if he'd tried. Not when Mattie was encouraging him on with the roll of her hips and every arch of her back. So instead he shifted sides to lavish the same attention on her other breast. To elicit the same heady response.

Just as she'd always done. As though…as though she'd always been his.

The realisation walloped Kane with unexpected force.

Lust flashed through every inch of Mattie's body. Through a haze of desire it occurred to her that she wasn't far away from coming apart just from Kane's tongue on her breasts.

Surely she ought to be embarrassed at how easily she fell? But she wasn't. Not remotely. Still, there was no harm in retaking the reins a little, was there?

Wriggling on his lap, she pressed herself against him, solid and ready even through their trousers, making him groan. Making them both groan. And making her realise, far too late, that she wasn't in control of anything at all. Least of all her thundering heart.

When Kane moved his hands to her hips, lifting her

off him for a moment, she actually felt bereft. But then he flipped her around, laying her down until she was lying on her back on the bedroll, and after pulling off his tops with one economical movement he lowered his body to cover hers.

Hard, and ready, and full of deliciously uncompromising promise. Mattie sighed in appreciation and ran her hands over the sculpted ridges of his back. Then her fingernails. She dipped below his waistband to cup his backside and pull him against her as she shifted her legs until the hardest part of him was settled against the softest part of her.

Bliss.

'If you carry on like that, I can't guarantee this is going to last long once I'm inside you,' he growled, and she might have giggled at the seriousness of his expression had her body not been roaring for him to do exactly what he was saying.

She shifted again and felt him flex against her heat, his sharp intake of breath speaking louder than any words could. And the idea that Kane was almost as close to the edge as she was was just too thrilling.

Kane seemed to think so too. Because the next thing Mattie knew, he was lifting himself up from her, like the most elegant push-up she'd ever seen, before rolling back on his heels and reaching for her boots.

She watched transfixed as he swiftly removed first her remaining clothes then his, all the while the moonlight and firelight seeming to take it in turns to dance across his bronzed, hewn torso.

Kane Wheeler. The first boy she'd ever loved.

And the man a part of her would probably always love. No doubt there were a million reasons why this—here, now—was a bad idea, not least because they could have no future together. Not the way things stood. Yet Mattie couldn't bring herself to care.

She'd tried moving on and look where that had got her. Her career as a colonel and as a doctor were her future, and that would be more than enough. But tonight she had one more thing. She had Kane, the only man who had ever been able to tease her until she'd gone practically out of her mind with desire.

Funny how she should remember that suddenly.

'One more night,' she whispered, not knowing whether she was asking or telling.

'One more night,' he rasped back, but it told her nothing.

Then, before she could speak again, he lowered his head and drew one hard nipple into the wet heat of his mouth again, cupping her other breast with his big hand and flicking the pad of his thumb over the pink bud.

Mattie's mind went instantly blank. She gasped as sensations surged through her, turning her inside out all over again. Wicked tongue, clever tongue, and all Kane. She gave herself up to the exquisite torture as he worked his way across her body. Down her body.

And then he was right…*there*.

His shoulders were between her thighs, nudging her legs wider, and wider again, as though he wanted to take just a moment to savour the view. She could feel his breath warm on her sex and only making her ache for him all the more. All her senses were so heightened, so taut, like any of those fragile ties could snap at any moment, and yet she held still. Her fingers were tunnelled into Kane's hair but she forced herself to hold still, not to give in to this desperation.

And then he licked into her and white heat slammed through her. She bit her lip to keep from crying out, but she lifted her hips and rocked, unable to help herself, especially when he grasped her backside in his hands and held her in place. Gentle yet firm, reminding her that this was *his* show as he kept on playing with her hot, wet core.

Mattie could hardly stand it, and yet she couldn't get enough. She wanted more.

Needed more.

She could hear her own ragged breathing loud in the quiet night air but she didn't care. She was nearly mindless, hurtling towards some invisible edge, and still Kane kept driving her on. Letting his tongue slide over her, drawing lazy patterns on her before dipping inside. He knew exactly what to do to send her wild.

Only when she thought she couldn't take any more did he finally, *finally*, draw her into his mouth and suck, slipping a long finger deep inside her. Then another.

Mattie cried out, her hips bucking as she came apart, right there in a ruined building in the middle of nowhere, and still Kane didn't stop. She fractured and splintered as if wave after wave of spine-shattering intensity were tossing tiny parts of her into the ether, never to be recovered.

Mattie had no idea how long it took her to come back to herself. Minutes perhaps. Or maybe hours. But when she finally did, it was to the blissful sight of Kane, hard and intense, and the most masculine sight she'd ever seen in her life, moving up her body.

He drew her into his arms as he settled himself between her legs, nudging her with his sex and, incredibly, making her begin to ache already. Cupping his face, she met his searching gaze, almost believing that he was trying to see right into her soul. Right into her heart.

The thought was simultaneously thrilling and terrifying. Yet she held the contact, refusing to let her eyes drop away. And then he slid inside her, slowly at first, giving her chance to recover. She let her fingers drift down his jawline. Tight and locked and intense as if it was costing Kane dearly to keep the pace low. As though with one swivel of her hips she could send him hurtling off into the same oblivion he had just sent her.

She found she liked the idea.

He slid carefully inside her again and, without warning, Mattie twisted her body, drawing him in deeper. Faster. His low, almost feral grunt was wantonly satisfying.

'Be careful, Mattie,' he gritted out. 'My self-control is rapidly slipping.'

'I'm counting on it,' Mattie breathed, hooking her legs around his hips and pulling him in hard before locking them at his back.

A fresh wall of heat and need surged over her, as if she hadn't already come apart only a short while ago. She clung to him, helpless to stop her fingers from biting into the solid muscles of his arms, his back. But it was Kane, muttering darkly as he lost whatever remaining grip he'd had on his own senses and plunged into her, driving home, that really sent her spinning again. Shaking with the intensity of her hunger.

Then, *at last*, they were moving together. Riding the same waves of pleasure, faster and higher than ever before. And this time, when Mattie shattered into a thousand bright, tiny splinters, calling Kane's name as she broke apart, he followed her.

She was never going to be the same.

They were lying snuggled together in the double sleeping bag they had made by zipping their two bags together, and Mattie snuggled her back tighter into Kane's chest, wallowing in the feel of his arms wrapped tightly around her. His body was so hot against hers and she wanted to bask in that glow forever.

But they didn't have *forever*, did they?

How had she ever thought it would be different? Why had she pretended that she could control this...*thing* that had always arced between her and Kane? Had she ever really thought, deep down, that one more night would be enough?

As if it would *ever* be enough for her.

Because the simple truth was that she loved him. She always had and she always would. They just could never be together. There wasn't room in the army for both of them if they wanted to be together. But the worst of it was that she didn't even know if Kane felt the same way.

Was this one night—or these two nights, if she including the one back in Castleton—enough for him?

Mattie couldn't bring herself to ask. Instead, she stared into the dying flames of the fire in front of her, telling herself that wasn't an ominous sign.

For a moment Mattie faltered, uncertain what to say next. And then she began to speak before her brain even knew what she was saying.

'I told you that I thought I'd imagined seeing you at my wedding rehearsal, before I called off my engagement.'

'You did.' His tone was careful, and she didn't blame him. 'You also said you called off your engagement because marrying George Blakeney meant having to give up your army career.'

'Yes.' She moved her head slowly, still not turning. Still relishing the feel of his strong, capable body at her back. 'But also…because at that moment I realised that I *wanted* to have seen you.'

She felt rather than heard his sharp exhalation.

'Say again?'

'I wanted it to be you. I wanted you to have come for me. I think that's why Hayden called you, because a part of him knew that.'

'What are you telling me, Mattie? You never loved your fiancé?'

'No, I did. I did love George,' she began. 'In some way.

He was good, and kind, and caring. I knew we wouldn't be unhappy together. But I wasn't *in love* with him.'

'You looked like you loved him,' he managed tightly. Painfully. 'That night I watched you on that stage together.'

'I tried to, but…' She shook her head. 'Fourteen years and I've never moved on. I tried to, you know that, but I couldn't. You were always there, haunting my thoughts.'

'There's never been anyone else for me either,' Kane bit out almost harshly so that, for a moment, Mattie wasn't sure whether he felt that was a good thing or a bad one. 'But we can't be together like this. Both still serving.'

Silence swirled around them.

'I know,' she acknowledged eventually. 'But I can't leave. I almost made that mistake once before, but I know it would have been the wrong choice. I would have ended up resenting George. And I refuse to ever risk resenting you.'

The silence grew heavier. She was almost surprised with Kane broke it.

'Are you asking me to quit?'

Was she?

Mattie hesitated for a heartbeat before answering.

'No,' she told him firmly. 'I'm not asking that at all. I'm just…explaining why I can't leave my army career.'

'Neither can I.' His voice was hoarser than she expected. As though the words were painful for him to say.

In an odd way, that helped.

'I'd guessed as much,' she whispered, shifting onto her back so that could turn and finally face him.

The expression on his face was dark, making her stomach dip and roll.

'If I was going to leave for anyone, it would be you,' he told her fiercely, his hand tilting her chin up as he stared into her eyes in a way that made her heart actually ache. 'But I can't. I won't.'

Her whole world was beginning to crumble, like the

tide coming in to reclaim the castles they'd build on the beach as kids.

Yet she hadn't even realised her world had been made of sand.

'Kane, I never said—'

'This is my life, too,' he cut her off quietly. 'It might not have been my dream since birth, as it was for you, but the army has made me the man I am. It's who I am now.'

'You were always that man to me,' she told him. 'Even as kids. If you hadn't been, you never would have kept yourself away from the life that your father led. Or your brothers.'

She heard him wince, even if she didn't see it. Like she'd landed some blow she hadn't even been aware she was throwing.

'I didn't keep away from them, though. Not until it was too late anyway. You always thought I was so different from my brothers, and from my dad, but the truth is, before you came along, I was pretty much the same. I just wasn't as far down that path.'

'You're talking about this thing you did when you were a kid?'

He didn't answer, and she faltered for a moment then shrugged, as though it didn't matter. Though every fibre of her being was crying out for him to tell her. To finally let her in.

'You don't have to say anything more. Not if you don't want to.'

Still, she held her breath. Right up until he finally started to speak.

'The night it all happened I was with my brothers in a stolen car. They were wasted so I was driving.'

'You were fifteen,' she cried, unable to help herself even as she instantly regretted interrupting.

Kane watched her closely, a dark frown clouding his features and making her fingers long to smooth it away.

'Anyway, we stopped at an off licence. That Eight-Till-Late over on Beech Street, you remember? It was where my brothers always got their gear from.'

She remembered it. Some hole in the wall notorious for alcoholics, and the night staff selling illicit drugs.

'Only when we got there, they weren't buying anything. They both had guns, goodness knows where they got them from, and I realised they were holding up the place. Worse, I was their getaway driver.'

She sucked in a shocked breath.

'Tell me you called the police, Kane. Tell me you drove off and called 999.'

He raked his hand through his hair, and she could *feel* his despair and regret.

'I should have. Of course I should have. But… I didn't think the police would believe me.'

She opened her mouth to argue then closed it again.

She remembered only too well what Kane's experience of the police had been back then. The Wheeler clan had been hated and feared in equal measure. If something went wrong in Heathdale, from house invasions to drunken brawls, from the cobblestone set on the dock road being taken up to the copper on the church roof disappearing, the Wheeler clan had likely been involved. People—everyone—had been desperate to get rid of them. All of them. And Kane was a Wheeler.

Still…

'You waited for them, didn't you, and then you drove them home? Or wherever they were going.'

'I didn't know what else to do, Matz. I was fifteen and I was in shock. I knew they were bad but even I had no idea what they were capable of.'

'And afterwards, when the shock wore off?'

She hated the bleak look that clouded his dark eyes.
Hated it.

'I ditched the car and I went home. I expected the police to show up on the doorstep any minute. I was ready to confess everything, and I was ready to take whatever punishment I was given. But one hour turned into two, then twelve. Then a day, a week, a month. So I stayed quiet. But from then on I tried to keep my distance. I told them to leave me out of whatever they did next, or I'd turn them in. I never let myself get dragged into anything with them ever again.'

'My God, Kane.'

'That was also when I got myself a motorbike. I figured I couldn't be tied to them if people always saw me around town on that thing.'

'I remember it.' Her body flushed in spite of everything. It had been a few more years until they'd started dating, but the number of times she'd been on the back of that bike. The delicious *things* she and Kane had done on it. 'Why didn't you ever tell me?'

He shook his head.

'Why would I risk losing you? You were the first person who had ever treated me with anything other than contempt. You told me that I wasn't like them, and that I was better than anything my life had to offer. I couldn't stand to see the look in your eyes when you realised that you were wrong.'

'I would never have thought that!' she exclaimed. 'I would have believed you and I would have helped you.'

'Would you, though? Really?' Kane challenged. 'You knew my family's reputation. Would you really have been that quick to trust me over anyone else if you had known?'

She opened her mouth to argue, then closed it again. As much as she balked at admitting it, maybe he was right.

'You changed me, Matz. *You.* And your family showed me there was a different way. A better way.'

'So what happened?' she asked at last. 'How did you end up leaving that night?'

She was afraid to hear, but afraid not to. It was impossible to shake the feeling that his story was leading somewhere she didn't understand. And yet the urge to finally understand the truth, after all these years, was sharp and driving.

'In the end, my past caught up with me.' Kane twisted his mouth into something that was more bared teeth than any kind of smile. 'I was heading home after being with you when the police came for my brothers. They'd held up another off licence, but this one had CCTV.'

'The police identified them?'

'They had a hunch but no clear identification. Still, I saw the lights, heard the commotion, as I was about to turn into the street, so I just kept going. I didn't stop. But I figured it was only a matter of time before the police put the two crimes together and came for me. I couldn't think of any way out. So... I rode straight back to your house.'

'You came to my dad.' She froze, her brain desperately trying to make sense of it all, piecing the puzzle together slowly.

Yet at least now she actually *had* the pieces.

'I came to see you. To apologise.'

'Why?' she whispered.

He paused.

'Because you were the only one who ever believed in me, and I had betrayed your trust.'

It was too much, and at the same time not enough. She wished she could go back and change it all. Though whether for Kane or for herself, she couldn't be certain. Possibly both.

'You never found me,' she finally managed.

'No. Your dad caught me about to try to shimmy up that drainpipe at the back of your house. He demanded to know what the hell I thought I was doing, and I'm not sure if he wasn't about to kick me into next week, but I ended up telling him everything.'

'He never said.'

Not in fourteen years. And yet, if she was to understand it now, he'd tasked Hayden with contacting Kane in the run up to her wedding to another man.

'He went straight to some high-ranking police chief he knew, and they made a deal that as long as I made a statement testifying against my brothers, they would never prosecute me. To this day I don't know how long I was with them, answering their questions. Then your father put me in a car with some old army buddy of his who drove me to the army barracks where I signed up on the spot. He called it my one chance for a fresh start.'

'I just can't… It's so…' She stopped.

Her whole world was spinning sideways, and she had no way to stop it. For over a decade she'd believed that Kane had walked away from her. She'd even considered that her father had offered him money to leave, though a part of her had never quite been able to believe it. Not of either of them.

But she'd never contemplated that Kane hadn't had much of a choice. Or that her own father had played such a part in getting rid of the boy she had loved.

'It was the best thing he could have done for me, Matz.' Kane's voice tugged her back to the present, reading her mind. 'I was able to reinvent myself in a way I never could have done anywhere else.'

'You could have—'

'No, I couldn't have. I owe your father so much. I like who I am now. I like what the army made me. I owe them.

And that's why I can't leave. Becoming some security firm guy—for the money—isn't the way to repay anyone. It doesn't make me proud.'

Mattie clenched her arms around Kane's, wanting to respond but not knowing where to start. None of this was what she wanted to hear, yet the hardest part about it was that she understood exactly what was driving him.

She was even proud of him for it. And proud of her father for being there for Kane when no one else had been.

But in some ways that also made it that much worse.

'So we're back to square one?' she managed at last, her voice flat and emotionless. 'Fighting this chemistry yet unable to be together. *That* isn't what I want either.'

It felt like losing him all over again, only this time it was worse, because this time it came down to their choices.

'It can't be both, Matz. I'll leave in the morning. We did our job, we decided on new scenarios and it looks as though we've found the perfect location. Once we get back to the hospital in the morning, I'll write my notes up and take them to my CO.'

Something moved through Mattie. Swift and certain. They had made their choices, as impossible as they were. And they were for the right reasons. She and Kane ought to be proud that they'd allowed logic to prevail over emotion.

She could cry about it or she could make the most of the rest of this one opportunity. The words were out before she could second-guess herself.

'We still have the rest of tonight.'

'We do,' he agreed slowly.

'After this you'll be going back to your infantry company. We'll never see each other again.'

'We won't,' he growled, the roughness of it rolling right through her.

'Then brace yourself, Kane.' She lifted her hands to his jaw and held it fiercely. 'It's going to be a long, sleepless night.'

CHAPTER TWELVE

'MATTIE, CAN YOU join the MERT team?'

Mattie's head snapped up from her desk as her second-in-command burst through her office door with barely a knock. She was writing up her own notes and pretending that she wasn't nursing an aching heart since Kane had left camp a couple of hours earlier.

But now she was up on her feet before she'd even replied.

'What is it, Kath?'

'Emergency call just came through on the field phone. Infantry soldier, penetrating chest wound, possible thoracotomy, and Clark is already in Theatre. You're the next best choice.'

Wordlessly, Mattie rounded her desk and raced down the corridor with Kath to the HEMS area, knowing every precious second counted. Such severe injuries on exercise weren't common, but this was a live firing exercise and so accidents weren't unheard of.

As a specialist cardiothoracic surgeon, Clark was the go-to guy for this, which was why they had tried to incorporate this training into some of the exercises recently. But this wasn't one of her scenarios. This was a real-life trauma, and if a thoracotomy was going to be performed in the back of the helicopter and Clark wasn't available, she was the best person to do it. She had been on more tours and had more experience than anyone else here.

'Cole, Nilson, Jones, with me,' she commanded, grabbing her gear and heading to the door.

There would be a full thoracotomy pack on board, but she grabbed an emergency serrated wire, clamps, scalpel and heavy scissors.

They had minutes to get their kit on, helmets, body armour, pelvic protection, knee pads, and to sprint to the helicopter with their gear. But it was a drill Mattie knew well, and all too quickly the chopper was dipping as it sped through the skies, reached the zone and landed.

At least with an exercise things could be halted, which meant that if surgical intervention was necessary she would be able to do it on the ground, and not in the back of the chopper whilst it was on the flight back.

If the injured soldier hadn't gone into cardiac arrest she would keep him stable on the flight back. But if he had, the maximum time for surgical intervention following the loss of cardiac output would be ten minutes. And the flight out would take up a hefty chunk of that.

She just had to fight off any paralyzing thoughts that the infantry soldier she was flying out to try to save could, so easily, be Kane.

By the time the helicopter landed and Mattie's team was leaping off the back, the combat medics already had the injured soldier intubated and were ventilating him. And it wasn't Kane.

This time, a tiny voice needled.

'Get full IV access and get him into a supine position,' she ordered her team.

A rapid application of skin prep would have to do— there wasn't time for full asepsis. Taking the scalpel and forceps, she felt for the fifth intercostal space and made a series of deep midline lateral incisions, then waited. If tension pneumothorax decreased, and cardiac output returned, she wouldn't continue with the procedure.

There was no change. *Dammit.*

'Okay, let's push on. Scissors.'

Nilson handed her the scissors and Mattie connected the thoracostomies, then she inserted two fingers to hold the lung safely out the way whilst she cut through the all the layers of intercostal muscles and pleura, leaving only a narrow sternal bridge between the anterolateral thoracotomies.

'Saw,' she demanded. The scissors were taken from her and the serrated wire placed into her hand instead.

Time to cut through the sternum.

She worked as quickly as she could, cutting with long, smooth strokes from the inside out. There would be retractors in the full thoracotomy pack but there was no time for that.

'Grab here…' she indicated to Cole '…and open up the chest cavity as far as you can. I need access. Scissors.'

Then, tenting the pericardium to minimise the risk to the nerves that ran through the lateral walls of the pericardial sac, Mattie made a longer midline longitudinal cut with the scissors, evacuated the blood and clot and began inspecting the heart for the site of the bleeding.

Her hope was that the heart would spontaneously restart, with a return of full cardiac output. Her fear was that it would remain in asystole. She held her breath and continued her rapid but systematic inspection.

And then the heart flickered. Began to pump again. Slowly. *Too slowly.*

'We have a heartbeat,' someone—Cole possibly—exclaimed.

Mattie shook her head,

'Reduced output. We need to find the wounds and close

them, then try massaging the heart. Wait… I think I see the hole.'

It was small. *Thank God.*

'Here.' Grabbing Nilson's hand, she pulled it into the soldier's chest. 'Plug your finger right…*there*. Good. Now, don't move it. Jones, get ready with the anaesthesia. If the procedure is successful, he's going to start to wake up.'

Slipping her hands around the heart, one on the posterior surface and the other on the anterior, Mattie began to massage from the apex upwards whilst ensuring she kept the heart horizontal. All the while she counted under her breath, trying to achieve optimal beats per minute of around eighty.

And then she felt the heart begin to take over, beating harder, faster. A return to full cardiac output—along with more bleeding.

'Don't move your finger.' She looked grimly at Nilson. 'We're going to need to get him back to the field hospital for surgery and a full repair. It's down to you to keep that hole in his heart plugged until we get there.'

And the moment Operation Strikethrough was over she was going to head back to the UK to see her father. If she could catch him on a good day—though they were rarer now—maybe she could ask him about Kane and see what he had to say.

Because if today had taught her anything, it was that it was true what they said—life really was simply too short.

'He's worse than I last time I was here, Hayd.' Mattie held onto the kitchen doorframe, her back to her brother as he prepared fresh tea for their father.

'I know,' Hayden replied grimly. 'I wish it hadn't been so long but…'

It hung there between them, unspoken. Between tours of duty, exercises away and compulsory courses there was no possible way that they could see their father more frequently. It was why they had employed a live-in carer, not just so that they knew he was being looked after but also because it provided him with the company and stimulation he needed. As well as allowing him to remain in his home where everything felt familiar to him. Safe.

The military was the life they had chosen, just as it had been the life that he had chosen. Still, it didn't entirely diminish the guilt.

'He keeps thinking I'm Mum.'

'He keeps thinking I'm his buddy from the Falklands.' Hayden arched his eyebrows and Mattie laughed, some of her sadness receding for a moment. 'There's no point trying to correct him, Mattie. If it gives him some pleasure, why not just leave him?'

'I know, I just…' She wrinkled her nose. 'At least with you, you're getting all the secret stories he never he told us over the years.'

'True. Some of them are shocking, even to me. Dammit, we're out of milk.'

'Vera will be back in an hour with the shopping. No doubt she'll bring some in.'

They'd both offered to do it for her, but the older woman had tutted them away and told Mattie that they were here to visit the Brigadier and not to do errands for her. It had surprised them both when she'd also told them that their father usually liked to accompany her to the shops, taking his time to potter up and down the aisles, even if he couldn't remember what they were doing there.

'I'll nip to the corner shop, if you're okay with Dad?'

'Of course.' Pushing herself off the doorframe, Mattie plastered a bright smile on her lips and smoothed her jumper, which was in her mother's favourite colour. No wonder her father was getting confused.

She strode confidently back into the living room.

'Hey. Dad, Hayd is just going out for milk for our tea.'

'Hayden?' Her father lifted his head from his paper to frown at her. 'Mary, darling, he's at university—how can he go to the shop?'

'It's Mattie, Dad. Your daughter. Not Mum… Mary.'

'Mathilda?' His peered at her harder, before covering smoothly. 'Of course. I was just miles away. How have you been?'

'I've been well, Dad.' Mattie smiled, relieved he had recognised her. Sometimes he didn't realise even when she told him. Soon it wouldn't matter what she said.

'Another tour?'

'There's a plan for a new army battalion,' she told him, even though she knew he wouldn't remember. 'I was running the medical support arm, seeing if the new strategies would hold up.'

'I remember testing a new strike plan back in 1992, or was it 1993? In between operational tours.' He smiled a soft, almost haunting smile. He was sinking back into his memories already. 'Operation Strongarm, we called it.'

'This was Operation Strikethrough,' she told him, trying to pull him back to the present even though she couldn't have said why. And then another thought hit her. 'I saw Kane.'

'Kane?'

'You remember.' She flicked out her tongue to wet her lips. 'Kane Wheeler? I never realised he had joined up all those years ago.'

Her father stared out of the window, blinking slowly. Mattie had no idea she'd held her breath until he suddenly spoke again.

'What are we going to tell Mathilda about the Wheeler boy, Mary?'

Mattie opened her mouth then closed it.

'What about Kane?' she asked cautiously. Hating herself.

'He's gone, Mary. And we're going to have to be the people to tell her. It's going to crush her.'

'What did you do?' she asked carefully. Not certain that she should be doing it but unable to help herself.

She had Kane's side of the story, but she still needed to know—to understand—what her father had thought all those years ago.

Why he'd never told her the truth.

'I had to help him, Mary,' her father said firmly. 'Mathilda won't see it that way, of course, but that can't be helped. There was no other way. That young Wheeler boy doesn't deserve to get pulled down by the rest of his abominable family.'

'Where did he go?' Mattie could barely recognise her own voice. She had no idea how she managed to sound so calm, so collected.

'It's best you don't know, Mary. It's best that no one knows. He's given the police enough to send those brothers of his away for a decent length of time. So neither they nor that father of theirs can find out where Kane is. They would hunt the kid down and they make him pay.'

Mattie blinked. It almost sounded as though her father was protective of Kane, yet all these years she'd thought her parents had hated him.

How could she have been so wrong?

Her heart felt as though it was about to beat right out of her chest.

'Surely he could have said goodbye to…Mathilda.' She faltered for a moment.

Her father snorted, though there was still tenderness in his voice. 'Don't be foolish, Mary—do you think our little Mathilda would have left it at that? She'd have inveigled the whole story out of him—you know that Wheeler boy would do anything for her—and our daughter is nothing if not hot-headed.'

A proud smile touched his lips now, despite everything.

'She would no doubt march up to the Wheelers' house and give the lot of them a piece of her mind. But those boys are both facing jail sentences so how safe do you think she would be, Mary? As it stands, they have no idea where Kane is now, or that I had anything to do with it. This way both the boy, and our family, are guaranteed to stay safe.'

Mattie started, then went cold. When Kane had told her, he'd deliberately left out the more sordid facts. The danger he'd been in.

Plus, her father was right, she *had* had a tendency to act before thinking back then, and Kane's brothers had never been the most rational, predictable of boys, and both had racked up a long list of violent offences, as far as she was aware. She could have caused no end of trouble not just for herself but for her whole family if she'd gone off at the deep end on them.

'Besides, he asked me not to say anything to her.'

Mattie turned back, watching her father carefully.

'Who asked you not to say anything?'

'The Wheeler lad, of course.' He clicked his tongue impatiently.

'Why not?' she pressed, reining in her impatience when he didn't elaborate.

Her father pulled his eyebrows together, the slight shake of his head almost imperceptible. 'Shame, I imagine, Mary. He didn't want Mathilda to know. I suppose he thought it would change the way she looked at him. Taint it slightly. He'd always been the only one in that dreadful family to stay out of trouble with the police. I think he wanted to preserve that image she had of him, rather than know the truth.'

Mattie stared. She could practically feel the cogs spinning and slipping in her head. She probably wouldn't have understood at the time, but in hindsight it made sense that

Kane might want to hide the truth from her. But her father? All these years she'd thought her father hated Kane. She'd imagined that he'd have taken any opportunity to convince her that her first boyfriend hadn't been worthy of her.

Instead, the truth was that her father had protected the one secret Kane hadn't wanted her to know. And she loved them both for it.

'Is there anything else?' she pressed quietly, but her father had switched back to staring out of the window and she knew he was lost in his own thoughts, leaving her to try to pick her way through the unexpected bombshell.

She was still musing when her brother walked back in with the milk and a huge round box of chocolates in his hand.

'Who are they for?' She forced a laugh, grateful for the distraction. 'Dad, or you?'

'Their Dad's favourite.' Hayden, oblivious to the turmoil in her head, at least had the grace to look sheepish as she followed him into the kitchen and dropped them on the island.

'But you quite fancied them?' Mattie lifted her eyebrows.

He lifted his hands, palms up.

'I admit nothing.'

She sank into a chair and toyed with the plastic seal on the box as he set about making fresh tea. It was only when she heard her brother clicking his fingers by her ear that she realised he'd been talking to her and she hadn't heard a word.

'Sorry, what?' Sitting up straighter, she affected levity.

She might have known Hayden wouldn't be fooled.

'What's happened, Mattie?'

'Nothing.'

'Mattie,' he chastised, but then turned his back as though concentrating on the hot drinks.

Knowing that would somehow make it easier to talk.

'Dad thought I was Mum again.' She stopped. Waited. But Hayden didn't press her, leaving her to continue in her own time. 'Did you know he helped Kane to leave because his brothers had held up that Eight-Till-Late in town?'

Her brother didn't answer immediately, but eventually he half glanced back, his head over his shoulder.

'Dad helped Kane leave because he gave evidence against his brothers.'

Whatever she had expected, it wasn't that. She tried to process the information, but her head was spinning hard. Beginning to pound. Another thought walloped her.

'You knew? Wait, is that why you invited Kane to London? To my wedding rehearsal?'

She heard silence as he stopped stirring the tea. Then the clink as he set the spoon down. Finally, Hayden turned around.

'I contacted Kane because Dad asked me to.'

'Dad did?' She kept her voice low because as much as shouting wasn't her, right now she wanted to yell and roar, and probably beat her bloody hands on her chest. 'What did he say?'

Hayden folded his arms over his chest.

'Not much. He was already into the illness by then, you know that.'

The pounding in her head grew louder, like a marching band made up of every drummer in the entire military.

'He must have told you something.'

Her brother met her gaze head on.

'He contacted me out of the blue a few weeks before your wedding. Told me Kane was in the military and that I should contact an old army buddy of his from way back. He wanted me to tell Kane that you were getting married.'

'And?' she prompted.

'And about what happened that night with Kane and his brothers. But that was pretty much all he said.'

Mattie shook her head in disbelief.

'He must have told you more than that.'

'I shouldn't need to remind you how closed Dad could be, Mattie.'

She knew. But, still, it didn't entirely make sense.

'And you did it? Just like that? No questions asked?' She recognised that expression. Knew that lock of his jaw. 'What aren't you saying, Hayd?'

He still didn't answer.

'Please?'

He eyed her a little longer, still not speaking.

'I don't know, Mattie.' Hayden shook his head eventually. 'Dad was never exactly clear, but I got the impression that he wanted to make amends. And…maybe he thought that you didn't really love George.'

'And you didn't think to *tell* me?' Her voice rose an octave, and she had to fight to bring it back down. 'To pass on this information.'

'I thought about a million things,' Hayden declared at length. 'You were getting married, Mattie. To a guy who seemed perfect for you and who you said you loved. I didn't want to rake up the past at what was supposed to be such a happy time for you. Plus, I didn't know how much of what Dad said was accurate and how much was the Alzheimer's playing tricks.'

He had a point. A part of her could see that, even with her head whirling like she was some kind of mad, spinning-top ride.

'But what about afterwards?'

'Afterwards?'

She didn't mean to cluck her tongue.

'After George and I called it off?' she pressed irritably. 'After Kane had come up that night?'

'How was I to know that you hadn't spoken to him, Mattie?' Hayden shrugged. 'When you didn't say anything, I assumed you just didn't want to talk about it.'

She balled her hands into fists, trying to slow her racing mind. And heart. Yet slowly, *slowly*, even now, certain things were coming into focus.

'I didn't speak to him. I didn't even realise he had really been there. I thought I'd...conjured him up in my head or something. Until I saw him at Operation Strikethrough and he told me about being there that night.'

'You saw him? Out on exercise?'

'Yeah. He's a WO2. Percy Copperhead's CSM.'

'Ah.'

There was so much sentiment loaded into that one syllable that it lifted the tiny, fine hairs on the back of her neck.

'*Ah*, what?'

'*Ah*, so that's why you've been in such a weird mood ever since you got back.'

She opened her mouth to deny it but then snapped it shut. This was Hayd. What was the point in lying to him?

'You still should have asked me about him at my wedding rehearsal,' she said instead.

He leaned against the surface, arms across his chest, assessing her carefully.

'Maybe,' he conceded at last. 'But ultimately what difference would it have made? Would you be with Kane now if I had said anything?'

'How would I know that?'

'Okay, then answer this. Now you've met him again, what's changed? Clearly you can't both stay in and still be together, so are you leaving your career? Or is Kane leaving his?'

'Are you suggesting I should?' she snapped. 'Weren't you the one person who told me—repeatedly—that I was crazy for getting ready to give up my army career for George. But you think it's okay to give it up for Kane?'

'No, I didn't say that.' He arched his eyebrows at her. 'I used to think it was crazy to give up something you love for anyone else but yourself.'

'Used to?' She frowned and despite all the rowdiness inside her head, she couldn't help picking up on such an un-Hayden-like comment.

'Oh, no, this isn't about me right now.' He refused to be baited. 'This is about you. And my point is that you can blame Dad and me as much as you like for not telling you the truth back then, but this is now. You've had a chance to put things right *if* that's what you really want. But if you're both choosing your careers then that's on you two, Mattie. No one else.'

Then, turning around, he picked up her mug of tea and passed it to her. She cupped it in her hands and slid her fingers through the handle.

Mattie still glowered at her unconcerned brother over the rim, changing the subject as though it could somehow resolve the issues tumbling around her head.

'So, what's your next task anyway?'

'I'm supposed to be DS for a training exercise on Salisbury Plain.'

'Supposed to be?'

Another uncharacteristically Hayden comment but as he answered her, Mattie found herself losing focus, her head was still echoing with his earlier words.

He'd made a good point. She *did* have a chance to put things right if she really wanted to.

The question was, what *was* she prepared to do about it?

CHAPTER THIRTEEN

'MORNING, WILLIAM,' MATTIE greeted the adjutant, after checking the room to ensure he was alone.

'Hey, Mattie.' William stood up from his paperwork to step around his desk and greet her. 'How are things? Congratulations on your promotion, by the way. I hear it's going to be officially announced any day now. Especially after Operation Strikethrough was such a success, in no small part down to the work you and WO2 Wheeler put in.'

'Thanks,' she croaked out, plastering a bright smile to her lips, and told herself that William couldn't possibly know that she was about to resign her commission.

In fact, getting the call from William that the colonel wanted to see her couldn't have come at a more opportune moment.

She had been wrestling with the situation ever since her conversation with her brother. Two weeks of going back and forth, listening to her head and then her heart. It had consumed her every moment. She had barely eaten, barely slept, only work had provided some relief from her buffeting emotions.

When she'd been ready to resign her commission for George it had been because it was what had been expected of her as the new Lady Blakeney, and she'd ignored the niggling doubt that it would breed resentment in her marriage.

So surely it was foolish to be considering giving up her army career for Kane? Only her heart was telling her otherwise. It was reminding her that she would still have a great career as a civilian doctor. And what about when—if—she and Kane had children? She had always imagined herself as a doctor and a mother. But she'd never imagined herself as an army doctor and a mother. Much as she loved her father, she could remember all too clearly how much of her childhood, and Hayden's, he'd missed when he'd been away on exercise, or training camps, or courses.

It wasn't something she wanted for herself.

And then there was the fact that Kane had never once asked her to leave. They had never even discussed any real future together because it had seemed like an impossibility. All the same, she'd known her heart had been winning the debate. In fourteen years she hadn't moved on because of one simple truth: she was in love with Kane and she always had been.

Nothing had ever changed that. So if she didn't put herself out there and take that bold step, somehow, deep down, she knew she would regret it for the rest of her life. And if he rejected her then at least she would finally have closure.

Surely that was worth something?

'Mathilda.' The colonel's voice broke through the room, cutting William off as he was about to speak again.

'Colonel.' She braced slightly but he gestured for her to stop and go through to his office.

'Schedule's a bit tight today and the call I received from Major Copperhead of the new infantry force rather caught me off guard.'

Percy Copperhead? Kane's OC? What could *he* want?

'Before you start, sir,' Mattie began, 'I wonder if I might say something?'

'One moment, Mathilda.' The colonel halted her as he sat down. 'Come in and close the doors, please, William.'

He sat down as his adjutant closed the doors between the two offices, then gestured for Mattie to also sit and, with William also in the room, she found she didn't want to say anything she'd come to say after all.

'Everything you and WO2 Wheeler pulled off during that pre-phase of Operation Strikethrough was quite impressive. My counterpart from Infantry said that medical support kept the pressure on, and it really helped to test the new tactical battle group to its limits. Outstanding work.'

'Oh. Well. Good.'

She wanted to feel relieved, but she couldn't. Her resignation was rolling all around her mouth.

'This is rather a delicate part.' The CO steepled his fingers. 'It's about how well you know WO2 Wheeler.'

Mattie's stomach dipped and tumbled in an instant. She hadn't been prepared for this. She and Kane had been so discreet, how could anyone possibly have known what had happened between them? This certainly wasn't how she'd wanted to go out—under some cloud—but if it was going to happen then at least she knew it was for the right person.

It wasn't like it had been with George, because Kane had never been Blakeney. She would always have gone to the ends of the earth for Kane. And she knew she wouldn't live to regret a single moment of it.

'You want to know how well I know WO2 Wheeler?' She unglued her tongue from the roof of her mouth.

'This is all in strictest confidence, Major Brigham.' Her colonel reverted to her rank for a moment, as if to impress upon her the gravity of the situation. 'But Division have been considering WO2 Wheeler for LE in the next year or so, having been put forward by his previous commanding officer.'

Mattie's brain skidded, the smell of burning rubber filling her head.

Kane was being considered as an LE? Mattie paused, somewhere between being shocked and not being surprised at all. An LE—Late Entry Officer—was one of few soldiers who jumped the non-commissioned officer and commissioned officer divide. Usually only a very select number of Warrant Officers First Class were considered for the role.

He would be commissioned into the army as a captain, able to either take up a staff officer role or to serve as a CSM and WO1. More importantly, as a captain it would mean that she and Kane would be commissioned officers together. They could both remain in the army whilst any personal relationship between them would be entirely acceptable.

It was like Fate was somehow spinning everything perfectly together.

'That doesn't surprise me at all.' She had no idea how she managed to sound so controlled. 'WO2 Wheeler was easy to work with. Extremely knowledgeable and efficient. He would make an exceptional officer, in my opinion.'

The best part about it was that it was completely true.

'And mine,' her CO concurred. 'However, it seems Major Copperhead doesn't agree. Ever since he took over from the previous CO, he has been trying to quash WO2 Wheeler's recommendation.'

A thousand thoughts skittered through her head, but she couldn't voice a single one of them. They were too personal, too revealing. In the end she settled for a pointed, 'I think that's a mistake.'

'I agree. And so, it would seem, does Division. They would like to bring WO2 Wheeler's consideration forward.'

'Bring it forward?' she hedged, not even feigning disinterest.

'Forward to this year. Percy isn't happy about it, of course, but it's gone over his head. They asked me if I would like to second the recommendation, which I do.' He glared at her, as though she was going to argue. 'I rather hoped your recent experience working with him would help me to do that.'

For the briefest of moments Mattie couldn't answer. Kane was exactly the type of officer the army needed—far more than any of the Percy Copperheads. From where Kane had started, he was exactly the kind of role model the soldiers needed, and his experience would make him a knowledgeable but fair leader.

Something moved inside her chest. Happiness. And pride.

'Yes, sir, of course I can do that.'

'Good.' He looked satisfied. 'I'd like a report on my desk by this afternoon. Mattie, for our eyes only, please?'

'Understood.' She dipped her head, a thousand thoughts crowding inside it.

'In fact, Kane's been earmarked as the next Army Sergeant Major,' William confided unexpectedly, at some unseen gesture from the CO.

'Say again?'

It was more than Mattie could believe. The most senior member of the other ranks in the British Army, the post had only been created in a few years before, and both previous appointment holders had been former WO1s, later commissioned as captains.

Kane would be the newest holder. And Mattie couldn't think of a more deserving individual.

'That's…phenomenal,' she managed, a wave of nostalgia walloping her suddenly.

What she wouldn't have given to be able to tell her father that the kindness he'd shown Kane all those years ago hadn't been wasted. He would have been so proud.

She was only sorry that it had taken her until now to know it.

Kane removed his headwear as he stepped through the doors to his battalion headquarters, as protocol dictated, and made his way up the long, winding stairs to his adjutant's office to get an appointment with his CO.

No doubt relaying his decision to Percy Copperhead would give the guy the kick of the year, but Kane told himself he didn't care. He'd spent too many weeks without Mattie, and he'd hated it.

Dedicating himself to his army career had been one thing fourteen years ago. But now, after those nights they'd spent together—and all those revelations—his career had lost some of its lustre. At least, when compared to what he had with her.

If he could have had both, it would have been perfect, but having to choose made it a no-brainer. He would have been to see his CO earlier, if the guy hadn't sent him to run yet another needless training course, as if to take up as much of his downtime as possible.

The guy wasn't to know that Kane had welcomed every moment of it. It had kept his mind busy whilst he'd tried to grapple with the gravity of giving up his entire career for the woman he loved—with the risk that she might not even want him.

But it didn't matter, he had to try. He would never forgive himself if he didn't.

Mattie had been right, back in that ruin the last night they'd been together. He had more prospects now than he'd had had as a kid. People head-hunting him. He would earn more money to provide for his family. He had something to offer her. Which was why it wasn't the impossible decision he'd feared it would be, to walk away from it all for her.

The last thing he anticipated, when he reached the top of the staircase, was to see Mattie leaving Copperhead's office, a grim expression on her face.

Everything fell away and in that split second there was no army, no building. Only her, and him. Something bubbled inside him at the mouth-watering sight of her walking down the corridor, every step a picture in elegance and barely restrained anger.

'Mat... Major,' he growled, changing his term of address at the last moment.

She stopped abruptly, her head snapping up to look at him, and Kane had to draw in a steadying breath, scarcely able to believe how much self-control it was taking him not to simply stride over and take her in his arms.

But there were too many people around and, as far as they were concerned, she was a major and he was a warrant officer.

'Hello, ma'am, what brings you here?'

'Mr Wheeler.' She inclined her head politely, her eyes taking in everyone around them without appearing to be looking anywhere. 'A little bit of final business on Operation Strikethrough.'

She was lying. He couldn't read the look that danced over her lovely features, but he knew there was something going on.

'Actually, it's fortuitous that I've seen you. Do you have five minutes?'

Only he could know her well enough to hear the shake of anticipation in her voice. Was the same buzzing thrill zipping madly around her body at this very moment, the way it was his?

He'd really wanted to speak to Copperhead before he

spoke to Mattie, but there was no way he could refuse her. No way he wanted to.

'Certainly,' he acquiesced. 'Which way?'

'This is your battalion HQ, Mr Wheeler, I wonder if you would lead the way.'

Wordlessly, he led her along the corridor to one of the quieter training rooms, set up a little like a classroom. He opened the door for her then followed her inside.

She moved around the other side of the desks and looked at him.

'So what *are* you doing here, Matz?' he asked quietly. 'And don't flannel me with final reports on Operation Strikethrough.'

'I can't tell you.' There was the vaguest hint of anguish in her tone, making him believe her, before she turned the question back on him. 'What are *you* doing here, Kane?'

'Me? Oh, I've come to buy myself out.'

He rather liked it that her mouth actually fell open a little. Though the urge to close it by claiming it with his own was incredibly powerful.

'You're leaving?' she breathed.

'That's the idea.'

He didn't miss the way she reached out, clutching the table beside herself, almost as if she needed the solid surface to keep herself from stumbling.

He liked it that he had that effect on her. *Still.*

'Why?' she choked out after a few moments.

'Why do you think, Matz? It's the only way we can be together.'

'No.' She began to shake her head. *'No!'*

This wasn't quite what he'd had in mind.

'Why not? That's what I want—to be with you. I should have seen it before, but the fact is that I've seen it now.'

'No, Kane, you can't do that.' And this time there was no hesitation in her tone.

A heavy beat started up in his chest, echoing through his head. He pretended he didn't hear it.

'That isn't quite the reaction I was hoping for, Matz.'

'I don't want you to leave.'

'Well, I want to.'

'For me?'

'For *us*.'

Again she shook her head, and Kane found himself grinding his teeth.

'I don't want to play this game, Matz. We love each other, we both said it. But neither of us were prepared to give up our careers for the other. Only now I *am* prepared to. Because after all that's happened between us, I realise that this career means nothing if I don't have you.'

'I still can't let you buy yourself out,' she gritted out.

He pushed off from the desk, taking a step closer to her, that fresh, citrusy fragrance pervading his senses, and that fire in her eyes stoking the flames that burned inside him.

'I want to be with you, Mattie. I thought the army was the most important thing to me, and perhaps it was. But only because it was the only thing that filled the void that had opened up when I lost you.'

'You're saying you would choose me over the career that you love?' she asked breathlessly, finding that her soul ached to hear the words.

'I would. And I am,' he told her simply. 'But I know you, Mathilda Brigham. This isn't your cue to start feeling guilty because you don't want to quit too. That isn't what it's about.'

'I won't,' she replied promptly, but there was a teasing quality to her tone that made him take stock.

'Am I missing something?'

'You might be.'

Okay, now she was definitely teasing him. Tentatively, given where they were, but it was there.

He studied her more intently.

'What's going on, Matz?'

It was there, bursting to get out of her. He could read it in every exquisite line of her body. And how he wanted to press that body to his again.

'I already went to my CO to resign my commission to be with you.'

Of all the things he'd considered she could have said, that wasn't one of them.

'Say again?' He heard the anger threaded through his tone before he felt it.

'I decided the same thing that you have. That I wasn't willing to sacrifice a relationship with you for a career in the army. Not when I could still do the thing I really love—being a doctor—in the civilian world.'

'You love being an *army* doctor, though,' he ground out.

'I do. And you love being an infantry man.'

'Not as much as I love you.'

She faltered. He saw it. She almost circled the desk back to him but caught herself, and Kane was glad. He wasn't sure he'd have had the self-control to resist if she'd done that.

'So…you really quit?' he demanded. And it didn't make him anywhere near happy. 'You can't. I don't ever want you to grow to resent me because you lost the career you love.'

'I wouldn't have. As much as I love being an army doctor, I know people are what matter more. *You* matter more.'

'No, Mattie, I won't accept that.'

'Well, we can debate that another time, but look at it this way instead. In the end I didn't resign.'

For the second time is as many moments he felt winded. So she *had* loved him enough to leave but had then changed her mind?

'You don't know why your CO has called you, do you?' she asked with a soft laugh.

'I don't care,' he told her, his expression intense and serious, making her sober instantly.

'You should,' she chastised him. 'And I shouldn't tell you this, but I don't want you to blow it by asking to buy yourself out. You know Percy will jump at the chance, and then everything everyone else is doing will be for nothing.'

He shouldn't be curious, yet he was.

'What do you mean, *everything everyone else is doing*?'

'I mean, your former CO put you forward for a recommendation as an LE. And my CO, following my report on our working relationship during Operation Strikethrough, has completed a second recommendation. Of course, it's no guarantee, especially as Percy is trying to talk us all down, but two recommendations don't come around very often, Kane. And they have for you.'

He didn't answer. It was impossible to know what to think, let alone what to say.

'We can have it all, Kane. Our army careers *and* each other.'

'I don't care, you know. I'm happy with my decision to give it up for you. For us.'

'As am I. And maybe we'll still choose to do that one day. But right now that isn't a decision we have to make, so why not take the opportunity being offered?'

She was trembling, he could see it from here. And he'd never wanted so much to take her in his arms and hold her. Kane had no idea how he held himself back. He dropped his hands to brace them on the cool surfaces of the desks, his fingers brushing hers.

She stared at them then back up at him, her expression so charged he thought the air around them should crackle with its intensity.

'It means waiting, though, Matz. We still can't be together until I'm a commissioned officer.'

With another glance down at his hands Mattie slowly—as if it was painful for her to do—lifted her own hands from the desk and took a half-step back.

'We've waited for fourteen years, Kane,' she whispered. 'I think we can wait a little longer.'

'I don't know how,' he growled, forcing himself to take control.

'Neither do I,' Mattie confessed. 'But we'll manage it.'

CHAPTER FOURTEEN

THE OFFICERS' MESS fell silent as Kane's old CO walked the newly commissioned Kane into the room.

Mattie's eyes prickled, hot and stinging, as she watched Kane walk across the room and ring the bell—the invitation for orders allowing every officer to order a drink at the bar, all of which would go on the newly commissioned officer's mess bill at the end of the month.

She watched with incredible patience as he navigated the social waters filled with the many officers who had worked with him over the years and who wanted to congratulate him on his success. And then, at last, people began to drift into groups, and she found herself facing Kane from the other side of the room.

Mattie wasn't sure who moved first, Kane or herself, but suddenly they were standing practically toe to toe, and for the first time ever she could call him Kane in front of anyone, and no one would bat an eyelid.

'Congratulations, *Captain* Wheeler.' She smiled. 'Be grateful it wasn't an official dinner, or they'd have had you popping a champagne bottle with a ceremonial sword.'

'Then I'm glad I got the bell.'

'You won't be when the bill comes.' She chuckled. 'I'll warn you now that first one is a bit of a shocker.'

'I've been warned,' he agreed. 'Still, can I buy you another drink?'

A frisson of excitement rippled through her.

'Actually, I was just going to retire for the evening,' she said clearly, for anyone else around to hear. 'But you can walk me back if you're heading that way.'

'Of course.'

Taking their leave, they walked out of the mess in step but apart. Like any other pair of officers who happened to be leaving together. It was more thrilling than she could have imagined.

'I booked the taxi,' she murmured quietly, when she was sure they were far enough away not to be overheard by anyone.

'I booked the hotel,' he said, and grinned into the night as they headed towards the main gate.

And then they were slipping into the taxi and speeding down the streets, back to the place where it had all pretty much started again only a few months earlier.

'I feel like I'm sixteen again!' Mattie giggled softly, her thighs pressed against Kane's, his arms slung around her shoulders. He dropped his head to her ear and his breath tickled her skin, making her neck goose-bump.

'If we were kids again we'd probably be making out in the back of this cab.'

And, oh, how she was tempted. Long, long months of keeping her distance, just waiting for Kane to finally get his commission. They'd waited so long, and this last leg felt like the longest wait of all.

Now, sliding her hand up the hard ridges of his muscular thigh, she stopped just shy of going too far, delighting in the long breath that Kane hissed out. He dropped his arm down her back, circling his hand around to draw lazy whorls on her hipbone and down to her backside.

'That's unfair,' she protested weakly.

He didn't look remotely repentant.

'Then in future I suggest you don't start something you don't want finished.'

And then they were there, pulling up outside the hotel, and Kane was thrusting a note into the driver's hand and telling him to keep the change.

'In a rush?' she teased.

He cast her a sidelong look.

'Would you prefer me to take my time?'

They could barely keep their hands off each other on the ride up in the lift, grateful for the deserted corridors as they stumbled along, locating their room. And then they were falling through the door and all she could think about was finally, *finally*, reacquainting herself with the body that had made her ache with longing for far too long.

It was the flowers on the bed that stopped her. Pretty lupins, like they'd found in that ruin back during Operation Strikethrough. And on top of them was a distinctive square box.

Her heart caught in her throat.

'Kane? What's going on?'

'Open it and find out,' he told her hoarsely.

Her fingers were trembling as she reached over and took the box. This wasn't what she'd expected, but she couldn't seem to stop herself from imagining. Hoping.

It took her two attempts to open the heavy hinge on the box, and then she thought her legs might buckle beneath her because it wasn't a modern ring, some exquisite, contemporary thing that Kane had scoured jewellery shops for.

This was her mother's ring.

'How...?'

'I asked Hayd's permission to ask for your hand—in lieu of your father.' Kane shrugged. 'He went straight upstairs and brought it down. So I guess you could say he approves.'

She didn't answer him. Especially when he dropped to one knee in front of her.

'So, Mathilda Brigham, after a decade and a half of waiting, of trying to live lives that were never going to be complete without each other, will you do me the honour of marrying me, and making my life whole once again?'

Mattie heard an incoherent sound and it took her a moment to realise it was her. Her chest was still tight and aching, but this time she knew it wasn't because her heart was breaking. It was coming back together, each little shard slipping seamlessly back into place.

Like a little miracle that made her chest swell until she thought it might explode.

'I can't believe this,' she breathed.

Rising up again, Kane cupped her face in his hands and dropped a smooth kiss on her forehead.

'Believe it, Matz.'

She shook her head, swallowing the lump of happiness that was lodged in her throat. Fighting to speak. She gripped his hands and held them in place.

He caught her against him, and she sighed at the way their bodies seem to mould perfectly to each other.

EPILOGUE

THEY WERE MARRIED the following year in the glorious, Grecian-style Guards' Chapel in London's St James's Park, with a uniformed usher trumpeting Mattie's arrival and an honour guard with their arch of swords over the happy couple's departure.

Mattie, walked down the aisle by a delighted Hayden in lieu of her father, had chosen a sleek off-white gown with lace shoulder detailing for modesty, whilst Kane was resplendent in his new officer's uniform.

'I'm still not sure I can believe we get our happy ending,' she whispered as she smoothed her dress in the back seat of the vintage car, and Kane slid in beside her, scooping his willing new wife into his arms.

'It's been a long time coming,' he agreed, his lips brushing hers and instantly setting her body on fire. Making her suddenly wish they didn't have to rush to the hotel to attend the wedding breakfast 'But it *is* finally here. And it's ours to enjoy.'

'Do you think the guests will have time to get to the venue before us?' She affected an air of innocence. 'Or should we give them a little additional time, do you think?'

'Colonel Brigham,' he murmured against her mouth, 'are you suggesting you can't wait?'

'I'm suggesting we've spent years waiting. Today, for

once, is about us finally getting what we've longed for. I don't want to wait any longer.'

'Neither do I,' Kane agreed.

And for the first time in forever they felt as if they had it all. And it felt *right*.

* * * * *

REAWAKENED BY
HER ARMY MAJOR

CHARLOTTE HAWKES

MILLS & BOON

To Vic.
Thank you for being such a fab—and patient—editor!
xx

CHAPTER ONE

'Relax, Bea, you look great.'

Stopping outside the doors to the nightclub, where a muffled bass beat was already audible, Bridget Gardiner smoothed down the shimmery short dress she'd borrowed from her friend and tried not to look awkward or out of place.

Not feel like some scraggly stray next to the strikingly sophisticated Mattie Brigham.

'You're sure?' Bridget shifted uncertainly.

'I'm definitely sure. Perfect for finally breaking out of your shell and trying something a little bit crazy.'

'Yeah…about that…'

'Oh, no. You can't back out now, Bea. Weren't you the one who originally said that tonight was about having fun?'

'Yes…' Bridget trailed off uncertainly.

Tonight *was* supposed to be about fun. Only *wanting* to do something crazy and actually *doing* something crazy were two very separate things.

'Weren't you also the one who said that we spend most of our careers being serious?' Mattie continued. '*Too* serious sometimes. Tonight is about just cutting loose, right?'

'I know…'

'Got to take a few chances. Life's too short not to. Trust me.'

Bridget eyed her friend for a moment. She couldn't put her finger on it, but Mattie seemed different tonight. Perhaps a little…agitated? Not obviously so, just flashes every now and then. Certainly not the cool, collected army major and doctor that Bridget was accustomed to seeing.

'Everything okay, Mattie?'

Mattie hesitated and, for a moment Bridget thought she was going to say something. But then her friend seemed to pull her shoulders back and roll her eyes.

'Ghosts from the past.' She shrugged, back to her usual self. On the outside at least. 'Gotta shake them off. Maybe I should try something crazy too, just so you're not alone.'

'It's fine.' Bridget plastered a bright smile on her face and tried to look earnest. 'Actually, I'm looking forward to tonight.'

'Liar!' Mattie laughed softly, reaching for the door handle and pulling it open as the thrum of music spilled out into the street. 'I know you'd be ten times more at home in some aid post in a disaster area. And a hundred times more confident. You can handle rebels and guerrillas in the middle of some refugee camp thousands of miles from home, Bea.'

'You make me sound a lot cooler than I really am…' Bridget wrinkled her nose.

'You *are* cool, Bea. But the fact that you're practically quaking at the idea of meeting a bunch of my army buddies, not to mention my thorn-in-my-side big brother, *isn't* so cool. In fact, it's daft.'

'I know that, too,' Bridget admitted.

Although, to be fair, it was meeting Hayden that was worrying her most. Mattie might grumble about her brother—also an army officer—but there was absolutely no mistaking the fact that she loved him without reservation. How many times had she lamented the fact that their respective army careers meant they didn't see each other—or their retired army brigadier father—enough?

And then, as if on cue, the doubts began creeping in. As familiar and painful as ever.

Bridget gritted her teeth and tried to shut them out, but it was impossible.

What if Hayden didn't like her? What if he told Mattie that she wasn't good enough to be Mattie's friend?

Stop it, you're not fourteen any more.

She wasn't *that kid* who all the cool kids pointed at and laughed at. The one whose father was a fraudster and a conman.

'Good. So, *fun*,' Mattie said firmly, oblivious to the sudden turmoil in Bridget's mind. 'Good, clean fun. Then back to the serious stuff tomorrow, okay?'

'Okay.' Bridget paused then returned Mattie's gentle smile with a rather sheepish one of her own. 'I'm ready.'

'Still a lie, but more convincing.' Mattie grinned. 'Trust me, Bea, we've been through this, they're a nice bunch and they'll love you.'

With that, her friend ducked into the club, leaving Bridget to follow, coming to an abrupt halt for a moment as a heavy wall of heat and sound hit her with such a wallop that for a moment she forgot how to breathe.

She watched Mattie accept the two proffered welcome jelly shots from the girl at the door, then let her friend place one in her hand.

'Open your mouth, pinch the container, and swallow.' Mattie demonstrated. 'Wow. Now, they *are* strong!'

Closing her eyes and sending out a silent prayer, Bridget followed suit. It slid down her throat surprisingly smoothly, the taste sweet but with a kick nonetheless. Then Mattie grabbed her hand and plunged them both into the gyrating bodies.

Like Alice down the rabbit hole.

And whether it was the crowd, the music or the insanely strong shot, Bridget found her body heating up and her brain beginning to loosen its grip just a fraction. People bumped her—or perhaps she bumped them—and swept her along, as if her feet weren't always quite touching the ground.

She was almost grateful when Mattie came to a stop in front of a small, friendly looking group who erupted into shouts and laughs, all of them jostling a little in their obvious eagerness to greet their friend. And before she realised it, they were turning to acknowledge her, too. Warmly, but not too over the top. Mattie had been right, her friends were a nice bunch, and this was actually...*fun*.

Right up until the moment when Mattie gave a low cry and hurled herself past Bridget.

'Hayd. You're here.'

Bridget turned, amused, but instead something jolted through her. Like a shock of electricity. Her body didn't even feel like her own any longer or, if it did, she certainly didn't have any control over it. Instead, all she could do was stand there, frozen in place like one of her teenage nightmares, her eyes struggling to refocus. To take it all in.

So, this was Mattie's brother, the infamous Major Hayden Brigham. He wasn't at all how she'd pictured him.

Then again, she wasn't sure *how* she'd pictured him. Good looking, certainly, since Mattie had never made any bones about that fact, but Bridget had put it down to indulgence on the part of a loving sister. Hayden was apparently a very eligible bachelor—and what was more, he knew it—so he didn't sound at all her type. If she actually *had* a type, that was. Still, she'd thought she'd been fully prepared for meeting him in person.

But she'd been wrong. In truth, surely nothing could

have prepared any woman for the reality of meeting the guy in person.

He wasn't just good looking—such a description was too pedestrian for a man like Major Hayden Brigham. He was…arresting—*magnificent*—and if there was a perfect specimen of male beauty, it was him.

Less of a man, more of a mountain, yet unequivocally male. Bridget was fairly certain she heard a collective sigh of appreciation from the female contingent of the entire club. Or maybe that was just her?

And she hated herself for it. It was so *not* her to lust over a man. *Any* man. But certainly not one who was also the brother of the closest thing Bridget had had to a best friend since she'd been a kid. Certainly not one with whom she was going to be working—out in the middle of nowhere on the African continent—for the next three months.

Well, not *working with* exactly. But close enough. Which was why, no matter how insane her body was going right now, she *didn't* fancy him. She refused to.

Yet what was to be done when everything about him, from that crop of short yet deliciously tousled dirty-blond hair down to the jaw—so square that a carpenter could have used it to take perfect right angles—was stunning? Not to mention those Baltic-blue eyes that seemed to peer into her very soul, holding her own and making it feel as though her entire face was on fire.

She couldn't move, could barely even breathe. She had no idea how she managed to wrest her gaze away, but suddenly it was dropping. Down over those broad, strong shoulders to which the fitted shirt clung so lovingly, and did absolutely nothing to disguise, and over the indisputably defined chest as it tapered to the sexiest set of male hips she imagined had ever existed.

She couldn't look down any further. She didn't dare.

And so they lingered there—shamefully—somewhere around his belt buckle.

Fleetingly, Bridget considered making her escape. Rushing for the Ladies' to douse herself with some much-needed cold water. Naturally, it was that exact moment that her friend chose to introduce the two of them.

'Bridget, this is my brother, Hayden. Hayd, meet Bridget Gardiner, who I've been telling you about. Though she's off limits, right?'

More heat—if it was even possible—rushed to Bridget's face, even as her mouth became too parched to begin to respond. Not that it mattered, as Hayden was already speaking, his rich, deep, yet slightly wry tone doing…*things* to Bridget's insides.

She needed to get a grip. Draw on some of that strength she always had in one of those refugee camps in the middle of some foreign country.

'Thank you, Mattie…' the low, rich voice rolled through her, despite the deep pulse of the nightclub bass line, leaving her altogether too…*aware* of her own body '…for making it sound as though I pounce on every friend you introduce me to. And, Bridget, I've heard a fair bit about you, It's a pleasure.'

He held his hand out, the movement breaking her stare, and she snapped her eyes back up in an instant.

His blue eyes glittered. All-knowing. Clearly amused.

Her flush intensified as she thrust out her hand to his proffered one, shaking it clumsily. She'd never, *never* reacted to anyone like this. She'd thought it was something reserved for films, or books. But, lord, how Hayden positively *oozed* authority. And power.

It was…intoxicating.

You can resist him. You can resist him… Bridget began to chant it furiously to herself, like some kind of new mantra.

As if she would actually need to try.

As if Hayden would even look twice at a woman so quiet that she could make wallflowers look like prima donnas.

But, then, that was what happened when you'd spent the first thirteen years of your life gliding around the most glittering, monied, social circles, only for absolutely everything to tumble down in the most shameful way when your father had got arrested for fraud.

Was it any wonder, then, Bridget thought, not for the first time, that she'd spent the next thirteen years making herself as inconsequential and invisible as possible, fighting to shake off those associations?

Only now, right at this minute, standing in the spotlight of Hayden's stare, she didn't feel inconsequential or invisible, or gawky and out of step. Instead, she felt raw. Wobbly. Naked.

And a raft of other things she couldn't—or didn't want to—identify.

Get a grip.

'Hayden.' Thrusting her hand out to take his proffered one, she wasn't prepared for the jolt of electricity that zapped right through her, from the tips of her fingers right to her core. Right...*there.* Bridget was frankly astounded that she managed to make her voice sound remotely normal. 'Likewise.'

'Call me Hayd. Everyone does.'

Hayd. Even his name sang a new song inside Bridget's head. It should have been laughable but instead, shamefully, she found that she was entranced.

'I don't think you pounce on every friend I introduce to you,' Mattie's firm, all-too-shrewd voice cut in. 'Just those who have something about them.'

'I take it she's always this complimentary about me?' Hayden...*Hayd* turned to Bridget with raised eyebrows, but the twitch of his mouth was almost mesmerising.

It was all she could do not to let her legs crumple. They were certainly shaky enough.

'Incredible brother, amazing commanding officer, but unashamed playboy.' She ticked off each trait on one hand, as if entirely amused and not the least bit affected.

'Playboy?' He frowned.

'Well, not those words exactly,' Bridget confessed.

Though she'd added the *playboy* bit to keep her own head screwed on, if nothing else. How he couldn't hear the deafening hammering of her heart was mystifying, though perhaps he was altogether too accustomed to it.

'I think it was more *women always throwing themselves at his feet*. But I get the impression you're not exactly a monk.'

'He definitely isn't a monk.' Mattie clicked her tongue. 'Are you okay for a minute, Bea? I ought to say hi to everyone.'

How was it possible to simultaneously want to grab her friend's arm and make her stay, and yet to push her on her way and tell her not to rush back?

'Sure.' She managed to smile instead, though it felt like a rictus.

'I'll take care of her.' Hayden's voice sent goosebumps chasing up her skin.

'Yeah, well, not *too* much care.' Mattie skewered him with a glower before bestowing a smile on Bridget. 'He's not what I meant by doing something crazy.'

'Of course not,' Bridget agreed, wondering why her voice sounded so robotic. And then Mattie was gone, and she was left alone with her friend's brother. And her body launched itself into another insane fever.

What was the matter with her?

Hayden Brigham was positively lethal and according to Mattie any woman worth her salt should steer clear of the man, or at least be able to steel herself against his natural charms.

She'd been confident she'd fall easily into that category. Now she feared for her own sanity. Less than three minutes in this man's company and her body was already feeling out of her control, and alien. What would three months of working with him be like?

'Something *crazy*?' he echoed, and for a moment she couldn't be sure if it was a question or an invitation.

Bridget stuffed down the sudden thrill that rose within her and told herself it was entirely unwelcome.

She didn't believe in that stuff. *Love, lust, sex*, whatever one wanted to call it. She'd seen firsthand how destructive that could be. How her father had used her mother's love for him, and her gullibility, to defend him. To lie for him. All because she had refused to believe what was right in front of her eyes.

Such was the power he'd had over her mother that for years she'd made Bridget—too young to know any better—lie for him, too. And as Bridget had grown up and had seen for herself what kind of a smooth-talking con artist her father was, she had assured herself that she simply couldn't see how anyone could be that naive.

Right now, however, she was terribly afraid she could begin to understand all too easily. Not that she was saying Hayden Brigham was anything like her father, of course... just that it was suddenly all too easy to see how one could succumb to someone with boundless charisma and incredible looks.

'Never mind,' she managed to choke out quietly, before raising her voice. 'I've heard a lot about you.'

'Judging by my sister's comments, I'm not altogether convinced that's a good thing.' His lips twitched in amusement and Bridget found herself helplessly bewitched. 'Let me assure you that whilst whatever I do in my downtime is my business, I am strictly professional when it comes to operations or exercises.'

'Right,' Bridget muttered.

And what did it say about her that a hint of disappointment rippled through her at Hayden's reassurance? Or that his gaze slid lazily over her as though he could read her reaction in every line of her body.

'Relax, no need to be nervous.'

'I'm not,' she lied, silently trying to bolster herself.

'Is that so? Your shaking hands say otherwise but, trust me, I won't bite.'

'Not unless I want you to—isn't that how the saying goes?' The quip was out before she even realised what she was saying.

Something pulled sharply in his gaze, but Bridget couldn't even begin to read it. She was too horrified at herself.

'I'm sorry... I don't...'

'And here I was, under strict instructions from Mattie that that's exactly the sort of remark I'm not allowed to make.'

He was laughing at her, and she couldn't blame him. Still, she prickled uncomfortably.

'I apologise unreservedly, Hayden,' she began. 'That really isn't the—'

'Hayd,' he reminded her, and she faltered uncertainly.

'Seriously, no one really calls me Hayden except my father, and the general if he isn't happy with me. Although I admit that doesn't happen often.'

Out of all the questions and responses swirling around her head, it was inconceivable that the one she came out with was, 'Isn't that a little arrogant?'

'No. Just factual.' He shrugged, but that smile still toyed with his lips.

A mouth that was more sinfully tempting than Bridget could ever have thought possible.

What was happening here?

'Are you always so…*factual*?'

'It depends on the subject, I suppose. But, yes, I try to be. I prefer that to people saying things they don't really mean.'

'I prefer that, too,' she said, before she realised she was even speaking.

'Yes. I think that's one of the reasons why my sister has taken to you so well.'

'Mattie has talked about me?' Surprise bounced through her. 'To you?'

His eyes skated over her face, leaving Bridget with the distinct impression that he was able to read altogether too much, just from her face. She tried to smooth out her features into whatever might pass for a passive or neutral expression. But that only seemed to elicit a ghost of a smile from his wickedly tempting mouth.

'She said you've been working for the charity for years. From Chad to South Sudan, in outreach clinics and major foreign aid hospitals alike.'

'I first met her after the earthquakes in Nepal,' Bridget heard herself say. 'I was a nurse for an NGO, and Mattie's army medical unit had come to help because of the sheer scale of the disaster.'

'Yeah, I remember her saying you were with the medical charity already on site. You and she dragged all the patients into the street when an aftershock ripped through the hospital building?'

'In a nutshell,' Bridget agreed, surprised he knew.

Even now, she could remember the moment with such clarity. The shock had rocked the buildings they'd been using as a temporary medical facility, some of the ceilings had fallen in with the intensity, and even the walls had shown signs of crumbling. If she closed her eyes, Bridget could still hear the shouts and screams in the streets.

She remembered looking for the patients she knew were the most severely injured, just as Mattie had taken charge, quickly and calmly instructing not just her army medics but *all* the staff. Determining that it was no longer safe to treat them indoors and designating the order that the patients needed to be stretchered outside, even as she sent a recce team to find a safe location and begin to set up large tents and temporary beds.

At that moment she'd seen Mattie as a mentor. A woman who might only be a few years older than she herself was but who was years ahead in terms of her career. A woman whose unique attitude had allowed her to easily adapt from being commanding officer to empathetic doctor—exactly the kind of doctor that Bridget had once hoped that she herself might have become, if things had been different.

If only her father's suicide following his arrest hadn't left her already fragile-minded mother a wreck, needing to be taken care of, leaving Bridget no room for studies or a career. Not that anything she'd done had ever been good enough for her mother.

Not until her mother had finally met a new man to fill that obvious void in her life and make her feel complete. And then Bridget had finally been able to start making a life for herself. First as a nurse and then as a volunteer for foreign aid charities in the hope that one day one would sponsor her to finally realise her dream and become a doctor.

If only her life had been different.

But it hadn't been. Bridget steeled herself as she had so many other times when her mind had threatened to take a little detour down this particular memory lane. What was the point thinking about something she could never change?

'So now I'm going to be working with another Brigham sibling.' She managed a laugh, trying to divert her mind. 'You're a major in the Royal Engineers?'

CHAPTER TWO

'I AM.' HE GRINNED, and she had to steel her legs from going as jelly-like as the shot she'd had when she'd walked into the club.

It was surely *that* which was making her feel so...*odd*.

'How does that work?'

'Your charity is working in a camp, providing medical aid, yes?'

'Camp Jukrem,' she confirmed. 'The country has been through decades of civil war, and now it's over they need to get back on their feet. We're there to help them with medical aid, water, sanitation, supplies. But the peace is new. Fragile.'

'Which is exactly why the new government decided to rent a some of its land to the British Army as a training ground, about a thousand square miles of it.'

'That's quite significant.' Bridget emitted a low whistle, which was easily absorbed in the noise of the club.

'Yeah, it's a twenty-five-year agreement that gives the new country's fledgling government money to start the rebuilding process. In addition, our presence should help to deter any unrest, and as part of our use of the land we'll be putting in infrastructure for them. Roads, bridges, buildings.'

'So you chose to come to Jukrem?'

'Actually, I understand your charity has camps all over the region, but they set up Jukrem once they knew we were starting from that point. They asked us to work in conjunction with them.'

'I hadn't realised that,' Bridget admitted, 'but it makes sense. Jukrem is the furthest south we've ever gone—usually the area gets hit by the rains, and roads and airstrips get washed out. If the British Army is there, putting in bridges, we'll be able to reach refugees who might never get to any of our camps further north.'

'So what was the last project you worked on?' he asked.

'The last one was a TB facility. Part of it was for treating *normal* tuberculosis, for want of a better term, but the other side had a village for patients suffering from a drug-resistant strain of TB.'

He drew his eyebrows together, and she had to clench her fingers to resist the urge to reach out and smooth his forehead.

'I thought TB could be cured with antibiotics. How does a strain become drug-resistant?'

'Do you really want to know, or are you trying to be polite?' She pulled a wry face, only too conscious of the fact that he'd touched on a topic that bubbled inside her. 'Only we're meant to be here to celebrate Mattie's promotion.'

Despite all her usual social awkwardness, her job was a subject about which she could chat to anyone, any time. It was more than just a job, it was a passion, and she loved being out there, helping people who wouldn't have had anything otherwise.

'Is it something we're likely to encounter where we're going?' he asked, and she liked it that he seemed to have actually taken a moment to think about his answer.

'It is,' she confirmed. 'The fact is that TB thrives in communities that live very close together, and where their immune systems are already weakened. We're heading into an area where there are refugees and displaced persons with no homes, no access to fresh water, and who will be malnourished. Their immune systems would already be in the toilet, if it weren't for the fact that the sanitation will be poor, too.'

He laughed. A deep throaty sound that made her feel insanely good about her attempt at humour. Like he found her fun, and amusing. Mostly people found her too serious back here in the UK. It was strange how she felt like a different person as soon as she stepped out of that plane in a foreign country, ready for her next medical mission. Freer, and more *herself* than she had ever felt back here.

'There you go, then. I'm genuinely interested.' Hayden stepped closer, making something surge inside her, even as she told herself it was just so they could hear each other better. 'I've spent almost half my life as an officer in the army, I've completed multiple tours in war zones, and I've been part of hearts and minds missions before. But this is the first time I've ever been part of one quite like this. I'm curious to know what to expect and I think you're the perfect person to tell me.'

'I don't want to bore you,' Bridget said.

It was the truth, but without the inconvenient fact that a part of her wished she was the kind of sexy, confident woman who could hold a guy's attention without having to resort to conversations about what, halfway around the world, they called sputum positives.

'Besides...' he grinned, as if reading her mind '...I can't say I'm much of a club-goer. I wouldn't even be here if this wasn't about the only time all our group had downtime at the same time. At least teach me something to make my night feel less wasted.'

He was teasing her. She knew it, and his words rolled through her, making heat bloom wherever they went. Making her feel *interesting*.

'Okay,' she began, unable to help herself. 'You want to know about drug-resistant TB, or XDR TB, as we call it. So buckle up.'

'Consider me warned.' His eyes glittered with amusement, though Bridget didn't realise she'd been staring into the deep blue pools until she ran out of breath and realised she'd forgotten to keep breathing.

'We've been running TB clinics out in places like Jukrem camp for years. The main problem we face is that treating TB usually takes about six months in normal conditions, and necessitates oral drugs and daily injections.' She pulled a wry face. '*Painful* injections. You have no idea how long I spent on my first mission, thinking that the local people were particularly susceptible to hip or leg bone problems, only to discover they were in pain from the injections they had to have in their bottoms.'

'Ah.' Hayden winced in empathy, and she liked it that he seemed to get it.

'They're confined to small wards or mud huts, and can't really mix with others. Often they've been separated from family. All too frequently, they leave before their treatment course is complete.'

'I'm beginning to see where you're going.' He raised his eyebrows. 'If they leave before they should then they won't be fully cured, but their body will have been exposed to the drugs and begun to build up resistance.'

It had to be the least sexy conversation in the club, and yet she could have kissed him for making her feel so engaging.

She ignored the voice in her head telling her that she could have kissed him for a very different reason, too.

'Right,' she continued, dragging her mind back to the infinitely less sexy conversation. 'So, we end up with a patient who comes back to us later, having developed XDR TB. As it is, we often get an all-clear patient returning home, only to be reinfected by a family member who hadn't yet been treated, or even screened, for TB. But the worst thing about XDR TB is that it can be spread the same way. So suddenly we get swathes of villages or cities that *all* have the drug-resistant strain, and there's very little we can do about it.'

'You're passionate about this, aren't you?' Hayden said suddenly, making her blink as she met his gaze.

'It sounds silly, doesn't it?' she noted, her voice flat even to her own ears.

'It doesn't sound remotely silly. It sounds like you care about other people and about trying to do what's best for them. And it sounds like you love your career, which is something I, of all people, can truly understand.'

Bridget didn't answer, she could only jerk her head awkwardly up and down, entranced by the quiet intensity in his eyes. As though they were forging some kind of bond. Here. In the middle of a nightclub.

And it was suddenly inexplicably important to her that Hayden see her not as a socially awkward wallflower but as the confident, competent woman he would be working with over the next few months.

Is that all it is?

She stamped the needling voice out quickly, scrabbling around for something to divert her and falling back on the safety of their previous conversation.

'It's hard sometimes,' she heard herself admitting. 'Especially when it's a husband and wife where the wife is afraid to sleep away from her husband, but they need to because one of them is entering an intensive phase of their treatment. And they may only live in a one-room hut or shed.'

'So what do you do?'

'Talk to them. Try to explain.' She lifted her shoulders slightly. 'But sometimes the best thing you can do is just find a hospital room where they can be at opposite ends but see each other. And where there are plenty of windows in between.'

'It's a fine balance.' He smiled gently, and it tugged at her. Hard.

Again she floundered for some kind of response.

'It is,' she managed, before fading out awkwardly.

This time, she knew, the conversation had reached its natural conclusion.

Bridget braced herself, mentally preparing for him to turn away and strike up a conversation with someone less...*serious.* More alluring.

'So you're Bridget,' he continued smoothly, not moving away even a fraction, she noted. 'But you prefer Bea?'

'Actually, I don't really,' she heard herself admit out of nowhere.

Hayden frowned.

'I thought that's what my sister calls you?'

'It is.' Bridget pulled a wry face, not really understanding what had come over her. 'I've never really liked being called Bea, but... I never told her.'

'I see,' he noted, and she wondered what it was that he was filing away for later. 'What about Birdie?'

It walloped her out of the blue. For a moment she wasn't sure her lungs would even kick back into gear.

'Birdie,' she whispered, too softly for him to hear over the music.

'No? Just Bridget, then?'

It was odd, this wistful sensation that suddenly wound around her.

'Birdie's what I used to be called as a kid.'

By her father before...everything. She'd loved that name, but then he'd tainted it somehow.

'Right.'

She was dimly aware that Hayden was watching her, but she couldn't quite bring herself to focus.

'You used to like it? Or dislike it?'

'I loved it,' she admitted, ignoring the fact that no one had called her that since the day her father had taken his own life.

And the fact that she'd never wanted them to.

'Birdie it is, then.' Hayden's voice unfurled through her, low, edgy and hot.

And then he flashed her a smile that was surely so maddeningly dazzling that it could have caused a major power outage in any city. Every caution in her head evaporated in a puff of smoke.

Birdie—she liked the way it rolled off Hayden's tongue.

Snapping her eyes to his, she tilted her chin up, feeling a long-lost surge of confidence. It reminded her of the way she'd used to be—once, long ago. Spirited and happy, bold and fun-loving. The way she only ever felt these days when she was thousands of miles away from the place she called home. Yet this relative stranger—the playboy brother of her friend and mentor—was making her feel that same boldness right now.

More than that, he was making her feel alive in a way she wasn't sure she'd ever felt before. Making her body feel as though it was waking up from a slumber she hadn't known she was in.

How was that even possible?

If she didn't get a handle on these unchecked, uncharacteristic emotions, she was going to make a fool of herself with this man before she'd even got out to Jukrem camp. And then how would they be able to work well together?

What the hell was he playing at?

Flirting with Bridget Gardiner was a distinctly bad idea, and not just because his sister would rip him a new one.

He knew a bit about Bridget from Mattie and, from everything his sister had told him, he'd been expecting her friend to be a sweet, shy, pretty in an unobtrusive girl-next-door kind of way. Someone who was unequivocally too innocent and saintly for the likes of him, which was good as he was rather more partial to a bit more of a sinner.

Yet what had smacked him across the face the moment he'd been introduced to Bridget had been that there was nothing *saintly* about her at all. Nothing *unobtrusive* and nothing low-key. Rather, Bridget Gardiner looked very much like she was a sex symbol stepping right out of the nineteen-fifties or -sixties.

And his body had ached on sight.

A figure-hugging dress moulded itself around her, as though she'd had to be poured into it, encasing generous breasts that made his palms long to cup them, a tapered waist that made his fingers itch to span it, and slinky hips that made his entire body hunger to press up against them.

It was all so ridiculously…*adolescent* of him.

He was never this out of control. He tried concentrating on her face, but that didn't help at all. His mouth felt parched even as his eyes drank her in like she was the longest, coolest drink he'd ever had. He didn't know if it was her large, dark eyes with their slightly startled expression, the pretty oval face framed by the mass of thick, glossy black hair, or the sultry pout that Hayden didn't think she was even aware of. And as for that tiny but deliciously naughty gap between her front teeth…he wanted to lower his mouth to hers right now and taste it.

Forcing himself to take a step back, Hayden folded his arms over his chest as if it could help him resist this unexpected pull that this woman had over him. This couldn't happen. It was wrong.

He was about to spend three months working alongside her in the middle of nowhere, thousands of miles from anywhere. And the fact that she was clearly so damned passionate about her work only appealed to him all the more. Yet having a fling with her would be worse than simply a *bad* idea, it would be a downright *catastrophic* idea.

As much as he had a reputation—not entirely fair since he wasn't anywhere as indiscriminate as he knew rumour painted him, although he would freely admit that he was no monk—he had a strict rule about not mixing professional with personal.

Only right now, at this instant, his head was wrecked and his body was in the process of ripping up the rule book and hurling it out of the window. If he didn't retake the reins on what little self-control he had remaining, he feared he was going to lose his grip completely. And then...well, he'd have three months in the middle of nowhere with a woman who would want more from him and be hurt and upset that he couldn't give that to her.

Not to mention a sister who would rip seven shades out of him for devasting her friend.

It might not seem like it now, faced with all the temptations of that luscious body, but it really wasn't worth the hassle.

'Your champagne, sir?'

Hayden blinked as the bartender approached them, several bottles in a couple of buckets of ice, along with enough flutes to go around. It took him a moment to recall that he'd ordered them earlier because they were all here to celebrate his sister's promotion. A fact he appeared to have forgotten in the event of meeting Bridget, despite her mentioning it earlier.

He didn't care to analyse why it was that he both welcomed and resented the intrusion at the same time.

'Do you always drink champagne in nightclubs?'

'Not exactly,' he told her, taking the magnums and setting them down. 'We don't usually do either. But tonight we're celebrating something big for Mattie. And sometimes it's good to cut loose, especially after a hard tour. Or before one. Plus, it's not often we're all in the same place like this, but with the RAF base down the road and all of us here at the same time, even if we are flying out to different locations, it seemed like the perfect time.'

Bridget didn't answer, and Hayden turned back to see her staring at the bottles with an expression he could only describe as agonised.

'Birdie?'

She didn't react, and before he could stop himself he reached out to gently take her chin in his fingers and tilt her head up to him.

He pretended he didn't feel the sparks that arced between them.

She startled, freezing for a moment before wrenching her head away, muttering as she did so, 'It's nothing.'

It was a patent lie and he shouldn't want so badly to call her out on it. What did it matter to him if she told him the truth or not?

'Excuse me, please.' He turned away to stop himself from pressing Bridget any further when she clearly didn't want to talk and picked up a bottle before deftly popping the cork.

'How did you do that?' she asked suddenly, touching her hand to the inside of his wrist until he opened his hand and she picked up the cork. 'I had visions of it flying across the room.'

He told himself that his pulse wasn't leaping at the contact. That it wasn't the reason why he'd forgotten to pour the champagne into the first flute and it was now effervescing over the top.

Hastily, he remedied the situation and set the bottle down where one of his and Mattie's mutual friends picked it up, telling him they'd pour if he opened. But his attention was on Bridget, whether he liked it or not.

'The trick's in the wrist,' he told her, taking the second bottle. 'You take the bottle in one hand and hold the cork with the other, like this. Now hold the cork steady and twist the bottle.'

It made a distinct pop as it opened, and this time Hayden reached for a flute to pour out the first bit before setting it on the table as before. He took the last bottle and held it out to her.

'You try.'

She eyed it for a moment, her body language revealing how tempted she was. But instead she shook her head.

'I might drop it.'

'It's all a matter of confidence.' He smiled.

She hesitated, but ultimately shook her head again.

'Want me to show you?' He knew it was a bad idea, but the words tumbled out all the same.

She slid him a curious look.

'How?'

Hayden didn't give himself chance to rethink the wisdom of what he knew was damn fool idea when he reached out and placed his hands on Bridget's hips, spinning her round as he stepped behind her and circled his arms around her to bring the champagne bottle to her front.

'Are you left- or right-handed?'

She didn't answer at first, her body tense, like something was coiled inside her, ready to run.'

'It's just opening a champagne bottle, Birdie,' he murmured.

Only…it wasn't *just* that, was it? He was lying to himself if he thought it was. He was complicating an already problematic situation. In a matter of days they would be working together and it was like he didn't even care. All he could think about was the heat of her back against his chest, the feel of her trembling slightly in his arms, and the faint vanilla scent pervading his nostrils.

'Now, hold the bottle here…' he lifted her hand, covering it with his own '…and put the other hand on the cork. Good, okay. Hold the cork in place without moving that hand and slowly turn the bottle with the other.'

In one easy movement the cork popped.

'Well done,' Hayden told her, stepping away as he reached for a flute.

But the damage was done. He was more intrigued than ever—or at least his body was. He wanted her. So badly that he could feel need advancing through him like an infantry unit on a forced march. If this is where he was after a few minutes on a night out with Bridget, how would it be after a few hours? With dancing? And the added headache of alcohol?

It all made for a distinctly potent cocktail. That meant the wisest course of action would be to abstain. He would stay long enough to toast Mattie, and then, when she went to buy a round of drinks as per tradition, he would make his excuses and leave.

It was the right thing to do. The responsible thing.

Before he was tempted to do anything he would regret with the delectable Bridget.

CHAPTER THREE

BRIDGET WAS STILL shaking as Hayden stepped away and prepared to toast his sister.

Never, in her entire life, had anyone affected her this much. This badly. He'd been so careful not to actually let their bodies make contact and yet she'd felt him everywhere. *Everywhere.*

It had started with a delicious tingling at her hairline, whether from his breath on her skin or just the simple fact that he'd been so close she had no idea. Then, as he'd closed his arms around her, a wave of tiny goosebumps had swept over her entire body. Her breasts had felt a sudden heaviness, her nipples pulling tighter than she'd ever known. But it had been the ache inside her that had scared her the most. Pulsing right through her body. Pooling right *there.*

The softest, hottest part of her. Where she longed for Hayden—this virtual stranger—to touch her. And it terrified her. She had never, *never,* craved something so much.

It had taken all she had not to edge back into Hayden's arms and press her body up against his. To find out if he wanted her anywhere near as much as her body seemed to be screaming out for him.

Like it knew things that her inexperienced brain didn't understand. All she did know for sure was that she needed to stay far, far away from this dark, greedy thing that was winding its way up inside her.

She needed to stay away from Hayden.

Taking a proffered champagne flute, she backed away until she was on the other side of the gathering, all the while acutely conscious that his eyes were on her. Tracking her.

And then he moved his gaze to the group, that dazzling smile back on his face, leaving her feel oddly bereft.

'My little sister, Major Mathilda Brigham, soon to be Lieutenant-Colonel Mathilda Brigham.' Hayden raised his glass at last, ensuring his voice could be heard over the deep pulse of the nightclub bass line. 'To Mattie.'

'To Mattie,' the handful of friends echoed.

As the group began to split, Bridget watched Hayden chatting proudly to his sister, unable to drag her gaze from his profile. What was it about him that captivated her most? she wondered. Was it as simple as the stark beauty of his physique, or was it more the way he held himself, or the ease of his body language? She couldn't work it out.

She was still staring when a shadow fell across her vision moments before one of the other guys in the group stepped in front of her. Effectively blocking off her self-indulgent ogling.

'Bridget, isn't it?'

It took her a moment to pull herself together.

'Yes.' She even managed a smile. The one she'd perfected over the past decade—the one that convinced people she was fine.

'I'm Ellis.'

'Hi.' She shook his outstretched hand. 'You're army too? Like Mattie?'

And Hayden. But for some reason she didn't add that bit.

'Yeah. I've done a couple of tours with Mattie over the years. You're a civilian doctor?'

'Nurse,' Bridget corrected, softening it with another smile.

Another mask to hide her regret at not being able to go to university to study medicine. Oh, she'd got the grades, but when she'd told her mother about her plans to move away from home, another breakdown had ensued, and Bridget had never broached the topic again.

'Oh.' The guy seemed surprised. 'Sorry, I'd just assumed... Anyway, Mattie holds you in high regard.'

This time, at least, the smile was more genuine.

'The feeling is mutual.'

'Yeah, Mattie's cool.' He grinned. 'But enough about our mutual friend. Can I interest you in a dance?'

'You want to dance?' It was too late to bite the words back. 'With me?'

First Hayden, now this guy. It had to be the dress. *Mattie's* dress. It wasn't *her*.

'I rather thought it might be a good plan, especially as we're in a nightclub. I don't know about you but us lot don't get that much chance for a night out like this.'

'No, Hayden was saying that earlier.' She bit her lip, wondering if lust was etched into every line on her face.

'You and Hayd have something...going on?'

'No.' She shook her head quickly. Maybe too quickly.

Bridget fought to smooth her face and offer a nonchalant shrug.

'I'm with the charity working near where his army unit will be working.'

'Operation Ironplate?'

'I guess.' As though she wasn't burning to learn anything new about Hayd. 'Like I said, I'm with the charity.'

Could the guy—Ellis—hear her heart hammering in her chest? She felt as though it was about to pound its way out, but he didn't seem to notice, so maybe she was okay.

'So you're not army barmy like us lot, then?' He

laughed. 'Well, I can tell you that Hayd is a great soldier and CO. You and your team are in good hands.'

'Right.' She nodded, forcing out the closest thing she could manage to a laugh.

'It's good to see Hayd back on operations.'

'He's been out?' Bridget's ears pricked up.

'Only recently. We've all done several back-to-back tours over the years and we're lucky we all got through them pretty much untouched—physically anyway. But Hayd was on a parachute jump about six months ago when some kid on his first jump passed out.'

Bridget sucked in a breath, not sure where Ellis's story was going.

'Oh, it's okay. Hayd had to cut his own parachute to dive and catch the kid in mid-air—not as common or as easy as the movies might lead you to believe—and he only had enough time to pull his emergency chute before the hit the ground, but he saved the kid.'

'Right…well, that's good,' she managed to choke out, telling herself that it was the drama of the story that had a wave of nausea sloshing around inside her. Nothing more.

'No, he's not likely to tell you either. But I've entrusted him with my life more times than I care to remember.'

Bridget nodded. And smiled again. Even though her teeth were gritted and her head felt as if it was jerking up and down. Knowing Hayden was such a true hero didn't really help her remember she was supposed to be staying away from him.

'So, how about that dance?'

She tensed instantly but tried to look as apologetic as she could.

'I…sorry… I don't actually…dance.'

'You look like you should,' Ellis tried again, but being encouraging rather than pushy. 'A couple of the others are out there on the floor, it doesn't have to be just the two of us.'

She relaxed a little and shook her head.

'Sorry.'

'Fine.' He looked disappointed but didn't push it as he headed for the dance floor, pausing to shoot her a final, open invitation. 'If you change your mind, you know where we are.'

Then he headed for the others, leaving Bridget wishing she'd had the courage to join him after all. And then Mattie was heading over, and Bridget relaxed even more.

'You okay, Bea?' her friend asked, before adding something else she didn't hear over the music.

'Sorry?'

Mattie leaned closer.

'I asked if Hayd has been looking after you?'

Heat rushed her again, making her cheeks feel hot.

'Yes,' Bridget managed. 'But you didn't really have to ask your brother to babysit me.'

'I *did* have to.' Mattie pulled an apologetic face. 'We were supposed to be working together at Jukrem camp— until I got called away for this new mission. I was really hoping to be able to show you the ropes out there.'

'It doesn't matter. I need to learn to be bolder anyway.' She forced a smile. 'Stronger.'

Like finally shedding the ties of her past and beginning to live the life she wanted to. Which probably included accepting an invitation to dance from a nice guy like Ellis and resisting this mad attraction to Mattie's brother.

'You're stronger than you realise, Bea,' Mattie suddenly said. 'You know what they say, fake it until you make it.'

'Yeah, well, I don't know how to fake it.'

'Sure you do.' Mattie laughed. 'Pretend you're that bush-veld lizard you told me about. The one that pretends it's a boogie-oogie beetle, or something like that, to frighten away prey.'

'*Oogpister beetle*,' Bea corrected automatically, but she still laughed back just as she guessed her friend had intended her to do. 'I don't know what I'm more impressed with—your analogy or the fact you even remembered my story.'

'Both.' Mattie grinned. 'But either way my brother will be there for any advice and support. Don't be afraid to use him.'

It certainly wasn't what Mattie had intended, but suddenly a thousand X-rated images of exactly what it might be like to *use* Hayden Brigham flooded Bridget's head.

And her body.

She flushed deeply and tried to shake her brain clear.

'Well, thanks.' The images were still there. In gloriously vivid colour. 'Anyway, enough about me, can I get you a drink to say congratulations?'

'Actually, it's traditional for me to buy you guys the drink since it's my promotion.' Mattie laughed, standing up and leaning over the table to address the members of the group who were left. 'Same again?'

And then she headed off, leaving Bridget to talk to the group and wish that she wasn't so very aware of where Hayden was, or what he was doing.

Or wondering whether maybe, just for once in her life, she might not do the sensible thing...but instead do the last thing in the world she should do.

And let her very first time with a man be with someone who would know exactly how to make her body come alive.

'Who's the guy? And why are you glaring daggers at him?'

He'd been avoiding her for the last couple of hours, but Bridget's voice cut unexpectedly across his thoughts.

Hayden, moments from making his escape—having congratulated himself on thinking with his head and not other, less cerebral parts of his anatomy—turned quickly, arching his eyebrows at her.

He may have been avoiding her but that didn't mean he hadn't found himself sliding into group conversations when she was talking to others. Getting to know her whilst pretending he was keeping his distance.

He kept expecting this inconvenient and unexpected attraction to fizzle as he learned more about her. Telling himself that it was just the fact that she was a stranger— and a rather enigmatic one at that—that was causing him to react in such an uncharacteristic way.

Yet far from losing interest as the night had worn on, the more Hayden had seen and heard, the more attracted to her he'd become. Until in the end he'd had to tear himself away, telling himself it was time to head home.

But he hadn't gone, had he? He'd lingered around the booth where she'd come to join him, to talk to him. The music was louder now, and she was so damned close, and even though he knew it was the only way they could hear each other, he revelled in it all the same.

'So, do you know who he is?' Bridget reiterated, once it became clear that he'd forgotten to answer her.

Hayden tried to refocus his brain.

'His name is Kane. And I wasn't *glaring daggers* at him, as you so eloquently put it.'

'Well, I overheard you talking earlier. Mattie asked if you thought it was a bad idea for her to talk to this Kane guy, and you asked her if she needed you to tell her that,' Bridget observed softly. 'And now you don't look happy that your sister is still talking to him.'

He had to concede her point.

'Kane and Mattie knew each other a long time ago,

when they were kids. They got together when she was sixteen, maybe seventeen,' he calculated. 'He hurt her.'

'That must have been about fourteen years ago.' Bridget whipped her head around to look at them. 'They look so... *involved* now.'

'Tell me about it,' Hayden grunted. 'Like the intervening years barely happened, and they're as close as they were back then.'

'Are they?'

'Are they what?' he asked through gritted teeth. 'Involved? I don't know but if they are then it's Mattie's life. Her choice.'

'But you don't like it?'

'Honestly... I don't know. She was devastated when Kane left her, and she's my kid sister. Part of me stills feel like I should look out for her. But she's also a grown woman, an army officer and doctor. She doesn't need me pulling big-brother rank on her.'

Bridget nodded, eyeing the pair of them again.

'I think it's kind of nice that you care, though.' She sounded almost wistful. 'I don't even have a brother.'

And, though he couldn't put his finger on it, Hayden couldn't help feeling that her casual comment revealed more than she'd intended it to. Even before she shook her head and pasted an overly bright smile onto her lips.

'Where were you going anyway?'

She was deflecting, and he couldn't have said why that caused something to scrape at him. To make him wish he knew what she was really thinking.

He pushed it aside.

'Actually, I was leaving.'

'Already?'

Something he fancied to be disappointment flashed in her eyes for a split second. Then it was gone, leaving him wondering it had been real or if he'd simply imagined it.

'We're leaving on operations in a couple of days. I might as well prep for it.'

'Tonight? No wonder you're such a good officer.'

Was she…flirting with him? If so, she was either doing it against her better judgement or she was simply not very good at it. Either way, he should take it as his cue to leave.

It was that or risk breaking every promise Mattie had elicited from him when she'd asked him to look after Bridget in her absence. Not that he was certain she needed, or even wanted, protecting, especially after she'd just handled Ellis's advances just fine.

Not that he'd been watching them, of course.

Not that he'd been *willing* her to turn the guy down.

'Yeah, tonight,' he confirmed. More for his benefit than for hers. 'The toasts have been done, everyone is breaking off into their own groups, it seems like a good time to leave.'

She frowned and Hayden realised he wanted, very much, to reach out and smooth her forehead flat again. With his mouth.

He forced himself to take a step back. Imperceptible to her, but hugely significant in his own head. Instead, she closed the gap, placing her hand on his forearm, making him *feel* her, all over.

'Take me with you.'

His chest pulled. Tightened. As did other parts of his anatomy.

'Say again?' he demanded, his voice somewhat gruff even to his own ears.

And then she flushed becomingly.

'I just… I just meant that… I only came to celebrate Mattie's promotion.' The words tumbled out.

'You mean my sister bullied you into it?'

'I wouldn't say *bullied*.' She frowned again.

Hayden pulled his mouth into a thin line, as if that could temper these odd urges.

'The point is,' she continued, a little firmer this time, 'I came for Mattie, and now she seems…otherwise occupied. I don't really know anyone else.'

'Ellis seems to want to remedy that,' he managed evenly, although he felt anything but.

What was the matter with him? He sounded like a young boy in a school yard.

'No.' Bridget shook her head, blushing as prettily as ever. 'I think he's just being polite.'

She couldn't be serious.

'It's about more than just being polite, Birdie.' Her eyes met his then slid away. 'You must know that.'

The scarlet stain was creeping its way down her neck now. And lower. Hayden couldn't help wondering how far below that sexy neckline it extended, and he couldn't stop wishing he could find out.

'You really don't have any idea how attractive you are, do you?' he realised with surprise, as she startled, tried to shoot him a defiant glare, and then shrugged with embarrassment. 'Even without this.'

As if he couldn't help himself, he lifted his hand, making a small circling gesture, unsure whether he meant her screen siren body or the dress currently showcasing it so perfectly.

She took a step back, as if searching for the wall to lend her some support, taking refuge in the corner where the dark wall met the edge of the booths. Protected from the sight of the rest of group. Even most of the club.

But her eyes were on him and he was pretty sure she was flirting with him. Badly, but still. Just as he knew that she was as caught up as he was in this…*thing* between them. Somehow he made himself stay still and not step towards her. But that didn't mean he wasn't intrigued.

Sure, Mattie had asked him to look out for her friend because, in her words, Bridget was 'unworldly'. But he was beginning to suspect it was more than that.

He knew she was younger than Mattie by about five or six years, which would probably make her around twenty-six, maybe twenty-seven. So was it more that Bridget was inexperienced? If so, how much?

'You've had boyfriends before who've paid you compliments?' he mused, apparently idly.

'Hmm?' She pulled her eyebrows together and cocked her head, clearly not hearing him.

He took a step closer and tried not to feel like a bull being pulled around by its nose ring. Then he repeated the question.

And there was no disguising the way the blood was beginning to thunder through his veins in a way that made absolutely no sense at all.

'Of course.' She jutted her chin out but refused to meet his eyes. In his experience, that was a tell-tale indicator that she was lying.

But about having had boyfriends? Or about them having paid her compliments?

'If not actual boyfriends,' he amended, leaning in closer like she was drawing him down, 'then those who might want to be?'

'Boyfriends?' she asked, and he could hear the shake in her voice before she jerked her chin higher. 'Or those who might flatter a girl to get into her underwear?'

There was something about the snippy way that she said it that made Hayden take notice. As though she was trying to appear more sophisticated and knowledgeable than she really was.

As if...

But, no, that couldn't be right. Still, he turned to face

her fully, sliding his fingers to her chin and lifting it, just like he had before.

'And how many men have got into your underwear, Birdie?' He barely recognised his own voice. Or that primal, driving edginess slicing through him. 'A few? A couple? One?'

He could feel her breath, hot and fast on his hand. See the way her chest was moving quickly, shuddery. Hayden couldn't help it, he wanted to stop himself, but he couldn't, she was too damn intoxicating. He dipped his head until his mouth was brushing her ear.

'None?'

She licked her lips, and it was all he could do not to catch it in his mouth.

'I don't really think that's any of your business,' she managed. 'Do you?'

And then, before he could say anything more, she lifted her trembling hands to his chest and spread her palms over him as though she meant to push him.

Only she didn't.

It was ridiculous that the action should burst inside him like a detonation. Before he could stop himself, Hayden stepped closer, pinning her to the wall, no longer able to pretend that he could resist her when his entire body was roaring at him to claim her as his own.

Shooting out his arm, Hayden rested his entire forearm on the wall by her head, not missing a single detail from her parted lips, from her rapidly rising and falling chest to the heat pouring off her—and into him.

And then he stopped noticing anything more as he dipped his head and fused his mouth to hers. Plundering her heat and raking his tongue against hers—ruthless and demanding—the way he'd wanted to do all night.

Something carnal and dark tore through him, and it was all he could do to keep it at bay. He'd never felt anything quite as *electric* as this before, and somewhere deep inside he knew that should have worried him a lot more than he was currently prepared to acknowledge.

And then Birdie surged against him, pressing her body to his as she angled her head to deepen their kiss, her hands reaching up very tentatively to cup his jaw, and he stopped thinking at all…he merely *experienced.*

He claimed her mouth over and over, learning its feel, its shape, its taste, sending him spiralling, half-delirious. And the fact that it was from a mere kiss only seemed to make it that much more insane.

His breath scythed between them, his body pushing him closer to edge than he could ever have imagined, and then Bridget raised her hands to loop them around his neck and pull him down to her with the most beautifully greedy sound he thought he'd ever heard, her body pressed against his.

Need shot through him. Lifting his hands, Hayden threaded them through the glossy, thick curtain of her hair. Subtle notes of coconut danced in his nostrils as he moved it, making him think of tropical beaches and hot sun, and Bridget's body naked beneath his.

He let himself explore some more. His hands moved down the long line of her spine, his mouth down the elegant line of her neck. Everything about this woman wound through him, making him hunger for more.

His hands learned the contours of her body, her backside, and then lower, abruptly coming into contact with the smooth, velvety skin of the back of her thigh.

White lights burst in his head. Her bare skin was so soft, and so damned hot. He should stop, he *ought* to stop, but when his fingers brushed her skin and she arched her body against his, he found he was lost.

Her mouth was still open under his, still inviting him in, still learning how to scrape her tongue against his as though dancing a sensual tango of their own. He pressed his body against hers even harder, needing to feel her heat against the hardest part of him.

Then, fanning his fingers out, he allowed them to slip slightly under the hem of her shimmering dress to that delicious crease where her legs met her peachy derrière. The greedy little sound she made was almost his undoing.

Hayden had never ached so badly in his life. He hadn't known it was possible to. He'd never felt as though he'd self-combust if he didn't get a taste of her, there and then. Yet with Bridget that was exactly how he felt. Before he knew what he was doing his hands spanned her thighs, his thumbs just creeping under the dress, the front of which—already short—had ridden up dangerously high, and stroked between her legs. Just once. But brushing right *there*, against a whisper of lace where she was searing hot, and so sinfully, perfectly wet for him.

Her moan rolled right through his body, and Hayden wasn't entirely sure how he didn't embarrass himself on the spot.

'You asked me how many men…before,' she managed, on a choppy little breath.

'Say again?' he muttered, his brain so fogged up he could barely think straight with wanting her.

'What if it was none?' she managed huskily, only the fact that his head was so close to hers allowing him to hear. 'Would that make a difference?'

Dear lord, she was a virgin, and she was offering herself up to him to be her first. He needed to walk away, but his legs refused to move.

He might have a reputation, but despoiler of virgins wasn't part of it. He preferred experienced partners who could enjoy a sexual encounter every bit as much as he did. Who knew what they wanted, and what they were prepared to give back—and said so.

Virgins had never been his thing. In fact, he'd always steered well clear of them in the past.

But this was different. *Bridget* was different. A fact that should set off more alarm bells than it was currently ringing. What was it about her that stirred something so intensely primal and feral within him? That made the idea that she could have lost her virginity to any number of suitors over the years but she'd saved herself to give such a precious gift to him?

He should be walking away.

All of a sudden, the sounds of the nightclub crashed back over him and he blinked as he came back to himself.

How had he lost all sense of where they were? Of who she was? Not just kissing in a public place but what he'd been doing to her had been practically indecent. In his whole life he'd never lost control like this.

He ought to be ashamed.

Instead, all he wanted was to pin her back in that corner and bury himself so deep inside her that neither of them would know where one of them ended and the other began.

It was insane.

'Take a moment to sort your dress out,' he told her through his teeth, turning his back to ensure no one had seen them.

Relieved to realise that no one had.

'I can't believe…' Bridget's voice sounded shakily in his ear once she had readjusted her clothing. 'I don't make a habit—'

'Trust me, neither do I,' he grated back.

'I think… It isn't… Can we just forget it happened? Just leave?'

'I think that's the wisest course of action.' He nodded grimly.

Just as long as they weren't leaving together.

CHAPTER FOUR

'THIS IS TOMMY, nine years old. At approximately ten o'clock this morning Tommy began suffering an asthma attack. By the time we got there he was in respiratory arrest and the ventilating was deteriorating. There was vomit in the airway.'

Bridget listened to the heli-med doctor as he gave the MIST report—the Mechanism of Injury, the Illness pattern, the Signs or observations, and the Treatment given—to her team. It was her last case of this posting, before she was scheduled to fly out to her briefing for her new foreign aid mission in three days' time.

Less than a week from now she would be at Jukrem camp. And a few days after that Hayden and his regiment of Royal Engineers would be arriving.

Her pulse fluttered weakly, just as it had on each of the occasions she'd thought about him since that night at the club. And there had been far too many of those thoughts.

Cross with herself, she pulled her head back into the present as the A and E doctor running the case began to address them.

'Let's get him stable so that we can get a scan and check for fluid in the airways,' the doctor running the shout concluded, and they each began to do their part. Putting on the monitors and administering the anaesthetic and the medications to try to regulate his stats.

Hour after hour. Interspersing it with other patients whenever there was a long enough lull. And then it was over. Bridget's shift was done and it was time for her to go home. Or rather to the cramped rented flat that passed for home.

No more cases of asthma, or diabetes, or emphysema—a few of the many things that had constituted the bread and butter of her UK work. Instead, she had to get her mind back into malaria, TB, measles and, almost always underlying it all, malnutrition.

And then there was the added complication of Hayden.

No matter how hard she tried to block it out, memories of the other night flooded her head, flushing her cheeks with heat—and her body with something even more molten. She shook her head viciously, as if that could somehow dislodge the inconvenient attraction, but it didn't work.

Had she really expected it to?

She couldn't ignore what had happened any more than she was going to be able to avoid seeing Hayden. The only solution was going to be to find a way to deal with it.

Lost in her thoughts, she was halfway out of the hospital grounds before she realised she'd walked past her bus stop. She could turn back around but it had stopped raining, and a perverse part of her welcomed the walk. As if it could somehow help her to clear her head.

Hayden was five miles into his eight-mile run when he saw her heading up the pavement towards him. The shock of it almost winded him, far more than the punishing pace he'd meted out to himself had managed.

He supposed he could have run past her as her head was bowed so low that she wouldn't have even noticed him until he was in line with her. Plus, he'd expected to have longer to wrap his head around how carried away he'd been the other night at the club. And he'd expected it to be in an army camp in the middle of the desert.

Still, much as he hated to admit it, he'd wanted to see her. Why else would he have chosen a running route that passed so close to the hospital in which she worked?

He slowed down. Stopped.

'Hello, Birdie.'

Her head snapped up in undisguised shock.

It was strange how seeing her again was a lot harder than Hayden had anticipated.

'Hayden.'

'Hayd,' he corrected. As though it mattered.

'Hayd,' she repeated carefully, like she was rolling it around her tongue.

And just like that he was back to the randy schoolboy of the other night, his mind full of all the other ways she could roll him around her tongue.

What the hell was it about her?

'What are you doing here?' she managed, breaking the silence. Looking altogether too cute and vulnerable for his peace of mind.

'Running.' He tried to suppress the smile that toyed with his mouth, not liking the way she got under his skin so easily.

'Running. Right.' She waved her hands at his shorts and tee in self-deprecation, and he found he didn't like that either. The way she always seemed to put herself down. 'Sorry. Obvious.'

And then, suddenly, a mask of indifference settled over her delicate features, and he found he liked that least of all.

'What about you?'

'I'm heading home.' She shrugged. 'I just finished my shift.'

'No car?'

Another shrug.

'I had an odd shift. Parking is always a nightmare.'

'Right.'

It was so stilted. So damned awkward. Like nothing he'd ever experienced before, which made him wonder how the next few months were going to go. They might not be working together per se, but their paths would certainly cross.

'Maybe we should…have a conversation,' he began.

Bridget, however, looked as though that was the least appealing activity she could think of. She shook her head vigorously.

'I don't think we should.'

'We're about to head out into an unfamiliar environment where we're going to be working in close enough proximity for three months. It's going to be difficult enough as it is, but if we don't resolve whatever…*this* is between us, it's going to be hell.'

'I think you made your feelings pretty clear when I basically…offered myself up to you and…and you rejected me.' She stumbled over the words in her haste to get them out, leaving Hayden to unravel them in her wake.

'Wait. I didn't reject you.'

She bit her lip.

'Of course you did. And I can't say I blame you. But I really don't want to talk about this with you. Especially in the middle of the pavement on a busy main road.'

'So go home, I'll head back to my hotel room to shower and change, and I'll pick you up within the hour. Maybe we could go for a drink.' Except what had happened the last time he'd been out with this woman, drinking? 'No, not a drink. But perhaps…grab a bite to eat.'

'To what? Talk about it some more?' She looked horrified. 'In the middle of a restaurant while trying to eat. No, thanks. I've had enough humiliation for one year. Admittedly, I probably brought it on myself.'

What the hell was she talking about?

'You didn't bring anything on yourself,' he countered, wondering why he was so fascinated by her.

Why even here, even now, his body was beginning to surge back into awareness.

'We need to resolve this, Birdie,' he said softly. 'Before we get into an environment where your inability to be around me causes problems for other people.'

'You're turning this on me?' she demanded incredulously, and that little spit of fire he remembered from the other night seemed to spark back into life.

'That depends. I'm willing to work this out. Are you?'

Then, as if things couldn't have gone his way any better, her stomach growled. Loudly. Hayden grinned.

'See, you *are* hungry after all.'

She spluttered for a moment then glowered at him, but he didn't care. If anything, it gave him a bit of a kick low in his belly. Because at least it didn't mean that she was indifferent to him.

'Fine,' she huffed out at last. 'One hour.'

'I'll pick you up.'

'I'll meet you in town,' she countered. 'Where?'

He could argue the point, but did it really matter? At least she was meeting him.

'There's that Italian restaurant,' he suggested. 'Unless you have any objections.'

He refrained from goading her by adding *to that, too.* Still, she glared at him as though she could read it on his face.

'That's fine.' Her tone was clipped.

And then, before anything else was said, she turned away from him and stalked up the road, this time with her head held high in the air.

He watched her for far longer than he should have done, all the while telling himself there was no reason for his heart to beat so strongly, until finally he made himself turn and try to get his head back into his run.

And then he heard it. The roar of a large vehicle, the splash of water, and what was indisputably a shriek.

Spinning around, he saw a white van zooming past him. And Bridget, shouting furiously and soaked to the skin, next to a puddle the size of a small swimming pool. For half a moment he paused, waiting to see if the traffic lights ahead would turn red, ready to sprint down there and haul any one of the laughing men out of the van and show them exactly what happened to guys like them.

But the lights stayed mutinously on green, and the van sped off into the distance.

Turning back to Bridget and breaking into a run, he raced towards her and hauled her out of the way before any other vehicle could pile anything more on her obvious indignity.

'What did they do that for?' she cried, tears glistening in her eyes despite the water dripping from her hair. Her skin. Her clothes.

'Maybe they didn't see the puddle until it was too late.'

It wasn't true but he had no desire to upset her any further. He didn't want to examine that further, but then she lifted her head.

'Oh, they saw me,' she gritted out, the unexpected show of spirit drawing him in in spite of himself. 'They did it on purpose. Just for a laugh.'

'Be that as it may, the priority is to get you out of those clothes and dry. How far is your home?'

'Too far.' She shook her head, her voice quivering. A combination of anger and shock. 'The hospital is closer.'

But it was still a good mile back in the other direction. Hayden's mind spun, but there was nothing else for it.

'My hotel is closer. If we cut across the park, we can be back there within five minutes.'

'Your hotel?' She froze, blinking at him. 'Aren't you in barracks or whatever?'

'Usually,' he admitted. 'But every so often I like to get away from everyone else, and I fancied a few creature comforts.'

'That's exactly what I've heard Mattie say.'

'Not really a surprise, it was what our father used to do when he couldn't get home but couldn't face another night in the mess.'

'Right.' She nodded slowly, but her teeth were already beginning to chatter. 'Makes sense.'

Quickly he peeled her rucksack and wet coat off her, slinging the bag on his back and folding up the dripping material.

'Can you run? It'll keep up your core temperature and get us there quicker.'

'And what happens when we get there?'

She eyed him speculatively, and he tried not to point out that she was getting colder and colder the more she stayed immobile.

'If you're worried about being in the same room as me, I'll shower in the hotel's gym downstairs and you can have my bathroom. I wouldn't even enter the suite until you're happy, okay? I'll even get them to find you some dry clothes.'

He told himself he was being gentlemanly and ignored the growing suspicion that he simply didn't trust himself around this woman. Still, another moment passed before Bridget replied.

'No need. I have a change of clothes in my rucksack. They're in a dry bag so they should be fine.'

'Good.' He exhaled slightly. 'So if you're all objectioned

out, maybe we could get going before you start making yourself ill?'

With a terse nod Bridget began moving. A little stiffly at first, but soon her legs seemed to loosen up and they were jogging across the wet grass. By the time they'd ducked around the railings and crossed the far road to his hotel, she seemed to have calmed down slightly, and he even heard her call out a cheerful greeting to a couple of elderly guests, who looked startled at her sodden appearance, suppressing her gurgle of laughter until they were in the lift.

And then she sobered again as they reached the door to his suite and he swiped the key card into the reader.

'I thought you weren't coming in?' she commented tensely, as he followed her inside.

Hayden held his hands up.

'Just getting a change of clothes then I'll be out of your way.' He efficiently opened the wardrobe and drawers to select fresh gear, before heading straight back to the door. 'Okay, I'm out of your hair. Take as long as you need.'

Closing the door behind him, he stood in the corridor and wondered what it was *exactly* that he thought he was doing.

Because far from clearing things up, as he told himself he had intended, it seemed to Hayden that all he'd succeeded in doing was making an awkward situation all the more complicated.

CHAPTER FIVE

BRIDGET WATCHED THE hotel-room door close behind Hayden and then stood staring at the white panelling for an inordinately long time, trying to work out what it was that wallowed clumsily within her chest.

Why there was a part of her that seemed to be silently willing him to come back into the room. The *bed*room. And revisit with her everything they'd started in that nightclub.

Before he'd done the one thing that any true playboy surely shouldn't do...and listened to his conscience.

Which, if she was honest, didn't do much to reanimate her already moribund ego. It only fed into the fears that already lurked in her mind that she wasn't the kind of woman who was pretty enough, hot enough, sexy enough to appeal to a man like Hayden.

In short, she wasn't *good* enough.

Much as she'd stopped being *good enough* the night her father had been arrested. Overnight she'd gone from being a popular kid, an *it* kid, to being a pariah. No one had wanted to be seen even talking to her, let alone the girls wanting to hang out with her. And boys wouldn't have been caught dead dating her—although many of them had suggested quick sex in the back of a car, or an abandoned barn, or anywhere else they wouldn't be *seen* with her.

And she was proud that she'd never been so desperate that she'd allowed herself to fall for it.

Instead, she'd become an outcast, spending her teenage years living in the shadow of her father's disgrace and taking care of her ever more fragile mother, and her self-worth had never quite recovered. Holding onto her virginity had become less of a matter of pride and more a matter of embarrassment. How to explain to a potential lover that she was still a virgin in her twenties when everyone she knew had long since—willingly—lost that title.

Was that why she'd found herself so attracted to the idea of finally losing that burden with Hayden? A halfway playboy who would know what he was doing. A man who'd had enough partners that he wouldn't remember her and her inexperience.

Or was the truth that she hadn't been thinking at all when he'd kissed her the other night in the nightclub? Making her feel giddy and light-headed. All her senses spinning so hard that she hadn't even been able to remember her own name, let alone the fact that she was letting him touch her so intimately in a dark corner of an otherwise public place.

As if he, too, had been carried away at that moment. Right up until the point where he had rejected her.

Oh, get over yourself! A sharp little voice sliced through her head. *So he doesn't want you.*

He was only here because he'd promised Mattie he would look after her. The best thing to do now was to shower and get ready, release him from this unnecessary duty as soon as he returned, and then get out of here.

Oh, Lord. Then again, weren't they supposed to be going for something to eat to discuss what had happened in that nightclub? To clear the air before the joint charity/army mission to Jukrem?

Forcing herself to start moving, Bridget made her way

to the chair—deftly avoiding even looking at Hayden's bed—and let her rucksack drop from her shoulderbefore reaching for her change of clothes.

The shower was hot, and powerful. Better than the shower she had in her own apartment, and certainly better than the solar showers she'd be having over the next few months. Five minutes stretched into ten, and Bridget took her time washing her hair, and her body. Cleaning away not just the dirty rainwater from that grimy puddle but also the hateful memories, and her sense of inadequacy that Hayden Brigham had inadvertently unearthed. She scrubbed at it all until it was gone, leaving her feeling shiny, and fresh, and *whole* once more.

Then she let the water sluice over her as if she was under the most luxurious waterfall in the world—and breathed.

By the time she had finished, blasting her hair quickly with the courtesy dryer before slipping into the soft pair of charcoal yoga pants and cropped tee that she had brought, Bridget felt new again. Happier.

More in control.

Until the soft knock at the door set her chest fluttering all over again.

Not so in control after all, she thought wryly.

Padding across the room, she drew in a deep breath and opened the door. Even before he entered the room, it felt to Bridget as though the walls were sliding in, making the space feel smaller and more cramped.

No. Not cramped. Full.

Hayden filled the space. Just as his very presence filled her chest with something she had never experienced before and couldn't identify even if she'd wanted to—though she didn't want to.

She didn't want to admit that, at twenty-six years of age, she had never experienced anything quite like it before. She'd heard about it from friends, of course. Even read about it in the books they shared around the medical camps, thrilling in the happy-ever-after stories that offered them a glorious escape for as long as they stayed lost in the pages.

But she had never *experienced* it. Not even close. She hadn't even believed it really existed. And then she'd met Hayden, and he'd upended everything she'd held to be true.

'I'll just pack my things back up and I'll get out of your way,' she managed, trying not to scurry across the room.

'You don't have to feel awkward,' he told her softly.

She had to be imagining it to think there was a hint of triumph in his tone.

'Of course I feel awkward,' she retorted, her voice clipped but not quite enough to disguise the tremor in it.

She felt like a drowning woman struggling to break the surface and grab deep lungfuls of air.

'I let us…myself…get carried away in that club.' She made herself say the words, as ugly as they were. 'I did things I've never done before with anyone…and then you rejected me.'

Something flared in those Baltic blue pools, and it almost pulled her straight back under.

'No one else?'

'You think I make a habit of it?' She gritted her teeth.

Hayden didn't answer, he merely stood straighter and folded his arms across his chest, as though planting himself in place.

Why? Because he wasn't tempted…or because he was?

The questions chased one after another through her head—no matter how much she tried to squash them.

'Forget it,' she blurted out, reaching for her things, her hands shaking. 'I should go.'

'Wait.' It was a command. Low but unequivocal, and

she found herself straightening slowly. Obeying. 'Let's get one thing straight. I did *not* reject you.'

'Please.' She tried to stay neutral but knew that self-disgust and shame had made her pull a face. 'You couldn't get out of there fast enough.'

He hesitated, and for a moment she thought he wasn't going to argue. That his silence was going to confirm her fears. She felt wrecked, and lost, and wholly confused.

And then his expression changed. Softened. As though he couldn't help himself.

'You're wrong, Birdie. I couldn't get out of there fast enough because I was about to lose my head. I *did* lose my head. I forgot where we were and nearly took you right there, against the wall in that club, you remember?'

She remembered. Oh, how she remembered.

How they hadn't been caught was a miracle and yet, even now, she wasn't sure she could have stopped if he hadn't.

'If we both wanted that...then why did we stop?'

'Apart from the fact that we were about to get it on in a public place, you mean?' His face twisted at the memory. 'Or that you're a virgin?'

'Is that what offends you most? That I'm a virgin?'

'Of course not. But you've been saving yourself all this time for a partner who will deserve you. I'm a player, Birdie, even my sister warned you off me. I can only end up hurting you.'

'You don't get it, do you? It isn't about deserving it or saving it. It isn't about getting hurt. It's about picking who and what I want.' She stopped, licked her lips, swallowed. 'And I want you.'

She wasn't even sure she recognised her own voice at that point, loaded as it was with something that felt dangerously like raw desire. *Need.*

'You don't want me.' He shook his head, but his voice was too thick. 'Trust me, you don't know me.'

'I want you. One night, that's all.'

'You're not the kind of girl who does *one nights*.'

'I might be, I just haven't tried it yet.'

'You're not.' His voice sounded strangled, and she liked it that she was getting to him. 'You're the kind of girl who holds out for more. Who deserves more.'

'You don't know as much as you think.'

'I know I'm not a good man, Birdie,' he warned her.

But his voice rumbled deliciously, and something shifted through those clear blue pools, sliding inside her and working its way down her body.

'Maybe I don't want a good man,' she bit back. 'Maybe a bad man is exactly what I need.'

'Birdie...'

There was no denying the answering note in his voice. As greedy and demanding as the call roaring through her entire body. And when she allowed her hungry gaze to roam his body, she realised the tell-tale shadow—right where he was hardest—gave away all the things he was trying to keep from her.

Hayden Brigham *did* want her. *Badly.* It was the headiest feeling she'd ever known. Bridget felt her hands begin to shake, her entire body start to tremble. But not with fear or uncertainty, but anticipation.

Either she had to be bold now or she had to live with regret for the rest of her life. It really was now or never.

Sliding her hands down to the waistband of her yoga pants, she hooked her thumbs inside and then pushed them down in one smooth movement until they were lying in a soft puddle at her bare feet. She stepped out of them.

'What are you doing?' It was a warning, but it was hoarse and lacked any real punch.

Bridget chose to ignore it. Instead, she took the hem of

her tee and pulled it over her head, leaving it to fall on top of her trousers. And then she was standing there wearing only her prettiest, wispiest thong.

And an expression that dared him to make the next move.

'Birdie,' he muttered, but he didn't add anything else. And he didn't move.

For a moment she almost faltered, but she could hardly stop now. Not when she'd already stripped. At least Hayden looked tormented rather than, say…*disgusted.*

Slowly, very slowly, she took first one step towards him. Then another. And Hayden shook his head weakly but he didn't speak.

'Cat got your tongue?' she asked sweetly, pretending that her heart wasn't clattering noisily behind her ribcage.

'You'd better be sure this is what you want, Birdie,' he growled at last. 'Because if you come much closer, I can't guarantee my actions.'

'How much closer?' She barely recognised that husky, needy voice as her own. 'This much closer?'

She took another step.

'This much?'

Reaching out, she slid one finger down the front of his trousers, to the part of him that fascinated her most, revelling as the sound seemed to hiss out of Hayden.

He was hard. So hard she felt a resounding throb between her legs.

She was the one who had got him that way.

'Birdie.' He circled her wrist with his fingers. Not painfully but firmly. 'All these years you've waited. To give that gift to me…be certain that it's what you want.'

'I'm standing here in front of you, for all intents and purposes naked,' she choked out. 'How much more certain can I be, Hayd?'

She had no idea if it was the words or saying his name,

but he gave in to her with a groan, snaking his hand around her neck and hauling her to him, crushing his mouth to hers and setting her alight like he'd dropped a match into a tank of petrol.

Bridget went up in flames.

He tasted her, sampled her, possessed her. And all she could do was cling to him and let him sweep her along on the ride, opening her mouth to him and feeling his tongue raking against hers just as it had the other night.

Just as she'd dreamt about every night since.

He angled his head, deepening the kiss and taking her mouth over and over again. Almost as if he'd forgotten that she was practically naked in his arms.

She didn't know whether to think that was a good thing or a bad thing. Then again, she didn't know that she could think very much at all, especially when his mouth slid so slickly across hers, his teeth stopping every now and then to draw one of her lips between his.

And then, suddenly, he let his hands drop. Skimming down her body, tracing her shape, testing her, as if trying to memorise every curve and every contour. Her skin leapt under his touch, sizzling and scorching, making her want to press her body as close to his as she possibly could. It still wasn't enough.

Pulling her arms around, Bridget sought out his shirt, fumbling with the hem until he stilled her, and she could feel his lips curving against hers.

'There's no rush.'

'I want to feel you,' she managed. 'Against me.'

'I am against you.'

They both knew he was teasing her. Testing her.

'Naked,' she clarified boldly.

'Ah.' Taking the T-shirt in his hands, he swept it over his head and launched it somewhere across the room. 'Why didn't you just say so?'

But Bridget didn't answer. She couldn't. All she wanted to do was feast her eyes on Hayden's chest with its defined muscles and never-ending ridges. Like nothing she'd ever seen before.

Slowly, almost reverently, she ran her hands over him. Fingertips first then palms. Up and round his chest, his shoulders, those arms. If she'd had the courage, she could have followed it up using her mouth, but she still wasn't sure enough of herself. Or of her effect on Hayden.

Though that was becoming clearer.

And then, before she could think what else to do, he dipped his head down to her neck and planted a host of devastating kisses in the sensitive hollow between her neck and her shoulder.

Bridget was helpless to resist. Letting her head fall back, she arched against him, and as she did so her nipples, already tight and aching, brushed against the fine hairs on his chest, making her gasp aloud. Her hands were pressed against his shoulder blades, her fingers biting into his skin.

'Hayd…' she muttered, wanting more. *Needing* more.

As if he could read her mind, he dropped his head lower, trailing kisses down over the swell of her chest and straight to one aching, straining nipple. And he sucked it straight into his mouth.

Everything began to spin. She felt desperate and wild, feverish all over. All she could do was try to hold onto the edge of her sanity as she finally began to regain some kind of footing.

And then he scooped her up and carried her across the room to the big bed, laying her down until she was sprawled in front of him for his eyes to feast on, before he groaned and removed the rest of his clothing with shocking efficiency.

Lord, how beautiful he was. And honed. And male. Very, *very* male.

Almost mesmerised, she used her elbows to push herself into a sitting position, her hands reaching for him as if on autopilot.

'No.' The low guttural sound shuddered through her, sinful and perfect.

And then, before she could rationalise anything, he gently pushed her back on to the bed, lifted one leg, and began to kiss his way up it.

Bridget watched, mesmerised, as he made his way from the inside of one ankle up to the inside of the knee, indulging, meandering, taking his time. She watched, even more hypnotised, as Hayden progressed from her knee up the inside of her thigh, his kisses growing hotter and more laden with promise as he advanced up the ever more sensitive flesh. Until he was...*there.*

Right there.

And her body was quivering wildly in anticipation of what was about to happen, even as her brain was struggling to take it all in.

She watched, bewitched, as he lifted his eyes to meet hers, that naughty curve of his mouth still working its way up the last inch of inner thigh.

'Hayden,' she muttered, only half understanding.

His grin broadened, even as those pools of blue darkened, and suddenly he lowered his head between her legs.

Bridget cried out. Loudly. She heard herself through the fog but was helpless to stop. She'd heard about it, read about it, even had female friends go into detail about it, but nothing could possibly have prepared her for how the pure sensation of it felt.

Or perhaps how it felt when Hayden did it. His mouth on her sex, his tongue licking its way into her core, went way beyond all that she'd ever imagined it would be. It felt like rocketing up through the troposphere, the stratosphere, to the very exosphere. It felt like she never wanted it to stop. Or to come back down again.

She wanted more yet she didn't know if she could stand it. Gripping his shoulders, Bridget writhed and moaned, barely recognising her own voice, and the low growls of approval that Hayd made—the sounds that rumbled their way from the back of his throat and into her very body—only turned her on all the more. Wantonly bucking her hips up to meet his mouth, shamelessly begging him for more.

'Please, Hayd.'

'Please?'

'Please?'

And the worst—or best—of it was that she didn't even know what she was begging him for. Not until he closed his lips around her and sucked. Hard. One finger slid easily inside her and sent her soaring into space all over again as everything turned into a brilliant, white light. She was hurtling into nothing, and she didn't care. And then, suddenly, he twisted his hand and slid another finger inside her, and Bridget heard herself shatter with a glorious scream, calling out his name as though it had always been meant to be this way.

She had no idea how long she was out of herself, but by the time she came back down to earth, Hayden was lying next to her, a dark, unfathomable expression on his hewn features. Who knew what it was about it? But if she'd been able to capture that look and put it in a bottle, Bridget suspected she'd be able to hold onto this incredible, intense sensation forever.

'That was…' she began hesitantly.

'Only the start,' he assured her with a grin. 'Are you ready for more?'

Was she? She didn't know if she could handle more. But she certainly wasn't about to say no.

Before she could answer, however, Hayden was leaning

over to the drawer, reaching for a foil packet—and part of her considered that she ought to be ashamed that the thought of protection hadn't even entered her head, she'd been so caught up in the moment—and deftly dealt with it.

Then he was sliding his sublimely solid body back over hers, gathering her up in his arms whilst her legs opened up to him as if by instinct, and all other thoughts fled from her mind.

He nudged against her. Velvet and steel where she was hot and so very wet. She could feel herself blush again, shifting slightly in her uncertainty, but then he let out a low, carnal groan, and Bridget wondered if she perhaps had a little more power than she'd realised.

Lifting her smaller hands to his well-defined shoulders, she shifted again, drawing him inside her, deeper than he'd intended to go.

A slow sound hissed out of Hayden's mouth as he gritted his teeth, clearly trying to regain some control as he drew back out of her, and Bridget found it inordinately satisfying that she'd caught him off guard, wresting some of his power from him.

She waited until she felt him flex again and then carefully, experimentally, she shifted once more and drew him deeper inside.

'Careful, *Birdie*,' he growled deeply, and the sound thrilled her ears. 'If you push us any faster, I can't promise you I'll be able to hold back.'

'And here was I thinking you were some kind of expert playboy,' she teased, not knowing from where this sudden show of courage was coming.

'I was,' he gritted out again. 'Until you.'

Then, not allowing her the chance to argue, he reached down between them and started playing with her. Long strokes, fast swirls, anything that made her head drop back and her breath come in short, choppy bursts all over again.

The man was far too devilish for his own good.

'I want you,' she whispered, her hands gliding down his back and her fingernails gently grazing as they moved.

He shivered against her, sliding in deeper, and she gasped.

'You're not helping.' His voice sounded half-strangled and Bridget found that she loved that most of all.

'I'm not trying to help,' she whispered back. 'I'm trying to make you come apart the way you just did for me.'

'This time we'll do it together.'

She lowered her eyes, not wanting to meet his. Not liking the idea of reminding him how inexperienced she was.

'I don't think I can.'

'Oh, Birdie…' He sounded amused even through his pained tone. 'I'm going to prove to you how many times you can.'

As she opened her mouth to respond, he started moving, slowly at first but still every sound was snatched away from her.

There was *pain*…only not. It was there for a brief moment and then it wasn't. Leaving instead a dull sensation. She might have to say a kind of…stretching. But along with it the shocking realisation that Hayden was sliding inside her.

His long, thick length was going all the way inside her, and her brain was thrilling at the notion, even as her body was making its objections known.

'Relax,' he murmured. 'I promise I'll be gentle.'

'It…pulls.'

'So give it a moment.' He dropped his forehead to connect softly with hers, as though he was having to control himself more than she'd realised.

Bridget didn't know what it was about that fact that made her want to shift her hips—but she did it. And then, as his eyes held hers, the expression in them darkening with desire, she tried it again. And again.

'Better?' he demanded hoarsely.

She grinned.

'I'd say so.'

'Fine,' he announced grimly, beginning to move. And only then did Bridget realise her mistake.

Awareness flooded her. And need. As he set a leisurely pace, she felt herself melt around him. Her body cried out for him and her knees began to rise up to draw him deeper. Instinctively, her hands moved down to his backside to encourage him further.

'I don't know what you're doing to me,' he gritted out, 'but I swear you're killing me, Birdie.'

'I don't know what I'm doing either,' admitted Bridget. 'I only know I want you. Inside me. Deeper.'

If this was sex, she had no idea what it must be like to be in love.

'I'm trying to go gently,' he managed.

She nodded, her words little more than whispered.

'I know. But I don't think I want you to be gentle with me.'

As if to prove her point, she lifted her legs entirely and wrapped them around his hips, plunging him deeper inside her. He groaned, a visceral, carnal sound, and then he began moving faster. And each time Bridget lifted her hips to meet him, he plunged into her deeper and faster, as though he was no longer in control, until all she could hear was their ragged breathing. Proof that she wasn't the only one so close to the edge.

Dipping his head, Hayden found the juncture of her neck and shoulder again, making her arch her back and thrust her breasts against his chest, her nipples raking across his smattering of hairs and driving her wild.

With every stroke she clung to him harder, opened to

him more. Deeper, and faster, and stronger. And for a moment everything hung around her, captured in a perfect snapshot in time.

But then she was flying again, rushing towards a brilliant light, unable to stop herself. Only this time when she fractured, and splintered, and finally fell, all the while screaming Hayden's name, he followed her, calling out her name, too.

It was pitch black when Hayden woke, with her still in his arms. The subtle coconut scent of her luxurious hair infiltrated his nostrils, making him want to inhale deeply. To breathe in the essence of *her*.

They'd made love—*had sex*, he corrected himself swiftly—twice more since that first time. Once in the shower and once back in bed. And even now his body started to harden, aching to take her again. And again.

He couldn't quite shake the odd sensation that moved through him. As if this woman was different from any other that he'd known. As if he was never going to quite get enough of her.

The next instant he shoved it aside.

Ridiculous.

Still, he didn't want to move. He didn't want to break contact with her. But, perhaps sensing his wakened state, Bridget stirred in his arms, stretching elegantly before opening her eyes.

And blinked at him.

He might not be able to explain it but there was no stopping the grin that spread across his face. He found that he was captivated by her. And he had to tell himself, several times, that he didn't like that fact.

It wasn't until she shifted in his arms, her expression shutting down, that he realised he'd started to frown.

'Should I…go?' she asked hesitantly.

'No, don't.'

He hadn't meant to say it. In fact, he'd been telling himself that if she left it was probably for the best. As if to compound things, he opened his mouth again, his voice just as rough and abrasive.

'Stay.'

'Stay?' she breathed, clutching the sheet in her delicate hands and pulling it up to cover her breasts.

A fact that his brain—and his body—were already lamenting.

'Stay,' he repeated, reaching over to pull her back down onto the bed. And onto him. 'A little longer.'

'With you?'

He heard his own laugh, like a roll of thunder, and wondered how it sounded like nothing he'd ever heard before. Yet he laughed. Not infrequently either. But never like this, with such pleasure.

'Definitely with me,' he growled, before settling her astride him.

Her entire, sublime fifties pin-up body on show for him. Her glossy, black hair cascading over her shoulders, down her back, sneaking over one breast.

He reached out and brushed it away, his body tensing even more as she exhaled and shivered on him when he brushed one already taut nipple.

'Is this just muddying things that we've complicated enough?' she asked, but he couldn't help but notice that she said it with more than a little reluctance.

They both knew what they were doing was insane, but neither of them could bring themselves to stop.

'In less than a week we'll be in a foreign country,' he noted. 'You'll be looking after people, and I'll be looking after your clinic, making sure there is adequate drainage, fresh water, power.'

'I know that.' She pursed her lips. 'So how does that help what we're doing here? Now? Surely it's…inappropriate.'

'It's a complication perhaps. Though not inappropriate. But in any case it means there's a clear line between the two things. Here, and there.'

And he was damned well going to ignore the niggling doubt that it wouldn't be that easy. That drawing that line, and sticking to it, were very different things. Especially, it seemed, where his libido and Bridget Gardiner were concerned.

'A line,' she repeated carefully. 'Like *What happens in Vegas stays in Vegas*?'

'Exactly,' he declared, fighting the almost overwhelming urge to move his hands to her hips.

She eyed him dubiously.

'And that works? It's that easy?'

'Why not?' he answered, shoving aside the simple truth that he'd never had to worry about it before because he'd never been tempted to cross his own self-imposed lines before.

Or the fact that, with Bridget, he hadn't merely crossed them as much as skidded over them, blotting them out altogether.

'Or we can stop,' he forced himself to say, even though he knew that stopping himself from touching this particular woman might well kill him.

Colour flushed her cheeks and she dropped her eyes to his chest, following the trail as her hands moved over the ridges they found.

'I don't think I *could* stop,' she whispered.

'Then we won't,' he ground out, need overtaking him once more.

And he used his hands to guide her onto him, wanting to take his time but driven on by the sight of her body moving on him, and as she dropped her head back, pushing herself down onto him, he thrust his way home as though it had always been this way.

CHAPTER SIX

THE FLAP TO the ICU room was snapped back and one of her colleagues burst through, carrying a young child in her arms, malnourished and pale. Bridget snapped her head up from task of finishing up loose ends at the end of her shift and hurried over.

'He was brought into the paediatric outpatient feeding centre. But he isn't breathing, and his pulse is slow,' Lisa announced, laying the child on the bed.

Swivelling around, Bridget grabbed the bag mask ventilator and connected it to the oxygen and began prepping the adrenalin as another nurse called the time, and Lisa began chest compressions.

Briefly it crossed Bridget's mind that the weight loss could be a symptom of malaria, TB, measles or any number of other issues out here on the African continent, but until they got him breathing and stable, there was no way they could even begin to diagnose. She wasn't sure how long they worked for, sweat pouring off them in the forty-degree heat, but eventually the boy was breathing on his own again, albeit wearing an oxygen mask, his pulse returning to normal.

She sent out a silent thanks that it was a better outcome than the previous day when they'd worked for thirty minutes, only for the little girl to have to be declared dead.

This time, at least, it was a happier end to what had been a long, draining shift.

'It's quiet this evening,' she observed, looking around the room.

'There were no new admissions so the clinic was shut down early,' Lisa agreed. 'Skeleton crew on for tonight—some last-minute plan, I heard. Anyway, your shift is done. Go. Relax. I'll see you tomorrow.'

'Okay, 'night, then.' Bridget hesitated, looking around one more time to check there was no work still to do.

'Go,' Lisa ordered with a laugh, making her slink sheepishly to the door.

'Yes, yes, I know. I'm going.'

As Bridget walked out of the tent, she stood in the heat and turned her face up to the sun for a few moments. Breathing in the hot, fresh air, and trying to remember if she'd ever felt so tired. She'd only been in the medical camp for four days, yet it felt like a lifetime. It was terrifying, exhausting, and—when they managed to save a life—the most satisfying feeling in the world.

Not that she hadn't felt that way back home, but it was always different out here where even the most basic medical supplies weren't freely available to these people.

Her first day in—arriving by plane and flying over miles and miles of dry arid, pretty much barren land—she'd been brought to the clinic, such as it was, to witness a little boy of about six, comatose and seizing.

The probable diagnosis had been meningitis, which back home would have meant the young child would have been sedated and ventilated, and he would have been monitored. He would have a feeding tube and a catheter, whilst a central line would have been put in, and a neuro monitor would have been attached to catch low-grade seizure activity. But out here none of that was available.

Even now, Bridget could remember her very first case

on her very first mission, many years ago. A small child very similar to this little boy. She recalled listening as her mentor had explained to her that she would simply have to monitor regularly herself by lifting the eyelid and looking for faint flickering, or even just test the arm for rigidity, to determine whether there was seizure activity. Then it was a matter of using the vitals to determine fluid boluses or diazepam.

'How will I know how much to use?' Bridget could still remember such a feeling of helplessness as she'd asked the question.

And she could still picture her mentor's half smile, half grimace.

'Look at the vitals.' The woman had shrugged. 'Too little and the seizures will continue. Too much and you'll cause respiratory depression. We do the best we can out here.'

She'd returned to her accommodation feeling more frightened than ever. Yet, only a few days in, and Bridget had already begun to find her sea legs.

Now, several missions and years later it felt horribly *normal*.

She saw measles, malaria and meningitis on a daily basis, and she had already delivered more babies in four days than she would probably have delivered in four months back home. But she hadn't grown used to the deaths yet. She hoped she never would.

The main problem with where they were was that it was so far into the bush that there was no town, no market, certainly no hospital. Which meant that people simply weren't used to having medical help around—not unless they walked for two days or more to the nearest big town with its understaffed, under-equipped hospital—and so they didn't come into the charity's small clinic until it was too late for Bridget or her colleagues to be able to really help.

As she rounded the corner to the small *tukul* she shared with another nurse, Bridget stopped short when she saw her roommate painting her toenails a glorious shiny red.

'Bad day?'

'Thankfully not.' Sara smiled, barely looking up from her task. 'I just fancied feeling a little more…feminine. At least, as much as one can, dressed in combat trousers, a tee and dusty sandals all day long.'

She shifted around on the corner of her hammock to allow Bridget to enter the one-roomed mud hut, containing the two beds—each complete with mosquito net—and something that passed for a chest of drawer per person.

Ultimately, the plan was to use local expertise to build more *tukuls* so that each member of staff would have a small haven that they could call their own. But at the moment a broken roof in what would ultimately become the main accommodation area in one of the abandoned village's old buildings meant the rooms there were unusable, and many of them were having to share.

'Want to borrow it?' Sara waved her bottle of shiny red nail polish in the air. 'We can call it our version of party gear.'

Bridget frowned.

'There's a celebration?'

'Close enough.' Sara laughed. 'The army unit came in this afternoon, and we're throwing them a bit of a welcome party as we're going to be working together so closely for the next few months. See if we can't break the ice a little to make the *getting to know each other* process that little bit smoother.'

Bridget pitched forward, grateful that her hammock was there to catch her fall, not that Sara seemed to notice.

So *that* was why the clinic had been shut down early

and there was only a skeleton crew on. Usually, the charity tried to have roommates on alternating shifts, so that one would be working when the other had down time, thereby allowing each of them to get some valuable alone time in the *tukul*. But tonight the charity was hosting a sort of party for the army camp, an effort to get to know each other given how they were both working in the area. So she and Sara both had down time for the evening, unless an emergency came in.

It had been almost a week since she'd left Hayd's bed. But it had taken her a lot longer to get him out of her head.

Her mind had been full of memories of him the entire flight to the charity's headquarters, all through the briefings and seminars, and the whole duration of the flight out here. Even during the short plane ride from the capital city to the tiny airstrip closest to the charity's new camp in Jukrem—which she would normally have spent drinking in the stunning views of lush vegetation after the rains—had been filled with X-rated images of Hayden Brigham.

So much so that it had been a relief to be ushered into the clinic almost the moment her four-by-four had pulled into the camp, so that the outgoing nurse could begin her handover. The bedlam of the over-subscribed outreach clinic proved to be just the distraction that Bridget had needed. And today she'd almost—*almost*—forgotten that she was meant to be forgetting about him.

But now he was here. His regiment of Royal Engineers had finally arrived, and she was going to have to deal with him on a daily basis. And suddenly she wasn't so sure she could face him without remembering everything he'd done to her with his mouth, his fingers and more.

She shivered deliciously then instantly tried to quash it.

What had happened that night was over. Done. It wouldn't be happening again, and the sooner she remembered that, the better for everyone. She wasn't out here to further anything with Hayd, or anyone else for that matter, she was out here because she had a job to do. A job she'd performed perfectly on many previous occasions.

'Did you want to borrow it?' Sara's voice crashed in on Bridget, and she looked up to see her roommate screwing the top closed and holding it out into the gap between the beds.

Bridget hesitated. She'd been through enough camps to have seen doctors do similar things over the years. Sometimes nail polish, sometimes mascara. One had even had pretty rhinestone Alice bands. And she'd been tempted.

It was hard to feel feminine out here sometimes with all the muck, and dust, and disease.

But in the end she'd never wanted to enough, so surely there was no need to let herself get distracted now? Just because Hayden Brigham was finally at camp?

He meant nothing to her, she reminded herself. They'd drawn a clear line between the UK and out here, and out here he meant nothing to her. She wasn't buying it.

Indeed, even in the UK he was just the man who had finally helped her to offload her inconvenient label of being a *virgin*. Nothing more.

And certainly not the reason why she reached out and took the gloriously red bottle from her roommate, murmuring her gratitude and wondering what...anybody else might make of it.

Hayden held the neck of his beer bottle in his fingers and leaned on the pillar, only half tuned in to the conversation going on beside him between his second-in-command and the charity's mission leader as he watched the rest of the reception play out in front of him. Pretending he wasn't looking out for *her*. The woman who had haunted his thoughts for the better part of the past week.

No matter what he'd said, that night in his hotel suite, about drawing a line between what had happened between them in the UK and how they would be out here in a professional capacity, he'd found that his thoughts had wandered back to Bridget too many times to count over the last few days.

How many times had he woken up, his body hard and ready after worryingly vivid dreams of her? As though nothing would ever sate him the way that this woman had done.

He was, therefore, intensely grateful that his army camp was separate from the charity's medical compound. Whilst they were making use of the buildings in an abandoned village while the army effected some of the repairs for them, his Royal Engineers, along with a logistics unit and some other support troops, were no more than a couple of hundred metres away on the opposite side of a dried-up riverbed.

It wasn't much of a divide in terms of terrain, but it was the psychological divide that he needed. The reassurance that he could focus on his task in hand. The confidence that he wasn't going to run into Bridget on a daily basis.

Because whatever else that night back in his hotel room had done, it had convinced him that one night with her wasn't nearly enough. It hadn't sated this smouldering need inside him—it had stoked it up.

He wasn't entirely convinced that anything would douse it, bar taking her to his bed. Again, and again. And it didn't matter how many times he told himself that he didn't mix work and pleasure. Or that virgins weren't his thing. Or even that, as much as his parents had made their relationship work, he'd still seen how it had affected his mother, being married to a military man who had been away more than he'd been home. He'd promised himself long ago that he would never put any woman through the same.

Now he was fighting the nonsensical notion that he'd only found it so easy to stick to that promise because he'd never found the right woman before.

'What do you think, Hayd?'

The question crashed through his thoughts. Pasting a polite expression over his features, he turned to his companions.

'Say again?'

'I was explaining to Mandy that the surveys we've been conducting all week have primarily been recces to determine whether the intel sent to us back in the UK matches the actual set-up on the ground before we can decide which pieces of infrastructure should be our priority.'

'Yes, I completely understand.' Mandy, the charity's mission coordinator, bobbed her head enthusiastically. 'I just wanted to make sure you understood that the ground conditions you're seeing now are vastly different from the conditions we encountered when we first arrived here a couple of months ago.'

'In the wet season?' Hayden forced himself to focus. To stop looking out for a woman whose presence should have no impact on him whatsoever.

'Right,' Mandy agreed. 'This part of the country gets muddy, swampy. We'd intended to be in a month earlier, but we had to postpone it because even the airstrip had been close to being reclaimed by the mud. The dry riverbed you see out there now was close to overflowing. The locals build roads each year but each year they get washed away when the floods come.'

'So your concern is that we'll focus on what makes sense now, without appreciating the terrain could look very different in six months? Or eight?' Hayden confirmed.

'Yes. I'm just conscious that the army is only here as a bit of a Section 106.'

'I'm sorry?'

She shot him a look that was only half-apologetic, but he was beginning to like her anyway. She was direct and down to earth, and he'd always found that much easier to work with than trying to guess what someone *wasn't* saying.

'You know…a bit of *quid pro quo*. You're getting a training area in this region on the basis that you put in a little infrastructure. And I'm very grateful for that, believe me. But I've been working out here for a long time, mostly in the main hospital a few hours' drive away. It matters to me—to this charity—that we make the most of you whilst you're here. Put in the base work that will most benefit the villages here on a long-term basis.'

'Which is why I'm more than happy to take on board any and all advice you give us,' he told her sincerely. 'Aside from the fact that I *want* to do as much as possible to help the people of this region, it's also in the army's interests to do so. So if you want to accompany me on a recce tomorrow, and perhaps let me run you through where I'm up to so far, I'd be happy to get your feedback?'

'Great.' Mandy gave a pleased smile. 'I'd really appreciate that. I think it's going to be a pleasure to work alongside you, even if not on a regular basis. If you'll excuse me, I should make a social round of my people. I see a few of the new volunteers and I want to introduce them so that handovers are easier.'

'Of course,' Hayden agreed, as his second-in-command asked to join her.

Then, stepping back, Hayden watched as they left.

'Welcome to Jukrem, Hayd.'

He knew he shouldn't care, and yet he turned around almost eagerly.

'I was beginning to think you were on duty tonight.'

'I was…painting my toenails.'

He could tell she wished she could bite back the words

the instant they fell from her lips. Still, he couldn't help his eyes from dropping down to the dusty, unflattering sandals that the charity workers tended to wear around here. Although they probably beat the hot desert boots his guys had to wear in such heat.

Glossy, bright red nails stared back at him, and he felt the corners of his mouth tug.

'Very dainty.'

'You're laughing at me,' she accused.

'Not at all,' Hayden corrected. 'I'm laughing *with* you. There's a difference.'

She grunted slightly but didn't answer immediately.

'Looks nice,' he added.

'I know you might think it sounds silly,' she informed him airily, 'but it's amazing how a hint of something like this can restore some degree of femininity, especially in a place like this.'

'Right,' he gritted out.

The last thing he needed was to be reminded of how gloriously feminine Bridget was. Like he wasn't barely keeping a grip of himself as it was.

Her expression changed and she looked almost disappointed. As if he had somehow let her down.

It should concern him how much that got to him.

'I've been here less than a week, but I know that as the months go by something like seeing my toenails a pretty colour could lift my mood. We go around all day in combat trousers and neck-choking Ts, covered in dust, or mud, or worse—blood. A bit of nail polish helps you to feel like you're still a woman underneath it all.'

'I wasn't judging,' he heard himself say.

'Well…good,' but she still didn't look convinced, and before he realised it he was speaking again, a soft smile pulling at his mouth.

She had softened him.

'Have you ever read the diary of Lieutenant Colonel Mervin Willett Gonin?'

'I don't know who that is…' She frowned.

'He commanded a field ambulance brigade in Belsen concentration camp back in 1945.'

'Oh.'

'In his diary, he recalls how he and his men were crying out for supplies to help with diphtheria, dysentery, severe malnutrition. Their conditions were inhuman. There was so much equipment his brigade needed but couldn't get hold of. Then the British Red Cross arrived, and shortly afterwards a crate of lipstick turned up.'

She watched him closely, her attention piqued. Something shifted through him.

'It wasn't what his men wanted at all, it wasn't going to help heal those people, yet it ended up being an act of genius. After years of being treated worse than animals, nothing more than the number tattooed on their arm, the women were suddenly given something to restore their humanity. A humble red lipstick. It made them feel like they were people again, like they were alive. So, yes, Birdie, I understand how the simple act of painting your nails could be uplifting.'

For a moment he could see her pondering and he wished he knew what was going on in her head.

'I wish lipstick and nail varnish could help everyone.' She exhaled deeply at last. Relaxing a little and letting her guard down again. 'I had a patient this morning, a young girl barely older than fifteen who had been caught with a spear blade. The local men had been out hunting and she'd been in the wrong place at the wrong time.'

He nodded in empathy, though a part of him lamented the fact that she'd had to slip back into her old routine of dodging the personal and sticking with the work-related in order to talk to him.

'The injury was severe, and they'd treated her the best they could, using what medicines they had available to them, but she needed surgery. She was feverish, hallucinating and there were clear signs of sepsis, and we don't have the surgical facilities here in Jukrem, so we were lucky we happened to have a surgeon visiting from the main hospital for a couple of days, who was able to carry out a full hysterectomy and save her life,' Bridget continued, oblivious. 'But I realised that in a small community like this great value would have been placed on her fertility. Essentially, without being able to have children, she has fewer prospects.'

'Yeah. It's a crappy situation. You save her life on one hand but condemn her with the other. Sometimes you must feel like you can't win.'

Surprise flitted over her face.

'That's precisely how it feels. Every time. No matter how many times I see awful things happen to innocent people.'

'I'm not sure that feeling will ever go away, Birdie,' he said quietly.

'Neither am I,' she admitted. 'But, actually, I'm not too unhappy about that.'

'So tell me, Birdie,' he asked abruptly, 'what happened in your past to make you run away to help people in countries as far away from home as South Sudan, Nepal and Haiti?'

CHAPTER SEVEN

BRIDGET VALIANTLY TRIED to restart her heart, which appeared to have stopped beating. But it was impossible with what seemed like this spiked *thing* penetrating her chest.

The noise of the small party had faded fast into the night and all she could hear was a rushing in her ears. Then silence.

The worst thing about Hayden's question was that he'd asked it as though he actually cared. As if she really mattered to him, when they both knew that they'd agreed there was—and never would be—anything more between them.

'Who said I was running away from anything?' she choked out at last.

'I'm a commanding officer in the army,' he pointed out almost kindly. 'I've seen plenty of soldiers and civilians alike who have been running away from something. I can recognise the signs.'

'You're mistaken,' she said in a panicked voice.

'No.' His voice was so low that she had to strain to hear him. 'I am not.'

A charged energy arced between them and Bridget was forced to acknowledge that it was futile pretending to ignore it.

Worse, a part of her *wanted* to talk to him. She'd spent over a decade quashing her past and yet, with one seemingly solicitous question, she suddenly longed to tell him what he purported to want to know. As though sharing her story could somehow, finally, make it seem less defining.

But she couldn't speak.

The words simply weren't there and the silence lengthened between them. The seconds ticking slowly by.

'You can't run forever, Birdie,' he murmured at length, the compassion in his voice startling her. 'If you don't want to talk to me, at least find someone to talk to. There's no hiding place from who we are. At some point you're going to have to face whatever it is if you want peace. Trust me.'

'I don't have anything I need to face,' she managed. 'I have peace. Out here.'

'You have purpose out here,' corrected Hayden. 'That isn't the same thing.'

'So everyone is running from their past?'

'No.' He didn't rise to it. 'But *you* are.'

'You don't know as much as you think you do.'

She bristled. But it didn't stop her from realising that there was truth in his words. And what did it say about him that he could read that truth in her, when no one else had ever done so in all these years?

'I know that you're a different person out here. Even if Mattie hadn't said so, and even if I hadn't heard all the things people had to say about you today, I would have known it from the way you became so animated any time you discussed your work when we were back home.'

He'd been talking about her to other people? All day? She wasn't ready to scrutinise what that meant right now—if it meant anything at all—but she could file it away for later. For when she wasn't feeling so shocked.

'That's just a passion for work. You're the same, by all accounts.'

'But you're a whole different person out here. Freer. Happier. Like you've undergone a complete metamorphosis.'

Freer.

Wasn't that the very word she'd used when she'd thought about it herself?

Her heart, which had started beating again at some point, was now pounding wildly in her chest. Clattering behind her ribs.

'I don't want to do this,' she muttered in a stricken voice. 'Not now.'

Though she noted that she didn't say *not ever.*

Hayden regarded her for a moment, and then he dipped his head simply.

'Then we won't.'

'We won't?' she echoed weakly.

It was that simple?

'We'll talk about what I'm going to be doing for the next few weeks around the clinic,' he continued smoothly. 'Work-related topics that won't make you feel uncomfortable.'

And what did it say that she wasn't sure she liked that superficiality either?

'You're going to be working around the clinic?' she managed. 'I thought your purpose out here was to survey the area around the vast training ground the military has been gifted? I understood that your *quid pro quo* was to put in some road and light aircraft infrastructure so that the region won't be so cut off and isolated when the rains come and the ground becomes a quagmire?'

'It is. But the mission has been extended to include some wat-san work.'

Water and sanitation?

'You mean like inspecting old boreholes that have stopped working around the region? Maybe stripping them down and rebuilding? Checking the generators?'

None of which would mean he was right on site, where she could round a corner and bump into him at any time.

'That…' He dipped his head in acknowledgement. 'But also we've been asked to construct some flood defences for the clinic. The idea is that we'll dig a series of drains around the old town to allow for expansion from the facility you have now into a main hospital once the buildings of the former town have been repaired. The drains will gravity-feed water into a four-or-five-metre-deep soak-away.'

'I see.' She tried to swallow past the lump in her throat. *Nerves.*

She'd psychologically worked herself up to be within a few hundred metres of the army camp but knowing he could be working right outside the clinic felt like a whole different matter.

And wasn't that the problem?

She'd known from the start about Hayden the playboy. He'd even warned her himself. But still she'd let herself become too emotionally attached somewhere along the line—and she suspected she knew precisely where that *somewhere* had been.

Was she now supposed to walk around camp acting as though she knew him no better than anyone else? Bridget wasn't sure she could handle that.

'Where have you gone, Birdie?'

His voice snapped her back into the moment and her eyes flew to his.

'Sorry. Did you say something?'

If she didn't get a hold of herself then this was going to be the worst three-month medical mission of her entire career.

'I asked how your first few days have been?' he forced himself to ask casually. 'If it's different from other projects you've worked on?'

And he absolutely wasn't wondering whether she had

been thinking of him as much as he'd been thinking of her, because that made no sense.

None at all.

He still didn't understand what it was about this particular woman that fascinated him so. He might have enjoyed flings from time to time but he'd never had, or wanted to have, a full-on relationship either.

Before now he hadn't even considered it.

So what made him want to get behind those defences of hers and understand what made Bridget Gardiner tick?

Wasn't he the one who talked about lines in the sand? About leaving their night of intimacy back in the UK, and focusing solely on a professional relationship out here? The way he wouldn't have had any trouble doing had it been any other woman. Then again, he probably wouldn't have given in to the temptation back home had she been any other woman.

And now wasn't he the one blurring those lines?

As if to prove his point, Bridget cleared her throat, clearly pulling herself together.

'Okay, well, the last week has been eventful. More frightening, draining, and sadder than I'd imagined it might be. Every other camp I've been to has had a small operating theatre and at least one surgeon, but this time we haven't had even that. I don't think I fully appreciated how many extra lives we could save with just one more tent and one more medical professional. And yet...'

'And yet...?' he prompted when she hesitated, keen to get them back to a more stable point, though he couldn't have said why it mattered to him so much.

Or perhaps he could have said so if only he'd cared to admit it.

'It always feels so satisfying when we manage to succeed. Even when we've had to endure losing three others, four, more, that one life we managed to save makes it all bearable.'

'I can understand that, Birdie.' He reached out to touch her cheek, but stopped himself. 'So, what are you all working on now?'

She narrowed her eyes at him.

'Why are you doing this?'

'Why am I showing an interest in your part of a joint charity-military project, do you mean?' He arched his eyebrows.

'Don't be facetious. You know what I meant.'

The worst thing was that he did know, and he wasn't at all sure what had got into him. He would never be so interested if it was anyone other than Bridget talking to him. But the fact remained he did truly want to hear about what she was doing, and how she was.

'I want to know how you are, Birdie. We might be drawing a distinction between our personal lives and our work lives, but that doesn't mean I can't ask about you. About how you are.'

'So you're saying you really want to hear about my day?' she repeated sceptically.

'I really do.'

And he didn't care what that said about how blurred his so-called lines were becoming.

'Okay,' she began slowly. 'So, the main problems we get out here are complications during birth, water-borne illnesses, and one of the biggest diseases we're dealing with here is *kala azar*. It isn't something you learn about back at home, but other people told me it was a major issue out here, so I researched a little. Still, I didn't realise quite how many of our patients would be affected.'

'I don't think I've ever heard of it,' he admitted. Although, having been on operations in so many different countries, he'd heard of many diseases, even if he didn't fully understand them.'

'No, it isn't something you really study back in the UK.' Bridget exhaled, her passion and empathy twisting inside his chest. 'Another name for it is visceral leishmaniasis and, similar to malaria and mosquitos, kala azar is a parasitic disease spread by the bite of a sandfly.'

'That's concerning.' Hayden frowned, trying to concentrate on what she was saying, and ignoring the inexplicable urge to draw her into his arms. 'Sand flies are so tiny they can even get through the mesh on a standard mosquito net.'

'Exactly. And it develops slowly with initial symptoms being fever, swollen glands and an enlarged spleen, which basically lowers the healthy red blood cells, platelets and white blood cells in the bloodstream, leaving the victim prone to more infections, which, in a place like this, is like inviting any number of sick buddies to the party. TB, malaria, diphtheria, malnutrition, cholera, measles…the list goes on.'

'So I would guess that it's usually the complications of other illnesses that bring them to you, rather than the initial symptoms of kala…what did you call it?'

He might not know this particular disease, but he'd worked in enough areas to know the score. In places like this, hours' or even days' walk from medical help, from foreigners who the locals didn't necessarily yet trust, it was often too late by the time people sought help.

'Kala azar.' She tilted her head. 'And yes. The later symptoms usually include anaemia, severe wasting and/or anything else I mentioned. Left untreated, most cases of kala azar prove fatal.'

Sadness burned in her eyes and he wondered how many cases she had seen already to look that way. And how old the sufferers had been.

Not for the first time, he was grateful for his job. He

didn't envy Bridget—or his sister, Mattie, for that matter—the job of working with the sick and dying out here.

'But if they came to you earlier—' he tried to sound positive '—is the treatment straightforward?'

Bridget shook her head, her eyes slamming into his. As if they were doing more than simply discussing her medical cases. As if they were *connecting*.

'Actually, not really. The drugs are expensive to start with, but they need to be kept between two and eight degrees at all times, which is obviously a challenge out here.'

'Today was forty degrees in the shade,' he agreed.

'Right. And the treatment is usually anything from two weeks to over a month of intravenous or intramuscular injections on either a daily or once every two days basis. On top of all that, the drugs can have serious side effects.'

'It just gets better,' he commented dryly, as Bridget pulled a face.

'Doesn't it just. As if they don't have enough to deal with. And that's without the contraindications of different treatments the patient might need for the other diseases I mentioned. Or, if they're anaemic, the need for blood transfusion.'

For a moment they didn't speak, but it didn't feel awkward. It was an oddly comfortable, companionable silence as they pondered the situation, both acutely aware that they got to walk away in a few months. A luxury not afforded to the people forced to live in the region.

'Good evening, Bridget.' Bridget jumped at the sound of her project manager's voice. 'Major.'

'Hayden,' Hayden corrected with his trademark smile.

And good grief...was that Mandy actually giggling like a schoolgirl?

'Hayden.' She smiled broadly. 'Lovely name, my dear.'

Bridget blinked in shock. She knew Hayden was a

charmer, but a bold, forbidding, often matronly woman like Mandy? From one single word?

'I'm not interrupting, am I?' Mandy looked from one to the other.

'Not at all,' they both said in unison. Which hardly made their case.

Mandy, known for missing very little, eyed them with mounting interest.

'Do you two already know each other?'

'I used to work with Mattie.' Bridget didn't know why she panicked to explain herself. 'That is, Major Mathilda Brigham, Hayd's sister...'

'We've been introduced before.' Hayden cut across her simply. Not unkindly.

She cast him a grateful glance.

'I see.' Mandy peered at them a little closer, and Bridget was sure she could see the wheels spinning in the older woman's head. 'Well, that make things easier in terms of working together.'

Bridget's heart kicked up at the idea, though she struggled to rein it back.

'I didn't think we *would* be working that closely,' she tried to say airily, though she wasn't entirely sure that she succeeded.

'It wasn't the original brief,' Mandy acknowledged. 'But Jukrem is such a new camp we didn't know what to expect in terms of footfall or types of cases. The longer we've been in the area, the better idea I think we're getting.'

'Did you have a particular project change in mind?' Hayden asked, getting straight to the heart of the issue.

By Mandy's expression, Bridget could tell the older woman liked his directness.

'Your right-hand man—Dean, is it?—was good enough to pass on the copies of the satellite images of the area that you guys brought out with you, as well as the geographical aerial surveys your team took today with their drones, looking for any riverbeds, wells or reservoirs. So thank you for that.'

'My pleasure.' Hayden smiled again, his charm not dipping for an instant, and even Bridget felt herself reacting. Again.

'I'm super-excited about the potential water sources, of course, and I know you've been tasked to focus on building infrastructure north of here up to the main camp of Rejupe, but I wondered if you were up for making a little detour?'

'How little is *little*, Mandy?' Hayden teased good-naturedly.

'Little...medium little.' She pulled a wry face.

He shot her a glance and she had the grace to look abashed. Bridget was shocked. She'd never seen Mandy look remotely accountable to anyone. But Hayden had managed it.

'So *medium big*, then?'

'Medium medium' was apparently as much as Mandy was prepared to admit. 'The thing is, those images also showed me that there appears to be a bit of a makeshift camp about half a day's drive south of here where the people have had no direct route to our medical centre during the rainy season because there's a wide riverbed between us.'

Hayden's brow knitted together. Not exactly a frown, but close enough.

'Forgive me if I'm wrong, but now the rainy season is over and the river is already drying up, they'll be able to get to you soon enough.'

'Precisely,' Bridget cut in, unable to stop herself. 'The moment the river dries out completely and they can cross, they'll flock over in their droves, all at the same time. We'll be overloaded here in this tiny clinic. And we'll be at risk of any number of contagious diseases coming over as well.'

'Which you're here to treat anyway,' he countered. 'Or am I missing something?'

Bridget cast a quick glance at Mandy, who gave the tiniest inclination of her head, allowing Bridget to proceed.

'Yes, but what would be best is if we could get to them with a small outreach team before they come here. That would help us keep Jukrem and this other camp separate whilst we treat any different illness or strains of illness. It will reduce the pressure here. And because we've gone to them, we can step the consultations so not everyone is clamouring for our attention at the same time.'

'I was also thinking of sending a small distribution team, as well as a small medical team,' Mandy said earnestly. 'It might be a good opportunity to do it with the security of your team on the ground.'

But this time Bridget felt the older woman was addressing her more than Hayden. As though she thought that Bridget might have some kind of sway.

She tried not to feel flattered. But it wasn't working.

'We don't have a mandate to engage if there are any problems,' Hayden pointed out, but Bridget could tell he was open to suggestions.

He *wanted* to help them. She just had to give him a reason he could sell to his superiors.

'No, of course not. We realise that,' she hedged. 'I think Mandy's just hoping that the added bodies out there will be enough of a deterrent.'

'That's exactly what I'm thinking,' Mandy concurred brightly, but Bridget's eyes were on Hayd.

She watched him closely, knowing he was assessing the practicalities. She could see his side, but she could also see what Mandy was trying to say.

'The thing is,' she waded in again, 'there are a lot of refugees beginning to come into the area now that the rains have ended and the roads are starting to become usable again. Part of our role is to distribute non-food items, such as tents, blankets, cooking pans, even soap to them so that they can live.'

Mandy nodded—silent permission to continue. So Bridget did so.

'Obviously, at times like this, these are valuable items that can be stolen and sold on for a good price. So it's important that we only distribute them to the refugees who really need them and won't want to sell them on.'

'Which makes distribution a security risk,' Hayden concluded, catching on quickly, not that Bridget was surprised. 'Stealing, rioting, stampedes?'

'Right. We try to keep information scant so that our arrivals are a surprise and no organised groups have a chance to get there and pretend to be refugees. We take a few hundred kits each time. And we try to do it at night so that we can get to anyone who might have to leave early in the morning to walk a couple of hours to their jobs.'

'Then can I leave you to discuss it, and hammer out any details?' Mandy asked. 'Bridget here has worked on enough projects that I'm happy she has a good grasp of the situation. And clearly you two already know how to work together. I think appointing you as the liaison instead of Lisa is going to be the best choice on this occasion.'

And with that, the older woman moved away briskly. On to the next concern on her never-ending list.

'I'm sorry.' Bridget pursed her lips as she watched Mandy leave. 'I didn't mean that to happen. I'll have a word with her later.'

'It's just a task, Birdie,' he answered casually.

'I thought you wanted us to keep some distance?'

'That doesn't mean we let it interfere with the job in hand,' he countered. 'Besides, I think we would work well together.'

'Do you?'

'Are you saying you don't think we would?'

Yes. No. Whatever. That was exactly what she was saying. Because it was now abundantly clear to Bridget that she, unlike Hayden, couldn't sleep with someone one week and then act normally around them the next.

Or maybe that was because it was *Hayden* she'd slept with. It wasn't as though she had anyone else to compare it to.

She felt trapped. As blocked in as this vast, landlocked country, and just as full of conflict.

'No,' she lied. 'Of course I'm not saying that.'

He grinned broadly and she knew that she'd just walked into that one.

The oddest thing was that she actually agreed with Hayden that they had the potential to be a good team. She happened to think so too. It was galling that the fact that he'd seen her naked and so...exposed had robbed her of the ability to act like she wanted to around him. Like the professional that she normally was.

Well, that stopped now.

'All right, let's discuss the feasibility. I think an army presence will just give the illusion of additional security without you having to act on anything. And I know it would be a morale boost for the teams.'

'Teams?'

'A logistical team and a medical team,' she elaborated. 'I would be going on the distribution mission anyway as a medic, in case something were to go wrong and someone ended up getting hurt.'

Hayden frowned, something shifting in his gaze. If she hadn't known better, she might have thought he was actually concerned for her.

But that would be nonsense. Hayd was a self-confessed playboy who had slept with army officers who put themselves in danger on a regular basis. He wasn't going to

around worrying about the her security just because…
well, *because.* Bridget rushed on quickly.

'But also I've been told that, a few months back, Mandy
had been talking about sending out a two- or three-man
medical team in order to carry out a measles vaccination
campaign if we were going to be out in those villages
anyway.'

'Measles?'

'I know it's not a major problem back home, but out here
it's second only to kala-azar in terms of serious paediatric illnesses,' she told him earnestly. 'It hits under-fives
very hard, and unfortunately even with prompt diagnosis
and our care, many, many of those children simply won't
survive it.'

'And vaccinating them will prevent that?'

'It will give them a better chance than they would
otherwise have,' Bridget confirmed. 'Certainly out here,
where immune systems can be non-existent given the
conditions. A mass measles vaccination campaign is
something that I've done before elsewhere, but we didn't
think we'd be able to here because of the security concerns.'

'Is that so?'

'Come on, Hayd.' The teasing tone was out before
Bridget could stop herself. 'You know you want to help,
deep down.'

She couldn't identify the look he shot her, but it made
her stomach pull tight and heat pool between her legs.

'Okay.' He nodded. 'You've sold me. I'll put a dozen
or so men together to accompany your teams. We'll put
it to regiment as a support task as part of our mission to
support the charity.'

'Thanks. I'll prepare the gear tomorrow. I'll drive the
medical team in one of the charity's four-by-fours, and I'll

get Christophe to drive the logistic team in the other. We can be ready to head out the day after.'

'Those timings work,' he concurred. 'But, Birdie, you'll need another driver. You'll be travelling with me.'

CHAPTER EIGHT

IT HAD BEEN a hectic night.

Bridget had been on call but hadn't slept well—if at all—and not just because of the conversation with Hayden. She'd lain on her bed, worrying, right up until a teenager had been brought in with a soaring fever. She'd had to strip him and administer a cold water sponge bath and paracetamol, before carrying out a malaria test.

She'd barely got back to her mosquito-net-protected bed, pretending that she wasn't still dwelling on the way Hayden had looked at her every now and then. When their conversation had flowed and he'd suddenly let his guard down.

And she'd schooled herself each time she'd risked imagining Hayden in his own hammock right then, in the army camp barely a couple of hundred metres away, on the other side of the wide but shallow dried-up riverbed.

Then the radio had crackled into life again. This time for another kid with fever but also convulsions. All tests led to cerebral malaria. Which meant stripping, cold baths, rectal paracetamol and plenty of fluids, along with an IV of diazepam.

The cases rolled in, one after another, and Bridget worked through each of them in turn. Methodically.

Oral rehydration and an overnight IV for one little boy, and skin-to-skin contact with the mother for an hour or so for another hypothermic little one. Then a snake bite, probably from about five days earlier, which meant it was probably a dry bite with no envenomation. Bridget assessed the site. There was no emergency but there was certainly a risk of infection, so she administered a tetanus booster and prescribed antibiotics.

But now they were in the army four-by-four as Hayden himself drove the two of them in the second vehicle.

'I didn't think you were allowed to drive yourself,' Bridget said as she slid into the passenger seat of the four-by-four, and Hayden swung into the driver's seat. 'I'm sure Mattie once told me that an officer had to have a driver.'

'Generally that's the case.' Hayden lifted his shoulders. 'Mainly because in the event of an RTA, an officer would have to go in front of a brigade commander if they were driving. Which isn't good for your career.'

'What if the RTA wasn't the officer's fault?'

'It doesn't matter,' he told her casually. 'If the only contact you've had with a brigade commander is a disciplinary, even for something as unfair as an RTA that wasn't your fault, when it came to a promotion, that could be all it takes for them to pass you over in favour of the next guy on the list who has nothing going against him. Especially if you're talking promotion to Major or above.'

'So why would you take the risk of driving now?'

'We're in the middle of nowhere. There are no roads and few vehicles. An RTA is more than highly improbable. And, frankly, I'm damned good at what I do. If my brigade commander wants certain, specialist roles carried out, he comes and talks to me directly, he doesn't even bother with the charade of going through my commanding officer.'

'Modest,' she teased, unable to help herself.

'I've never pretended that was one of my traits.' He flashed his teeth in another of those wicked grins that melted her bones.

She struggled to hold herself together, searching blindly for a more neutral topic.

'Here's one thing I didn't fully understand,' she managed. 'The charity I work for has hundreds and hundreds of medical camps all over the world. How did the army come to be involved in this one?'

'It's a *quid pro quo*,' he answered. 'The government of this country gave the British, American and Canadian armies access to a one thousand square miles training ground on the basis that we help with infrastructure in the surrounding areas, after so many years of their civil war.'

'But how did that come to involve this charity?'

'You were already in the area, doing an incredible job with health, water, education. It made sense, rather than come in and do the same things that you guys do but not have the trust of the local people, to instead come in and support you guys, boosting your resources and manpower, enabling you to reach more people, faster.'

'Right,' she considered. 'And build roads.'

'And bridges. Yes. Like you said the other day, the rainy season has made everywhere impassable for so long that everyone has to move at the same time around here. People, cows, goats. Permanent roads will allow for freedom of movement throughout the year.'

'But that's going to take months and months, surely? Even years?'

'You appreciate that my guys can build a bridge in under ten minutes?' he asked, amused.

'Sorry? Ten minutes?' Bridget blinked at him, and suddenly all he wanted to do was stop the vehicle and pin her up against the beaten-up seats, tasting that luscious mouth of hers again.

'You mean…something like a little foot bridge?'

CHARLOTTE HAWKES99

It took a herculean feat of self-restraint to keep his hands—and his body—to himself.

'No, I mean something like a man portable medium girder bridge that can span a nine-metre gap and support up to seven hundred and fifty tonnes.'

'Then with machines, surely? Tanks?'

'You're thinking of light armoured. No. I mean eight men.'

'And...you can set up one of those in under ten minutes?'

'We can when we're not under enemy fire. Takes a bit longer when my men also have to fire back.'

'Now you're being facetious.' She frowned.

How was that possible to make him want her more than ever?

'No, I'm just teasing.'

'Well, I hope you're enjoying yourself.'

'As it happens, I am,' he confessed with another grin. 'But wait until we get to our first river and you can see for yourself how we do it.'

'You're really serious, aren't you?'

'Like I said,' he told her breezily, 'this is something we have to do regularly, even in contact situations. If the rest of the army needs to move somewhere fast, we have to be able to make it happen.'

She pursed her lips, clearly tempted to agree. He could almost read the reservations as they paraded through her mind.

'Relax, Birdie. It will be fine.' He shrugged, ignoring all the alarm bells clanging in his head.

They'd been ringing ever since he'd heard himself tell her, the night of the welcome party, that she was going to be driving with him rather than in her own charity's vehicle.

Since when had he ever wanted to spend time with a woman so badly he was willing to bend the rules?

The answer—should he have admitted it rather than ducking the unspoken question entirely—was...*never*.

So much for concentrating on the incredible show being carried out less than twenty metres in front of her—so slick, so elegant, and so well rehearsed that it might as well have been a West End performance—all Bridget could think about was the fact that Hayden's leg was pressed sinfully close to hers.

She felt like a tangle of nerves and nothing else, leaving her jumpy and restless. Hayden, on the other hand, looked completely relaxed and at ease.

'So, right now the guys are putting together a five-bay, medium girder bridge which can span a nine-metre distance, and once fully built, ramped and decked, can take up to one hundred and thirty tonnes if it's a wheeled vehicle, or if it's a tracked vehicle up to eighty-five tonnes.'

She tried not to consider the fact that the glorious early morning sun was painting the sky a stunning, cloudless blue whilst she was standing here with Hayden, leaning on the bonnet of his four-by-four, feeling utterly peaceful.

'Tracked vehicle?' It was a tousle to drag her mind back to the matter at hand. 'You mean...a tank?'

'Tanks, armoured personnel carriers, mobile platforms for high-velocity missiles.'

'You lost me after *tanks*.' She laughed weakly. 'But put it into context for me. What do tanks weigh?'

'On average? I'd say about seventy tonnes.'

'So you're telling me that those eight men out there can put a bridge in place in under ten minutes and it will get a tank across a nine-metre gap.'

'Steady on.' Hayden grinned, and her stomach flip-flopped all over again. 'They can put the bridge together in that time, but it takes a bit longer to push it out over a gap. Okay, so the initial part of the bridge you can see there is called the horseshoe, and the smaller part you can see at the front is called the nose. The pieces you can see each two-man team picking up right now weigh about two hundred kilos. But those beams over there—we call them bank seat beams—weigh around five hundred kilos each.'

'So that's why you guys suffer so many musculoskeletal injuries.' Bridget laughed, but it cracked at the end when her mind decided to suddenly conjure up an image of Hayden's body and the tiny scars she remembered seeing that night at his hotel.

The scars she'd touched, and kissed, and tasted.

'Yeah, they're quite heavy bits of kit.'

'Hmm?' Guilt lanced through her as her mind whirred. *Something about heavy bits of kit?* 'But your guys are making it look like a walk in the park.'

She shifted position, moving against Hayden. Everything sizzled through her. Working with Hayden was thrilling but simultaneously fraught.

Every time she thought she was succeeding in dampening the attraction between them, he said something, or did something, and it flared up again.

Exciting, yet wholly inappropriate.

'How do they actually get the bridge over the river?' she asked, valiantly working not to be distracted.

'They use the nose as a counterbalance and simply push it out.' He used his hands to try to demonstrate. 'Once it's fully across, they'll jack it down and begin decking it.'

'And you really built these bridges and used them whilst under fire?'

'Sure. But out here we can be quite casual. In theatres of war we'd be wearing body armour and all that kind of thing. It makes progress a whole lot harder out there.'

'So if you're here to build roads and bridges, why don't you simply leave the bridges you're building now in situ?'

'Honestly? Because we only have a few man-portable bridges here, so we need them with us. The idea is to put down more permanent bridges once we've finished assessing the area.'

'How will it get in?' she frowned. 'By road? Isn't that a bit of a catch-22 situation?'

'We'll probably have it parachuted in,' he said. 'With the country being land-locked it's going to be easier to fly over than to try to drive everything across potentially hostile terrain.'

'Oh, my word,' Bridget cried suddenly, jerking up to watch the men. For once her attention was where she wanted it. 'They're done.'

She didn't miss Hayden consulting his watch. Checking their time, making his mental notes, no doubt. Ever the OC. She smiled to herself.

'Will you have to collect that bridge again once we've crossed?'

'No, we'll be heading back so soon that we might as well leave it in place.' Then he grinned, pushing off the bonnet of the four-by-four and hoisting himself inside.

'Come on, Gardiner, let's go and save a few lives.'

They reached the camp in good time and in the end over six thousand families received plastic sheeting and blankets, food and a jerry can.

'Good morning's work,' Hayden commented, as they helped the logisticians pack up their now empty vehicles and begin the trip to Jukrem camp.

'Very good morning,' said Bridget happily.

Although she had been setting up her medical twelve-by-twelve over near the shade, and hadn't been needed for the distribution because of how smoothly everything had gone. And being away from Hayden had helped her to regroup.

'Now they've got something to protect them from the elements, to eat, and to collect clean water from the pumps already in the area, and from the new ones when you've drilled the new boreholes.'

'And you're good to go?'

'I just need to hang a flag.' She waved a well-worn but well-looked-after piece of cloth in one hand. 'And I'm waiting for an extra table that one the carpenters of the community is making for me.'

'Then you're doing the measles immunisations.'

'Yeah, but depending on take-up, my team is also hoping to screen for malnourished kids.'

'There's a test for that?' He looked surprised and she didn't blame him.

'More like a band for measuring mid-upper arm circumference.' She rolled her eyes. 'Not very high-tech, but it works. If the arm is in the green part of the band the kid is healthy—in the red and the kid urgently needs to be admitted to one of our hospitals. If it's in between they don't need urgent hospital care but they do need treatment.'

'And you're expecting red?'

'Actually, no. It's the end of the wet season so the cows and goats are healthy and producing plenty of milk at the moment, so the kids are usually well fed and fall into the green category. At least, that's what I'm hoping for because we're now heading into the leaner season. The next harvest isn't due for a few months so there's a bit of a hunger gap.'

'Right, well, you go and immunise or screen. I'm going to see if I can't find some liquid gold.' He tapped the survey map in front of him.

'Okay.' She laughed. Surprisingly happy. 'See you later.'

Like they were a couple. And the strangest thing about it was that Hayden didn't react to it at all. He merely shot her a smile and lifted his hand.

Her heart stuttered, though she told herself she didn't know why that would be.

'What is it?' he asked, as if reading her mind.

'Nothing,' she lied, her mind racing. 'Just, maybe, take some of the local builders with you and see if you can't teach them about gradients and gravity-fed soakaways.'

'Say again? I don't want to be patronising.'

'That isn't being patronising.' She frowned. 'It's acknowledging a reality. There are things they build or make out here that we wouldn't have a clue about, at least I wouldn't. Like baking their own bricks for construction, or the way they build those beautifully crafted *tukuls*. In the same way, whilst we understand water and gradients, it's currently new to them.'

'I see.' Hayden looked thoughtful but unconvinced.

With anyone else she might have left it there, not wanting to press her point. So what did it mean that she barely thought twice about explaining herself to this particular man?

'Listen, you and I might think putting a gradient on a pipe is intuitive, but it isn't, it's a learned technique and out here people haven't yet had a chance to learn it. They just think that because water flows, it won't matter in which direction, up or down. Our water, sanitation and hygiene expert has spent the last few days explaining the importance of putting a gradient on pipes or drainage channels but the simple truth is that she's a woman so they find it hard to believe her.'

'Will your WSH expert really want me taking over, then?' Hayden looked sceptical. 'Won't that just make it worse for her?'

Bridget offered a light shrug.

'Don't take over, then. Work with her instead. Whether we like it or not, it's just the way it is out here at the moment and we're here to help, not to judge or tell them they need to change. Change can happen in its own time—we can't force it.'

'I see.' Hayden looked thoughtful again. 'Okay, I might have a few experiments I can use to highlight the point. Leave it with me, I want to run it by your WSH expert first.'

It was all she could to stifle the broad smile that suddenly threatened to spill over her face. She really needed to stop reading so much into so little.

It was all she could do not to skip back to the medical tent. But as she stepped through the flap, expecting everything set up ready for the immunisations, she was confronted with a grim-faced colleague and a local woman at the end, blood all over the bed.

'What's going on?' Bridget hurried forward.

'Emergency.' Her colleague lifted her hands into the air. 'Her family brought her. We told them she couldn't come in here, but they carried her in anyway. She gave birth quite a few hours ago but the placenta still hasn't come out.'

'Okay.' Bridget nodded. 'She's going to need manual removal.'

It wasn't ideal as the place had been set up for measles vaccinations and there was no way they could use it now. But these women were well accustomed to giving birth at home, so if she'd come here then there had to be a real issue.

'Can you bring me long-sleeved gloves?' she asked, reaching into the boxes for a gown. 'Damn, no long gown.'

'No long-sleeved gloves either,' her colleague apologised, handing her a pair that covered hand and wrist only. 'These are all we have.'

Bridget fought to keep her expression neutral in front of the already worried family, but there was no denying it was an issue. She would need to insert her arm into the woman's uterus, sweeping the blade of her hand around the side in order to find the plane where the placenta met the uterine wall. Then try to manually work the two apart. But that meant inserting her arm right up to the elbow, and without latex gloves that was going to be a problem.

'What if we cut up several pairs of gloves and kind of arrange them around my arm in overlapping rings?'

'We can try.' Her team looked dubious as one of them lowered her voice. 'Do you think I should get her family out? They're here to donate blood if it's needed to keep her alive, because if she dies, she would not only leave her beautiful newborn an orphan but also its four siblings. And the family, as much as they might care, simply wouldn't have the means to take on four young children.'

It was an added pressure, but one that was painfully familiar.

'We'll do our best.' Bridget nodded without looking up, her focus solely on cutting the fingers out of the gloves. 'But get the family outside and take their blood for cross-matching.'

A few minutes later the family was safely outside whilst Bridget slid her arm into the uterus and felt around for the placenta.

'I've got it,' she confirmed. 'It's free at the back but still attached anteriorly... Wait... There.'

Feeling it sheer off the uterine wall and fall, she slipped it out easily and the job was done.

It was going to be a successful mission. She could feel it.

CHAPTER NINE

HAYDEN COULD SLEEP on a clothesline. Over a decade and a half in the army had allowed him to perfect that technique. But tonight he couldn't even lie still. His thoughts were keeping his mind on a veritable assault course because he couldn't pretend he wasn't feeling this sleek, warm thing that moved around inside him every time he was with Bridget.

It was a madness, he knew that. Just as he knew he needed to put an end to it.

Yet he couldn't seem to be able to.

The rational part of his brain tried to pass it off as little more than a *sex* thing. The fact that no man had ever touched her the way that he had done, had even slid inside her, meant that she had given him the most precious gift indeed. It was only logical that it should have brought out a primal response in him.

But it was more than that—more than just the physical. It was as though she made his life better, brighter, more vibrant, even though he'd thought his life had been just fine as it was.

And that was part of the problem.

It was making it impossible for him to distance himself from her the way that he should, because really what could he offer her in return? A life like his mother had led whilst he lived his army life as his father had? Who would want that?

Yet if he tried to explain it to anyone, he wasn't sure they would have understood. How could they when his parents had appeared to have a happy marriage? And had loved each other?

Other people hadn't seen what he had. Those moments when he'd caught the utter loneliness in his mother's expression before she'd smoothed her face out and smiled at him with so much love that it had been blinding. He could still recall the first fifteen years of his life—Mattie was much younger, of course—when his family had moved once or twice a year, following his father up and down the country for each new posting and promotion.

He and his mother had felt as though their entire lives were a series of packing up, moving, unpacking, trying to make new friends, him trying to fit into a new school and his mother trying to find a new part-time job, finally settling in only to be told to pack up and move again.

But that was a road he didn't want to go down. Not now. So he found himself sitting by the fireside, chatting with the locals about nothing less beautiful than the carpet of stars that shone so brightly over their heads.

He'd learned how their names for the stars and the constellations differed so greatly from his own, and how their changing, flowing appearance throughout the year corresponded with the water missing from the sky during the rainy season, and the sky refilling during the dry season.

In turn, Hayden had answered their questions on why the moon was full some nights, yet not even there on others. And how the moon wasn't a great bowl that was lit up from the inside at night, as some of them had been taught to believe.

But now he sat, still and watchful, and finally alone, as

the reason for his apparent insomnia crept silently out of her tent and came to join him by the fire.

'I heard you out here earlier, but I didn't dare come out whilst the elders were here.'

'Indeed,' he managed, unable to drag his gaze from her as she settled prettily beside him. 'Shouldn't you be getting sleep before your main vaccination day tomorrow?'

'Probably,' she agreed mildly. 'How did the drilling go today? Did I hear you were planning on building a high tank where the water could be chlorinated before collection?'

'I thought that if we could increase the chlorination we might be able to reduce the number and severity of Hep E outbreaks that seem to occur in this region. Then again, there was a study carried out a few years ago that considered the likelihood of recontamination by the water bottles used by individual households before they even got the water back home.'

'What were the results?'

'I don't know.' He grimaced. 'I couldn't find them published anywhere. But I could rerun the tests if I use turbidity meters, chemical analysers.'

'Is that in your brief?'

'No,' he confessed. 'But I considered recruiting and training some locals to help us collect data in the field.'

How odd that her approval should affect him as it did.

'That's a good idea, Hayd. The locals really appreciate being taught new skills that can benefit their community. It makes them feel far more valued that if they had to simply stand by and watch others—outsiders—doing it for them.'

'I figured as much.'

'Sorry.' She looked sheepish. 'I guess you already know that. You must have worked with communities before.'

'A few times.' He smiled. 'But don't worry about it.'

For a moment they fell silent, each of them staring at the stars and losing themselves in their thoughts.

'Can I ask you a question?'

He didn't know why it made him tense, but he heard the forced note in his voice as he tried to tease her.

'Pretty sure you just did, Birdie.'

'Very funny,' she told him dryly, making him begin to ache.

As ever. As always.

'Fine, go ahead.'

'Why do you have such a reputation as a playboy?'

He paused, taken aback. Not that he was about to let that show.

'Do you really want me to demonstrate for you here? Now?' he teased. 'I'm more than offended you can't remember, of course.'

'My point is that I can't work out how you seem to have the time for all these women.'

'Why does it matter to you?'

'It doesn't,' she denied, unconvincingly. 'I was just curious.'

'Well, you know what curiosity did to the cat, don't you?'

'Then I've nothing to worry about, have I? Since, according to you, I'm the Bird.'

He didn't know why that should make him laugh, but it did. Hard, until he felt better than he'd felt in a while.

And closer to Bridget. Again.

He laughed for quite a while before an odd, sobering feeling began to creep up inside him.

'I don't know how my reputation came about, Birdie,' he managed softly, staring at the stars. Not addressing her directly. 'But I've always thought it was convenient for me. The perfect foil for the women who seem to think a single army officer must be on the lookout for a permanent companion.'

'But why?' she pressed. 'Whenever Mattie has talked about her childhood, it always sounded fine. Like your parents had a good marriage, and home life was great.'

And Hayden didn't know what it was, but something inside him...*shifted*.

'Mattie doesn't know what she's talking about sometimes,' he exhaled softly.

'She said they were happily married for twenty years before your mother passed away unexpectedly. She has always wanted to emulate your parents' marriage.'

'Well, she shouldn't. My sister isn't in possession of all the salient details.'

'Such as what?'

Hayden slid his gaze to her, this woman he didn't need to see in the darkness to be able to picture every line and angle of her lovely face, this woman who had slid under his skin when he hadn't been looking. And he heard himself begin to speak.

'My parents' marriage wasn't quite so perfect in the beginning, but Mattie's too young to remember, and I've never discussed it with her.'

He stopped, wondering why Bridget, of all people, should be the first person he had ever talked to about this. Giving her the chance to speak. But she didn't, she just sat watching him steadily and there was something encouraging about that.

'You know my father was a soldier? Yes, well, we got posted to different places a lot. Every nine months or so we'd move house, up and down the country, but because my father was away on exercises, it was my mother—and later me, too—who would have to pack everything up, clean the old home before the army would come and inspect the house and march us out, and then get to the new house and unpack everything.'

'That must have been difficult.'

'New home, new school, trying to make friends, every nine months.' He gave a ghost of a smile. 'Yeah, it was tough. But it was harder on Mum. Mattie was just a baby, and because we were always moving—not even always to where my father was, if he was on exercise—she didn't have a support network of friends and family. She couldn't have a career, although I think she would have liked one, she just had to find a part-time role to fit in around Mattie and I. And all the responsibility for family was on her.'

'I can't imagine,' Bridget said quietly. Sincerely. And he loved how she could convey such empathy without sounding either patronising, or gushing.

'She became depressed. Nothing suicidal, but meandering through mild to moderate depression, then back to being okay. Sometimes the house would be a tip. All the time. She could barely get herself moving. And other times she was so on top of it all that not a single thing would be out of place, and I'd almost be afraid to touch anything.'

'You're right, this isn't what Mattie has ever known.' Bridget shook her head gently.

'Like I said, she was a baby. By the time she started to get to the point where maybe she might have started to remember, my father got a promotion, and a more permanent posting in HQ. He was home a lot more. As in, every night. Everything changed.'

'She wasn't raising a family alone.'

'Right. She had support, and Mattie was older, so she actually went out and got herself her first job as a receptionist at a dental practice. It seemed to give her freedom and a new release. And that's the family life that Mattie remembers.'

'But it isn't the one you remember most?'

'No, it is.' He shifted in position, looking for the right words. 'I remember that, and I look back on it with affection. And although, looking back on it, Mum was clearly depressed, she kept herself together for the sake of Mattie and me. Home life was never miserable, and she was a good mum. A great mum.'

'But...?'

'But I remember how difficult it was for her because of my father's army career, and I think that any woman who wanted to be with me would have to put up with the same kind of stuff. I'm a soldier, it's who I am. I get moved around a lot, and I'm always away on exercises, or training, or operations. It's a great life for a single person. But my personal opinion is that it isn't conducive to good relationships. Or happy marriages.'

'I don't know,' she said thoughtfully, after a moment. 'I think it's different, Hayd. Or it *can* be different. You don't have a family, and not every woman is like your mum. What if you chose a woman who was also in the army, and career-minded like you?'

Or a medical charity worker, posted abroad for months.

The thought hung there in the air, and Hayden was sure Mattie could read it as well as he could. But he didn't say it.

'Then we'd never see each other.'

'That isn't true. And, even if it was, in time you would get promotions, and be offered more roles that gave you a more permanent situation, instead of postings here, there and everywhere.'

It was astounding how much he wanted that to be true. And how much he wanted it to be true with Bridget.

'It isn't just that, though,' he made himself continue. 'It's also the nature of what I do. You see my unit building roads, drilling boreholes, digging drainage channels. But that isn't all we do. We also deal with mine warfare, explosive demolitions, anything. How is it fair to settle with one person knowing that in the next operation you go on, you might never make it back?'

'It's admirable that you consider others,' she told him quietly, firmly. 'But that's not a choice you should be making on their behalf. That's a choice each individual should be able to make for themselves.'

'I disagree. There's often a romantic notion attached to what we do, and that notion is often a far cry from the reality. I *know* the reality, I've lived it. I've stood next to a best friend one moment, only for them to step on a land mine and be gone—literally vaporised from existence—a second later as we turn away from each other.'

And if he'd expected his resolute, focussed Bridget to drop her eyes from his even as she dropped the topic, he should have known she was stronger than that.

'Maybe you should try trusting people a little more,' she told him evenly. 'You might be surprised at what they've experienced themselves. And just how much they understand. Often more than you might think.'

How he stilled himself in that moment Hayden would never know. Every nerve ending in his body was on fire just keeping himself from crossing that invisible divide between them and hauling her to him.

He'd kept telling her there was a line between personal and professional, and that what had happened between them back in the UK could be kept separate from what happened between them out here.

But he suspected—more than suspected—that it was himself who he kept trying to remind. *He* was the one who, after years of being happily single and never wanting more, couldn't keep his mind from wandering back into territory it shouldn't be in.

Imagining Bridget. Like he had no control at all where she was concerned—she dominated his every waking moment. And, if he was honest, she haunted his sleep, too.

He told himself that it was just temptation. Purely a physical attraction. Undeniable chemistry. But whatever term he tried to use, the fact was that it was still here, hovering like a ghost in the periphery of his mind.

No matter where he was or what task he was on, a part of him was always aware of where she was and what she was doing. He could never shake this *longing* to go to her and talk to her. Touch her. Take her.

As if she could make him forget everything he'd ever thought was important in his life if he only gave her the chance. The thought was more frightening than he could have imagined.

And something else besides that he didn't care to examine in that moment.

Suddenly he didn't want to talk any more. He just wanted to act. Reaching out, he slid his hand behind her head and pulled her easily to him, his lips brushing over hers for a fraction of a second before he tilted his head and claimed her mouth with his.

Hayden was kissing her. *Again.* And it was even better than all the memories she'd been replaying in her head these last couple of weeks.

He was unrushed. Unhurried. Tasting her and sampling her, as if he'd never done so before. They said you could never experience a second first kiss, and yet this felt crazily close.

It was like he was pouring more into that kiss than she'd known before. More of *himself.* Telling her things with every scrape of his tongue, every slick move of his lips. Hot and demanding. Only she was afraid to believe them, in case she was reading too much into the unspoken words.

So, instead, she just gave herself up to the kiss. Submitting to the sensation of his calloused thumb pad against her cheek and indulging in the magic as if it was a spell from which she never wanted to be released.

She had no idea when she moved, or even that she had, only that suddenly she found herself against him, wrapped in his arms with his chest hard against hers. He kissed her over and over, his hands cupping her jaw, his fingertips gliding softly down her neck, as if he couldn't get enough of her.

As if she was the most precious, beautiful thing he'd ever held. And then he kissed her some more, licking his way over her lips and kissing a path down the line of her neck. Heat bloomed right through Bridget, as her skin seemed to grow taut over her body in some kind of visceral response. Like her insides were liquefying and he was turning her core molten. She was sure that if he hadn't been holding her so tightly, she would have fallen in a puddle, right there on the hard ground.

As it was, she was helpless to control the greedy little sounds that kept escaping from her. She couldn't stop her mind from spinning in some dizzying, glorious, calamitous waltz that could only end with her either soaring to vertiginous heights or crashing agonisingly on the ground.

He moved his hand lower, his palm raking over her tee, making her skin prickle with the need to feel his touch. Lower still, until suddenly he was covering her breast with his palm, his thumb grazing over the tight bud. All she could do was arch into it as a kind of jagged wildness ripped through her, leaving her wanting more. *So much more*.

Vaguely she heard the alarm bell in her head, warning her that if she didn't stop now she wasn't going to be able to and for a split second she froze.

Hayden pulled back instantly.

'Hayd…' she whispered, the loss of contact leaving her feeling bereft.

'No.' His voice was ragged, like glass. 'You were right to stop. That should never have happened.'

'Not here anyway,' she managed weakly.

'Not anywhere,' he corrected, and she hated the grimness in his tone.

Hated that he regretted the kiss they'd shared. Because as much as she knew they couldn't have continued, she couldn't quite bring herself to wish it hadn't happened.

She wanted to tell him that, but the moment was gone. Lost forever. And as he stood up, hauling her to her feet beside him and settling her before taking a clear step away, she knew that there was no trying to reclaim it.

Her heart was beating hard and fast in her chest. The simple truth was that Hayden had convinced himself a long time ago that he didn't want a woman in his life, and if he was ever going to change his mind then he needed to come to it in his own time.

On the other hand—she vacillated as she so often did when it came to this man—it was worth remembering that just because he'd confided in her about his childhood, it didn't necessarily follow that *she* was the woman he would ultimately want.

If anything, it was possibly somewhat arrogant of her to believe that she held an allure for him that no other woman who had gone before her had held. And yet…the flame of hope flickered in her chest.

'I should go back to my hut,' she murmured eventually, trying to eradicate the shake from her tone.

Pretending that it wasn't a fight to keep her distance from him.

'You should.' His voice was clipped, and still she didn't think she was imagining that undercurrent.

'I'll see you in the morning,' she added softly.

He dipped his head once in silent affirmation, but she knew instinctively that he wouldn't be in camp when she woke. Maybe he would drive to the site of another potential borehole, or perhaps he would head off to conduct more ground surveys of the area. Either way, he would be putting a bit of distance between the two of them.

And as much as Bridget told herself that was a good move—a wise decision, given that that ever-shifting line in the sand—she couldn't help feeling that Hayden was fighting her for all the wrong reasons.

That maybe he was trying a bit too hard to tell her that she didn't mean anything to him.

CHAPTER TEN

'WILL SOMEONE CALL the doctor again, and tell him this is an emergency?'

Hearing Lisa's frazzled voice from outside the emergency *tukul*, Bridget hurried over. It had been a frantic few days since she'd returned to Jukrem camp, her measles vaccination programme a success. And in some respects Bridget had been grateful for the bustle to distract her.

She'd suspected that she wouldn't see Hayden after that kiss they'd shared a few nights ago, and she hadn't been wrong. But now, far from lamenting it, Bridget felt it had been just what she'd needed. She'd still been shaking over the sheer intensity of it up until yesterday. Seeing him could only have made things a hundred times more intense.

'Can I help?' Bridget asked, pushing open the plastic screen that served as a door. 'I can...'

'Stop.' Hewa, a local nurse trained by the charity, hurried to the door to block Bridget's way, but Bridget's attention was already dropping. Down to the floor and the blood-soaked earth. Then the blood-covered shoes of the nurse.

'Retained placenta,' Lisa told her grimly. 'Baby is okay, she's over there. But the placenta didn't come away even though I tried the usual procedures. And then she started haemorrhaging.'

Carefully sidestepping the blood, Bridget made her way to the bed where a young woman, lay, the life literally draining out of her.

She couldn't focus on that, though. She could only focus on Lisa.

'Did you run a manual removal?'

'I tried,' confirmed Lisa. 'I ran the usual procedure of sliding my hand in to run the blade of my hand around the uterus… I did it to the letter, Bridget. But it's stuck fast, she's still haemorrhaging and there's nothing I can do.'

'Is the placenta abnormally deeply embedded?' Bridget asked.

'Abnormally,' Lisa echoed with a nod. 'Yes.'

'Okay, so we can't risk anything more, she's going to need surgery. Hewa, can you get this girl's relatives together to see if they can donate blood? Lisa, de-glove and clean up. Then maybe see if you can get a bucket to try to catch some of this blood before it hits the ground. No point having us slipping and sliding as we try to treat the poor woman.'

Usually a birth was a glorious event. But not right now. Not when the beautiful, healthy baby the midwives had just delivered was lying, swaddled but untouched, his mother only metres away, unconscious, and at any moment could need to be resuscitated.

As soon as she could, she would look to get something to clean up the blood that was already all over the delivery room floor. It wasn't going to help anyone to see it, let alone anything else.

Janet appeared just as Bridget was passing the door. The doctor was sweating in the forty-degree heat and looking like she hadn't been to bed for days. Bridget knew exactly how she felt.

Being here was utterly demanding, but it was also fulfilling.

'You radioed me?'

'Patient with retained placenta. It's abnormally deeply attached, and our patient began haemorrhaging.'

As Janet entered the delivery room to see her patient, Lisa began to run through her actions to correctly detach the placenta.

'Okay, so it's embedded in there,' Janet confirmed at length. 'Let's give her fluids and something to get her blood pressure up before she crashes.'

'Right,' Bridget concurred, all too aware that the blood pressure medication was potent.

They were going to have to count the drops to infer infusion rate as it was going to need very careful titration. The sooner she could get donated blood from any suitable relatives, the sooner they could start to reduce this incredibly powerful blood pressure medication. But the fact remained: the placenta was embedded and they didn't have the means in this camp to get it out.

'Surgical solution,' Bridget muttered. 'Meaning transfer to the main camp at Rejupe?'

'Only choice,' concurred Janet. 'But I'm afraid I heard the heli was on a run elsewhere. And there's no other way.'

'What if she could be driven?'

'The ground is still too unpredictable. Not all the riverbeds are traversable.'

'And if the army did their bridge-building stuff…? I saw them when we went to the outreach camp. They're fast and direct. It's probably this girl's only chance.'

For a long moment Janet considered it. Her mind working on one problem whilst her hands worked on another. The biggest concern was that their patient was going to start bleeding into her uterus.

'Go,' she urged Bridget abruptly. 'Speak to the OC. If he agrees, we'll leave straight away.'

Stepping outside, it took a mercifully short time for her

to locate Hayden, engaged in discussion with one of his men, a set of plans in front of them.

Hayden was poring over a map when Bridget called his name.

It was probably a good job, as his mind was so active that he couldn't have seen a single contour line or feature if it had leapt up and engaged him in a fist fight.

He made himself turn slowly, willing the few days away to have dulled his irrational reactions to her. But when he saw the expression on her face, everything else dissipated.

'What's wrong?' he demanded. 'What do you need?'

'We've an emergency,' she told him without preamble. 'A young mother we have to get to the main hospital in Rejupe for immediate surgery. We've requested a transfer, but the helicopter is already on site elsewhere.'

'So you need us to head out along the route and lay any bridges or sections to ensure you get a smooth run?' he surmised.

'It would save us hours and ensure our safety.'

'And the patient?'

She looked him straight in the eye, causing that habitual flare of electricity.

He stamped it out.

'We can carry her in the back of a one of our four-by-fours, but we're going to have to carry mobile monitoring equipment, rig up some kind of pole for the IV, and ensure she has a medical escort with her as well as a driver. That means needing room and, more importantly, tying up two of our staff.'

'I'll give you a couple of drivers and a four-tonner,' he said without preamble.

'Thank you.'

He glanced quickly at his watch 'When do you want to go?'

'As soon as possible. The longer we wait, the more

chance she will bleed out into her uterus. We just need to get a medication pack for transport and make any last-minute infusion changes.'

'Who is the medical escort? A local nurse?'

He didn't know why he asked. It wasn't as though it made any difference.

'I don't know,' she replied, but there was the faintest hint of a blush under her tanned cheeks. Not that he knew what that meant. 'Probably a local, yes. Though it should be someone who can handle a critical care situation like this, and who will know how to deal with any possible complication that may arise *en route*. But we can't spare any of the doctors. They're all needed here.'

'Sort your medication pack, I'll jury rig a pole for your IV line to the canopy of the four-tonner. When you're ready to bring your patient out, my guys will come and carry your stretcher.'

'Understood,' she confirmed. 'Thanks.'

And then she was gone, and he was striding to the mess tent to find his second-in-command, to hand over command. Logically, he didn't need to go. But a trip to Rejupe camp would be a good opportunity to get the lie of the land, especially as it was a main site.

And that was the only reason, he told himself obstinately.

'Hey, Dean, just need to brief you,' he stated, walking into the ops post.

'What's up?' Dean asked, looking up and seeing he was alone.

'The charity has just asked us to assist with a cas-evac to Rejupe. I'm going to need a four-tonner and driver for the patient and medical escort, along with their mobile monitoring equipment. Also, an MGB on a DROPS, with an eight-man team.'

The DROPS would be the perfect vehicle to carry the Medium Girder Bridge.

'What's the lead time?' Dean asked, already going through his task sheets.

'They're ready to transfer the patient, timings are on us, of the essence. Send a runner to use the charity's radio and find out what billets will be available at Rejupe, so let's go for an O group in fifteen minutes to let the guys know what gear they need to bring.'

'Understood. I'll also let Lieutenant Johns know that he's going to be your second-in-command while I'm gone. It'll be good practice for him.'

'Better let him know he'll be *your* second-in-command.' Hayden deliberately held his tone neutral. 'You'll take command here while I head to Rejupe. With it being the main hospital and camp, I might as well do the recce we were planning to do there next month anyway.'

'Makes sense,' Dean agreed, taking it at face value.

'Great, right, I'll go and grab my kit and be back for the O group.'

He heard Dean answering over his shoulder, but Hayden was already heading out of the ops tent, telling himself that it was business. The mission.

Nothing more.

'How's the baby doing?'

'Hungry,' Hayden growled, ignoring the amusement in Bridget's eyes as she watched him trying to cuddle the newborn.

She'd basically shoved it…him…into his arms as soon as her patient's stretcher had been carefully manoeuvred onto the vehicle amongst the equipment, ignoring his objections. Not that he'd many the moment she'd told him that the baby's mother was all the kid had, his soldier father having been killed by a rebel group a few months earlier.

It was a point that had served to remind Hayden how the country's civil war had raged for so long that even now the peace they had was painfully fragile.

'I'm really not sure that I'm the best person to look after him.'

'You're fine,' she'd answered in a tone that had invited no argument. 'I need to have my hands free for the mother in case anything goes wrong. And babies around here don't get put down, they're held all the time, even if it's in one of those intricately woven newborn baskets the women carry on their heads.'

'I'm not carrying him in a basket on my head,' he'd said with a grimace.

Not that Bridget had seemed to care.

So now he was stuck holding a baby—literally—whilst watching her deal with any problems with her patient, as their vehicle made careful progress along what didn't even pass for roads around this place. And he found himself drawn in by the way Bridget kept talking softly to the unconscious mother in what seemed to be quite a decent grasp of the young woman's language.

Caring.

Then the baby began to grouse again, causing him to have to start the jiggling and soothing of his own all over again.

'Sing him a song,' Bridget suggested.

'Say again?'

'Babies love songs, right?'

'How the hell should I know?' he demanded, but it lacked any real heat. 'And I don't sing.'

'Well, you'd better start now.' She chuckled as the baby had made its objections even clearer. 'Either that, or show him the birds outside by the river, or the purple lily beds, or the sorghum in the fields.'

'Egrets.'

'Sorry?' She frowned at him.

'The *birds* you mentioned are egrets. Yellow-billed egrets, to be more precise. They nest in the trees along the riverbank at night.'

'I didn't know that.' She rocked back on her heels, surprised. 'Although I *do* know that the river in this area offers good fishing opportunities, especially at this part of the season, right when the locals are caught between the rainy season and the next harvest.'

'So I understood.' He laughed, loving the tiny glower it earned him.

How was it that he'd come to relish those moments more than anything else? Because those were the times when she struck him as being the most *herself.*

'We're not far out now.' She peered around the back of the vehicle and out at the landscape, which was, to be fair, rather boringly flat.

As everywhere was in these parts.

'About an hour by my calculations.' He checked his watch.

Again she poked her head out the back and peered around.

'I'd say a little longer. There's something of a deceptive dip in the terrain around here. Takes you by surprise if you're not careful.'

Yes, he knew all about things around these parts taking him by surprise. He was staring right at one of them. Two, if he counted the precious being currently nestled in his arms, so tiny that it was almost fragile.

Almost.

He'd been around them long enough to hear that cry and know that these babies were a lot more robust than they seemed.

'Are you really hating this?' she asked suddenly, taking a break for a moment from checking her patient.

'Hating what? Doing a recce in the middle of our training ground that I was going to be doing anyway?'

'You know what I mean.' She dropped her voice until, even in the back of a four-tonner, it felt almost…*intimate.* 'Being in the back of this lorry, holding a baby.'

He pondered her question for a moment, almost tempted to lie, before wondering why he needed to.

'Let's just say that I'm disliking it a lot less than I thought I would,' he answered honestly, and then, as if to prove the point, he found himself peering down at the baby to check he was all right, before snuggling him tighter.

As if he was somehow protecting this tiny, fragile bundle from the potential of becoming an orphan in the next few hours.

'Quite a compliment,' she told him, and he couldn't tell if she was serious or not.

'Maybe our patient here will call her baby *Hayden.*'

For a moment she looked bleak, and he didn't need to be a doctor to know that the chances of the mother surviving were low as it was, and getting lower with every moment. Not that his drivers could go any faster with the sick patient on board.

Then Bridget gathered herself together and made herself answer. And he liked it that she kept her voice upbeat and her words positive, even though they were both fairly sure that the mother was too far out of it to hear. And that, even if she could, she wouldn't be able to understand.

'Maybe.' She forced a smile.

And she didn't contradict him.

For a long, long while they continued in silence.

'You'll like Rejupe,' she told him at last. 'My team acclimatised here for a couple of days before we headed out to Jukrem. Unlike back there, where we have hole-in-the-ground latrines, the guys here all have individual bathrooms, plus they live in purpose-built accommodation blocks. It isn't five-star but it's plush compared to where we are.'

Not that she would be anywhere but Jukrem.

'Quite a luxury.' He matched her grin with one of his own and something delicious shivered through her. She tried to ignore it. 'So, what's the plan when we arrive?'

Bridget shrugged her shoulder but kept her voice deliberately even.

'Hopefully we'll get to the camp in good time, the surgeon comes out to assess, and they take her straight into surgery.'

'And then for us?'

She knew he didn't mean anything by the word *us*, but it rippled through her all the same. As if there was a possibility of that word meaning something more.

No, it probably wasn't what he'd meant at all.

She shook her head imperceptibly and tried to concentrate on the question he had more likely been asking.

'It will depend on how the surgery goes. If it's successful, Mandy suggested returning with our patient on the supply plane since it's scheduled to fly into Jukrem in a couple of days.'

'And if the surgery isn't successful?' he prompted gently when she stopped.

Her throat felt suddenly tight. She couldn't explain what it was about this patient or her baby that had got to her as it had. She saw plenty of sorrow and death in this job, and it was never easy to accept, but one grew accustomed to it.

What other choice was there?

'If it isn't…' she gritted her teeth '…then I guess I'll be returning with your team at first light tomorrow.'

'Understood.'

She nodded, forcing herself to remain upbeat for the sake of the mother and baby if nothing else. They might not be able to hear or understand her, but either way she wanted to keep the atmosphere around them a positive one. It mattered to her.

'So, at Rejupe we'll get to sleep in decent beds for a night or two, enjoy hot showers and eat food that doesn't come from a can. Maybe we'll even have the opportunity to go into the local town and buy some gifts for back home.'

For a moment he just watched her, making her feel as though her body was turning inside out. And still the word reverberated around her head. *Us.* Hayden and herself. Was it possible? Did she even want it to be?

'Sounds good.' He spoke at last. 'I want to speak with the project coordinator here anyway to get the lie of the land, so to speak, and then I think I like the idea of a hot shower. But maybe after that you can show me around this market of yours.'

Surely her body shouldn't so instantly thrill to the notion? As though a part of her was hoping for…what? A repeat of that kiss? Or more, such as a repeat of their night together?

And why not? a voice whispered in her head.

No matter how much she tried to avoid him—admittedly, she hadn't tried that hard at times—it was as though *fate* kept throwing them together, telling her to be bolder and have some fun. Again.

But then what? Where would it go from there?

Relationships out in places like this, in NGO camps in the middle of nowhere, weren't exactly encouraged. Back at training they were frowned upon, usually because any tension between the couple inevitably fed through to the rest of the team.

Then again, she'd known plenty of couples to hook up on missions and if both parties were discreet, putting their roles first and not allowing their relationship to make anyone else feel awkward, it went largely ignored.

It was just that she'd personally never had a hook-up. She'd never wanted to. Never even been tempted. Until now.

Until *Hayd.*

The devil on one shoulder was whispering that this was a second chance to break out of her usual shell. To pursue something with Hayden, safe in the knowledge that it couldn't last past the three months' time limit imposed on them by the date when he and his unit were due to return home.

She couldn't get hurt if she put a definitive end date on it. *Right?*

But the good girl on her other shoulder was reminding her that getting together with a colleague was a potential distraction. That she had a job to do, and that didn't include acting like some kind of lovelorn teenager around the brother of the woman who was—for all intents and purposes—the closest thing she'd ever had to a best friend.

The issue was that she didn't seem to be able to control herself where Hayd was concerned. That gave her two options. She could either roll with it and indulge in the attraction for the first time in…well, *ever.* Or she could consider removing herself from temptation altogether and ask the project coordinator for a transfer away from Jukrem—and Hayd—altogether.

Bridget knew what the logical solution was. So what did it say that it was definitely *not* the choice she wanted to be making?

CHAPTER ELEVEN

SEVERAL HOURS LATER Bridget was standing under the shower and simply revelling in the glory of the hot water rolling over her.

The handover had gone as well as she could have hoped, with her accompanying the mother as she'd been whisked into surgery, whilst Hayden—still carrying the baby—had been led to the neonatal ward.

The surgery had been promising and the team had done everything they could. Now it was just a matter of waiting. And hoping. And that meant enjoying the shower, which was nothing like the power showers of back home but certainly better than the solar showers she'd been having in Jukrem.

And pretending that she didn't feel wrecked by Hayden.

Why was it so impossible to shake the man from her head?

Refusing to give in to any more distractions of the six-foot-three variety, Bridget soaped up quickly, rinsed, and shut off the precious water supply. A bit of revelling was one thing, but even though the infrastructure here at the main town of Rejupe was better than at the mobile camps at Jukrem, she was still sensitive to the resources.

As she changed into a fresh set of clothes, Bridget raised her hand to the door of her temporary two-metre-by-three-metre room and promised herself a quick check on her patient's surgery, a bite to eat, and the first full night's sleep she'd have had in a couple of weeks.

So why was her heart hammering at the idea that she was about to embark on the closest thing to a *date* with Hayden, taking him into Rejupe town to sample the gastronomic offerings of the market, as she'd promised?

For a moment she debated feigning exhaustion and crying off. But then, suddenly, there he was, standing in the middle of the square in the charity's compound, waiting for her. His long, muscular legs stretched out in front of him, apparently oblivious to the two women crossing the area behind him, their eyes riveted.

'Ready?' he asked, taking a step towards her.

Her chest constricted. So tightly she could actually feel her breath squeeze out. All she could do was smile and nod, trying to keep steady as he fell into step beside her and they headed out of the gates together.

'I heard the mother's surgery went well,' he said after a moment.

'It did,' she managed, forcing herself to say more. 'We're waiting to see how she goes overnight.'

'Right.' He nodded, falling silent again and leaving Bridget to mentally kick herself for sounding so strained.

But she didn't need to worry, he spoke again after a few moments, sounding as relaxed and unconcerned as ever.

'Do you have anywhere particular in mind for eating?'

'Quite a few,' she answered gratefully. 'I'm trying to think of the best one. There are marketplaces in the main town and even pizza restaurants and a bar where the staff—foreign and locals alike—go to decompress.'

'Sounds great. I'll follow your lead.'

'Okay.' She grinned, and there was something about the way he wasn't trying to take control that made her relax that little bit more.

For a while they wandered around, soaking it all up, and Bridget found herself recounting some of the stories from when her group had last been here earlier in the month.

'What about eating here?' She stopped at last by some tables near a street stall she remembered, which showcased some of the tastiest local cuisine. 'There should soon be some entertainment in that open area opposite.'

'Here it is,' he agreed, looking around for a moment. 'Any recommendations?'

'Lots.' She laughed, the delicious cooking smells making her stomach rumble loudly. 'As you can hear. And it's kind of like tapas, so we can try plenty.'

'I definitely like the sound of that.'

So, a few minutes later, they sat at the table with a selection of little pots in front of them from which they both tried green beans flash fried with onions and garlic, dough balls with a variety of dips, and bowls of chicken with different sauces.

'This is a little better than the Friday night offering we have at Jukrem.' She laughed, popping the last mouthful of local cake, complete with a creamy frosting, into her mouth.

'Isn't it.' Hayden grinned. 'It seems like they have a whole host of stuff on offer on a Friday night. When I was in the neonatal ward I heard that tonight is movie night for them.'

She grinned, easily able to imagine that one of the single girls had invited him to join her there. But instead of accepting, he was here. With her. It made her feel...*special.*

'Yeah, they had that when I was here. No worries for them about conserving power and electricity shutting off from midnight onwards, like we have to back in Jukrem.'

'Evidently.'

'The guys here don't know what roughing it is. Did you know they even have their own cook?' She paused and cocked her head to one side. 'Wait, you guys have your own chef out in your army camp, don't you?'

'What can I say? The army knows how to live.' She loved the way he laughed.

'I thought I saw you with some local builders the other day, trying your hand at *tukul* maintenance?'

She tried not to flush as she thought of quite how she and, if she was being honest, a couple of the other nurses had taken the long route between the outpatient building and the wards a few too many times that day whilst Hayden and his men had been working.

'Maybe you can repair some of the huts back at Jukrem? Though probably not the large one, which was once the kitchens area, I believe.'

'No, that hut is definitely too far gone,' Hayden agreed. 'You're better off staying in the temporary kitchens in the twelve-by-twelve for now.'

'And the open stone barbecue, that's a decent cooking set-up.'

His eyes held hers over the table, making her heart pound for no reason other than it reminded her it was just the two of them.

'I'm not saying my guys will rebuild the entire *tukul* village, but I did think we might have a go at mud hut repairs before we go. Maybe get the army to fund us enough to employ some of the local builders, once we get back to camp, to teach everyone.'

'That isn't a bad idea,' Bridget mused. 'As long as you pick a new gang at the start of each week, you won't fall foul of the local labour laws.'

His gaze turned more serious.

'Good to know. I think the more we try to integrate and use locals, even in the construction of the roads, the better we're going to integrate into the area, especially when we've got full brigades here for training. Before we left

Jukrem I discovered a couple of very traditional builders who still know how to build the ancient way, and *tukul* construction is quite similar to traditional Celtic round-house builders.'

'Isn't it like a woven stick—walls packed with mud?'

'It is, but they have a particular way to do it that ensures structural integrity. Enough to support the long conical poles that reach up to that crown in the centre. And the most intricate part is the stunning, handmade, local rope that binds it all together.'

'Did you learn to thatch it too?' she asked, Hayden's enthusiasm beginning to infiltrate.

'Not from the locals, although I have tried thatching before, back in the UK.'

'I tried that once back home, too. Maybe one day we could learn together,' she began, and then stopped.

What was she doing? It had been a throwaway comment that had made it sound like she was making plans for the future. Hayden must be cringing. They might have started to talk a little more, or it felt as though they had anyway—certainly recently—and things might seem good between them right at this moment, but that didn't mean she wanted to go ruining it by sounding as though she was pressing him for more than they'd already agreed. Or by getting too personal.

Hadn't he already told her that he didn't envisage seeing her again once they'd left this country? He had never suggested that getting involved in a relationship had ever been part of his plans.

But was tonight a tiny hint that he just might be changing his mind? No, she was probably only fooling herself, if she believed that.

'I meant the charity and the army could learn together,' she clarified awkwardly. 'Not just *you* and *I*.'

'I understand that,' he replied smoothly, much to her

relief. 'The point is, I figured that rather than trying to re-pair that kitchen *tukul*, which, as you said, is a bit far gone, I might just rebuild it altogether.'

'Wow, that would be great.' She blinked, trying to clear her head. That unwelcome awkwardness from her blunder still lingering in her mind. 'Somewhere us charity workers can maybe eat together?'

'A bit more of a social space,' he agreed. 'And if that project goes well I was considering contacting HQ whilst you guys contact your team back home to see if we can't get the go-ahead to construct a small village in Jukrem. Once we've got in a few more fresh water stations, we'll know how the dwellings could be arranged for the best.'

'I think that's a great idea.' It was amazing how quickly he could make her start to feel at ease again. 'Jukrem is growing a lot faster than we'd imagined. It was only meant to be temporary, a bit more than a mobile medical camp, but certainly not the main medical hub that it seems to be turning into.'

He nodded as she warmed to her topic.

'But that's hardly surprising with its proximity to that refugee camp. And with more and more people flood-ing in every day, it really is a good outreach site. Now it needs to be more.'

'I agree.' Hayd dipped his head gravely. 'Now the rainy season is over, more displaced persons and refugees are going to start arriving *en masse*, by road and by river. If Mandy is on board as the charity's project coordinator, she is best situated to contact your charity's HQ.'

'Yeah, she is.' Happiness spread through Bridget and she couldn't pretend it was just at the thought of Hayd's team helping the charity. 'And she'll be delighted. So, these *tukuls* of yours, will they come complete with the wildlife?'

'Say again?'

'Well, mine came with a hedgehog, Lisa's has a mouse, and Janet's has a couple of lizards.'

'Hedgehogs, lizards, and mice…' He pretended to jot it down. 'But no spiders or cockroaches, I'm guessing? I'll see what I can do.'

It was nice, Bridget thought as they headed back to the compound an hour or so later, the way they could banter and take time together. They'd spotted some of the other staff in the town, along with a group of Hayden's men, all enjoying the unexpected downtime, with Hayden lamenting the fact that he was now going to have to ensure he sent all his men for a couple of days' R&R to Rejupe in the interests of fairness.

And then, all too quickly, they were back at the compound, walking through the gates together, and she had to tell herself that she was only imagining the fact that they'd both slowed down, as if trying to prolong the night that little bit longer.

She really needed to get a grip on herself. Since when had she been the kind of person to read non-existent things into situations? Biting the inside of her cheek, Bridget made herself stay quiet as he walked her to her room.

'Well, this is me, then,' she managed, as she stood with her fingers on the handle, unable to make herself actually push it open.

'Yes.'

She wanted him to say something, *do* something, and yet at the same time she didn't. It was painfully confusing.

'I'll see you in the morning,' she managed stiffly, flinching with embarrassment.

He didn't answer straight away, and she didn't blame him. Who knew she had a long-hidden skill of turning a perfectly innocent moment into something insanely uncomfortable?

With a great effort she pushed the handle down and began to open her door.

'We could check out the film?' Hayd suggested brusquely, halting her.

It was incredible how badly she wanted, at that instant, to pull the door closed and go with him.

Go anywhere with him.

Bridget would never know how she managed to hold her nerve. How she managed to push that door wider. How she managed to make her legs work long enough to carry her those couple of steps inside.

'Thanks, but I think I'll get to bed. It's been a long, long day and I haven't had a good night's sleep in a decent bed in what feels like forever.'

And she shut out the fact that every fibre of her being was screaming at her not to be such an idiot.

One more night, it cried. *One more night with Hayd before he goes back to Jukrem in the morning.*

'If you're sure,' he replied, his voice altogether too husky.

Too tempting.

His head was dipping towards her. Barely a fraction but enough to convince her that this time she wasn't imagining anything.

And, Lord, how she wanted to say yes *to whatever it was he might be offering.*

'I'm sure,' she rasped instead.

'Birdie…'

'Don't.' She shut him down before she could think. 'It would be a mistake.'

And then she slammed the door and pressed her back against it before she could do something stupid, like grabbing him by those all-too-solid shoulders and dragging him into her tiny room.

It took her a minute or so to catch her breath before she could push herself off the door again. Another minute to walk across the room to her bed, pull the covers back and then stand there, staring blankly at the sheets.

She wanted him. Incredibly, he wanted her too. Just like he'd wanted her that night at the club. And the night they'd shared after that. And maybe that didn't mean they had a future together, but who said they had to have one?

Who said she couldn't enjoy just one more night with him? Because she *wanted* to spend another night with him. She wasn't sure she'd ever wanted anything quite so much in all her life.

Abruptly, her body working overtime before her brain could process what she was doing, Bridget found herself snatching her door open again and striding back into the corridor.

Striding back down the hallway and to his room, even though she had no idea if that was where Hayd had even gone. And then striding into his room before any could see her, having barely waited for his answer after she'd offered the tersest of knocks.

'Birdie?' Half a question, half a growl, his voice rumbled through her. 'I thought you said it would be a mistake.'

'The second one we'll have made in less than a month,' she pointed out shakily. 'But we still have next month to work together. And the month after that.'

'Do you have a point, Birdie?' he rasped. 'Or are you just pointing out my failings? Failings I never had, I should point out, before you came along.'

It was the most backhanded compliment she'd ever heard, although she was sure he hadn't intended it as a compliment at all.

'I was thinking that I could ask to transfer.'

For a long moment he merely stared at her. His blue gaze darkened by the moment as he pinned her to the spot.

'Say that again?'

She ran her tongue over her suddenly parched lips and

wished he didn't follow the movement so intently. It made her want things she knew she couldn't have.

'I could swap job roles.'

Bridget had absolutely no way to read what that almost infinitesimal shift in facial expression meant, she just knew it had happened. In the silence she heard herself adding more.

'If it would make things easier.'

And still Hayden didn't reply.

'It's just that, when I left our patient heading into surgery earlier tonight, one of the project coordinators was telling me that a new role had opened up in a different camp and she wondered if Mandy might want to send anyone from Jukrem to fill the gap.'

'And you volunteered?'

'No, I just...said I'd ask Mandy once we return. But now...well... I just thought that if I left Jukrem it might make things easier.'

'Do you want to leave Jukrem?' he asked simply, breaking the silence at last.

Everything tilted inside her.

'No,' she admitted.

She just hoped he didn't ask why, because she wasn't as ashamed as she should probably be to admit that that he factored into that choice more than he had any right to.

'I don't want you to leave, either,' he ground out instead, taking her by surprise.

Then, before she could answer, he strode across the room, cupped her face and lowered his mouth to hers.

CHAPTER TWELVE

As EVERYTHING EXPLODED around her, all Bridget could do was cling to him. A thousand tiny detonations burst out of her like her own body wasn't enough to contain them.

His tongue invaded her mouth, scraping against her own, and she welcomed it. When he angled his head to deepen the kiss, she rejoiced in it. It was like her entire being was singing an aria that it only knew when Hayden was there to conduct.

But it wasn't enough, she wanted to be closer. Sliding her hands from his shoulders, she let her palms graze their way down over his rock-hard abdomen, tugging gently to pull them out.

Abruptly, Hayden wrenched himself away, leaving her feeling bereft and confused. But then he headed for the door, spinning a chair around and lifting it up in one hand as he went. Jamming it under the doorhandle and testing the improvised lock with impressive dexterity.

They weren't likely to get interrupted, but Bridget was grateful for his additional care.

And then he was back with her, his mouth fusing once more with hers and hands releasing her hair from its confines and tangling his fingers into it as he let it tumble around her shoulders. As if he couldn't get enough of her.

It was an intoxicating experience.

At some point, without her even realising it, his hands moved from her hair and over her body, like he was trying to learn its contours. The slope of her shoulders, the indentation of her waist, the dip in the hollow of her back. And then they were moving over her chest, testing the shape of her breasts through the thin tee, grazing her hard nipples with the pads of his thumbs and making them both groan a little in appreciation.

But as much as she arched her back, pressing herself into his palms in a silent plea, he seemed intent on torturing her. The sweetest torment she had ever known but a torment all the same, when all she really wanted was to feel his bare skin on hers, his hot, wet mouth closing over her aching nipple.

Again and again he teased her until she thought she would go out of her mind. Then, when she thought she couldn't take any more, he hauled the tee over her head, undoing and removing her bra in one slick movement. And then his mouth was closing over her, and Bridget thought she could burst with pleasure.

Need punched through her, hollowing right into her core. She slipped her hand into his hair, cupping the back of his head, her body arched into him. *This* was what she'd been missing. *This*. Right now. Wild sensations, and primitive.

And she wanted more.

Reaching for his clothing, the buttons, the zips, Bridget fumbled a little in her haste, and the curve of his mouth against her sensitive skin practically seared through her.

'We have time, Birdie,' he muttered, though she didn't answer.

She couldn't.

All the same, he let her push the jacket off his shoulders and then tug his T-shirt over his head until they were finally, gloriously, skin to skin. The hard planes of his chest feeling all the more muscular under the softness of her breasts, abrading her nipples and making her almost mad with desire.

All this time she'd been telling herself she'd built up that night with Hayden to be more than it had been. Now it was clear to her that she'd been downplaying it in her mind. So this time—on the basis that this was all there could ever really be between them—she was determined to preserve every perfect moment of it in her memory forever.

She dipped her head forward to kiss his chest. To taste him. To smell him. Sandalwood and musk, and something that was all Hayden. She moved slowly, thoroughly, determined not to miss a single inch of bare, solid, chest as she blazed a trail over him. His low murmurs of approval spurred her on. Making her drop to her knees in front of him as her chest tightened in anticipation, her breath coming in short starts just as his was. Particularly when she reached for his trousers and unbuttoned them.

'Bridget...'

It was a caution, but she didn't want to hear it. She couldn't quite understand what it was inside her that *wanted*, so badly, to do this. But it drove her on, making her curl her hand around him and draw him out.

'Shh...' she managed, her voice thick with expectancy as she felt a deep shudder course through his body.

And it was strange, wasn't it, the unexpected sense of power that instilled in her. How, even though she might be the one on her knees in front of him, she felt as though she held him in the palm of her hand. And not just literally. She smiled to herself, her lips curving along his hot, velvety length.

Then, lifting her eyes to his to make contact and hold it, she ran her tongue all around him and took him deep into her mouth.

* * *

Hayden had no idea how he managed to stay standing upright. He'd been pleasured before by women far more practised than his former virgin Birdie, yet never before had he experienced such a primal reaction as he did at that moment. His legs actually shook as though they might give out underneath him at any moment.

Her mouth was hot and perfect around him, but it was the shots of pure lust that jolted through him that pulled at him the most. Threatening to unravel him in an embarrassingly short time.

Desire and something far, far more dangerous coursed through his veins. And he couldn't bring himself to care. He couldn't bring himself to do anything but focus on her. *Birdie.* She was making him feel hotter, and greedier, than he'd ever felt in his life.

It was like he'd tied himself up in an inaccessible parcel all these years, but she was freeing him with every sweep of her tongue and each graze of his teeth. Teasing him one moment and worshipping him the next. Driving him closer and closer to the edge…until he feared he was going to topple off.

Hayden would never know how he managed to rein himself in, pulling himself out of her willing mouth and catching her off guard. Even when she rocked back on her heels, her wide eyes staring up at his in surprise, he feared he would still fall.

Before she could speak he was lifting her up, shucking off the rest of their clothing and carrying her to the single cot bed that surely couldn't take their combined weight. It didn't even look as though it could take a man of half of his stature.

But he couldn't let that stop him. *Them.*

Hayden had no idea what it was about Bridget that made it impossible for him to control himself when he was around her. But, then, he wasn't sure he even cared, just as long as he could taste her plump lips. Hold that incredible body against his. And slide inside her like he had over and over that night in the hotel.

Wordlessly, he pulled the mattress onto the floor and laid her down, almost reverently, on the clean white sheet he'd only put on it moments before she'd walked in and he'd proceeded to lose himself in every perfect inch of her.

Propping himself on one arm, he cradled her cheek with the other hand.

'That wasn't...good?' She blushed prettily.

'That was perfect,' he growled. 'But if I hadn't stopped you when I did, I don't know that I'd have been able to any later.'

'I didn't want you to stop me.' She glowered at him from under those long, thick lashes of hers. 'I didn't want to talk about it. I just wanted to...*do*.'

Insanely adorable, but he wasn't about to apologise.

'If you don't want to talk, Birdie,' he managed wryly, 'perhaps you'd consider stopping.'

And then, before she could object any more, he set about reacquainting himself with each long line of her and every delicious curve. Relearning her, as though it had been a lifetime since she'd last been in his bed. In many ways, it felt as though it *had* been.

He dropped his mouth, intent on kissing every inch of her satiny skin, all the while knowing that he couldn't get enough of her. He kissed, he licked, he grazed, revelling as she arched into him, seeking more. Demanding more. She began to move her hands over him on an exploration of their own. She let them glide up his arms and to his shoulders, before slipping down his back, using the leverage to arch up into him let her hard nipples rake over his chest and set him alight all over again.

And then she slid her hands lower, cupping his backside, and she opened her legs to him until he was nudging against her wet heat before he could stop himself. The heat outside was making the room that much hotter, and it was that much easier to slide against each other.

He heard a moan and wasn't sure if it had come from him or her. Possibly both. A dark, urgent need moved within him. A madness that he didn't think could ever be controlled.

'Please, Hayd,' she whispered. 'Now…'

And he was lost.

He'd told her that she'd come here to run away from something. But it had never occurred to him that he'd done the same with the army. Maybe he hadn't wanted to see it, or maybe it had taken these events to bring him to it, but the simple truth was that he'd been lost, and he'd only realised it when Bridget had found him.

Holding himself above her, Hayden slid inside her. Only a little way at first, then out. Then repeating it again. Slowly. Lazily. As if it wasn't killing him to do so.

'Deeper,' she gasped on a ragged breath, tearing down the last vestiges of his self-control.

This time, when he tried to slide into her slowly, Bridget gripped his backside and lifted her hips.

He drove home with a groan and all his ease and skill disappeared in an instant and the rhythm became harder and faster. He ran one hand up her silken thigh as she wrapped it around his back, letting his head drop until his mouth was pressed in the flawless valley between her breasts. And still the rhythm didn't let up.

The entirety of his long length was buried so deep inside her that neither of them knew where one of the ended and the other began.

As though it was *meant* to be that way.

Always.

When he felt her shift around him, he reached down between them and found the centre of her need, his fingers playing with her until she was gasping with every stroke. She clenched around him, arching right up off the bed and muffling her voice against his shoulder as she cried out his name, shaking deliciously around him.

And Hayden finally let himself go. Throwing them both into the fire and taking him higher than he'd ever been before. Higher, he feared, than he ever would again.

Bridget had no idea how long it took to come back to herself. She only knew that when she did, her body was still pressed up against Hayden's. Fitting to him as though they'd been hand-crafted to go together—as ridiculous as she knew that notion was.

A thousand questions hovered on her lips at that moment, but she didn't dare utter a single one of them lest it break whatever spell had wound its way around the tiny room.

She suspected that she wasn't alone because Hayden didn't speak either, he just held her close as if he never wanted to let her go.

Or perhaps she was just being fanciful. Perhaps that was why the confession slipped out of her.

'You were right when you told me that I used this place to run away. I didn't want to acknowledge it before, I don't think I was ready to do so, but now it seems far clearer.'

His pulled her closer, his hand drawing circles on her skin. Encouraging her to keep talking in her own time.

'I had a relatively privileged childhood. A nice house, a good school, lots of money, and we moved in quite elite social circles. Then, when I thirteen, my father was arrested for fraud. Every single thing we had was off the backs of other people, some of whom were meant to have been our friends.'

She loved that low rumble of objection from him, making her feel as though, had he been able to, he would have protected her. It helped her to continue.

'Overnight our whole lives were torn apart. Mine and Mum's. We were thrown out of our home, understandably, and all our assets were frozen. We had only the couple of bags we'd been allowed to pack, under the watchful eye of the police, of course, but nowhere to go. No one wanted to help us, or even be associated with us, since the media couldn't accept that my mother hadn't known about it.'

'Had she?' he asked gently, his arms still around her making her feel safe. Secure.

'No.' Bridget shook her head. 'I really don't believe she ever did. My mother was very beautiful but not very worldly. At all. I truly believe she was foolish enough to fall for all the lies my father fed her, but the media didn't believe that. Or else they didn't want to. It was a national scandal.'

'I think I can believe it.' Hayden paused, and she tensed. 'Did your father take his own life before his trial?'

Nausea rolled through her, but Bridget fought against it. *She* was the one who had brought up this subject, she wasn't going to let it beat her or make her cower the way it had for the past thirteen years.

'Yep.' She tried to sound flippant. 'Mum and I were devastated. For all that he'd done, I was only thirteen and he'd been the father that I'd idolised my entire life. But Mum fell apart. My dad had been her whole life. She'd lived vicariously through his successes—although, of course, they were never successes at all—but she'd thrown all the parties, all the PR events, all the social functions for him. It was the only thing she knew how to do. He'd brought in the money—she'd never earned a penny in her life.

'And, worse, with Dad gone the media had no one else to blame. We were hounded. For years we couldn't go anywhere or do anything without someone recognising us. Mum became depressed, spiralling into one addiction after another. Losing herself in anything that could make her forget, for a day or a night. And I became her carer.'

'You don't have to talk about this if it's too difficult for you,' Hayden said tenderly 'But I'm here for you, as long as you need.'

Bridget nodded. It was tempting to stop, but she wasn't even sure that she could put the lid back on the proverbial box. She'd opened it up and memories and emotions she'd thought long buried had spilled out all over the place.

And somehow it felt good to be able to start to talk through it.

'I'd dreamed of becoming a doctor for as long as I could remember. I'd always been good at school but finding myself without friends had just given me more time to throw myself into my studies. At least schoolwork was always there for me and didn't care what my father had done. So I had the grades to go to university and study medicine, but I didn't have the money to support myself. Besides, I soon realised that I couldn't leave Mum.'

'Is that why you became a nurse?'

'I suppose. It brought in money to keep a roof over our heads, and it kept me in medicine one way, but it meant I didn't have to go away for my studies. When she died five years ago, that was when I became a volunteer.'

'You reinvented yourself,' he acknowledged. 'I can see why that would have been far easier to do if you were thousands of miles away from everything you'd ever known.'

'Crazy, isn't it?' she commented wryly. 'But I don't want to run away any more. Besides, ever since I met you, I don't think I've been running *from.* I think I've been running *to.*'

'I was wrong, Bridget Gardiner.' His voice slid over her like the honey that families here poured over their wounds. 'I don't think you run anywhere. I haven't thought that for some time. You stride with confidence, and you inspire wherever you go.'

'Even with you?' she asked, only half teasing.

'Especially with me,' he growled, making it sound altogether too much like an unspoken promise.

Before she could second-guess herself, she found herself pulling out of his arms to straddle him.

An echo of their first time together.

'Show me,' she whispered, spreading her palms over his chest and moving her hips over him, revelling in the way his body had pulled hard and tight in an instant.

For her.

'Your wish is my command,' Hayden growled, his hands moving to her hips to lift her up as though she weighed nothing and then settle her back where he wanted her.

Heat bloomed in an instant. And Bridget let her head fall back and be guided wherever he wanted them to go.

CHAPTER THIRTEEN

'WHAT'S GOING ON?'

The sun was just peeking over the horizon the next morning as Hayd's men lined up their vehicles at the compound gates and Bridget threw her grab bag inside one, trying not to glance at Hayden himself for fear that ridiculous emotions would be written all over her face.

Her body still ached lusciously from their night together. In truth, they'd barely been able to keep their hands off each other long enough for her to sneak out before anyone caught her, less than a few hours before.

Now they were due to head back to Jukrem, after deciding with the doctors at Rejupe that although both mother and baby were doing remarkably well, they would stay for a few more days to recover, before being brought back on the supply plane in the middle of the following week.

But whilst the Rejupe volunteers had been relaxed and calm an hour ago, there was suddenly a bit more of a flurry than usual, and before she could ask anyone what was going on, she saw one of the Hayden's men rushing over to speak to him.

'Sit-rep, please,' he ordered.

'Sir, there's been some kind of an attack at a camp called... Luerina.' The man checked his notes. 'No reports of casualties.'

Wordlessly, Hayden waved her over and she hurried around the vehicle.

'Do you know anything about the camp at Luerina?'

'Luerina is about two days' journey north of here,' Bridget replied. 'It's a small outreach camp like our own. If you think about a clock face, with Rejupe here at the centre and Jukrem in the seven o'clock position, Luerina is at about the one o'clock position.'

'Right.'

'You're sure there were no casualties?' She turned to the young man.

She knew volunteers who had gone to Luerina. People who weren't just colleagues but friends.

'None that we know of, ma'am, but our intel is sketchy. We've never had any communications in the area so the reports coming through now are through the charity. You'll probably know it from your team before we get the report.'

'Thanks,' Bridget acknowledged as she turned back to the door and jogged out over the courtyard towards the hospital cluster. The charity had their own communications facility, and the project managers here would surely have more information.

Her head was so full that she wasn't expecting it when Hayden fell into step beside her. But she wasn't surprised either.

'Slow down.' He placed his hand gently on her arm. 'It won't help anyone if you end up with a broken ankle.'

Reluctantly, Bridget slowed.

'Do you know the team?'

She bit her lip. It had to mean something that he could he read her so easily. Didn't it? A sob bubbled inside her, and she fought to choke it back.

'I know, I know,' he said softly. 'You're all out here for the same reason, working for the charity. I get it, it's like a brotherhood. Or sisterhood, if you prefer.'

Despite everything, she managed a wry smile.

'I understood what you meant.'

Reaching the hospital, she headed for the radio building where plenty of others were milling around, the volume louder than usual.

'What's going on?' Bridget asked one of the nurses whose face she recognised from the previous day, even if she didn't know her name.

Hayden had already slipped across the room, no doubt going to see if his men could lend support.

'Apparently Luerina got hit a few days ago. A couple of pick-up trucks of rebels. They got medical supplies, food and a charity vehicle, but fortunately no one got hurt.'

In the grand scheme of things that was, at least, some good news.

'And the guys who were working there?'

'They're all on their way here,' the nurse answered. 'The charity called them back straight away, until local police can apprehend the rebels. They still had another vehicle, so they were okay. We understand they're less than an hour out.'

Relief coursed through her.

'Thank goodness for that.'

'You're heading back to Jukrem with the army unit?'

'I'm heading back with part of the unit. Hayd…that is, the major in command, is taking a group of his men out on a recce into the area around Luerina.'

'That's good.' The nurse nodded. 'We could do with someone seeing what's going on out there. How many rebels there are and what they're after. The reports coming in are conflicting and no one is quite sure what the situation is.'

And Hayden was the perfect guy to do that. So why did her chest ache so badly? As if a part of her wished he didn't have to go?

'Anyway,' the nurse continued, oblivious to Bridget's unease, 'if you can wait just for an hour or so, I think the project coordinators are working out a group to send out with you.'

'A group of medical volunteers?' Her attention switched immediately back to the nurse. 'To Jukrem?'

'I think they decided that a bunch of extra medics at Rejupe wasn't the best use of resources. If we have that kind of skill on hand, and we aren't safe in the Luerina area at the moment, we might as well send a mobile vaccination team out towards Jukrem, maybe help alleviate some of the sudden influx you guys have been getting by intercepting those refugees closer to the border. Especially the mothers and babies.'

It was a great idea, and one that offered Bridget the perfect lifeline. The ideal distraction from worrying about Hayden going to follow up a group of rebels.

Being part of that mobile medical team would certainly help to refocus her on the job she'd always loved—being a nurse in places like this. And she had no doubt that once she spoke to Mandy back at Jukrem, the woman would be only too happy to send her with the team. Not least because it might help to take the pressure off them in camp.

'Sounds good. Think they'll need an extra pair of hands?'

'They usually do.' The nurse laughed. 'I should have been that quick off the mark.'

'Well, maybe I'll see you there.'

Jogging over to the comms unit to see if she could contact Jukrem and confirm her plan with Mandy, Bridget felt a little happier with herself.

Hayd would have a plan. She knew him well enough to know that. But now she had a plan, too. One that didn't involve sitting around and worrying about him.

She only hoped it would work as well in practice as it did in theory.

* * *

'This is Waeya. She's three years old,' the triage nurse told Bridget as she stepped around the makeshift bay in the mobile clinic her new team had set up near the refugee camp just over half a day's drive from Jukrem.

The plan had been a sound one. As anticipated, the increase in new refugees coming over the border had meant a significant uptake in the number of visitors to Jukrem camp itself, and Mandy had jumped at the idea of a vaccination team being able to get to hundreds of them sooner. Another week, she'd told Bridget, and Jukrem simply wouldn't be able to get through the backlog.

Even now, both Rejupe and Jukrem were recruiting and training both local nurses and healthcare providers in their scores.

In many ways, it was a compliment. Testament to how well their charity had integrated into the area and become a trusted source for the local people. All the teams in the region deserved to be proud of themselves. Bridget knew that she was.

And she wasn't remotely thinking about Hayden, and whether he'd been safe out there. Days away from camp. Days away from *her*. Or the fact that he'd apparently arrived back at the army camp near Jukrem the day before, in time for a parachute drop that night. She wondered if he'd even been across to the charity's camp, only to find out that she wasn't there.

Then she hated herself for even thinking about it. For even caring.

Because Hayden wouldn't care. It had been a one-off, that night. Logic told her that it didn't mean anything more than that.

As soon as that call had come in, he'd forgotten all about her, focusing on his job instead. *Exactly* the way that he was supposed to do. Just as she was.

And still something ate away inside her. The fear that she couldn't pigeonhole her emotions the way that he could. The fact that a part of her was ignoring every warning she was trying to heed, and instead it wanted more.

And Hayden had made it abundantly clear that he didn't have *more* of himself to give.

'Waeya's mother brought her in whilst you were away,' the nurse prompted, and Bridget snapped her head round instantly. 'She has coughing, chest pain, and is severely emaciated. She weighs about ten pounds. We've diagnosed TB and begun treating with first line oral antibiotics and second line injections.'

'*Male*, Waeya,' Bridget whispered to the oblivious little girl on the makeshift floor cot, the huge mosquito net pinned all around her. 'Mum's being screened now, is she?'

'She's right next door,' Lisa confirmed. 'Come on, I'll show you our last, new patient.'

'Here?' Bridget turned expectantly.

'Next door.' Shaking her head, Lisa led her out and across to another tent with a couple of white mosquito net domes inside, where a pulse oximeter was emitting an unwelcome beep, warning of a low oxygen level as it tried to help those infected little wet lungs.

'Hamar is eighteen months old. He missed his measles vaccination when his family fled their village after an attack. I don't know how many weeks or months it took them to make their way here, or when Hamar contracted measles.'

'You've treated him with oxygen to help his lungs and antibiotics for secondary infections?'

'Yes, but he continued to deteriorate so we tried a course of steroids and have finally seen an improvement. Right now, we need to ensure plenty of fluids and good nutrition, and salbutamol to ensure the lungs are open. But it looks as though we may have turned a corner with him, so right now we're holding onto that.'

For the next six hours Bridget talked the older nurse through their patients, concentrating on the information that was never at the briefings but which made such an impact on the ground. By the time she emerged, stepping into the wall of heat and shielding her eyes from the sun, Bridget wasn't expecting the large crowd jostling excitedly in the market area. Instinctively, she headed over. And stopped in her tracks.

Whatever she'd expected, it hadn't been to see Hayden crouched down, sifting through muddy, dirty water.

What was he even doing out here?

Emotions charged through her and she found herself heading over, a thousand questions dancing on her tongue. But when she spoke, even she didn't recognise the light, teasing tone in her voice. So completely at odds with all the turmoil coursing through her at that instant.

'Having fun?'

Hayden twisted his head to eye her critically.

'Bad day at the office,' he answered simply.

As though he hadn't been away. As though nothing portentous had happened at all. And maybe, for him, it hadn't. Bridget swallowed hard and fought to keep her tone airy.

'Is that so?'

He stood up, glaring balefully at a dodgy-looking generator hooked up to an even more unreliable-looking control panel, before turning to face her. And then, suddenly, he lifted up one arm and brushed a stray hair from her face with the back of his hand.

Like flipping a switch to let light suddenly flood the dark, needling void in her chest. Making her feel almost... *joyous.*

'Some group got hold of this old jenny, but it keeps

pumping out mud and gunk along with the water, and the panel keeps giving people electric shocks. I figured I'd take a look.'

'Nice.' She grinned.

'Hardly.' He wiped his hands on the army-green rag from his pocket.

'Aren't you supposed to have men for that, *Major*?' she teased. 'What are you even doing here?'

'I heard a new team had come out here to try to help with the influx of people crossing the border. They said it might be a good place to start setting up a new transit camp so I thought I might as well bring a section and repair the old jenny at the same time.'

'You've dealt with the rebels back at Luerina?'

'They were well gone by the time we got there.' Hayden shrugged. 'We patrolled as far as we could with the local police but there was no sign of them. For now, we have to assume they got what they wanted and left, though the police are still up there, trying to stay on hand in case anywhere else gets hit.'

He stood up and moved to stand next to her, and she could feel the heat pouring off his wide, solid chest. Her body went into overdrive, though she tried to pretend to herself that it hadn't.

'And when you've finished playing superman here?'

'Then I'm going to check on the rest of my guys. They're building our first permanent bridge a few clicks away. The components got parachuted in last night.'

'I heard on the radio.' She laughed. 'Apparently the whole camp is buzzing about it. I heard all the kids ran out to the drop zone and you guys had to widen your perimeter fence?'

'Yeah, got a bit hairy for a while, but it was all good. If you're ready to get back to Jukrem tonight, can you give us another few hours? I'd really like to get this pump working properly again for them.'

Technically she was due back to ensure cover for the next shift, but she knew Mandy would rather wait a little longer if it meant the people of this village could regain access to clean, fresh water. Besides, there were so many potential patients to see that she definitely wouldn't be short of work.

'I can give you a little while,' she replied.

'That's all I'll need.'

He was already dropping back to the ground when she heard the roar of an engine as his second-in-command headed towards them at speed. The vehicle slowed down far enough away not to put any of the crowding villagers in danger, but as Dean jumped down and began running over, Bridget knew it was serious. No one ran in this heat unless there was a damned good reason.

Her stomach began to swan-dive.

Especially when Hayden stood abruptly and hurried to the captain. Close enough that she could hear them but far enough that the rest of the crowd couldn't.

'What's going on, Dean?'

'Conversation with the project coordinator,' Dean imparted. 'Message in on the charity radio is that Lawian village has just been hit by the renegades. Probably the same group that hit Luerina.'

For a moment, she had to think where Lawian was. A satellite clinic in a small town northeast of Jukrem and southeast of the main city and charity camp in Rejupe.

'Casualties?' Hayden asked.

'No serious casualties, just been roughed up a bit. However, some shots were fired.'

'Okay, so they're really moving around, and that's also an escalation,' Hayden said, waving her over. 'Did you catch all that, Birdie?'

She nodded grimly, hurrying over.

'Last time they just waved the guns in the villagers' faces and beeped horns.'

'Anything else?' Hayden asked Dean.

'Yeah, everything Mandy has gleaned suggests that they are heading south and they're getting more desperate.'

'Do we know if they're heading to us?' Hayden asked, his eyes flickering to her for a split second, and her heart gave a tiny leap at the idea that his instinct might have been concern for her.

Even if he'd then pushed it aside and focused on his task in hand, as he was meant to do.

'We've no way of knowing if the bandits are going to keep coming south, or if they'll veer off more southeast when they realise that we're in the area. *We* as in the British Army.' Dean swiftly turned to her. 'Not *we* as in your charity.'

'I understand that,' she assured him. 'What about the local police? Didn't you just say they were patrolling in case anywhere else got hit?'

'I said they were still patrolling up north of Rejupe,' Hayden confirmed. 'We didn't anticipate the rebels moving so far or so fast. If they hit Laiwan, that would make the police one or two days out by now.'

'Which is why they're hoping we can help,' Dean added.

'We might not need to do much more than look menacing,' Hayden said thoughtfully. 'The criminals are hitting small villages that can't really protect themselves, stealing what they can but leaving before anyone can get to them. It doesn't seem likely they'll attack this camp with us being so close by.'

'I thought the same thing,' Dean confirmed. 'Our mere presence might be enough to make them stay away.'

'We can hope.' Hayden looked grim. 'For now let's keep it between us and Mandy, no need to alert the rest of the staff and panic anyone. But is she prepared to evacuate the staff on short notice, like Camp Luerina did?'

Again his gaze flickered to her, as if he couldn't help himself. Dean, mercifully, didn't seem to notice.

'Mandy wants your assessment before she makes her recommendation, sir.'

Bridget opened her mouth to argue then closed it again. The charity would be legally obliged to err on the side of caution, but none of the staff would want to leave. But better to let Mandy tell Hayden that they would be staying put—after all she was the project coordinator.

Besides, that wasn't what was playing on her mind the most. The simple fact was that last time, back at Rejupe, she'd been daunted enough by the prospect of him heading out to face rebels, but she'd managed to quash it. She'd managed to convince herself that this was his job, just as the nursing was hers.

But this time, somehow, it was different. Perhaps because Dean had already confirmed that the scale of the attacks was escalating, and she knew that would put Hayden and his guys into greater danger.

It made it all the more real. All the more frightening. As she could lose him.

As if she was in a position to lose him.

'Okay,' Hayden decided, making her jump slightly as she listened to his commands to his captain. 'Let's put out a warning order to the guys to prep for escorting the charity vehicles in any potential emergency evacuation.'

Hayden began jotting down names.

All business. No time for emotion.

'They need to ready a DROPS to carry an MGB, and let's have these guys tasked with constructing that on the route out, and two four-by-fours. You're going to need to put them on driver rest so scrap any tasks they've got lined up over the next couple of days.'

'We'll want to evacuate a couple of the severely ill but stable patients that we can't afford to leave behind if we can help it,' Bridget interjected quickly.

'Mandy didn't mention it,' pointed out Dean.

'I know, but she *will* want to. I can guarantee it.' There was nothing personal in Dean's uncertainty, Bridget knew that, but she'd worked on enough projects over the years to be confident of her facts. 'I understand you'll need to contact her for confirmation but if you could factor it in. And if you could provide any additional support in that area.'

'How many?' Hayden asked her.

Later, she would take her time mulling over the glorious fact that he hadn't questioned her, he'd merely accepted. Later, though. Not now.

'We have three four-by-fours for staff and a couple of patients. I think we'll want to bring a minimum of four more who can't be left. More, if you could accommodate them.'

'Okay.' Hayden dipped his head, adding more names to the list. 'Dean, if you can ready a second DROPS to act as an ambulance. I'm thinking Dutton and Chester to drive, charity workers in the back with the patients.'

'I'd maybe swap Dutton for Gould,' Dean recommended. 'Dutton pulled some kind of injury doing some groundworks yesterday. Not serious but I'd rather have another second driver.'

'Fine. And speak to Carl, the infantry platoon commander, about picking a section to escort.'

'Will do. I'll head back now. Are you on your way?'

'My guys will finish up here and then we'll head out,' Hayden confirmed, handing his second-in-command the list of names. 'And, Dean, best let the embassy know.'

CHAPTER FOURTEEN

THE TENT WAS ROASTING. Packed with jostling bodies and feverish conversation. But everyone fell silent the instant Hayden walked in, flanked by Dean and Mandy.

'Okay, guys, as you're all aware there have been escalating attacks on several of the villages in the region,' Hayden began without preamble. 'You'll need to prepare for an emergency evacuation to Rejupe and the army will offer support.'

'What about the patients?' Bridget asked at once, her eyes on Mandy for fear that she'd give herself away if she looked at Hayden.

'It has been decided that you'll take the most serious of the patients only,' Hayden answered instead.

As one, the medical staff all turned to Mandy, waiting for her to argue the case for staying. The refugees needed them. But uncharacteristically Mandy was silent.

'How bad was the attack?' Lisa demanded after a moment. 'You're the army. Can't you guys fight them off?'

Bridget tried not to look at Hayden, but the draw was too strong.

'We were sent here to build infrastructure for the surrounding area, not as a fighting force. We didn't anticipate any hostile activity and we don't have authorisation to engage them. You need to get ready to evacuate.'

'We can't just leave,' Lisa argued. 'Mandy, please. You can't want us to leave?'

'I do understand how you feel,' the older woman replied empathetically. 'Really, I do. But it isn't a risk the charity can afford to take. I'll need most of you to be ready to leave in the first wave back to Rejupe if necessary, taking the most critical patients and as much kit as we can.'

'We can't just leave the rest of the patients,' Bridget pointed out. 'They still need our care.'

'We'll keep a small group here—I'll be one of them—to keep things ticking over,' Mandy confirmed. 'But if things get too dangerous, we'll have to leave, too.'

As if they truly just thought this was a genuine, if tense back and forth between colleagues.

'But we have a troop of Royal Engineers,' someone said. 'As well as a detachment of infantry a couple of hundred metres away. Surely these renegades would have to be crazy to attack us?'

Mandy nodded and shrugged all at once.

'All the more reason to believe that they're getting more and more desperate if they're heading down this way, knowing all of that.'

'And desperate groups are unpredictable groups,' Hayden added. 'We can't assume they won't get desperate enough to kidnap and ransom a charity worker.'

'And if they shoot you?' someone asked, from the back of the tent.

'Well, in that case we have the right to engage.' He paused, then clarified, 'To fire back.'

But Bridget was already gripping the metal table behind her, trying to stop this sensation that she was suddenly free-falling into nothingness.

If the rebels shot at Hayden and his men, it changed the parameters. How had she not realised that before? There

would be a gunfight…or what had he called it? A firefight?
It wasn't unrealistic to consider that he might get injured.
Killed.

Nausea raced to meet her.

She was an idiot. She'd let herself get too close to him.
Too invested. Despite everything she'd told herself. And
now she was terrified he was going to confront a group of
rebels and he could get hurt.

Worse.

Yet this was his job. It was what he did. What he *loved*
doing. She had no right to wish that she could stop him.
No right to wish that he would want stay…with her.

'Can't you build a compound around this facility?' She
fought to drag her mind back the present.

'We can, but in this short time it won't be big enough,
or secure enough, to encompass all the medical tents, the
new generators, and all the *tukul* accommodation.'

Her stomach pulled tight and twisted as she listened
to all the voices.

'Meaning?'

'Meaning we need to keep it compact and just incorporate the most necessary areas and a skeleton staff, who
also need to be ready to evacuate on command.'

Bridget had no idea how she managed to tear her gaze
from his, but somehow she managed to slide her eyes to
Mandy.

'Fine. Then I'm volunteering to be one of the staff who
stays behind.'

'No.'

His voice cracked out around the room. She could hardly
breathe. She certainly couldn't face him. He sounded so
cold. So hard. She opened her mouth to argue but nothing
came out. Not that he gave her the opportunity in any case.

'I can't allow staff to decide for themselves who evacu-
ates to the main hospital now and who remains in camp.

As project chief, Mandy and I have discussed all staff in terms of medical capabilities as well as previous experience in the potential risk voluntary confinement camps such as this one will become.'

It was all Bridget could do not to reel at the force in his tone. She understood that this was his job, but it didn't explain his brusque attitude. As though he somehow blamed her for something.

Her head ached, trying to work it out.

Perhaps he thought the night with her had stopped him from seeing something earlier? Acting to stop the rebels. Although she didn't see how that could make sense.

But what else could account for this sudden, awful hostility?

It was like her heart was cracking in her chest and every word was being ripped from her mouth, and yet her colleagues seemed utterly oblivious to the undercurrents between her and Hayden.

'We've unanimously agreed a list of five names. Don't bother arguing, Nurse, your name isn't on it, and you'll be wasting everybody's time.'

'Actually...' Mandy spoke up, her eyes scanning her notes, seemingly equally unaware of the undertones. 'I could do with you staying, Bridget. You went through this kind of scenario a few years ago, didn't you?'

'I did.' Bridget nodded, keeping her gaze firmly away from Hayden, even though she could feel his eyes boring into her.

It was the oddest sensation.

'Good, okay, I'll add your name.' Mandy scribbled her name on the page before nodding her confirmation to Hayden.

Was she the only one who could feel his disapproval bouncing around the room? And yet, like the soldier that she'd known, he quashed it before he spoke.

'All right, the staff staying back will be briefed by Mandy now to prep any patients the first wave will be taking with them in this initial evacuation.'

There wasn't even a low grumble of protest as the group, evidently jolted by Hayden's unequivocal tone, moved forward to check the list.

'The rest of you have ten minutes to grab your personal gear and get back here to collect those patients. The transport will be leaving in half an hour and nobody will be late, are we clear?'

'Clear,' came the chorus as people checked the list and then spilled out of the tent to carry out their designated roles.

But as Bridget headed off, she wasn't prepared for Hayden to snag her arm, pulling her into one of the *tukuls* under repair the moment no one was watching.

Her heart hammered against her ribcage. Whatever this was about, she didn't think it was going to be good.

'You need to remove your name from the volunteers staying behind.'

He shouldn't be doing this, he knew that, and yet he hadn't been able to help himself. And now, even as Bridget blinked at him, her lovely eyes looking hurt, he hated himself in a way he never had done in his life before.

But he didn't relent.

He couldn't.

This was the right call for the right reasons, wasn't it?

Hayden stared grimly across the *tukul* and into a face he was sure would haunt him forever. He had never—in his entire career—had to second-guess his motivations before. He didn't like it.

But he was forced to concede that he liked even less the idea of anything happening to Bridget.

'Remove your name, Birdie,' his voice rasped out.

Her brow furrowed and Hayden found himself clenching his fists to stop himself from reaching out and smoothing it flat.

'Why?'

'Because it's not safe.'

She eyed him with astonishment for a moment, before she bit back.

'It's a lot safer than what you're doing.'

'I don't care.' It was all he could do to keep his voice down, knowing all too well how sound carried out here. 'You can't stay here.'

'Why not?'

He didn't want to answer. Yet he couldn't not. Everything in him was railing at what he was doing but he didn't care. He had to stop her. He had to keep her safe.

'Because you're a liability.' He barely recognised the sound of his own voice.

He hardly blamed her for looking at him with shock. Then horror. Then fury.

'I'm a what?'

'You're a liability,' he repeated, even if through his teeth.

This wasn't him. This wasn't what he did. And yet here he was, unable to help himself.

'I am *not* a liability,' she managed to hiss, though there was no mistaking the shake in her voice. 'I am *very* good at my job.'

'You're a liability to *me*.'

Everything froze around him. The hut. The camp. The world. It was just him and her, and for a split second he wished it was all there would ever be.

'Say that again?' she whispered.

He didn't know if he couldn't or if he just didn't want to. It was an admission he hadn't imagined he would ever make. But the moment he heard it he realised the truth.

He cared for this woman. In a way he'd never thought he'd ever care for anyone. A part of him had realised it earlier, of course. A few days ago? A week ago? Longer?

Hayden didn't know. He just knew that he couldn't stand the thought of anything happening to her. Ever.

'You heard me,' he bit out instead.

For a moment he thought he saw a flicker of…something in her expression before she shut it down.

'I'm a liability?' she asked softly. 'To you?'

'Forget it. Just withdraw your name.'

'Because you care about me.' It was less of a question and more of a realisation, and yet he couldn't answer her. 'Say it, Hayd. Tell me you care.'

And the sickest part was that even though a part of him wanted to tell her—desperately—he refused to. As if that could somehow make this moment, this *weakness* disappear.

'I don't care.'

'Clearly you do.'

'No,' he denied, despite that fact that even *he* didn't believe himself. 'No more than I care about any of your colleagues. I just don't need the distraction.'

'If you don't care, why am I any more of a distraction than anyone else?'

Everything tumbled within him. This churning sea of… *feelings* he had never had to deal with before. Had never wanted to.

He was cool and detached. He prided himself on it. He didn't drag other people into his life because it was never steady or consistent enough. Hadn't his kind, caring but permanently unsettled mother taught him that much?

'This is your job, Hayden.' Bridget was speaking suddenly. Her voice was firmer than he thought he'd heard before. 'And it frightens me, what you do, but I accept it. It's who you are and it's what makes you tick. But nursing out here is who *I* am. This is what makes *me* proud of who I am. And you have no right to ask me to stop that because you've suddenly realised you care for me.'

'That isn't what this is about,' he growled.

'I think it is.'

'Remove your name, Birdie,' he bit out. 'Or I will go to Mandy and do it for you.'

And then, before he could betray his own code of ethics any further, he swung around and left the hut.

And the woman that he was terribly afraid he was beginning to love.

Bridget waited for the helicopter to come in to Rejupe on a rare, miserable, overcast day, and pretended it didn't feel portentous.

She'd asked Mandy for the transfer the moment their small team had been evacuated from Jukrem after all. There were any number of the charity's other camps in the region that were far enough away to be safe from the rebels and which were crying out for an extra pair of hands. Some of the Jukrem camp staff were filling in gaps in the main Rejupe compound, whilst others, like her, were transferring out to smaller camps across the area.

It was no big deal, she told herself crossly as she commanded her hands and body to stop shaking. When they didn't obey, she tried telling herself that it was anger.

She suspected it was more grief.

Up to that moment in the *tukul* a few nights ago, she'd been afraid that Hayden hated her. That he was trying to shut her out and disengage from her. And the idea of him pulling away from her had hurt more than she'd ever wanted to admit.

But the truth seemed to be that he didn't hate her, he *loved* her in his own way, and impossibly, devastatingly that was worse. Because his idea of love was dominance and control. Just like her father had dominated her mother.

Hayden didn't believe in equity or mutual compassion. He believed in her supporting him in his career, but him dictating what she chose to do in her life.

And the worst of it was that she had realised she was so in love with him that a part of her had actually considered taking her name off the list that night. Even if she'd only entertained the notion for a moment.

But, then, that wasn't love at all, was it?

It couldn't be. Which was why she had to leave.

All she needed now was for Mandy to get the final paperwork signed off for her to take with her on the flight, and in a few hours she'd be over one hundred miles away in another village, another camp, where she wouldn't run into Hayden Brigham.

It might not be a decision that her heart liked, but it was a logical decision. Her best choice, given the circumstances. She could complete the remaining months of her programme without her heart being constantly in her mouth in case she walked out of the clinic and turned the corner, only to walk into him.

How impossible would it be to keep focused on her job as she should—as she had always been able to do in the past—when a hopeless part of her was anticipating the next time they would be alone.

When her traitorous body kept reminding her what it felt like to be with him—the only man who had ever truly known her. And how it would feel again?

She stood up rapidly, pacing the bare room as if that could somehow dislodge the image of him that had pinned itself to her brain. That thatch of dirty blond hair. His dimpled chin. The chiselled body.

She picked up the pace abruptly, and she told herself that was relief she could feel spiralling through her. Not something that felt dangerously like something else entirely.

It had been a mistake to let herself get too close to him.

Hayden had warned her from the start, but she hadn't listened to him. She'd been too caught up in the...the *feelings* sloshing around inside her. Her inexperience, she supposed, in mistaking sex for emotions. Believing that their nights together—even their conversations—had meant more to him than they had.

That *she* had meant more to him than she had.

But there was no escaping the truth of it. The sexual chemistry between them—so powerful that it was almost self-destructive—was just that. *Sexual chemistry.* Not a connection, or bonding, and certainly not *love.* Which was why she couldn't go back to Jukrem.

Bridget held her hand to her chest as if the action could still the fluttering in her chest. Jukrem meant Hayden. And her weakness. They were bound to end up back in bed together, probably more than once, if she returned. The offer to take up a role at another camp couldn't have come at a better time, she reminded herself for the tenth time in the past hour.

She heard Mandy's footsteps in the dirt long before the project coordinator rounded the corner. Making herself stop pacing, Bridget adopted what she hoped was a wide, bright smile.

'Everything ready?'

'Not exactly.'

There was no way to stop her stomach from rolling and soaring, try as she did to rein it in.

'Hayd.' Her voice didn't sound remotely even. 'I was expecting Mandy. When did you get here?'

'About five minutes ago,' he growled.

'And the rebels?'

She wasn't quite sure how she even remembered them, her head felt so thick and muggy.

'Caught. Local enforcement arrived last night.' He

waved his hand irritably. 'I didn't come here to talk to you about some low-level criminals.'

'Well, it's what I want to talk about.' Not true in its strictest sense. But it was certainly the only thing she was *prepared* to talk about. 'There are so many patients still to treat in Jukrem, it's good to know the rest of the volunteers can return.'

'You can *all* return.'

'I won't be going.'

He cast her an exasperated look. And…something more. Something she didn't care to examine too closely, lest it sway her from her goal of leaving.

'You can't be serious about taking up a position at another camp?'

'Why not?' Smoothing her hands over her dusty combat trousers, Bridget tried to remind herself of everything she'd been saying earlier. Only it was rapidly sliding from her head. 'I've been offered the position of selecting and training a healthcare team of locals. It's a promotion.'

'You're one of the medical staff. Not admin.'

'That doesn't mean I can't be given a more responsible role.' Her voice cracked, and she stopped abruptly. 'Plus, this means I get to extend my assignment for a further three months. I gain more experience in this environment, which can only be good for my career.'

He sounded so disapproving. So dismissive. She needed a moment to compose herself, but he was already snapping out alternatives.

Commands. As though he thought he knew better.

'Ask Mandy for more responsibility at Jukrem. After everything you did on that emergency run last month, and the evacuation the other day, you've proved yourself to be one of the most valuable members the team has. And Jukrem is where you're meant to be stationed anyway.'

Her chest was pulling so tight she expected to hear her

ribs crack any moment. He was doing it again—telling her what he thought was best. Expecting her to agree because he'd said it? Again, exactly as her father had done.

So how was it possible to want, so badly, to agree to what Hayden was saying? She hated herself for being so weak.

'I'm not staying, Hayden,' she managed to bite out suddenly.

She didn't know where it came from, but she clung to it nonetheless.

'You have to stay,' he stated. The hint of barely disguised bleakness in his tone made her heart fracture. 'If you leave…'

She didn't want to answer, but she couldn't help herself. 'If I leave…?'

'If you leave, how will I know that you're okay? That you're safe?'

The admission hung, shimmering, in the air between them. So ethereal that she was afraid that if she reached out to touch it, it would disappear, never to have existed in the first instance.

'Hayd…' she began at length, before stalling.

He began moving again, so slowly that at first that she didn't even realise it until he came to a halt in front of her.

And then he reached out, his hand hovering millimetres from her cheek, making her want to lean into him. She would never know how she resisted.

'Hayd…' Her voice was barely more than a whisper, but that was all she could manage. 'I don't understand any of this. A few days ago, you were telling me I had to leave because you were mad you couldn't focus with me around. Now you're telling me I have to stay so that you know I'm okay. You must see how wrong that is.'

'To want you to be safe?' He let out a hollow laugh. 'I'm sure that's very wrong.'

'No.' She kept her voice even though she didn't know how. 'To ask me to run my life according to what works for *you*.'

'That isn't what I said,' he refuted.

Still, he let his hand drop, the frankness in his gravelly tone jolting through her. It made her forget, for a moment, everything she'd in which just been schooling herself. Every caution.

'Yes. It is.'

And the worst of it was that a part of her wanted to obey, as long as that meant being with him. Building something with him.

But what could they possibly build that could be real under those circumstances?

'I know the army is your career, your life. It's what you love. And I respect that. But the nursing, and this charity, is what I love. And you don't respect *that*.'

"I was keeping you safe the only way I knew how,' he ground out, and disappointment roared through her.

'Then you should have found another way than expecting me to fall in with everything you wanted. It wasn't fair. It wasn't professional consideration. It wasn't mutual recognition.'

'What did you expect?' he asked harshly. 'For me to tell you to crack on and stay until things got really close to the wire? Or for me to beg you to leave in the first wave because I didn't want you hurt and that I loved you?'

'Do you love me?' she asked abruptly.

'Do you think loving someone means choosing them over your job? Your career?'

Of course he wasn't going to answer her. She'd known it even as she'd asked the question. But suddenly the truth enveloped her, like a sandstorm, harsh and unrelenting. *She* loved *him*. She might have never really experienced it before but that didn't mean she didn't *know*. Besides, there was nothing else that this deep, roaring, all-consuming *thing* inside her could be.

Love.

Painful and beautiful.

But wholly unrequited.

Still, she didn't know how she broke contact, taking a less than steady step backwards.

'That wasn't what I was asking. And, for the record, I think a person can have both.' She barely recognised her own discordant voice. 'And I'm going to the new camp.'

'Bridget…'

She straightened her shoulders, hitherto unknown strength beginning to flow through her. Sluggish and reluctant, but there nonetheless.

'I have to go. For me. Not for anyone else and certainly not for you. I want to do something for me. Can you understand that?'

She turned, barely able think straight, but in the instant before she looked away she was sure that she saw him take pause for a moment.

Or, probably, it was some perverse wishful thinking on her part. The silence stretched out for what felt like an eternity and then, finally, he answered.

'I can understand it.' His voice rasped over her. 'Have a safe flight, Bridget. They'll be lucky to have you.'

'Thanks.' Her throat was so constricted she could barely answer.

And then Hayden walked away—as her silly, insubstantial dreams floated down around her like ashes.

CHAPTER FIFTEEN

'I CAN'T BELIEVE you're advocating that I leave the army,' his sister snorted at him as she sat, upright with back straight, at the kitchen table in their father's home. 'You were the one who told me—repeatedly—that I was crazy for giving it up for George. But you think it's okay to give it up for Kane?'

Did he think that?

Hayden faltered. For the first time in his life he wasn't one hundred percent sure what he thought. His head was all over the place and it was all to do with the woman who was still thousands of miles away right now.

Bridget.

It didn't matter how far away she was, she was nonetheless haunting every one of his thoughts.

He'd been so caught up in his own astonishing hubris, and the paralysing fear that something could happen to her out there that he hadn't accepted what she'd been saying even as she'd said it.

In that one idiotic move he'd effectively asked her to turn her back on her passion and her goals, the things that made her *her*. The things that had made him fall for her in the first place.

He would never have entertained any woman who had

demanded those things of him. In fact, he *hadn't* entertained them, and they *had* tried it.

There was an indisputable irony in that fact that didn't pass him by.

'No,' he heard himself answering slowly. Reminding himself where he was and who he was talking to. 'I think it's crazy to give up something you love for anyone else but yourself.'

And it was gradually dawning on him that although he was speaking aloud to his sister, in the kitchen of his childhood home, in his mind he might as well have been saying the same exact words to Bridget.

He could see Mattie turning to stare at him, no doubt wondering who he was and what he'd done with the brother she knew. Or *had known*, right up until Bridget had walked into his life. The least he owed his sister was to answer her questions, but instead of with his head he'd be answering with his heart.

'Be that George, Kane or the Queen of England—and you take the Queen's shilling every pay cheque. My point is that you can blame others as much as you like for not telling you the truth back then, but you've had a chance to put things right—if that's what you really want—and you've decided to stick with the devil you know. And that's on you, Mattie. No one else.'

Just as it was on him to put things right with Bridget, Hayden thought, turning around to pick up his sister's freshly brewed mug of tea and pass it to her.

He watched her cup it in her hands and slide her fingers through the handle, glowering at him over the rim. And still all he could think about was Bridget, and how he only had himself to blame for the way things had ended between them.

'So, what's your next assignment anyway?' Mattie asked.

'I'm supposed to be DS for a training exercise on Salisbury Plain.'

A few months ago he would have relished this task. It had to mean something that he couldn't muster up an ounce of enthusiasm for it.

'Supposed to be?'

Mattie narrowed her eyes, but Hayden was grateful that she was too preoccupied with her own thoughts of Kane to really be concentrating on what he'd said.

The truth was that he'd rather be somewhere else than the UK entirely. Somewhere thousands of miles away. Somewhere with a certain person. It was the most bizarre sensation. Certainly not one he'd ever had to contend with before.

Who would have thought that one woman could have turned his whole life on its head this way? And it had happened so quietly, so stealthily that he hadn't seen it coming for even a second.

Bridget Gardiner.

If he wasn't to change the dialogue with her, he was going to have to find a new approach. Soon, thanks to requests from the various charity project coordinators he had met in his time out there, his CO would be sending out a new contingent to the region for ongoing support. They would carry out similar infrastructure work to that they'd carried out at Jukrem, but this time at other camps such as Rejupe, and further afield.

Only one question remained: *was he willing to?*

Snatching up one of the few remaining paediatric units of O negative from the refrigerator unit in the lab, Bridget began decanting the blood into the sterile bags for paediatric use before taking a sample in order to allow her to conduct a bedside crossmatch.

'You paged?' Justin, the doctor, hurried in as Bridget was back at the child's bedside.

By the looks of it, he had just woken from what had probably only been his first hour's sleep in about the last twenty hours.

'You look like hell,' Bridget offered by way of apology. 'Patient is an eighteen-month-old baby, presented about ten minutes ago very pale, low oxygen, bloody diarrhoea, and a haemoglobin of two point nine.'

'How much blood have we got?' he asked grimly.

'Not a lot. But there are at least three donors out there so we'll screen them as quickly as we can.'

'Okay.' He began to examine the baby, no doubt taking in the same muscle-wasting, anaemia and malnutrition that she had. 'It's going to be hard to find a vein.'

If by *hard* he meant *basically impossible*, she concurred.

'IV line to normal saline?' she suggested.

'I knew you were here for a reason.' Justin nodded grimly. 'I know you've been on duty all night but you're the best crossmatcher we have.'

'I'm not going anywhere,' Bridget assured him, pushing back against the wall of exhaustion that threatened to crash over her.

'That's good, because the new army units are due in today.'

For a fraction of a second Bridget froze. And then she threw herself into her task, but this time the wall threatening to crash over her wasn't one of exhaustion but of memories—forceful but unwelcome. Thinking of the new army units arriving made her think about Hayd, whom she couldn't think about without her chest feeling as though an entire herd of elephants was sitting on it, crushing it.

What made it all the more laughable was the fact that the charity had only decided to extend its working relationship with the British Army because they'd been so impressed with how well the relationship had worked in Jukrem.

Now other medical camps in the region were getting Royal Engineers to work on infrastructure, whilst the relationship between Hayden and herself had died a pitiful death.

And still an even more foolish part of her had half imagined that now Operation Ironplate was over for him, Hayden might have tried to come out on one of the new charity/army operations, this time in her area. But he hadn't, and she hated herself for that traitorous voice stirring things up.

She hated herself even more for the other voice that told her it was merely telling the truth.

Four months, and she still hadn't learned. But volunteering out here had always brought one thing back to her more than anything else. Life was too short for grudges.

She was still cross-matching the first patient when one of their colleagues rushed in.

'Another emergency on its way. A two-year-old girl with high fever, suffering convulsions and diarrhoea. Haemoglobin three point one. Preliminary assessment in the clinic is that it's malaria.'

'Another IV line,' Justin confirmed. 'Intramuscular injections, and malaria tablets, and, Bridget…?'

'More cross-matching.' Bridget nodded. 'Got it. Is her mother in with her?'

'Yes. I'll take her to the lab for screening,' the nurse assured them, hurrying back to the door. Then turned. 'Also, the new army unit has arrived. They've already started investigating the pump in the south quarter so we might even have additional fresh water by nightfall.'

It was the kind of thing Hayden would have done, Bridget couldn't help thinking. He would have launched himself into emergency tasks like that. If they succeeded, the limit of five litres per person per day could be raised to ten litres. Still less than the ideal minimum of fifteen litres out here, but quite an improvement for a few hours' work.

But it hadn't happened yet.

Thrusting the thoughts away, she focused on the two cross-matches over the next couple of hours, as well as third one that came in, only feeling she could breathe again when the life-saving blood was being transfused into all three of their tiny patients.

At last, exhausted yet with an enormous sense of satisfaction, Bridget called her shift done and left the medical part of the compound and headed for the mess tent to grab a bit of rather late lunch.

'I didn't think you'd ever come out.'

Whatever tiredness or hunger had been threatening to overtake her, it dissipated in that instant. Slowly she turned, half expecting him to be a mirage. That he'd disappear when she tried to look directly at him.

'Hayd. What are you doing here?'

'New orders,' he told her easily, but she didn't miss that expression in his gaze.

The one that caught at her, tugging on the loose thread until it threatened to unravel. She commanded herself not to react.

'New orders?'

'To check the boreholes. Strip down and rebuild any of the submersible electric pumps that need it. Get them working again.'

'I knew there was an army unit coming.' She was impressed with herself at how steady her voice sounded. She had no idea how she'd managed it. 'I just didn't think for a moment that it would be you. Is that a coincidence?'

Hayden's eyes slammed into hers so hard she felt as though he had physically winded her.

'No, Birdie, it isn't a coincidence.' His voice rolled through her like thunder. Like a prelude to the monsoon season that wasn't yet due. 'I put in a request to my CO to come out here, to be part of this follow-up mission, because I wanted to see you. I missed you.'

She wanted to believe him. So much that her heart felt like it was cracking. But something lurked in the periphery of her mind. A dark shadow that warned her not to be as gullible and foolish as her mother had always been.

Hadn't he already told her he couldn't offer her any kind of relationship? So what had changed?

'You missed the sex.' She hated the sound of every single word, yet they had to be said. 'Nothing more.'

'No, I missed you,' he corrected, reaching out to take one loose lock of black hair in his fingers and twirl it.

The tiny gesture felt so intimate that it almost stole her breath away. If she didn't steel her heart against him she was afraid he was going to shatter it all over again. But it still didn't explain what had changed in his head.

'You don't,' she refuted thickly. 'And I don't want to go down this road with you again.'

And then, before she could crumble, as she feared she surely would, Bridget found the strength to remove his hand and begin to walk away.

Whilst she still could.

'I was wrong,' he said quietly. Simply.

And she knew she shouldn't engage with him, but she couldn't help it. She stopped, but she didn't turn around.

'I don't know what that means.'

'It means I want more.'

The softly spoken words hung there in the dry, hot midday air. And Bridget didn't know which of them would reach for them first. Slowly, very slowly, she turned around, murmuring, 'Say that again?'

'You heard me the first time,' he answered, but there was no rancour to his tone.

This time when he approached her and reached for her, she couldn't bring herself to pull away.

More to the point, she didn't want to.

'More?'

'A lot more.'

Yet it wasn't the words that got under her skin—or, at least, it wasn't *only* the words—it was also that stunned, raw expression in his gaze that was her undoing. It made her throat parched and her voice scratchy.

And it also made her oddly, perhaps irrationally, angry.

'You suddenly decide you want more? You come haring up here on some pretext of a reassignment? And you expect me to drop everything and welcome you with open arms?'

'You think I'm going to change my mind,' he stated clearly. Empathetically.

She was *terrified* he would change his mind. But she didn't need to tell him that, not least because she was still trying to process what he'd said.

'I don't *think* you'll change your mind. I fully *expect* that you will,' she shot back. 'Because, no matter what you say now, your career comes first with you. Just as mine does with me.'

'There's no reason why we can't have both.' He lifted his hands to cup her cheeks. 'A wise woman once told me that, only I wasn't ready to listen to her.'

Bridget told herself that she wanted to pull away.

Only she didn't. Not a millimetre. She just stayed right where she was, her eyes locked with Hayden's and her feet rooted in place.

'And now you *are* ready?' she asked a little breathlessly.

He shot her a look she could only describe as solemn.

'For the rest of my life,' he assured her.

'The rest of your life?' she echoed, almost in wonder. This all felt very real, and yet wholly unreal. It couldn't be happening to her, surely?

'The rest of *our* lives,' Hayden corrected. 'You only have to say you'll take me back.'

She wasn't entirely sure it was a request. It sounded more like a command, albeit couched in the softest terms. Yet it was a command she felt she could obey.

For the first time since she'd walked outside she smiled.

How could it be that her smile shone brighter than the equatorial sun? And seared him twice as strongly?

He'd never dreamt he'd ever find a woman like Bridget, who made him feel complete when he hadn't known he'd even been broken. He'd spent years congratulating himself that he hadn't fallen into the same relationship trap that friends and colleagues alike had fallen into. One night with Bridget and he'd stepped right into it and had never even realised it.

'I'm not a man of words, Birdie,' he told her apologetically. 'I'm usually a man of action. I don't know how to tell you what you've come to mean to me, but I hoped by coming up here with my team it would prove it to you instead.'

'I think I'd like both,' she told him with a half-laugh.

She was probably joking, yet because she'd asked, something inside him wanted to try; wanted to be the kind of man who could tell her what was in his heart.

'Okay.' He held her. 'How about this? I've spent all my life ducking the idea of settling with one person. Believing that it was better to be like this than give any woman the life my father gave my mother. However much she loved him.'

'Hayd—' she began, but he dropped his lips to hers and momentarily silenced her.

A mere brush of their lips, yet it was enough to almost send him over the edge.

'I think I loved you the moment you walked into that damned nightclub with my sister as your personal bodyguard.'

'Was it the danger of being attracted to your kid sister's friend?' She grinned, but he could see the hint of uncertainty in her and he loved the fact that he could read her even when she was trying to cover herself.

'No.' He shook his head, his eyes dangerously sexy. 'It was most definitely not that. It was the danger of *you*, Birdie. Pure and simple. I couldn't resist.'

'You certainly made me think you were going to,' she teased.

'I've no idea how,' he groaned, stepping forward and gripping her shoulders. Not tightly enough to hurt but enough to hold her in place and make sure she was listening. 'It damned near killed me, Birdie, and I never want to have to do that again.'

'Is that so?'

'That's so,' he confirmed. 'One month in your company and I realised that what was *really* better was to find a woman who actually wanted to live the life that I did.'

He loved the way her eyes glittered, like crystals of demerara sugar dropped into the richest, darkest pools of strong coffee.

'But not always, Hayd.' She pursed her lips ruefully. 'What about in the future?'

'I don't know what the future will hold. I only know that I don't want to face it unless I'm by your side. You and I. Together.'

'You should know now that I want a family one day. Maybe that will be ten years from now. But one day.'

'I want that too, with you,' he told her, knowing that there wasn't a part of him that doubted it. He wanted everything with her. Now he understood what Mattie had been going on about.

And then, before either of them could waste any more breath talking about it, he lowered his head and claimed her mouth with his own.

The first kiss of the rest of their lives.

* * * * *

MILLS & BOON

Coming next month

FALLING FOR THE SECRET PRINCE
Alison Roberts

'Roberto Baresi is our father.'

Emilia actually shook her head. 'But your surname's
Di Rossi, not Baresi.'

'I go by my mother's maiden name. I didn't want my
background known when I came to study and work in
America. I didn't want special treatment or media attention. I wanted to be like everyone else. Like you,
Emmy… Being able to work hard and achieve my dream
of becoming a doctor.'

Emilia's head was spinning. 'Wait…you're telling me
that you're the son of a king? That would make you
a…a prince?'

He was holding her gaze again and she could see the
absolute honesty in his eyes. 'Yes.'

A single word but one that suddenly opened a gulf
between them that was wider than an ocean. He was
nothing like her. They were suddenly so far apart that
they could have come from different planets. He was a
prince. Part of a royal family that could be traced back
for centuries and she was a girl who hadn't even known
who her father was and had to be taken away from her
mother's damaging lifestyle. He was a man who'd always
had a privileged lifestyle and a future to look forward
to, whereas she was a girl who'd been labelled wild

enough to get shunted from foster home to foster home, becoming more and more lost until someone—that amazing teacher she'd had in the eleventh grade—finally believed in her enough to let her dream of a different future.

So she'd been bang on the mark in thinking she didn't know very much about Dom, hadn't she? It was, in fact, so much of an understatement that it should have laughable. But it wasn't. This wasn't remotely funny. Emilia couldn't quite identify the swirl of emotion that she could feel building inside her head—and her heart—but it wasn't pleasant. And it was powerful enough to be preventing any speech right now. Having opened her mouth and then closed it again, she had to give in and wait for the initial shock, or whatever it was that was paralysing her, to wear off.

Continue reading
FALLING FOR THE SECRET PRINCE
Alison Roberts

Available next month
www.millsandboon.co.uk

COMING SOON!

We really hope you enjoyed reading this book.
If you're looking for more romance, be sure to
head to the shops when new books are
available on

Thursday 29th
October

To see which titles are coming soon, please visit

millsandboon.co.uk/nextmonth

MILLS & BOON

WE'RE LOOKING FOR NEW AUTHORS FOR THE MILLS & BOON MEDICAL SERIES!

Whether you're a published author or an aspiring one, our editors would love to read your story.

You can submit the synopsis and first three chapters of your novel online, and find out more about the series, at **harlequin.submittable.com/submit**

We read all submissions and you do not need to have an agent to submit.

IF YOU'RE INTERESTED, WHY NOT HAVE A GO?

Submit your story at:
harlequin.submittable.com/submit

MILLS & BOON

LET'S TALK
Romance

For exclusive extracts, competitions
and special offers, find us online:

f facebook.com/millsandboon

▼ @MillsandBoon

⊙ @MillsandBoonUK

Get in touch on 01413 063232

For all the latest titles coming soon, visit
millsandboon.co.uk/nextmonth